This book is the first step on what promises to be a wonderful journey.
I would not have been able to accomplish this without help
Thank you so much; BatSam, Raven, Gary, and all of my wonderful
Friends and Family who supported me and helped to get here.
From the bottom of my heart, thank you!

1:

As the final bell of the school year rang, a collective sigh of relief swept through the student body. The halls soon became filled with the sounds of summer plans and regrettable parties that were bound to take place. Everyone seemed to brim with joy; except one senior, who walked to his locker with heavy steps. He reached his locker and opened it with a heavy heart.

"Jesus in a race car, Xavier; don't look like someone killed your favorite kitty." Snapped a female voice from behind him.

Xavier swore and clutched his chest; he hated how she always found a way to sneak up on him. He turned around to see her smiling at him. She was dressed in her signature black jeans and pink shirt with a skull on it; her hair in infamous pigtails. To anyone else, she was a dream for guys who were into adorable looking women. To him, she was a source of constant annoyance and the closest thing he had to a friend.

"Millie! Do you really have to scare the crap out of me every day?"

"I've been doing it for years, it's a lovely profession, but that's beside the point. What's with the doom and gloom?"

"Go away, and I'm not being gloomy. Just a little down. School is over."

"Ordinarily, seniors are happy to escape the prison of the public-school systems. You don't have to come back. You know, ever."

"Ordinarily. But when am I ever ordinary?"

"Don't be so dramatic. So, you're not happy that you graduated?"

"I'm not happy about a lot of things."

"I see… We should hang out during the summer. Enjoy our last days of childhood."

Xavier put his last notebook into his book bag and slammed his locker closed. Millie meant well, but her lack of knowing anything about him really irritated him.

"When do I ever have free time, Millie?"

"That's because you have school. Now that it's done…"

"We have college to think about."

"Seriously?"

Xavier slung his book bag over his shoulder and fixed her with a blank stare.

"Seriously."

He was about to begin his very long walk home when he felt a hand grip his arm and wrench him around. Millie got very close to his face and glared with a level of malevolence that both impressed and infuriated him.

“What is wrong with you? I’ve always been there for you. I’ve always been the only one who’s willing to even talk to you. The least I deserve is you to be honest with me and not make up any retarded excuses for why you don’t want to hang out.”

“Get out of my face.” Xavier understood why she was angry. It was an obvious lie, but the truth was something he didn’t trust anyone to have. She wouldn’t understand. His personal hell was just that: his.

“What are you gonna do if I don’t? I kinda like being in your face.”

“Millie…I’m warning you…” Xavier started to feel his blood boil. She may be his ‘friend’, but she was crossing a line that no one could cross.

“I’m listening.”

Before Xavier could even control his body, he had punched Millie in the jaw. Fortunately, he had swung poorly and only clipped her, but the force was still enough to knock Millie off her feet. Xavier had immediately felt bad, kind of, but he held the thought that she had it coming. Millie looked at Xavier with a confusing blend of what seemed like anger and pity. She got up and rubbed the left side of her jaw and smiled at Xavier. Xavier felt his insides churn as he knew that smile had no good intention behind it.

“Can’t say this is the first time a man has swung at me for standing my ground. But I can promise you, it will be the last time you ever do it. Have a nice life, Xavier. Try to trust the next person dumb enough to be your friend.” Millie waved and then proceeded to walk past Xavier with her head held high.

Xavier sighed and instantly berated himself for being so stupid. Millie was honestly the only one who went out of her way to speak to him. She was the only one who had ever shown any type of care towards him, and he just ruined it. Xavier shook his head and started to walk towards the school’s front door. As he slipped his earphones on and began to hum along with whatever tune his iPod decided to play, he glanced up and watched as the buses start to pull off.

"Guess I missed the bus yet again," he whispered.

It would take him at least an hour and a half on foot to get to his house, but he wasn’t fazed in the slightest. To him, home didn't even exist. While students everywhere claimed that school was a prison, he reveled in it. It was the only place he was truly free. He began his long trek home with heavy steps and an even heavier heart. He knew he would be punished severely when he got home, however it was Friday and he didn't care.

He crossed yet another street, this time at an intersection when the rays of the setting sun finally caught his attention. He had been so caught up in his own mind that more time than he thought had passed by unnoticed. With a sigh of exasperation, he made a beeline for his street and began to quicken his pace. As he passed by familiar houses and familiar faces, his feet grew heavier and heavier. He hated all those people who he had feigned politeness to and most of all, he hated that house. He finally came to a stop when he saw it.

To anybody else, the house was a simple blue, two story single family house with a nice sized garage. To Xavier, it was the truest definition of hell on earth. With slow and calculated steps, he walked up the sidewalk leading to the front door. He retrieved his keys out of his pocket and slid the house key into the door knob.

From that moment, he knew something was wrong.

Normally he would hear his uncle yell some inane comment of what took him so long, or see his shadowed outline waiting for him. Except this time was different; he heard nothing and saw no one at the door. He quickly opened the door and looked around. In the living room, he could hear the filth that was usually playing on the television but saw no sign of its owner. He looked up towards the ceiling while he strained his ears to hear if someone was there.

Nothing.

Xavier cast a concerned glance to the kitchen and quickly retrieved a knife. If this was a game, he was not going to play willingly.

As he crossed the kitchen to head to the den, he heard a soft squelch. His brow furrowed and he his mind began to race. There was no way that company was over. Not on Fridays, anyways. It wasn't allowed. As he crept towards the den, the noise was more prominent. As if someone was stepping in something squishy and not realizing what they were stepping in. He made his way into the den and he dropped his knife and screamed in fearful disgust. Lying in the middle of the floor was a mutilated body; his uncle's body. The head had been nearly bitten off and the chest cavity had been torn open. The only identifying feature was the tacky skull tattoo on the left forearm that his uncle constantly bragged about.

The worst part, the thing sitting next to the body. It was almost human sized and covered with a dense black fur. The creature sat on its hind legs that were rippled with muscle. A spiked tail twitched to and fro and its hands and feet were adorned with six-inch claws that dripped gore and blood. Whatever it was, it had an elongated snout; like that of a dog, and rows of serrated teeth which were currently chewing into the innards of the victim. Just when Xavier thought the “thing” couldn’t get any more terrifying, he caught a glimpse of its eyes. They were black ringed with a small amount of green. Staring into those eyes were like staring into a pit, with no hope of light ever escaping.

His scream had caught its attention and the beast dropped the guts it had been feasting on. It stared directly into his eyes and began to breathe faster and faster. To his dismay, the thing seemed to be laughing at him. He began to slowly back away when the beast stopped its laughter and flashed a grotesque grin. Before he could react, Xavier felt a searing pain in his left shoulder, as if hot blades had run across his flesh. He stumbled backwards and recoiled as he saw that the thing was now on the other side of the hallway, blocking the door. He looked at his shoulder and discovered three tears in his hoodie extending through his shirt and into his flesh. He attempted to grip his knife tighter, before remembering he dropped it. Xavier cursed under his breath while the creature once again began its vile form of laughter.

"What do you want with me?!" Xavier screamed, struggling to his feet.

It cocked its head at him as if he were an oddity and began laughing even harder. "Death..." it replied in hushed whisper, its voice gruff and strained.

Xavier felt taken aback. It could talk? That didn’t improve his fear at all. The thing ate people and was intelligent. He chanced a small glance at the kitchen. If he was going to die today, he was going down with a fight and seeing as he dared not turn his back on the creature to retrieve his knife; the kitchen was his best bet.

"Why do you want to kill me?" He asked, inching towards the kitchen’s doorway.

“Prey…” the being replied, tail twitching.

There was an immediate loss of words. While biology had been incredibly hard to pay attention to years ago, he knew the mention of a talking human-eating monster would have easily caught his attention. Whoever or whatever this thing was, it wasn’t widely known. As he inched farther and farther towards the kitchen he noticed that the beast was watching him with unnerving intensity, as if daring him to make a move.

Whatever it was, it was ticking him off; though he was still terrified. Fine, if the creature wanted to mess with him, then he would hate to disappoint. Xavier raced into the kitchen straight towards the drawer. He felt something slice a thin line in his cheek and noticed that it was on the other side of the hallway and stalking towards the kitchen. Xavier grabbed a knife and immediately swung it backwards as he had a sneaking suspicion that the creature was right behind him. His swing only met with the empty space behind him and the force of his swing flung him off balance and onto the ground.

His knee called out with searing protest as he got back to his feet and began searching frantically for his opponent. He kept looking all over but could not catch a glimpse of it. He was becoming frantic; there was no way that thing was discouraged by his pathetic attempts at fighting back. His heart danced in his throat when he heard the grotesque noise that was the creature's laughter. It sounded almost like a scraping snort, as if an arrogant chalk board were laughing at him. Dread filled every fabric of his soul as he slowly raised his head. Sure enough, the creature was hanging from the ceiling by its claws and laughing at him. Xavier screamed with frustration and fear as he ran for the door. He soon felt the cold pain of what he now knew was its claws in the middle of his back. The force of the slash caused him to drop to his knees. After a few quick series of pain-filled breaths, he looked and saw that the creature once again stood in front of the door. Xavier could feel his rage mix with the rest of his emotions and began running at top speed with the knife poised at the creature. He may die, but he was determined to try and take that thing with him. The creature lifted its head his head and as soon as Xavier was within a few feet of it, it turned around and swung his tail right at Xavier's chest.

The impact was brutal. It felt as if Xavier had the air squeezed out of his lungs and time seemed to halt. He soon found himself launched down the hallway and embedded in the wall. He struggled to get up, but he felt as if every bone in his body was broken and only succeeded in sitting up. The creature flashed him a knowing smile and he felt despair gnawing at his very being. This was it. This was to be the end of his life with no one to bear witness and no one to help him. It would've seemed appropriate if he was ready to die, but as his attacker grew closer, he determined that he wasn't destined for death today. He wanted to live. He wanted to attempt having a life. He wanted to have a degree, a husband, and possibly even a family. He wanted all these things, but right now what he wanted most was for this thing to go away.

"Get away…" he found his voice saying. "Get away from me…"

The creature's smile grew even wider and it began to advance slightly faster.

"Get away from me you monster!" Xavier yelled. For some reason he felt hot. As if his anger at being hurt and helpless were boiling inside of him. His hands felt especially warm, as if he were holding his hands under hot water. The creature started to run even faster, and the heat intensified.

"I said, GET AWAY FROM ME!"

He lifted his hands to strike the creature as soon as it came within his reach and a fireball shot forward. It hit the creature in its shoulder and it hit the ground while letting out a high-pitched squeal of pain. Xavier looked at his hand incredulously. He wasn't quite sure, but he knew that somehow, that fireball came from him. A grim smile graced his face and he felt a sense of satisfaction and confusion.

"Now you're gonna pay," He said, slowly rising to his feet, "I don't give a crap that you ate him, but I didn't do a damned thing to you."

The beast immediately got off the ground before Xavier could react, and once again swung his tail into Xavier's chest, knocking him into the living room. As he rolled across the floor, Xavier cursed under his breath. He was sure he felt something crack in his chest and he was now powerless to move.

"Fool," the creature hissed. "I shall suck the marrow from your bones."

Xavier no longer felt the heat he once did and once again wallowed in despair. This was it, and this time there was nothing that could be done for him. He closed his eyes as the creature crept forward; he didn't want to see the thing eat him at least. His eyes were immediately bid to open as he heard a high squeal of pain. Considering how unholy it sounded, he assumed it was the creatures. As he was stuck on his stomach, he could only lift his head an inch or two without extreme pain. He saw a flash of silver and heard another squeal of pain. His neck sent jolts of agony and he lost what little strength he had to hold his head up. As his head crashed to the ground his vision blurred and began to dim. As images became darker and darker, Xavier swore he saw the sandaled feet of someone, but his vision dimmed even further, and he suddenly felt the need to sleep. He let his mind sink into an overwhelming darkness and he felt no more pain.

"Hey! Wake up! You've been healed, and I have questions!" Demanded a female voice.

Xavier felt something collide with his face and he groaned with discomfort. He didn't really feel any pain, but he still knew he was getting slapped. He opened his eyes and all he saw were colors blended together to form a confusing image. He blinked a couple times to clear his vision and found that he was face-to-face with a woman. He yelped in surprise and attempted to move backwards only to find that he was in a bed and had no shirt on. He took a moment to look around and was surprised to see that he was no longer in his uncle's house, but a large, circular room. The walls were bare and a dingy grey, but there were beds dressed in white sheets and pillows littered throughout the room.

Xavier shifted his attention when he heard the woman chuckle. She had very strong features for a woman. She stood at least six feet tall, had resplendent and flowing brunette hair that kissed the small of her back and possessed a gentle, angular face. She was clad in black leather pants and a leather vest that clung a body toned from years of working out, but the most prominent thing about her was her deep purple eyes. Xavier searched her eyes for the telltale signs of contact lens but couldn't see any. Her eyes were seemingly ancient and alien. They reflected a wisdom and experience that Xavier felt no woman in her twenties should ever have. Well that, and the fact that they were purple, too. She smiled and pulled up a chair from a nearby table that escaped Xavier's vision. She sat down with a small sigh and fixed Xavier with a stare that unsettled him beyond anything then what that thing had. At the thought of the creature Xavier's mind instantly began to race as memories flooded back into him like a roaring a river..

"Where am I? Where is that thing? Who are you?" The questions came out faster than he intended, but he really didn't care to stop them.

"Whoa there, dear. Take a breath first, calm down," the woman replied.

"Calm? I just got attacked by this thing that eats people and it slashed the crap out of me and..." Xavier reached up to touch his shoulder where he was injured only to find that the cuts were not there. He looked down at his arm and there was no sign of the cuts either. He reached and softly touched his lower back and again there was no sign of his injuries. There was no way he had imagined that creature and he wasn't on any drugs to his knowledge. The woman laughed again, and he gave her a look of genuine confusion.

"What's so funny?" he asked, anger mounting.

“I love that look that people get after I’ve healed them. They wonder if they’ve been smoking something or that they’ve gone crazy. Well you’re neither. I think.” The woman flashed Xavier a smile, revealing dazzling white teeth.

“You healed me? How? More importantly, who are you?”

“My name is Serea. And yes, I healed you. Magic tends to give one that ability. Especially when said magic revolves around blood.”

“Blood…magic?” Xavier heard the words but was highly unsure of if she meant them. Well, she did have purple eyes. This didn’t help his feelings that he was maybe better off with the creature.

“Yes, if you want to call it that. More specifically, powers that concern blood. Magic is just part of the package. Well, I think it’s safe to say you probably think I’m crazy by now.”

“You aren’t too far off…”

“Then let me put your doubts to rest.” Serea reached down to her left boot and pulled a small knife out by its handle. She then proceeded to cut a small line down her palm. Instead of the blood slowly trickling out the wound, it started to lift into the air and form a small ball. The cut soon healed, and a ball of blood now floated above her hand. Xavier felt his eyes widen. There was no way any normal person could do something like that. No possible way. He was about to throw off his blankets and run for the nearest door when another memory of his attack flooded his mind. When he was fighting the creature, he threw a fireball. No normal human could have done that either, yet he did.

“How…are you doing that?” he asked, eyes still fixated on the floating ball of blood.

Serea laughed and put her knife into her boot. “If you were listening earlier, I had already told you.”

“Magic…”

“Yup.”

“I don’t understand. How can this possibly be real? Am I just super high on a drug that I don’t know I took? Or is this the real Wonderland?”

“If you are, then we’re on the same drug and having the same hallucination. Although I must admit, going to Wonderland would be interesting. But no, you are not high, hallucinating, or otherwise mentally impaired. This is real. See?” Serea flicked in her hand and the ball of blood whizzed off towards the wall and resounded with a sickening splat on the wall. "I suppose you want an explanation or two as to what all this is about, yeah?"

"Please."

"What all do you remember?"

"I remember getting attacked by this creature of sorts. It looked like it came out of some horror movie or something. I threw a fireball at it. Don't really know how to be honest. I thought it was going to kill me and then I blacked out. Next thing I know, I'm here."

Serea remained silent for a while, her eyes unfocused as if collecting her thoughts. Then she spoke in a low and almost sad tone. "That thing was a demon. Most demons feed on humans in one way or another. They come in all varieties, shapes, and sizes. Even the weakest of them should not be underestimated as they are all dangerous."

"Wait, wait, wait. Demons? Like the opposite of angels, demons?"

"Depends on your faith. But yes, for sake of argument. What attacked you was a demon. You didn't do too bad, judging from your wounds. The fact that you survived at all is amazing, considering how weak you are."

Xavier immediately stiffened with anger but kept his thoughts to himself. He knew that Serea probably considered anyone who didn't have magic to be weak, but she didn't have to put it so plainly.

"So where do they come from?" He asked, determined to steer the conversation into slightly more comfortable waters.

"No one truly knows. They've been around since the start of humanity according to certain ancient texts and stories. They've done a great deal to remain hidden from the public. Hence why most people associate them with myth and fictional creatures out of a bad bed time story. But make no mistake dear, they're real. As for the demon that attacked you, if I hadn't received a tip from one of our informants, it most assuredly would have killed you. Though I must give you credit for trying to fight. Most humans would have just screamed and died."

"Why do you keep referring to humans like you aren't one?" Xavier asked, slightly afraid of the answer.

"Because I'm not human. Obviously." Serea then flashed Xavier another toothy smile, only this time he noticed that her canine teeth were several centimeters longer than usual.

"So, what are you?" he whispered, sinking slowly into the bed.

"Are you truly that stupid? Blood based powers? Fangs? Kids these days I swear… I'm a bloody vampire. And yes, that pun was indeed intended."

"So, are you going to kill me?"

"Oh God, really?" Serea sighed exasperatedly. "Why would I bother saving you if I just wanted to kill you?"

"No one does anything for anyone anymore unless they gain something from it. So, what do you want from me?"

"We'll come to that in due time. Now, you told me that you threw a fireball at the demon that attacked you, yes?"

"Yeah." Xavier narrowed his eyes and fixed Serea with glare. Vampire or not, he didn't like to be ignored when he had an honest question. And it was even more annoying to think that she could simply wave him off and change the subject. It was fortunate that she was giving him answers, for now.

"Well then, I have a bit of news for you then."

"Do tell."

"You, lad, are a Witch."

"…I'm what now?"

"A Witch."

Xavier stared blankly.

"I'm totally going insane and you're a figment of my imagination, aren't you?"

"Nope."

"You sure?"

"Positive."

"A Witch?"

"Yep."

Xavier's mind began buzzing with several thoughts, but prominent among them wasn't disbelief as he thought, but a calm acceptance. Her words sounded, right. He couldn't explain it to himself to make his brain understand but, for some reason he truly believed what Serea said.

"Aren't Witches supposed to be ugly old hags who ride brooms and speak in verse?" he asked, amusing himself with his poor Shakespeare reference.

"Heh, no. I truly do not understand how humans managed to make the jump from the truth to fiction, but in this case, I guess it's a blessing."

"Yeah…"

"Witches use their inborn ability to tap into a force of nature to do quite incredible things."

"Like throwing fireballs?"

"Exactly."

"So, is that it? I'm a Witch."

Serea grew quiet for moment then got up went to a nearby cabinet that Xavier hadn't noticed until then. She then pulled out plain red t-shirt and tossed it to Xavier. "Put that on," she replied, "I have something to show you."

"Is it a coffin?" Xavier retorted half-jokingly.

"Don't you trust me?"

"No?"

"Wise policy. Now hurry up."

Xavier was extremely hesitant to do as she asked but figured that there was little else he had to lose.

2:

"You sure you don't want to tell me everything now? Because now is a wonderful time to start sharing," Xavier called, trying to catch up with Serea.

"Yes, I'm quite sure, be patient. Good things come to boys who wait."

"Not even remotely funny." Xavier caught himself as he nearly tripped. He wasn't used to the combat boots Serea had given him. He wasn't used to boots in general, much less heavy steel-toed boots. What was wrong with a nice pair of sneakers? The boots however, were the least of his worries.

When they left the medical room, Xavier came face-to-face with a fantasia of sights and sounds. Almost immediately he noticed the vastness of his surroundings. The hallway was well over one hundred yards wide and the ceiling was easily forty feet high. The walls were painted a bland, pale grey that for some reason made him uneasy. The hallway was brightly lit with lights that dotted the ceiling like stars in the sky. He assumed that they were underground as there were no windows or sunlight. Although from the way it looked, they could have been in a heavily secured compound like the ones he saw on TV.

He felt a small chill go down his spine, though he was unsure if it was due to the temperature or his discomfort. The walls seemed so oppressive that he couldn't help but feel that he was in danger. Everywhere he looked, there were no signs of sunlight or even joy. There was a faint metallic tang in the air which did nothing to assuage his unease. Every fiber of his being was on high alert and he started to look at the other people around.

Everywhere he looked, there were men and women flitting in every direction. He started to get the impression of being in a crowded mall. He was bumping into people no matter how careful he was and yet, no one seemed to notice. As if their destination was vastly more important than being stumbled into by him. He began to observe the surrounding people a little closer and saw that while everyone wore different things, there were similarities. There were those in medical scrubs, some in variations of Serea's outfit, some in white lab coats, others dressed completely casual and folks dressed like they were attending a business meeting.

The one thing they all had in common is that they all looked like they had something important to do. There was no one who was idle or who seemed to want to engage in the usual idle conversations that people seemed to always have in hallways. While there were certainly conversations being had, none of them looked like the pleasant chatter that Xavier was used to being surrounded with. Everyone moved almost robotically in that nearly no movement was wasted. He wondered if they were even human; after all, he was following a vampire throughout this building.

"Stop staring about aimlessly. All will be explained soon," Serea chided, looking back.

"These people…are they vampires too?"

"A few of them are. But as I said, I'll get more in depth when we arrive at our destination. Turn left here."

Another hallway opened before them. This one was only a few yards wide, but it was littered with identical brown doors with small windows in them. As they passed a few doors Xavier could see various sights. Rooms filled with computers on desks, rooms shrouded in books, and some that looked like the science labs. Unfortunately, all of them were empty. He wondered at the reasoning behind so many empty rooms but decided to hold the question for when he and Serea arrived at their destination.

She stopped in front of a door on their right and motioned for him to go inside. When he opened the door, it revealed what seemed to be a large break room complete with vending machines, a round medium table and a couch. There were six people in the room, five men who all looked uncomfortable to be there and one woman who stopped mid-sentence and smiled and waved. She was sitting on the middle of the table cross-legged as if she were in kindergarten. She scooted off the table and her hazel eyes seemed to twinkle. Wearing an outfit almost identical to Serea's, he could see that she too was quite toned; though, unlike Serea, she filled out her uniform. Her caramel skin contrasted rather well with her dreadlocks which had been dyed a lighter brown at the ends. The only thing that marred her appearance was the presence of a large scar along her left cheek. She bounded towards them with a grin.

"Hello! How are you? My name's Szakiya," she chimed, extended her hand.

"Hi." Xavier replied, shaking her hand uncertainly. She seemed overly chipper.

"Another quiet one," she sighed. "This whole bunch is way too quiet, Serea. Can we trade them in for happier ones?"

"Let them be. They're all a little anxious to get answers," Serea chuckled before pulling up a chair and seating herself at the front of the room.

Xavier took this as a sign to join the other men in the room. He walked to the nearby counter and leaned against it. The room fell silent while Serea was seemingly collecting her thoughts.

"I think before we dive into anything, we should properly introduce ourselves. My name is Serea, as most of you know. My function here is a multi-faceted one, but for all intents and purposes, you'll be reporting to me most of the time."

"Hold up," Szakiya giggled, "we haven't even explained what here is. Let's keep it short and sweet for a sec. I already introduced myself, in case you missed my loud mouth."

"I doubt anyone missed hearing you, dear."

"…that was shady." Szakiya pouted, though the twinkle in her eye gave the impression of joking.

Serea chuckled before motioning to Xavier. He instantly felt his heart skip a beat and a surge of embarrassment immediately after. He hated introducing himself to a group. He always got the impression that no one really cared who he was, so what was the point in wasting time on an introduction? He straightened himself a little and muttered his name, staring at a random spot on the wall.

The man was nearest to him stood up and gave a small smile. Xavier felt his eyes widen a bit as he took a harder look. The guy was huge! Easily standing a few inches taller than him and covered head to toe with hardened muscles, he made Xavier feel so tiny. It didn't help that his golden skin and ebony hair seemed to shine under the lights. This was the type of guy you saw on the cover of those cheesy old lady romance novels, though Xavier would never admit to having read one.

"Um, hey guys. Name's Nate. What's up?" his voice boomed throughout the room with a resounding bass. He was good looking, and he had a godly voice. Xavier hated him already although he knew it was out of pure jealousy.

The man sitting next Nate at the table smiled as he watched Nate sit down. No mistaking that he was checking Nate out. As soon as Nate sat, he stood up. Xavier winced internally. Why on earth were his pants that tight? Did he not have genitals that were screaming in protest? His yellow shirt was also extremely tight that it showed every inch of his lithe frame. Xavier assumed that he was the sort that didn't want to leave anything to the imagination. He had copious dark brown hair which Xavier assumed had been straightened considering the man's cocoa colored skin.

"Hey everybody. How you doin'? My name is Justin." As he sat down, Xavier had to suppress a shudder. He didn't mind if guys were flaming, but he still didn't like when someone embodied the whole stereotype in one fell swoop.

The last one at the table stood up as he waved slightly. The poor guy looked scared half to death. Easily standing at Xavier's chin, he had that whole 'I've been getting beaten up since I started grade school' aura about him.

"Hello, everyone. My name is Maximillian, but you can just call me Max." His accent revealed his Middle Eastern roots, though he seemed to have been in America long enough to speak English like a native. Xavier wondered if he grew up in a less accepting area. Even in his Massachusetts home town, he would still see some lingering 9/11 grudges. Though upon further inspection, Max didn't strongly resemble most Middle Eastern men that Xavier had seen previously. His skin looked extremely tanned, but his eyes were an intense light blue with silver that seemed to exude sadness. He was also so incredibly skinny that Xavier wanted to make the poor guy a sandwich.

One of the guys on the couch then shot up, causing Xavier to jump slightly in surprise. The man had vibrant purple hair which instantly earned Xavier's approval. The man had snake bite piercings as well as one in his eyebrows. The slight slant in his eyes announced his Asian heritage, though it was nearly impossible to notice between the hair and piercings. He stood only a couple inches taller than Max, but he had an even greater presence than Nate. Everything from his beaming smile to the way his eyes lit up just screamed "let's party." Even though he knew nothing about him, Xavier liked this one.

"Sup, everybody? Name's Danny. I know things are mad weird but come on. Cheer up! We're safe right now. Might as well make the best of it." Even though he was smiling, it was obvious that he was just as uncomfortable as everyone else.

"Indeed, you are," Serea replied. "Now, last but not least…" She motioned at the other man sitting on the couch.

The man had flowing, dirty blonde hair that rested neatly on his shoulders. His eyes looked like they held an ocean as the light caught them when stood up. He looked as tall as

Xavier but was incredibly well toned. While he didn't have Nate's build, there was no denying this guy worked out. Xavier looked at his own skinny frame and heaved a defeated sigh. At least Max looked punier than him. That was something. When Xavier returned his gaze back to the man, his stomach clenched. The guy practically oozed apathy, which was strange considering the situation they were all in. His expression held so much boredom and contempt that Xavier almost felt like punching him. Who gives that little of a crap in a situation like this? Xavier's dislike increased exponentially when the man introduced himself with, "Adam".

As Adam sat back down on the couch his eyes met with Xavier's. A mutual glare grew between the two, the first of many Xavier assumed. Serea's chuckle broke the glaring match and Xavier pushed his current dislike aside. He had almost forgotten that there were far more pressing matters to discuss. He caught Serea's amused glance and felt himself scowl. He hated being anyone's entertainment.

"Now, now, boys. Save the aggression. You'll need it," Serea said, her chuckling switching for a somber expression.

"Why?" Max timidly asked.

"Time to get into the serious stuff." Szakiya's initial cheer had vanished, and its place an expected stern and almost cold countenance came forth. "There really isn't an easy to say this, so we'll just rip off the Band-Aid quick. Y'all have a lot in common with each other. Unfortunately, none of it is all that pleasant. For starters, all of you were attacked by demons and lived. Which, trust me, is extremely lucky for y'all."

This robbed everyone in the room of speech. What surprised Xavier the most wasn't what she had said, but how easy it was to hear the second time around. He always enjoyed learning the myths and legends of various cultures but never really put much stock into it. Even learning about the Yei was a simple interest. But now, there were no other explanations available to him. And why should he search for any other explanation? He saw what Serea was, so in all reality if vampires were a thing, why not demons? He looked around the room and saw that Justin and Nate seemed to accept Szakiya's words. The others didn't look too convinced, however.

"Demons?" Max whimpered, wringing his hands slightly, "that's impossible. We aren't dead. Are we?"

"I'm afraid you're wrong on both accounts, my dear," Serea answered, a look of pity creeping across her face. "Demons are indeed real. And you yet live."

"But what? How? And why didn't you tell us this yesterday?"

"We aren't sure. Tales of demons can be found in almost every civilization throughout history. They have plagued humankind from the shadows for what seems forever. I'm roughly eight-hundred years old and I've heard tales nearly ten times my age. As for our not telling you, you were a bit…hysterical yesterday."

"But what did they want with us?" Xavier found himself asking, a train of thought suddenly hitting him. "If demons have been hunting humans for as long as you say, then the six of us getting attacked shouldn't really be that special. But you went out of your way to not only save our lives, you healed us and brought us here. Why? And don't say you did it simply to be nice. Being nice would be dropping us off at a local hospital. What do you want from us?"

Serea fixed him with what oddly seemed to be a look of pride. "You're correct. But there are other things you must know before we get to that. As I was saying, demons have been around for a long time. No one knows where they came from, nor has any effort to forge peace succeeded. These monsters came in all shapes and sizes and bear terrible and unique abilities. Whether humanity will ever admit it, demons very nearly drove them to the brink of extinction. But like all things on this planet, humans evolved. Wielding the six forces of nature, the first of the Witches came into being. They-"

"You're kidding, right?" Adam's eyebrow was cocked and his face dismissive. "Witches? What's next? Werewolves? The Fair Folk?"

"Says the one healed by a vampire," Serea spat. "Try to keep an open mind. And don't interrupt me again."

Adam snorted in disbelief before crossing his arms and readjusting his position on the couch. "Fine."

Serea let her eyes linger on Adam for a few more seconds before she continued. "With nature's power at their disposal, the Witches began to turn the tides and soon covens were springing up everywhere. Humans now finally had their champions. Some Witches even began to make a name for themselves. For millennia, the Witches waged global war against the demon population. Though nothing seemed to extinguish the demons for good. They always popped up somehow…"

"Fast forward to about few centuries ago," Szakiya added. "For some reason, new Witches stopped appearing. In any given area, there would be almost a hundred new Witches a generation. By the eighteen hundreds, that number had dropped to nearly three. This gave rise to the Heretic Witches. Heretic Witches were those who gained powers through other mediums. Usually a ritual to invoke a power not of nature."

"Was that a bad thing?" inquired a confused-looking Nate. "If the Witch numbers were declining, wouldn't it make sense to bolster the numbers in some way?"

"A smart person would say yes. But a wise person knows it's never that simple," Szakiya trailed off, looking hurt.

Serea's expression saddened and she lightly touched Szakiya's arm before continuing. "There is a reason they were called Heretic Witches. Natural Witches are born into their power. It is a destiny granted to them by birth. Heretic Witches were seen as an antithesis to that. Greedy humans who could not accept their lack of power. Then there was their power itself. The forces of nature serve as a stable means of a source of power. But there are other…unstable sources that caused certain Heretics to go insane."

"What are these forces of nature?" Justin asked.

"Fire, water, air, earth, lighting, and ice."

"Isn't ice just frozen water?"

Serea nodded. "In the scientific sense, yes. But in nature, ice is a monster all its own."

"And the unstable ones?"

"It ranges. Metal, light, darkness, even space. The point is that their powers were incredibly dangerous and seen as an affront to most of the Witch population."

"Let me guess," Adam cut bitterly, catching Xavier off guard. "The majority started treating the other Witches like crap. Tensions rise. Then boom, war."

Serea narrowed her eyes in what seemed irritation but said nothing of Adam's rude interruption. Xavier wondered if this guy had a death wish. "A little over-simplified but correct. What was known as Crimson Dawn took place. Witches slaughtering each other left and right."

"Nice to see humanity still hasn't changed."

"Jeez kid, what on earth made you so cynical at such a young age?" Szakiya muttered.

"Learning anything about human history."

"…Can't argue with that."

"If we could get back on track," Serea hissed, "there is still much left to explain. Now what neither side knew was that the demons were lying in wait. They washed over both armies like a swarm of locusts. Barely any survived. Those that did went into hiding. It was around this time that Zora began to implement stricter guidelines."

"Zora?" Danny asked.

"An international paramilitary group focused on keeping all supernatural threats to humanity at bay."

"So, there's more than demons to worry about?" Max replied, looking terrified. "What else is out there?"

Szakiya gave him a small smile, though her eyes betrayed a certain amount of worry. "Plenty, I'm afraid. As you know, there are vampires out there. Not all of them believe in leaving humans alone. Same with Lycans. There are also whole sects of Heretic Witches out there that are determined to corrupt wherever they can. Rogue psychics starting trouble. As well as shifters."

"Psychics are a thing?! And what're shifters?" Max squeaked.

"Calm down, sugar. Nothing is going to get you…yet. Psychics are the products of Witches having children with normal humans. Eventually it became a genetic trait which was then further bred. Every psychic can trace their roots back to a Witch. Shifters are the same, except between Lycans and humans."

"What can they do?"

"Psychics have a ton of different abilities. Telekinesis, telepathy, empathy, clairvoyance, psychometrics, and rare occasions possess spirit medium traits. Shifters are a bit different. Shifters can well…shift their shape into an animal. Powerful shifters can even have powers relating to the animal."

"So where do we fit into all of this?" Xavier asked, although he already knew the answer.

Serea looked him directly in the eyes and her face told him everything he needed to know. "The six of you are Witches."

Even as he heard the words, Xavier tried to refuse them. He knew that he wouldn't be let go because of his being a Witch. But when presented with the fact that every single one of them were the same, a heavy weight fell upon his heart. Any chance they had of talking their way out of this disappeared with one sentence.

The silence in the room betrayed a staggering amount of tension. As Xavier looked around, he could see that the others were having similar struggles. Poor Max looked so pale that passing out seemed eminent. Nate opened his mouth but closed it, looking as if he wasn't sure what to say. After a few moments, Adam broke the silence.

"So even if we believe you. What then?"

"Isn't it obvious?" Xavier replied harshly, perhaps more than what was necessary, but he was ticked, "They want us to stay here and fight demons."

"Pfft. No."

"You don't get it, do you? We don't have a choice."

"Like hell I don't!" Adam shouted, his face growing red.

"Do you really think they'll let us just walk out of here alive if we refuse?"

Adam's face showed a hint of surprise before he narrowed his eyes and looked towards Serea and Szakiya. Max and Nate both rose out of their seats slowly and backed away while Justin leaned forward in his seat. Szakiya had a very sad expression on her face that lent more proof to Xavier's theory. Perhaps she could be reasoned with, but not Serea. Her eyes wore cold determination like an elegant night gown. There was no swaying her and she was arguably the more dangerous of the two.

"So, what now?" Xavier felt his heart pound in his throat. While he was sure that the six of them could take two ordinary women, he had no idea what Serea was capable of and he didn't even know if Szakiya was human or not.

"That largely depends on you lot. But you are correct, if you refuse to fight or be detained here, we will kill you in this very room."

"Detained? So, fight, be jailed, or die?"

"Essentially. Please understand, we don't want to kill all of you, but you need to see things from our perspective. You six are untrained Witches with no clue how to use your magic or your powers and you now possess intimate knowledge of the world's dark past. You're dead no matter what you do. If the demons don't kill you, your abilities will. What's worse is that you would then pose a threat to the general populace. I won't allow that to happen."

"And what about the lives we have? You just expect us to give up everything we had?!" Nate spat.

Serea cocked an eyebrow before replying. "What lives? All of you were attacked by demons. With most of you, these were violent attacks that resulted in the deaths of others."

Nate's eyes widened as his mouth fell slightly open. "The kids…"

"All dead. Did you really think they would survive the wounds inflicted by that creature? By the time I got you out of there safely, they were already too far gone for me to do anything. And that goes for the rest of you as well. Do you think you all can come up with good alibis for why you survived a grisly murder scene? Because if not, you'd be the prime suspects. And considering how most of the American legal system works, you'd be lucky if you got an insanity plea for spouting nonsense about Witches."

"I'll show them," Max whispered. "I'll show them my powers."

"Ha! And then what? You and your family get taken away by government officials to never be seen again? They'll kill you just to figure out how you tick."

"I have rights!"

"Which pales in comparison to 'national security.' You think the government is gonna give a damn about your precious rights when you can freeze things, Max? Let me answer that for you: no, they won't. It's the same no matter where you go. Humans in power fear anything that could threaten that power. That hasn't changed in centuries."

"Please listen to her, y'all," Szakiya pleaded. "I know it sucks. But in the end, y'all don't have much choice. There's no home for you to go back to. At least fighting with us gives you a chance to learn about yourselves and you can help keep humanity safe."

"As your hostages," Adam replied bitterly

"As our brothers in arms." Serea heaved a sigh and rubbed her temples with her middle finger and thumb. "Look. If you agree to join us, I can't promise an easy life but it will be loads better than the alternatives."

"What type of life would that be? I'm not a solider. I don't think any of us are."

"So, you would rather be prisoners or die? You would rather waste the opportunity given to you to make a real difference in this world, simply because you find it distasteful?"

"Put yourself in our shoes!"

"I've been in your shoes!" Serea roared, her voice taking on a sinister quality. Her fangs suddenly grew longer, and her eyes began to glow purple. Xavier blinked, and she was then directly in front of Adam, staring at him with a scowl of sheer disgust. "I had no choice when I discovered I was Witch. I had no choice when I was made into the abomination I am now. I have never had a choice in what I was. The only thing I could choose was what I did with the things that were forced on me. So, instead of whining and moaning about my fate like a pup, I decided to fight. I decided to find a way to get as close to happy as I could while helping to secure the wellbeing of those who could not defend themselves. Do not cry about loss to me, human, because I have lost more than you have ever known and if I'm successful, you will never know it. Now choose."

Xavier felt his heart leap into his throat when he saw Adam's face adopt a glare of defiance. He could see Serea's body tense slightly as her eyes narrowed. If he didn't say anything, Adam was going to be killed and judging from Serea's glare, it wasn't going to be gentle.

"We'll fight!" he found himself hollering. "We'll fight. I can't guarantee that we'll be any good at it, but we'll try."

Adam and Serea both stared at each other unblinkingly for what seemed like an eternity. Xavier started to fear that Serea would kill Adam anyways. Just as he was about to start walking towards them Serea's fangs receded and her eyes stopped glowing. Her body slowly began to relax and Adam's followed suit.

"Thank the man, Adam," Serea whispered menacingly. "He just saved your life."

"Serea," Szakiya murmured, "that's enough. They already not gon' trust us. Can we all chill?"

Serea heaved a heavy sigh and her face surprisingly wore a look of weary exhaustion. "Now that we've gotten past the un-pleasantries, perhaps we can continue to converse like rational individuals."

"Death threats tend to elicit irrational behavior," Max spat venomously, shocking Xavier a bit.

"We don't mean to seem like the bad guys, but you need to understand the seriousness of the world you've stepped into."

"You sure you aren't the bad guys?"

Serea's eyes widened in what looked like shock and offense, but it was Szakiya who retorted.

"If you saw the monsters we face every day, you wouldn't have to ask. Look, I understand y'all are scared and angry. We all were. But this is bigger than the few of you. This is about protecting those that cannot protect themselves from the crap that really does go bump in the night. There ain't no runnin' from this. Might as well walk straight up to it and punch it in the face."

"Because that always works."

"It does when you're Witches."

"So, what now?" Nate asked, his eyes taking an almost alarming degree of emptiness. Xavier never saw someone so defeated. "We train or something?"

"Yes," Serea interjected. "Szakiya and I will handle the majority of your training as we're the only ones here with intimate knowledge of your powers and magic. We will train you in combat, magical education, and finding out what each of you are good at. Once you have the basics, other trainers will be introduced. You will also be given additional duties to provide support to both Zora and your coven specifically. Since you're all Witches, you will be fighting together. I suggest you all get used to seeing each other's faces."

"When do we start?" Justin's voice had suddenly become several octaves lower and took on a more refined quality. Had Xavier not seen the man speak with his own eyes, he would've thought someone else had spoken.

"Now."

Noticing the immediate looks of shock, disgust, and defiance on his fellow Witches' faces caused Xavier's heart to sink. Haven't they learned by now? "Serea, would it be ok if we had a few minutes. This is a lot to take in, you know?"

She flicked her eyes towards him, her gaze telling him that she knew he had saved everyone again. She nodded and touched Szakiya on the shoulder as she got out of her chair. "We'll be in the room across the hall."

The room had grown so silent that Serea and Szakiya's footsteps were clearly audible the moment they walked out of the room. When the door to room they entered closed, everyone seemed to release their pent-up breaths. Then there was silence. It was only a few seconds worth but it stretched for what felt like hours. Adam was the first to speak, looking at Xavier with the same defiant glare that nearly got him killed.

"So now you think you get to decide how we live our lives?"

"I made a decision that saved both our lives and yours," Xavier spat, feeling his temper flare. "Instead of being an ass, you could be grateful."

"Thank you so much for my life of forced servitude."

"Hey! At least we get to do something other than *die*."

"What guarantee do we have that we won't die fighting those demon things?! Have you seen them?!"

"Yes. I fought the one that attacked me."

"Oh yeah? How'd that work out?"

"Obviously I was almost killed. But that was before I figured out I'm a…Witch or whatever. We've got powers and junk. We can actually fight."

"I'd rather my neck get snapped by the vampire chick. At least then, it was my choice."

"You're an idiot."

Adam's glare deepened into one of fury and malice which elicited a small grin from Xavier. He knew he was being petty but sometimes it was nice to irritate someone who had irritated him. "How do you figure?"

"Because you're ignoring one very important fact. What's our best chance of escaping here? Being stuck up and uncooperative? Or playing the role of the good boys while they hand us the keys to our freedom?"

Adam's mouth fell open slightly before he closed it again. Xavier assumed he hadn't thought of it that way yet.

"They want to train us to be some kind of demon killing warriors. Which sucks, I get it. But think beyond that. From what I understand, this is a place that offers far more than just demon killing techniques. They're gonna train us on things like infiltration, information gathering, and above all else, magic. Are you really trying to tell me that the six of us can't put all of that to use and escape here?"

"We don't know how many of them there are," Max whimpered. "And they may come after us once we escape."

"We'll cross that bridge when we get to it. But for now, we need to watch each other's backs," Danny replied, giving Max a small smile.

"Screw that. Now all of a sudden we're besties and we're in this together?" Adam snarled. "For all I know, you guys might get used to all of this. Forget it."

"What do you really have to go back to, rich boy?" Nate snapped, revulsion distorting his handsome face.

"Excuse me?"

"I know who you are. What your parents are. Is that really a life worth probably dying to get back to?"

"First off, you don't know a damned thing about me. Second, no it's not. I hated that life and everything that went with it. But this is my life and I won't be told how to live it."

"Enough," Xavier cut, already starting to feel another argument brewing. "Look, I get where you're coming from. I really do. Nobody should have the right to tell us how to live our lives, but what use will it be if we let that anger end the life we're defending? I hate to admit it, but Serea was right. We don't have much of a life to return to. If we want to preserve the little chance of a life we have left, let's just play along for now."

If Adam had any other complaints, he fortunately kept them to himself. After a few more murmured words of affirmation, they began to slowly walk towards the other room. Xavier was the last to leave the room. He knew the moment he got up and followed the others, the last vestiges of what would be a normal life would be gone. He knew he was the one who suggested the new path they all had to walk, but he didn't want to walk it any more than they did. Heaving a heavy sigh, he straightened himself up and walked out of the break room. He hit the light switch and closed the door on what he was sure was his current identity.

3:

Xavier tried to lift his spirits as he heard the door close behind him. Yet, he walked across the hall, feeling hollow. He went to open the door to follow the rest of his soon-to-be teammates when he felt a chill creep down his back. He had never been the sort to be jittery, but thanks to his upbringing, he had recognized the feeling of being watched. He quickly turned to his left and saw a figure in standing down the hall.

Even at a distance, he could see that the person was huge. The first thing that came into view was the huge shoulders and matching biceps. They wore an outfit like Serea's, but this one seemed designed to highlight how massive this person was. Whoever this was, they made even Nate seem small in comparison. As the figure continued to close the distance, Xavier could make out more specific features; namely that the figure easily towered over him and was female. Her muscles seemed more pronounced now, which normally wouldn't intimidate him, but she was different. Her face remained hidden by shadow despite walking directly under several light fixtures and her shoulders were squared. As she grew closer, something in Xavier made him identify her as an enemy. When she was roughly ten feet away he could see a row of white teeth, all sharp. That was all he needed, he instantly went for the door to call for help.

"Too late." Her haunting voice replied.

Xavier saw a flash of movement out of the corner of his left eye and attempted to move out of the way. Pain erupted from his shoulder to alert him that he had failed. He grasped his shoulder with his hand, blood leaking through his fingers and started looking around for the mystery woman. Surprisingly, she was still in the same place, arms crossed. Even though he couldn't see her whole face, he could see her smiling at him. He looked around to see any sign of what she attacked him with. As his eyes flitted from here to there, never keeping his eyes off his assailant for more than a few seconds, another flash of movement appeared in his peripheral. Her fighting style seemed like it was focused on taunting him. She made it so that no matter what he tried, all he would be able to do is see it coming. He felt another slash, this time in his right shoulder blade, and screamed in pain. It was then that he noticed that no one had come out to his defense. He looked at the door to realize that a dark, shadow-like substance had covered it.

"Serea! Szakiya!" Xavier hollered, berating himself for not thinking of yelling for help sooner.

"They can't help you now, little Witch," the woman replied, her smile widening.

"Are you a demon?"

The woman's head straightened, and Xavier felt a small pang of panic. Next thing he knew, the hall was filled with cackling laughter. The woman leaned against the nearby wall and clutched her side. Xavier didn't need another invitation. Despite her size, Xavier was sure he could run into her with enough force to move her out of the way. He shot off in a wide sprint and, to his surprise, closed the gap between them within a few seconds. He had never been this fast before but chalked it up to having his life in danger. He tensed his muscles and aimed his left shoulder at the woman. The woman made no attempt to stop him. As he came to be mere inches from her, he could finally see her face. Instead of surprise or annoyance, the woman wore an expression of pure amusement, as if this was all a giant joke. As Xavier made impact with her, he found out why. She was so solid that it felt like Xavier ran head first into a brick wall. He let out a howl as he felt his shoulder make a sickening pop and he fell to the floor.

"Brilliant. Absolutely brilliant." The woman bent over and brought her face closer to Xavier's. While he wouldn't call her beautiful, she didn't have that haggard face that he had associated with large and muscular women. She had a small nose that seemed out of place compared to her startling black eyes and short red hair. She smiled at him again, displaying her teeth. Moving so fast that Xavier didn't even see her arm move, she wrapped her hand around his throat. While her hand didn't quite cover his entire neck, the strength of her grip more than made up for it. He thought she was going to break his neck well before he ran out of air. "It looks like you dislocated your arm. Here, let me fix that for you."

She stood up while lifting Xavier by his throat the entire way. At this point, the best he could do was hope the pain would make him pass out. The woman gripped his forearm with bruising strength and, with a quick jerk upwards, set his shoulder back in place. Due to the death grip on his throat, all he could do was groan in agony. The woman smiled again and lifted her free hand level to his face. Xavier then saw the familiar flash of movement. With great effort, he looked down and saw his attacker. Rising from the ground was a dark substance that seemed to writhe in the air like a snake. Xavier felt his heart drop as he realized that she could control shadows, or the horrors contained within.

"Took you long enough to realize," she mused, her amused grin returning.

Xavier brought his hands on her wrist, his entire left half throbbing in protest. He gripped her wrist and started attempting to pry her clawed hand off his windpipe. As his efforts became more and more futile, he began to kick her and attempt to bite her. Despite all his strength, she did not budge. She tightened her grip for a second and that was all it took to rob Xavier of his energy as a new wave of pain washed over him.

"Come on, that can't be it. You've got to have some fight left in you," she said, her smile widening.

For some reason, the sight of her smile enraged Xavier. He was being toyed with and treated like a weak, little mouse. He was a Witch, not some small child. Xavier felt his anger grow and it was then that he felt warmth within his hands. Xavier allowed himself a smile as he thought he had finally figured out how to summon his powers. He balled his right hand into a fist, allowing all the heat to flow into it. With as much effort and strength he could muster, he swung at the woman. His fist collided with her jaw and he was instantly thrown back by a small explosion. The woman left out a feral yowl and crashed into the wall a few feet away. Xavier landed on the ground with so much force that it knocked the wind out of him. He swore his lungs were going to give out as he slid across the floor. When he finally came to a stop, he took a few rattling breaths, grateful that his oxygen intake was no longer being hampered.

After a few more lifesaving breaths, Xavier started to slowly get up off the ground. He had managed to sit up when he heard a low malevolent growl tear through the air. His assailant started to stand, and Xavier felt his eyes widen when he realized the growl was coming from her. It was deep, angry, and oozed murderous intent. It was clear that she wasn't human and that she was furious. As she stood fully erect, her face caught the light of a nearby overhead bulb. While there wasn't the level of damage that Xavier hoped for, there was a fist-sized burn on her lower jaw. He couldn't help but smile at his accomplishment, which he instantly regretted. Upon seeing his smile, the woman's eyes widened in fury and her growl intensified. The growl seemed familiar to Xavier for some reason.

"I was going to play around with you for a while, but you need to be put in your place!" she snarled.

"You attacked me. Why wouldn't I defend myself?" Xavier replied hoarsely.

The woman's growl intensified to the point where it drowned out all other noise. Xavier had finally managed to stand and readied another fireball. He knew he couldn't beat this woman, but he intended to go down swinging. The woman's eyes suddenly turned yellow and her pupils became vertical opals, favoring a cat. Xavier swore under his breath as shadowy tendrils rose from the ground and formed an orb around the woman. The shadows opened and began to slowly swirl around to reveal what was now a large panther. Even though this woman wore a Zora outfit, Xavier was still sure she intended to kill him. This was cemented into certainty as he saw her body tense and her tail flick. What he didn't count on was her speed. He made the horrid mistake of blinking and the moment he opened his eyes; her fangs were mere inches from his face with the shadow tendrils wrapped around his arms and legs.

"Beatrice!" shouted a familiar voice.

Xavier, who had shut his eyes tight to avoid seeing his impending death, opened them slightly to see why he wasn't dead yet. He let out a small gasp as a great maw was wide open and had nearly encased around his throat. She was so close that he could feel her warm breath and sharp teeth grazing his neck. A shift of motion out of the corner of his eye caused Xavier to turn slightly to the right. There Serea stood, eyes glowing purple and her hand in the air towards who Xavier assumed was Beatrice. Even with a panther wrapped around his throat, he still felt more afraid of Serea. Though she had a human form, she exuded an aura that felt both ancient and incredibly dangerous. There was no doubt that she was the most dangerous person in the hall.

"Your job was to test him, not eat him." Serea's voice was venomous and bloodthirsty, as if she had found her prey. With a mere flick of her wrist, she sent Beatrice sailing down the hall.

Shadow tendrils once again formed an orb around her and Beatrice resumed her human form before twisting in the air and landing on her feet. Xavier felt himself being released from the shadows and nearly collapsed. Serea caught him and helped him steady himself. After a few seconds, he began to feel better. Shortly after all the pain began to subside. He had never been more grateful for someone with healing powers. When all traces of his encounter with Beatrice had faded, he finally felt safe enough to take his eyes off her. When he turned to Serea he felt his heart sink into the depths of his stomach. Her eyes weren't glowing, but the glare they threw was so frightening that he wished they were.

Beatrice seemed to have noticed the glare and made a growl of disgust, though her eyes never left Serea. Xavier felt a quiet dread press against his mind. He could barely stand up to Beatrice and yet here she was, visibly disconcerted with the look she was being given. Xavier couldn't help but wonder how powerful Serea really was and how he and the others would escape her.

"Szakiya! Drop the field, the test is over," Serea called, still glaring at Beatrice.

In that instance, Xavier felt a weight lift off him. He looked around frantically for a few moments before casting a questioning glance to Serea. She looked him and chuckled.

"You didn't realize it, did you?"

"Obviously," Xavier replied, still unsure what he was supposed to recognize.

"Szakiya is a Heretic Witch. Her force is time. She erected what we call a Stop Field, an area in which time is slowed to a fraction."

"Two questions. I thought no one liked Heretic Witches, so why is she here? And if she's not inside the field, then how was she able to hear you just now?"

"Both are very good questions!" Szakiya beamed, opening the door directly next to Serea. Xavier peered inside the room which appeared to be a small library. The rest of the witches were all assembled inside, most looking terrified and stressed out. Xavier figured that they must have been tested before him. Considering Szakiya's force, it would be entirely possible for all of them to have had short skirmishes with Beatrice despite only a few seconds having passed.

"To answer your first one, Serea herself had to insist on my being here. My powers are extremely rare and powerful in the right situations. When I'm not fighting in the field, I double as a scientist and researcher. This entire hall is mine, which shows you just how many people like me. And even if I'm not in the Stop Field, I am still very aware of what goes in it. Like Bea nearly killing you."

She turned and looked at Beatrice with a wide smile. "Coincidently, sugar, if you try to kill one of them again I will make death look preferable. We clear?"

Beatrice flashed a defiant glare and walked away while muttering under breath. As soon as Xavier was sure she was out of earshot, he turned and faced Serea. His face must have not been very pleasant because as soon as they made eye contact, a she scowled.

"Is there a problem?"

"What the hell were you thinking?" Xavier spat, feeling the rage building in him with every word.

"Excuse me?"

"You tell us we're Witches like five minutes ago and then you throw us against that?"

"We needed to see how you would respond to a life-threatening situation."

"Like any normal human would!"

Szakiya cleared her throat to draw attention. "We knew that, Xavier. But every human is different. For instance, only you and Justin thought to fight back. He literally punched Beatrice in the eye."

Xavier looked over her shoulder to catch a glimpse of Justin. He knew what the man looked like, but he assumed Justin would be the weakest out of them. He then mentally slapped himself for being stupid and turned his attention back to Serea.

"What now?"

Serea looked back into the library at others and sighed. "We start your training. Combat and powers for now. Everyone follow me."

With general muttering and snide comments of annoyance everyone in the library stood up and began to follow Serea down the hall. At the end of the hall, they made a left which opened into a larger hall, revealing a plethora of people. He noticed that there were an unusually high number of people wearing lab coats or sporting googles on their heads.

"Are we in the science wing or something?" he asked.

"Essentially," Szakiya responded. "This is part of the R&D unit."

"Where are we headed?"

"Somewhere else where you can blow things up." She chuckled.

After a turning into a small atrium, they arrived at collection of elevators. Serea pressed the down button and in a few more seconds the elevator to the left of them opened. They all filed in, and Xavier was surprised to see that the elevator was spacious enough to accommodate eight people. Serea reached in her pocket and withdrew a circular piece of plastic, no bigger than a coin. She pressed it against a black rectangle that was on top of the number buttons and then pressed B20.

"You need a fob to use the elevator here?" Nate asked.

"And why not? It's a basic security measure."

"Just figured with all the magic and weirdness you'd – whoa!"

At that moment, the elevator lurched and suddenly started descending. Everyone seemed to have lost their balance, especially Justin, who took the opportunity to fall precisely into Nate's arms. Xavier rolled his eyes and Justin gave him a wink as he apologized to Nate for falling on him. Unfazed, Serea simply picked up where they left off.

"Yes, we have a lot more…options in dealing with security issues. But that doesn't mean we should be negligent of the small things. For instance, let's say someone snuck in here and killed a member to get their fob. Every place that you must use that fob is also equipped with a camera. So, if said person pops up on the camera using someone else's fob, the elevator is automatically shut down and locked, or the nearby doors will all close and lock. Things like that."

"Things like that? Don't you think we should get more details than that?" Adam asked.

"Oh, all of you will be thoroughly briefed on that along with everything else. Every new member goes through about a month or so of basic training, and then another four months of basic specialized training in your assigned units. Once the basics are done, you start delving into the more advanced stuff."

"What units will we be in?"

"Haven't figured that out yet. Your training will be unorthodox."

The elevator finally stopped and opened to long hallway. Unlike the other ones they had seen, this hall was eerily empty and quiet. As they walked, they passed by several rooms. Each room had a door with a window and, much to Xavier's dismay, the rooms were also empty. Some rooms had weights, while others had nothing but mats. There were even a few that contained varying weapons, some Xavier recognized and others he did not. As they reached the end of the hallway there were a set of double doors. Serea pushed them open to reveal a giant room. There were common exercise machines along the right wall, a collection of weight machines on the across the room and to the left were an assortment of different colored mats. However, what was in the center of the room concerned him the most. In the middle was what appeared to be an unusually large boxing ring.

"Do you guys sell tickets, or…" Danny mused.

"Some of the tribes of Shifters feel it necessary to prove which one of them is the biggest and baddest. After a few years of unnecessary property damage, I came up with this. Disputes are often settled here. This also functions as a training ring to break in new recruits," Serea replied, smiling faintly.

"Don't you mean just break?" Szakiya retorted

"What? I wasn't that bad to you."

"How many of my bones did you break? I lost count."

"Hey, you healed, didn't you?"

"Um guys…not the best subject matter all things considered," Nate chimed in, nodding towards Max who had paled again.

"Oh, hunny. I solemnly promise that I won't hurt you in a way that I can't heal," Serea cooed, though Xavier swore he saw a twinkle in her eyes.

Serea took a few steps forward and jumped. The sheer height she achieved was unreal and with a small flip, she landed inside the ring.

"Did she just jump nearly two hundred feet in the air and land like she does that all the time?" Justin gasped.

Xavier nodded, in as much shock as everyone else.

"Jesus take the wheel…"

Szakiya must have heard him because she giggled. Before Xavier could ask her, what was funny, she leapt into the air. She landed beside Serea seconds later and flashed a toothy grin. She beckoned the rest of them to come closer. Xavier looked at his fellow Witches and they all wore the same look he did: a mix of defeat, shock, and fear. They all walked towards the ring and, one by one, climbed in.

Once everyone was inside the ring, Xavier noticed that he and the others had all gathered on one side of the ring, the opposite of Szakiya and Serea. Serea must have noticed too because she chuckled.

"You know that if we really wanted to get to you, you'd need literal miles to keep that from happening instantly."

"Not very endearing," Max muttered.

"Well, you're going to have to get used to this ring. Because this is where you're going to pretty much live for a while." Szakiya winked and stepped out to the middle of the ring. "Alright, boys, time to see what you're made of. You can rush me all at once or one at a time. Your objective: hit me."

Xavier felt his heart sink. He had gotten into plenty of scraps at school, but if his test with Beatrice showed anything, it was that he was horrifically weak compared to the monsters inside this building. After a few muttered words were exchanged, Nate started walking towards Szakiya. Xavier wondered for a moment how well he did against the panther from Hell as he watched Nate lower himself into a slight crouch. Xavier recognized the stance as one that the wrestling team uses.

Szakiya looked at Nate with a look of mild interest but made no move to assume a fighting stance. This worried Xavier more than anything. Nate towered over her and easily outweighed her by nearly a hundred pounds and yet there she stood, confidence never waning. It was almost as if Nate posed no threat to her and he saw it. Nate stiffened a little and a look of apprehension came over his face.

"Don't worry," Szakiya replied kindly. "I'm not going to use to my powers or magic on you."

The moment she finished speaking, Nate rushed her. It was obvious he was going for a hold. Xavier shook his head. He didn't know if Nate had some code about not hitting women or if he couldn't get over the size difference, but whatever his reasoning was, it was going to cost him. Even a child could see that move coming from a mile away. Although, if he was being honest with himself, his previous plan to ram Beatrice out of the way wasn't what he'd call a stroke of genius.

Szakiya moved to the right of Nate's arms, twisted to face him, smiled, and plunged her fist right into his stomach. The impact looked atrocious. Xavier could see all the wind and fight leaving Nate's body. Nate dropped to the ground and let out a groan of agony. Szakiya looked him with a sad expression on her face.

"Sorry, hun. But that was really stupid, and you had to pay the price for that stupidity." She turned and looked at the rest of them. "Next."

Danny whisked by the rest of them and leap into the air. With a slight shift, he launched a kick at Szakiya. Once again, Xavier could see the fault with the approach. He wasn't a martial artist by any means, but he didn't think it took a pro to see what was wrong. From the moment he left the ground, Danny was showing what he intended to do. Xavier knew that a lot of kicks suffer from being telegraphed, but they are usually so quick that it didn't matter. Unfortunately for Danny, Szakiya was quicker than any normal human. With a small pivot, she grabbed

Danny's leg and used his momentum to launch him at Serea. She may as well have thrown him at a brick wall. He bounced off Serea, who did not move at all, and just stayed on the ground with a groan.

Szakiya turned to look at Danny and giggle when a blur caught Xavier's attention. Max had a surprising amount of speed, but Xavier knew that it wasn't enough. Szakiya caught sight of him from the corner of her eye and reacted as Xavier thought she would. With one fluid motion, she snagged poor Max by the face and brought him to the ground. While Xavier didn't think the impact was enough to really hurt him, one look at him and Xavier could tell he was terrified. That left Adam, Justin, and himself.

Adam took one look at Szakiya and lifted his hands into the air. "I'm out. I'm not gonna be able to scratch you, much less hit you."

Xavier didn't know much about Adam, but from what he had seen of him made his surrender predicable yet still annoying. Xavier looked at Szakiya and took a deep breath. He started going over different strategies in his head. He strained to find the perfect solution that would allow him to at least land a grazing hit on her and his mind snapped to one conclusion he hadn't seen before.

"What are our restrictions on this fight?" he asked, looking to test his hypothesis.

Szakiya smiled at Serea, who returned it in kind, and replied, "There are none."

That was all Xavier needed. He reached deep within himself and tapped to the little bit of anger that was always yearning to be stirred and felt the familiar warmth of his powers. Unfortunately, his life wasn't in any real danger and all he could summon is a wreath of flame around his fists. He immediately let go of the anger and looked at Szakiya, who had been observing him with a look of mild interest. He knew he showed his hand, literally, but that didn't mean she knew how he was going to play it. He realized that it was only in the heat of battle that his powers worked. The problem was that he wasn't sure how much punishment he could take. He could maybe tank one or two solid hits, and that was pushing his luck. He shrugged off any concerns he may have had and decided that if he was going down, it was going to be in style.

He squared his shoulders and brought his fists up in the way his gym teacher had taught him and slowly walked towards Szakiya.

"Alright, I can get down with a little boxing. Don't blame me if your face gets jacked up, though." She assumed a stance like his and bent her knees to a slight crouch.

Her first punch came quickly, quick enough to floor him if he hadn't been expecting it. He blocked her jab, thankful his prediction had been correct, and responded with one of his own. She bobbed out the way and smiled. Next came a left hook from her. He had assumed she was right handed so he wasn't expecting a left hook so soon. He raised his right arm to block it and he saw it, the mischievous gleam in her eye. This was a fake out. Because he had seen how strong she was physically, he didn't want to chance taking a direct hit to the face. She counted on that and took full advantage of it. It was too late, even if he could move backwards fast enough, she would just grip his arm turn it into a gut punch. The only way he was coming out of this is sacrificing the use of his left arm to block. The force of her punch was incredible. He felt the bone break almost instantly as it collided with his arm. The punch forced him to take several stumbling steps back and left out a stifled scream of agony.

"Well done," Serea chimed.

"My arm disagrees." Xavier hissed through clenched teeth.

Serea walked to him and placed a hand on his right shoulder. He instantly felt a wave of relief and what was once an intense pain dulled into an annoying ache.

"Wow, Szakiya, you did a number on this."

"I admit I may have been a smidge curious and I wanted to see what he would do," she replied, shrugging.

"Still. I actually have to use magic."

"Well, they're gonna have to see it at some point."

"True." She looked at Xavier and winked.

"Why does that not reassure me at all?" He had come to realize that whatever those two were lighthearted about usually meant something life-threatening to him.

Serea held her hand out, presumably asking for his broken arm. With a couple seconds of hesitation, Xavier gently placed his arm in her hand. She wrapped her fingers around his broken forearm which elicited an exclamation of pain and annoyance from him.

"Sorry, but the next part is really interesting."

"Whatever you say." Xavier felt that if he gritted his teeth anymore that he was going to crack a tooth.

Whatever reservations he had were replaced by shock, fear, and wonder. An intricately designed circle of light suddenly appeared over his arm. It had lines going through it that made a six-pointed star along with some smaller circles and triangles; there was even a design that looked like two leather wings. The thing that made it seem almost sinister was the color. Cliché though it may be, it was the color of crimson. Like fresh blood had been spilt all over the circle. Serea met his eye and gave him a look of reassurance.

"Repair. Restore. Heal," she chanted.

Xavier yelped as he was besieged by strange sensations in his arm. Feeling the bone his arm snap back into place was almost worse than having it broken. His muscles spasmed and it felt like insects were crawling underneath his skin. It took all the self-control he had to prevent himself from trying to tear his arm away from Serea. After a few more seconds, the sensation ended. Xavier wiggled his fingers and began to slowly move his arm. All the previous pain was gone, and his arm seemed to be in fine working condition. He muttered a rushed thanks to Serea and stood over next the others. Evidently Serea had healed all of others when he wasn't looking. Each of them looking defeated and frustrated. Xavier wondered if they were all thinking the same thing; how could they escape from here when they're so weak?

"Well that just leaves you, sugar," Szakiya called, looking at Justin.

Xavier had almost forgotten about Justin. All this time he had remained quiet. From what Xavier saw of him, he expected Justin to do poorly in his fight. Although, now that he thought about it, Justin seemed to have been waiting on purpose. It was almost as if he wanted to go last. Xavier took a moment and looked at Justin. Despite the girlish figure, Justin was quite toned. What stuck out more than anything was his eyes. They looked like they were studying Szakiya. He seemed like he was desperately searching for a weakness yet taking special care to pay attention to every detail.

Xavier looked back at Szakiya and saw that she too had noticed Justin's critical stare. She walked to the center of the ring and assumed her combat stance; her smile having vanished. Justin followed suit. Xavier took notice that his hands were a little higher than he was taught, and his knees were only slightly bent. It was then that he noticed Justin's legs. They looked like they were pure muscle. It all made sense. As both fighters squared off, it became apparent: Justin was probably the best fighter out of the new Witches. Xavier assumed the reason that Justin went last was twofold. One, he wanted to see how the others fought and two, he wanted to study how Szakiya fought. Xavier was admittedly guilty of underestimating Justin due to his flamboyancy, and he berated himself.

Szakiya rushed Justin and began her assault with a fierce right hook. Justin used his left arm to push the punch away him while simultaneously turning his body to launch a round house kick at Szakiya. Xavier wondered why he would aim for her body and not her head but seeing Szakiya back away answered his question. There was no doubt about which fighter had the most physical strength and speed. Szakiya easily possessed several times the strength of anyone Xavier had ever seen. The only way Xavier could see Justin coming out of this on his feet is if he kept Szakiya at bay. Provided of course, she continued to show restraint in the fight.

Szakiya rushed in again, this time a little faster, and launched a flying knee at Justin's face. Justin instantly side stepped and again launched a kick. Before Szakiya even landed on the ground, she snagged his foot with a clawed hand. Justin leapt into the air and kicked with his other foot. Xavier thought this was a foolish move as all Szakiya would need to do is catch other foot. And sure enough, she positioned her other hand to catch his oncoming kick. But the moment she did, Justin adjusted the kick to sweep over her hand. Xavier felt himself being a little impressed because even though he was going to fall to the ground, he changed the trajectory of his kick while still midair.

Szakiya moved to dodge Justin's persistent foot and Justin fell to the ground as predicted. Szakiya must have seen this as her chance and responded with a kick of her own. Justin spun on the ground and avoided the kick while getting to his feet. The move was expected yet Xavier thought it looked almost graceful. He wondered if Justin was also a trained dancer. Szakiya heaved a sigh of exasperation and Justin resumed his stance.

"You know I'm holding back, right? Don't make me use actual effort, please," Szakiya said.

Justin scowled, but made no other move. Szakiya shook her head rushed Justin again, this time moving much faster. Xavier wondered if improved eyesight was part of the whole being a Witch package because he knew Szakiya was moving faster, yet he could see every step she took. It was almost if time had slowed down and, considering Szakiya was in the vicinity, he wondered if that was what was really happening. But as she approached, being within a couple inches of Justin, Xavier felt a sudden gush of wind. He smiled as he realized Justin's ploy. All of this was meant to frustrate and annoy Szakiya into using enough speed to pose an actual threat. Justin must have figured out how his powers work and waited until the right moment to blast Szakiya. Unfortunately, Szakiya possessed far greater speed than either Xavier or Justin thought.

As the wind blast collided with the ring where Szakiya was standing, she appeared right behind Justin and poked him in the back of the head with her finger.

4:

Justin's eyes widened in shock which mirrored Xavier's. Xavier began to doubt the whole improved eyesight thing as he didn't see Szakiya move at all.

"Well done," she purred, her voice having an almost sinister quality. "Your timing was flawless. I had only a fraction of a second to move."

"Alright, you," Serea chimed, shooing Szakiya away. "You're sending emails to the wrong inbox sweetie."

Szakiya giggled but moved off to the side to give Serea the center of attention. She took a moment to look at each one of them before clearing her throat.

"All things considered, most of you performed as we thought you would."

"Sounds like you're not too impressed," Adam retorted.

"I'm not. So far, only two of you have any real fighting sense about you. Although most of you at least tried."

Adam scoffed, which earned an additional giggle from Szakiya.

"That being said, you did display how you would react when faced when a creature that was stronger than you and fighter that outclassed you."

"Never mind the potential PTSD you may have triggered," Xavier snapped, suddenly becoming highly annoyed at Serea's lackluster opinions.

"You'll get over it."

"Sure, because that always works."

"Did I not make myself clear earlier? You lot are demon slayers. Warriors. Death, pain, despair, and hopeless odds are part of the dish that life has now served you. Whether you like it or not, whether you agree or not, you are going to have to deal with it."

"And for those of us who can't?"

"You better pray the demon, or demons, make it quick and painless. Spoiler alert: they don't."

"How charming," Xavier spat, mocking Serea's accent.

"Mock me all you wish; it won't change anything. If you want someone to cry to, we have counselors but when the time comes for you to walk into battle, you need to leave all hesitance and misgivings at the door."

"That might work on animals and creatures of the night, but we're human."

"No, you're not."

"Well, we still act and think like we're humans. We didn't grow up fighting. Well," he looked at Justin for a quick second, "most of us didn't grow up fighting. You can't expect us to be warriors at the drop of a hat."

"I don't. But I do expect you to remain open to what I must teach you. Because once you are done with your training, ready or not, you will be called on to fight. And, ready or not, you will either kill or be killed."

The room grew quiet with noticeable unease, which caused Serea to heave a heavy sigh.

"Look, I'm not trying to be a tyrant. I understand that this is all difficult for you. Despite being so old, I do still have feelings and what not. However, the brutal truth is that there is no escaping what you are. The more you struggle and fight against it, the harder it will squeeze. So, please, may I continue? Because there is much more I have to say and much more to be shown before the day is through."

There was a general grumble of agreeance, which caused Serea to frown.

"My point for testing you so early is because, as Witches, you will be faced with harrowing ordeals. Many times, you will either be outnumbered or outmatched. You must learn to be flexible and, above all else, think. I know you've heard the saying, 'the mind is your greatest weapon' or something to that effect?"

Xavier nodded, noting how much he hated that saying. Because if any situation made that apparent, it was his.

"Rest assured, we will teach you everything we can. I only ask that you learn. Your life is going to depend on it. Now, as we've seen how you…fight, we will move on to your powers. Your powers are as much a part of you as your eyes and nose. Yet only two of you thought to even use them. And, even then, both used their powers poorly."

"How so?" Justin asked, his deeper tone of voice once again making an appearance.

"Let me guess: you assumed your powers only kicked in fully when you're in life threatening situations, yes?"

"There wasn't much room for trial and error, but yes."

"It's a common mistake made by most fledgling Witches. Your powers require two things. Willpower and emotion. Your emotion fuels your powers and your will controls them and gives them shape. As your confidence and skill grow, you'll find some powers are easier to use. Some of them don't even require any effort from you."

"Like what?" Danny asked, looking honestly curious.

"Let's take Xavier here. As a Fire Witch, he is immune to extreme heat. He could stand in an explosion and never be burned."

Xavier felt his initial disbelief get crushed by a sense of recognition. He couldn't remember the last time he took a hot shower and had to stifle the urge to go run his hand under hot water.

"That doesn't mean he's immune to the impact from the force of the explosion," Justin quipped.

"You are correct, Justin. The heat wouldn't kill him but being blown into debris certainly might. Since we started with Xavier though, why don't we have him be our first volunteer in this 'how to use our powers' seminar?"

Xavier felt his annoyance flare up again. He hated being the first in anything. Because that meant either setting a bar that no one can reach or putting down a step stool that everyone steps on. He walked up to Serea and looked at her expectantly.

"Now hold out your hand, palm up. I'm going to show you how to properly summon a fireball. Now what do you need to create fire?"

Xavier scoffed mentally. While he was by no means a genius, this was basic. "Some kind of spark and fuel."

"Close. Technically you're correct, but you're not thinking outside the box, so to speak. Let me put it this way. What's in your hand right now?"

"Air?"

"More specific."

Xavier furrowed his brow in confusion before his mental lightbulb suddenly came on. "I can manipulate air particles?"

Serea smiled. "Close. I'd go closer to saying that you can agitate them. Enough agitation to…"

"Cause friction, which causes a spark." Xavier was kind of excited. Much like when his gym teacher taught him to box, he always relished in learning he could do something new. His excitement grew exponentially higher when a baseball sized fireball suddenly appeared in his hand. He stared at it in wonder until it started to shine brightly. He had enough time to brace himself before the fireball exploded. True to Serea's words, he felt no heat from the small explosion, but that didn't stop it from launching him across the ring. He landed and just rolled over onto his back, groaning in pain.

"So…" Serea asked, suddenly appearing over top of him, "what did you do wrong?"

"Too much emotion, not enough willpower?" he groaned, taking her outstretched hand.

"Indeed. Your excitement was understandable, but you have to learn to direct and channel that excitement." She pulled him to his feet and he felt the familiar sensation of her healing him. "Think of it this way: the emotion is the food and the willpower is the plate. Too much food, and it falls off the plate. Too much plate and the food looks tiny and insignificant."

"Understood."

"Good first try, though." She clapped him on the back. "Next, let's have Adam."

Xavier looked at Adam and met his eyes. He had never really noticed how blue they were, or how much fear they contained. It was hard to imagine someone as apathetic as Adam showing fear. As quickly as it came, it vanished; replaced by a veneer of calm and disinterest.

"Alright, Adam, your force is water and you can accomplish this by-"

"I know. Forcing oxygen molecules and hydrogen molecules together." Adam retorted, holding up his hand.

"Wait!"

"What?" Just like Xavier, Adam has summoned a baseball sized orb of water in his hand. "See it's easy…" Adam suddenly looked like he was sick and sunk to his knees.

"Idiot!" Serea snarled while gripping Adam's shoulder. "If you don't focus on taking the water molecules from the air, they'll come from your body instead! Why is that a bad idea, Adam?"

Adam looked at her defiantly before muttering, "It could kill me."

"Brilliant. Let's all try to listen to all my instructions before one of you kills yourself or others with your bumbling, please."

For a second, Xavier could see the fear return to Adam's eyes and his initial excitement began to dissipate.

"Alright, let's have Nate next."

Nate walked over slowly and looked to be apprehensive.

"Right. You're an Earth Witch. Before I was turned, I was an Earth Witch myself, so I'm fully aware of the potential you have."

"Really?" Nate gave a small smile. Xavier still couldn't figure out what Justin saw in him. He was tall, chiseled, and had a great smile, but still... he wasn't that pretty.

"Yes. Out of all the other forces of nature, yours grants you the most diverse power set. This can be both a blessing and a frustration. So, let's start slow and just cover the three basic ones."

"Which are?"

"Manipulating plant life, manipulating earth particles, and generating seismic activity."

"I can do that?!"

No sooner than the words left Nate's lips, the ground started to shake. Xavier groaned as the ground began to shake more and more violently. He held on to one of the ropes in the ring for support as he saw Serea smack Nate upside the head. The shaking stopped as soon as it began, with everyone glaring at Nate. He responded with a sheepish grin and looked at Serea.

"Didn't mean for that to happen."

"Yet it did. You'll find that there is little room for the word 'oops' in this line of work. When generating any seismic waves, do try to remember that you are the epicenter of the waves. You must concentrate on their direction or they will spread like ripples in a pond."

"My bad."

"Indeed. Moving on," Serea reached in pocket, and pulled out a something tiny. Xavier assumed it was a seed of some sort. Although the way Serea looked at it, it made him wonder. She seemed almost wistful, as if the seed was something she was both happy and sad to see. She handed it to Nate and resumed her usual demeanor. "As you can see, this is a seed. You'll get used to carrying these around when you're learning your powers. This seed is a rose seed. I want you to help it grow."

"Cool."

"A word of caution!" she yelped, throwing up her hand to stop him. "Making plants grow is a potentially dangerous process. Which is why Earth Witches are always given flowers to start. You must use your own energy to make it grow. You use too much of your energy…"

"Exhaustion, dehydration, and starvation all rolled into one package of near death?"

"Exactly. So…take your time. This is one of the few times where balancing willpower and emotion is crucial."

Nate nodded, took a deep breath and closed his eyes. After a few moments of silence, Serea gave a small exclamation of delight. Sitting on the middle of Nate's hand was a fully bloomed red rose. Nate smiled, Xavier could tell he was exhausted. Sweat was beading all over his forehead and he began to pant heavily.

"Well done, Nate, but you saw what I meant about growing plants?"

"Oh my god, yeah. I am so tired. Please tell me that moving dirt is easier."

Serea chuckled and nodded. "It is. Earth particles can be found literally anywhere. It's just a matter of focusing on them."

"That simple?"

"Well, you have to direct where the earth goes. If you summon all the particles to you, you'll wind up looking very dirty."

Everyone let out a collective groan which caused Serea to chuckle.

Nate once again closed his eyes. He slowly lifted his hand and pointed to a spot in the middle of the ring. At first Xavier thought Nate couldn't do it. Several minutes had passed yet he heard nothing move. Boredom caused him to look at the spot his was pointing at and he let a small exclamation of surprise. There was a small pile of dirt that had somehow gathered. Xavier guessed that the particles that Nate was manipulating were so small that they couldn't see it. He looked up to say something when he noticed that Nate looked significantly worse. Sweat now drenched him, distorting the color of his shirt and he wore a pained expression on his face. Serea seemed to be concerned as she looked apprehensive though she did nothing to stop him. After a few more minutes, Nate's face relaxed and he lowered his arm. He opened his eyes gave a small smile.

"Sorry, that's all I can do."

"That was more than enough. I'm honestly impressed. You have amazing amounts of endurance."

Nate smiled and then suddenly sat down on the floor of the ring, visibly exhausted. Xavier could feel his jealousy mix with his own feelings of amazement. This guy was handsome, built like a tank, and had the strength of ten men. Xavier had never felt so inferior, though he was still glad Nate was on his side. Given time and training, Nate would be a valuable asset.

"Alright. Let's have Justin next."

Justin walked up towards her, face construed in what seemed like deep thought.

"Now that I understand how this works, I think I've got it."

"Truly?" Serea asked with a laugh. "Go on ahead then. But keep it contained."

Justin lifted his arms until both of his hands were held parallel in front of his chest. Within a few seconds, Justin generated a small tornado between his hands. Xavier felt a pang of jealousy as Justin went to stand with the rest of them. Serea didn't even yell at him for not waiting for instruction. In fact, she just let him go to town. Xavier wondered if she saw something in him that made her trust him or at least his ability to learn.

"Well done, Justin. Danny, you're up."

"Sweet! I got this!"

"Wait!"

Xavier instantly felt like his body was on fire. He fell to the ground as his muscles no longer had the strength to hold him up. The feeling soon ended, and he let out a groan. He felt a hand on his shoulder and he turned to see Serea with a look of concern on her face. He felt the familiar rush of relief that her power brought, and he struggled to get to his feet.

"What happened?"

"Danny here didn't wait for instruction and didn't know that he needed to consciously control the flow of his bio-electricity or it will jump from his body to another."

"…did I just get electrocuted?"

"Yes."

"You okay?" Danny asked sheepishly.

Xavier nodded while resolving to get vengeance later.

"Fellas," Szakiya called, "You have got be more careful. Your powers can actually kill people."

"Don't bother with additional warnings!" Serea snapped. "When they stand over the corpse of their first innocent, they'll learn."

"Not helpful when the first victim could be one of them, Serea."

"Yes, yes, yes. Max, you're last. Since you lot want to rush things, let me give you your instruction now. Much like Adam, your primary powers involve water molecules. Whereas his naturally joins them in their liquid form, your combines them in the solid. Now, slowly form an ice ball, please."

Max, who had paled when his name was called, nodded feebly and lifted his shaking left hand. He closed his eyes and took a deep breath. The moment his lungs finished exhaling, Xavier felt a sudden and quite unwelcome shift of cold in the air. He looked at Max and felt himself gasp in surprise. Floating mere centimeters over Max's hand was a boulder sized ball of ice. Max opened his eyes and gave a small smile. Soon the ice ball decreased in size until it disappeared entirely, and the air resumed its former temperature. Silence made itself comfortable as Xavier and everyone else sat in quiet shock.

"Did I do poorly?" Max squeaked.

"Oh, goodness no!" Serea replied, seemingly getting over her own shock. "I just didn't expect quite the amazing show of power."

"Was I really that good?"

"Yes! Gracious."

Xavier walked over and tapped Serea on the shoulder as she took a step backwards while issuing further directions to the others.

"Max isn't just good, is he?" Xavier said.

Serea looked at Xavier and shook her head. "I've seen Witches who have become extremely powerful and have never shown that level of raw ability. You've quite the coven here, Xavier. I see great things ahead of you."

"I think the word you're looking for is 'terrible.'"

Serea snickered while beckoning him to follow her. "That depends on who you ask, my dear."

5:

Xavier let out a groan of boredom read yet another report. It had been almost two months since he was conscripted into joining Zora. His first month of basic training had been difficult to say the least. Learning how to use his powers and how to fight were easy to him; by contrast, magic had proven particularly challenging. Summoning the power to cast spells wasn't hard, but he was truly limited by his knowledge. In order to cast a spell, the caster had to know exactly what he/she was doing. It soon became apparent that most witches had been well educated physicists, chemists, and biologists by necessity and not choice. And those were the basics. Magic was literally the power to influence the world around oneself; barring that the user knew how the world actually worked.

Xavier looked at his office. All things considered it was normal looking. His large desk sat the back of the room, with this back to the wall. He had a desk top computer stationed to the left side of his desk, as well as a large calendar marked with reminders, scheduled meetings, and training dates. To the right was a various assortment of paper reports, memos, and office supplies. On the right wall sat a book case, littered with books ranging from standard operating procedures to historical texts to frivolous fiction for small breaks. There was a couch near the left wall for when he had more than two people in his office. While the office looked like something you'd see in an everyday building, the lack of a window made the office feel like more of a prison cell. He looked at his trashcan, which was to the left of the door and huffed in frustration.

He lifted his hand in the direction of the trash can called his power to bear. His magic circle appeared seconds later. He liked his circle. Much like Serea's, his circle was red and possessed the same six-pointed star. Unlike hers, his shown with the intensity of the flames he wielded. He also felt warm and soothed when he saw his circle. He looked at the trash can and concentrated on his desired action.

"Levitate." He barked.

The trash can shot into the air a few feet and hovered. With a smug smile, he moved his hand slightly to the right and the trash can followed. He moved it a little more and allowed himself a small chuckle. Then his door flew open and he immediately regretted his decision. The force of the door slamming into the trash can sent it flying directly into Xavier's face. Thanks to his spell still being active the trash can did not tip or flip, so none of the trash landed on him. Still, he did not enjoy a trash can flying into his face nor did he appreciate people barging into his office. He released the spell and placed his trash can next to his desk. He looked up to see Justin with an apologetic look on his face.

"My bad. I didn't realize you were…"

"If you had knocked, it wouldn't have happened."

"If you still weren't practicing baby magic, you wouldn't have had to worry about that." Justin quipped, a sly smile gracing his face. He was lucky that he had become the closest thing to a friend to Xavier.

"What do you want Justin?"

"You get Serea's email?"

Xavier turned to face his computer and logged in, reveling in how fast his typing speed had increased. Between the physical enhancements of being a witch and simple practice, typing at nearly a hundred and fifty words per minute was him being lazy. He accessed his email and skimmed until he saw Serea's name. He clicked on it and began to read. Evidently, she wanted to have a meeting with them within the next few minutes.

"What do you think it's about?" Xavier asked.

"Why you asking me? Ain't you the one who's supposed to be in charge?"

Xavier cringed internally. After clearing basic training, Serea had informed him that he would be leading his coven. He had argued for what felt like hours with her. He didn't get along with people, he didn't like making decisions, and he knew none of the others would listen to him.

Her final reply was, "Then make them listen."

His next task had been to assign each of them to a unit within Zora. Though he had spent a month training with them at that point, he really didn't have the time or desire to get to know them. Thus, assigning them had been an exceptionally daunting task. Due to his being Coven Leader, he had no choice but to be in the Tactics Unit. He assigned Adam to the Medical Unit and was extremely relieved that Adam actually aspired to pursue the medical field. Due to Adam's defiant and apathetic nature, Xavier feared his reaction the most. Everyone else went equally smooth. Nate was assigned to the R&D Unit, Justin the Engineering Unit, Danny the Intelligence Unit, and Max the Archives Unit. By some miracle, he had managed to assign everyone to units that suited them.

That, unfortunately, was the only stroke of good luck he had as Coven Leader. Now that he was in charge, he had been tasked with not only understanding how Zora worked, but figuring out where his coven fit in. There had already been numerous incidents of them rubbing certain groups the wrong way. Adam mouthed off to a group of lion shifters, Justin tore apart an office out of annoyance, and the Psychics all but declared war on them for some strange reason that he had yet to figure out. He felt that most of his day was filled with either training or wading through the latest slew of complaints against them. He let out a sigh of exasperation.

"We've been making waves since we got here, so your guess is as good as mine. You didn't blow up another office, did you?"

Justin's eyes narrowed in annoyance, "No I didn't. I've been good."

"Well then I suppose we'll just have to go see."

Xavier got up from his chair and followed behind Justin out of his office. The Tactics Unit was the largest unit in this branch of Zora considering that it was the first branch established in North America. The hallway was jam packed with the offices of all the leaders and the end opened to a large control room. There, assigned members were watching cameras, sifting through reports or busy having conversations with field operatives. Xavier and Justin skirted by on the edge of the room as to not draw attention to themselves. They entered another hallway which contained all the meeting rooms. They found the one labeled "Patience" and entered. Everyone else had already assembled and they all greeted them as they entered.

"Xavier, you know what this is about?" Nate asked.

"Nope."

"Great…"

"That may have to do with the fact that I didn't tell him." Serea's voice rang.

They all turned to the door and watched Serea walk in. Xavier felt his heart drop to his stomach. Whenever she had bad news, she'd always have this look on her face. As if she was trying to decide how to break the news. Since his appointment to his position, he had become accustomed to seeing that face.

"What did we do now Serea?" he asked, already trying to figure out what he could do to smooth things over.

"It's not about what you've done, but what you're going to do." Another voice replied.

The mood instantly dropped in the room and a visible tension took its place. Another woman walked in the room and stood next to Serea. She was lean and very tall, easily standing eye-to-eye with Nate. She had long auburn hair, which was tied in a neat pony tail. Her blazing green eyes held a permanent sneer that always made Xavier want to punch her in her pointed nose.

"Eliade. What can we help you with?" Xavier replied curtly. There was no hiding his contempt for this woman. Xavier had assumed that he and the rest of his coven would be trained by Serea and Szakiya for their basic training. Unfortunately, he was only half right. Serea handled teaching them about their powers and Szakiya taught them the nuances of magic. Much to his and everyone else's dismay, Beatrice was made in charge of their combat training and Eliade oversaw their training on general knowledge of Zora and how it interacted with the rest of the world.

Surprisingly, Xavier had developed something of a respect for Beatrice. She was brutal but had helped them develop as combatants. Eliade though; she delighted in attempting to prove how inept all of them were. Even Justin, who was easily the smartest out of them, was not safe from her critical stare and snide comments. One thing that tied all of them together was their mutual distaste for this woman. It didn't help that she was a shifter and field certified as well. Their first mission hunting demons was completed under her watchful eye. They had struggled due to the demon being a Chameleon Demon but were well on their way to killing it. Before they could even land the finishing blow, she swooped in and killed it. After making several comments on how weak they are, she had them burn the carcass and submitted a formal complaint to Serea.

"Is that anyway to speak to your superior?" she asked, her green eyes alit with a quiet fury.

"I didn't realize your name was Serea."

"Just because your training with me has advanced, that doesn't mean,"

"That's exactly what it means. Serea, please get to the point. My coven and I have things to do."

Eliade opened her mouth to retort but was stopped by Serea lifting her hand and shaking her head.

"We have come across a location of a possible demon hive." She said, giving Xavier her signature 'we'll talk about this later' look.

"Where?" Max asked.

"D.C."

There was a general groan that escaped everyone's lips. Fighting demons in a small town was preferable. Less likely to be witnesses or innocents involved. Less chance for collateral damage as well. Fighting demons in cities was another matter entirely. If there were any witnesses or police involvement, it required the efforts of at least twenty people to clean up. Psychics to erase memories, certain shifters to procure evidence, and anonymous funds donated to pay for damages. And with a huge city like Washington D.C., the chances of exposure were almost doubled.

"I know, I know. I hate fighting in cities too, but you lot need the experience. This will also be the first mission led by Xavier."

Xavier felt his stomach tie itself in a bow. He took a deep breath and pushed aside his feelings.

"Where is this supposed nest?"

Serea scrolled through her tablet. "In a small bar where they host local bands."

"Downtown?"

"Need you have asked?"

"How large of a crowd are we talking?"

"The bar is small, so no more than a hundred."

"I'll need a couple of field psychics."

Serea let out a snort.

"Ha! Good luck with that one."

Xavier scowled, but said nothing. He knew if Serea ordered it, they would have to comply, but of course she hated the psychics as much as everyone else, so she shied away from issuing orders as much as possible.

"Being as this is your first solo mission." Eliade cut across, clearly annoyed at being ignored. "You will be evaluated."

"Of course, we will." Adam muttered.

"We've been trained well, and this isn't our first hunt. We'll be fine." Xavier hastily added, preventing Eliade from saying anything back to Adam.

She lifted her head and nodded curtly before leaving the room. Serea shook her head and looked at everyone.

"Could you at least try to get along? I do actually have to work directly with her."

"Not a chance." Danny replied with a chuckle.

"She's right though. Everyone in Zora will be watching how this mission goes closely. I can't stress how important success is on this one."

"We understand." Xavier hated the idea of being judged by everyone in Zora, even though he knew it was inevitable. "We'll be fine."

Serea lightly punched him in the arm and turned to leave. A noticeable silence filled the room as everyone stared at Xavier, waiting for instructions. He racked his brain and settled on a course of action.

"Justin, what's the status of our gear and weapons?" he asked, hoping for good news

"Finished."

"Alright. Everyone go down to Engineering, so Justin can show you all the upgrades. I'll go to the Psychic wing and see who we can get. Then we'll all meet in Danny's office"

"You sure you wanna go alone?" Adam inquired, a touch of concern in his voice.

Xavier heaved a sigh, "No. But because I'm a Section Head they won't be directly rude to me."

"Good thing their powers don't work on us."

"Yeah well, they can't all hate us, right?"

Everyone else in the room made varying statements of disbelief before all filing out of the room.

Xavier cut off the light and exited the room. After travelling down a few more hallways he arrived at a nearby elevator. The Psychics had their own floor. It was sad really. As the offspring of the Witches and normal humans, they developed an assortment of abilities. Telepathy, telekinesis, clairvoyance, empathy, and psychometry were the most common. While they were certainly useful, they paled in comparison to the might of their magical parentage. This became painfully obvious as the Witches numbers declined. Except a select few, they were useless in a demon fight. This created a great deal of tension between the Psychics and the rest of the Shadow Factions. The Vampires, Lycans, and Shifters began to shun and belittle them. The result was an uneasy partnership rife with disrespect and anger.

When Xavier and the other Witches arrived, there was a significant shift in dynamics. This was the first time in nearly a century that a full Coven had been discovered. Despite their apparent weakness, there was a great deal of hope and relief when it came to them. Even Eliade, who seemed to express nothing but disappointment, seemed anxious to see their growth. But on the back half of that, the Psychics came under a new wave of poor treatment. There had already been several skirmishes between the Psychic field operatives and other groups. Any communication between the Coven and the Psychics was almost always routed through Serea. He felt a pang of dread as the elevator doors opened.

"Xavier!" shouted a voice.

A blur of motion and color collided with his chest and he felt the wind leave him as he fell to the ground. He instantly summoned a fireball and was about to smash it into the face of his assailant when he stopped short and unleashed a tirade of curses. Perched happily on top of him was bane of everyone at Zora's existence; Miguel. Or at least, that's what he was currently calling himself, according to Serea it changed every fifty or sixty years.

Miguel had the appearance of someone in his early twenties. His shaggy brown hair was kept under a green bandana and he wore tattered jeans with a yellow shirt that had a flower on it. Despite looking like an unwashed hobo, Miguel had the distinction of being exceptionally powerful. No one knew where he came from or what he truly was. Serea named him as being the one who helped her to sanity after she was turned and had been a horrid mix of a thorn in her side and valuable asset. He possessed the ability to literally be anywhere he desired and served as Zora's greatest information broker and spy, and thus his eccentric nature was tolerated.

"Miguel, I swear to God…" Xavier warned through clenched teeth.

“Aw, why all the hostility bro, bro?” Miguel replied, his face adopting a hurt expression.

There was something about Miguel’s voice that was soothing to hear. Almost like his voice was a warm blanket. It made it that much more difficult to remain angry with him, but Xavier was determined.

“You almost caught a face full of fire.”

A strange glint crept into Miguel’s eyes and he smiled. “You know that isn’t true. Besides,” he suddenly vanished. “I brought presents.”

Xavier saw a hand fly out of the corner of his eye and offer itself. The hand was attached to a woman who smiling at him. He took the hand and got to his feet, thanking her.

“You’re welcome.” She chimed.

Xavier took a quick moment to look at her from head to toe. Platinum blonde hair swept back into two cute pigtails, dazzling hazel eyes, incredibly white teeth, one of those jean jackets that only came down to her chest on top of a light blue shirt, a black mini skirt and some pumps. Xavier’s first reaction was that was a typical “spastic-plastic”, but something seemed to tell him that he was mistaken. The way she held herself was confident, but not like he had come to associate with women like her. The confidence was rooted somewhere far deeper than her looks.

“I suppose you’re the ‘present’.”

“We are.” She said nodding to her left.

Xavier looked towards the direction she indicated and noticed another woman. She was leaning against the wall and the moment her eyes met Xavier’s he could tell she didn’t like him. She was dressed in a simple leather jacket over purple shirt, a pair of faded blue-jeans, and a pair of sneakers. Her dark brown hair gracefully danced around her shoulders as she walked towards them. The look he received threw him off a bit, but he ignored it as he extended his hand.

She looked at it and rolled her eyes before shaking it and saying, “My name’s Ophelia and she’s Cassandra.”

“Cassie.”

Ophelia paused a moment and sighed with exasperation. “Cassie. A little birdy told us that you would need two field Psychics.”

Xavier nodded. He wasn’t sure how Miguel had figured it out, but he was glad he didn’t have to go to the Psychic’s floor.

“I’m guessing that face you’re making is relief.” Cassie asked, cracking a small smile.

"A little. Despite not really talking, there seems to be some issues between the Witches and Psychics."

"Yeah. Because who doesn't want to be compared to a group of people everyone thinks is vastly superior to you?" Ophelia cut across.

"Look," Xavier replied, determined to bury this hatchet, "I can't control what everyone else says or does. We don't think any less of you. But from what I've seen you guys are determined to keep fueling this crap."

"Right, you've got nothing to do with it."

"You think you catch hell? Imagine the pressure they're putting on us! We found out we were Witches like two months ago. Our lives taken from us and we get put in the middle of some type of war. Everyone acts like we're supposed to be experts overnight, but they don't care that we were 'normal' beforehand. They just want their weapons. At least you get to be a person."

"Alrighty then." Cassie walked in between both of them and then gave Ophelia a look. "We all have our issues here. We all have to deal with some a-hole who thinks they're entitled to say who's better than who. But we have to give him credit Phi-Phi. He was going to ask for our help."

Ophelia looked at Xavier and her brow furrowed. "Why."

The answer was simple, and he had no issue admitting it.

"We need help. And preferably not from Eliade. Since Miguel nabbed you two, I'm guessing one of you is a telepath or an empath."

Cassie raised her hand, "I'm an empath."

"There we go. We're investigating a possible demon nest. Said nest is in a club. With that many innocent people involved, we need a method of evacuating them without raising undo suspicion. Ergo, Psychic."

"Fair enough." Ophelia seemed to relax a little. "I'm guessing you don't know what else we can do."

Xavier shook his head.

"Cassie is an extremely powerful empath. She can affect the emotions of nearly a thousand people. She's also a telekinetic and pretty kick-ass one at that." This garnered a small giggle and an extreme case of blushing from Cassie. "Me, I'm psychometric and clairvoyant."

"How far in to the future can you see?" He always found the idea of seeing the future to be an unpleasant one. He pitied anyone who could.

"About five minutes. Ten if I really focus. Not much when it comes to prophecy, but what I lack in length, I make up for in accuracy. Especially in combat."

"Still has to suck though."

"Yeah it does. But, it's nice that you know that. It saves me the trouble of having to explain why it's not."

"Well a lot of people want to see their futures so that they know what's coming. But that's the trap isn't it? Knowing. Because once you know, you'll either do everything to make it come true or to prevent it."

"Yup. Fun fact, people always fail. Oh, and bless you."

Before Xavier could ask what she meant he felt a tickle inside of his nose. Seconds later he sneezed, and fire came out of his mouth.

"What the hell?! Since when is that a thing?"

Ophelia chuckled. "Yeah, pretty cliché if you ask me."

"Oh my god I know! The Fire Witch sneezing fire. Gonna ask Serea if there's an off switch or something."

"So, when's the mission briefing?" Cassie asked.

"In a few minutes." Ophelia replied. "Just as soon as he checks on his gear and Danny finishes his report."

Xavier wasn't caught off guard that Ophelia knew what he was going to say, but it still bothered him.

"I just realized something, how can you see me? I thought Psychic's powers don't work on Witches."

"I'm not using my powers on you. The future involves everyone, so I see everyone."

"Did I mention that seeing the future sucks?"

"Heh, yeah. Go ahead. We'll meet you at Danny's office."

Xavier nodded and went back to the elevator. After tapping his fob and looking directly into the camera, the floor buttons lit up and he pressed the B-20. The elevator lurched and began its descent. Nineteen floors later, the doors opened. Xavier had to shield his eyes as the sudden abundance of light began to hurt. He knew why it was so well lit as R&D and Engineering both needed to be able to see precisely what they were doing, but it was still incredibly jarring. Once his eyes adjusted he began to walk to Justin's office. Everywhere he looked he saw people with googles, gloves, tablets, or a combination of the three on. Everyone seemed busy, but in the good way. Like they honestly enjoyed what they did. When compared to his unit, Xavier was almost jealous. After turning down two hallways, he arrived at Justin's workshop.

"What you got for me?"

Justin looked up from his computer and a mischievous grin came across his face. "I finished your sword."

"Sweet."

After they began their basic training, everyone in the Coven was told to choose one to two martial arts to specialize in and a weapon. Initially, Xavier didn't understand why everyone didn't use guns. It seemed the easiest weapon to use against the demons. He didn't expect the answer to be as simple as 'guns make noise'. Since most their missions were covert in nature, the sounds of automatic fire drew far more attention to them than necessary. Although silencers were available, it was easier to use less conventional weapons. Xavier shook it off as an adherence to tradition that Zora could not resist. Either way, he enjoyed the training. Even though he had access to a multitude of ancient and obscure styles, he had always had a love for the Japanese martial arts; therefore, he chose to learn to Karate, Judo and Kendo. Despite Beatrice being a harsh instructor, he reveled in how easy the styles came to him. Though he knew he still had a long way to go, he couldn't help but feel confident in his new martial prowess.

Justin got up from his desk and sped across the room. He nabbed Xavier's katana and tossed it at him. Xavier caught it and he felt a rush familiarity. Once he had graduated to the use of an actual blade, Justin and his team had constructed his blade for him. Although they did not make it traditionally, it was still made with care and hope. Xavier looked at his blade and mumbled "Identify." His magic circle appeared over the sword. While many spells were beyond his ability to cast, he had a knack for being able to see what sort of spells have been cast on an object.

"Well?" Justin asked, looking excited.

"I see the reinforcement spell. I see a shielding spell?"

"To protect it from the force of impacting with another object."

"Ah. What's…this?"

“That would be an invisibility spell.”

“But its visible…”

“Tap the tsuba with your right index finger.”

Xavier did as he was told and watched in wonder as the sword faded from sight. Though he could still feel the sword in his hand, he could see right through where it lay.

“You figured out how to embed a sensory spell!” Xavier replied ecstatically. He remembered how Justin and Nate had been spending hours of their free time putting their heads together trying to figure it out.

“Yaaaaas.”

“Took you long enough. Finally stopped staring at Nate long enough to think?”

“First of all, he is gorgeous. You don’t not stare. Second, magic is a pain in the ass.”

“I assume you mean in a way that I don’t already know?”

“Our magic is literally based on how we think. It isn’t enough to know how something works. We have to also know how we want it to work.”

“I thought there was barely any wiggle room with stuff like that?”

“More than you might imagine. In order for me to imbed that spell, I not only had to know the how but also the when. And it’s there that you can determine the conditions.”

“This can’t work for all sensory spells though. Can it?”

“No clue. Sensory spells are a little tricky. Usually they involve us having to cast them immediately; which made embedding them a headache. How do you put a blinding spell in a cup without it blinding everyone who picks it up? The answer, you set the conditions when it activates. Like tapping it with your right index finger for instance.”

“Nice. What about gear?”

“Considering we’re going to a bar, we’ll have to have to wear regular clothes. We’ll have to enchant some clothes and call it good.”

“Don’t think I own anything non-Zora related.”

“Gurl. Do I have to dress you?”

Xavier flicked his eyes up and down and internally winced at how tight Justin’s clothes were. “No thanks. I’m not sure my brain would survive the sudden lack of circulation.”

“Boy bye. Sometimes you got to put on a show.”

“For?”

"A man?"

"What makes you think I want one?"

Justin let out a bark of laughter, "You got 'I'm so lonely' in neon printed on your forehead. Nate's mine though."

Xavier mimicked Justin's laugh, "What if that's who I want?"

Justin fixed Xavier with a glare so profound that it actually worried him.

"Hoe, I will cut you..."

Xavier quickly started laughing to diffuse the situation as Justin's deeper voice had made an appearance.

"Chill. I don't want him."

Justin let his gaze rest on Xavier for an uncomfortable amount of time before replying, "Aight."

Desperate to turn the conversation elsewhere, Xavier suggested that they head to Danny's office as everyone was probably waiting for them. Justin smirked and agreed before locking his computer. Even though he was just joking, Xavier didn't expect such a harsh reaction from Justin. When they got to the elevator, he saw Justin begin to relax and saw his opportunity.

"So…how long?"

Justin heaved a sigh, "Couple weeks. Didn't realize it until I noticed how happy I got when he would visit the lab."

"Look, I'm the last guy who should talk about feelings and junk, but you shouldn't sit on this."

"Oh, my bad, I thought I'd just be sick and sad for no reason."

"I'm just saying."

"Xavier, in case you forgot we're demon hunters. I'm not just an engineer. I can't afford to be distracted when we're in the field."

Xavier cocked an eyebrow causing Justin to scowl.

"Problem?"

"You're full of it."

"Excuse you?"

"Not acting on your feelings is going to distract you worse. Because it's gonna hurt. Trust me on that. At least if you throw it out there, you'll get an answer."

"Maybe I don't want the answer…"

"In the wrong business to be scared there, buddy. Even if he does say no, at least you can heal and move on."

Before Justin could answer the elevator opened. Xavier placed his hand on Justin's shoulder and smiled. As they headed towards Danny's office, unbidden memories began to flood Xavier's mind. Memories of a beautiful man with long black hair and piercing green eyes danced to the forefront of his thoughts. Xavier still regretted not having the courage to at least speak to that man and hoped that Justin would listen, so he could be spared that same regret. He shook the memories away as they entered Danny's office. As predicted, everyone else had already arrived. He acknowledged everyone and asked Danny to begin the briefing.

"What up guys? I've gone through everything I could find on this and I'm not gonna lie. This is gonna suck."

"Let me guess, a crap ton of different ways for things to go wrong?" Adam asked.

"Yup. I hate being a downer, but this has disaster written all over it."

"Why do you think they gave us this assignment?" Nate chuckled. "They want to see how we can handle a situation that's bound to go wrong."

"Bingo. Everyone in Zora wants to see what we can do. Some want us to succeed and others want us to fail. A lot want us to fail."

Despite the negative news, Xavier was immensely grateful to hear it. Danny had an amazing gift for information gathering. Due to his friendly and approachable nature, there were a multitude of people who opened up to him. Those who did not like him still made the mistake of underestimating his stealth and eavesdropping skills. Offices, computers, phones, memos; nothing was safe from him. Xavier felt almost a swell of pride at the fact that Danny had only been caught once and was still able to talk his way out of it due to his quick thinking.

"I thought Psychics were the only ones who hated us?" Adam asked.

"Afraid not. A lot of people here don't like the shift in focus. For decades Witches weren't a thing. There would be one or two, but they would be killed off pretty early. Then here we show up. We're strong, determined, and we're a full Coven. We have the potential to become the most powerful group in Zora. Not just in this branch, but globally. It doesn't help that we're being trained by Serea either."

"What's wrong about that?"

"You guys don't know? Serea isn't just the one who founded Zora, she leads all of it. The only person who doesn't have to listen to her is Miguel. And even then, he at least follows her lead. More than that, she's considered the mother of all Vampires."

"I've heard that rumor." Xavier replied, unable to recall where. "I always thought it was gossip. She can't be that strong."

Cassie let out a giggle which caused everyone to look at her. "Are you serious? She's a monster. Literally. Yeah vampires existed before she was turned, but they were more demon-y. No human ever bitten could keep their sanity due to the demonic corruption. Serea was the first person to ever regain her sanity. And on top of that she was a Witch. The corruption changed her powers and her magic. You think other vamps can wield blood the way she does? Nope. Not to mention, every non-feral can track their sires to her. She created the current vampire nations."

A stunned silence filled the room. After a few moments Danny cleared his throat and resumed speaking.

"We're getting a bit distracted. Let's just say that there are a lot of people in Zora from around the world that want to see us fail this, which complicates things considerably."

"While I get there's a possible hive in a public place, what makes this so difficult?" Justin asked.

"Let's start with the premises. The club only has two points of entry. But it's below a store which is below some apartments. It's possible that every level contains demons. We could easily be outnumbered twelve to one. Next, the high probability of collateral damage. Higher tiered demons are fairly smart and won't hesitate to nab hostages. There's the matter of the bar itself as well. One misplaced fireball or spark and we'll have some serious explaining to do. Our best bet is to have Cassie get the innocents out and watch her back."

"How fast can you get a group of a hundred out of a building?" Xavier asked, honestly curious as how powerful she was.

"Without causing a mass panic and drawing attention to us? Maybe an hour. It has to be a few at a time. The groups will be easy, but the people who came in by themselves have to appear that they're naturally leaving."

"We'll have to make that work then. What time do the shows typically start?"

Danny looked on his desk, presumably for notes, "Show starts at ten. Bands are always late, so we should get there at ten-thirty. We should go in two groups, so we don't draw too much attention to ourselves."

"I agree." Xavier replied.

After a few more details and some battle plans were exchanged, Xavier dismissed everyone to go get ready and rest, given that they had a few hours before it was time for them to leave. After a few additional words exchanged with everyone he headed for his room. One of the many things he hated about Zora was that almost all its new members were required to live in the branch. This was especially true for them as they weren't willing inductees. What better way to ensure they stayed put than putting them in a place where they were constantly watched?

His room was a little plain. Since they weren't permitted to leave the grounds for personal reasons, anything they wanted from the outside had to be submitted via a requisition order or simply bought online. Despite being paid an impressive stipend, Xavier couldn't bring himself to buy anything too personal. He didn't want to become accustomed to his prison. Thus, his room only had a bed, a desk, and a small bookshelf. He walked towards the back of the room which revealed a walk-in closet and a full bathroom. He cut on the light and heaved a sigh. True to his earlier words, he really didn't have much in way of regular clothes. He didn't see much of a point. As he tore through uniform after uniform, he stopped when he noticed a black t-shirt. He had always been a video game fan, despite not ever being able to play them and he couldn't resist ordering a particular shirt that featured a man with a flaming sword that seemed to be shooting a green energy dragon from his hand. The image had been the cover art from the last game he had watched a play-through for and he thought it looked cool.

With a shrug he snatched it off the hanger and put it on after taking his Zora shirt off. A few more minutes of hunting yielded a black hoodie which he put on. He walked into his bathroom and cut on the light. The sight that met him in the mirror caught him off guard. Due to the constant training and work, he really hadn't taken much time to really look at himself in the mirror. The changes were slightly disturbing. His muscles had grown and become more prominent. His hoodie clung tightly to his form, showing the beginning of a toned set of pectorals which prompted him to see what his arms looked like. He took off the hoodie and saw that the shirt hung tightly to his body showing muscular arms and a flat stomach to boot. Xavier felt like his body wasn't his own. He had enjoyed having a bit of tummy fat. It set him apart from the gym rats people expected him to emulate. He looked at his lower half and then rolled his eyes.

His once scrawny chicken legs were replaced by thick and stout thighs. He turned slightly and much to his dismay, his posterior had also followed suit. It was now more prominent and round than it had ever been. He laughed softly at the irony that he had the body that most people would kill for and here he is, wishing he didn't. He felt a fresh surge of anger towards Zora and whatever god or spirit saw fit to make him a Witch. He looked back at the mirror and stared at his face. He ran a finger along his jaw. Had his face always been so…chiseled? He had always thought he looked ugly, despite being told by people that all 'Natives' looked good. He had scoffed at the sheer ignorance at the generalization and disagreed completely. Being Native American didn't guarantee good looks and he certainly didn't think he was all that attractive. That is, until now. Now he thought he was at least average. He let himself enjoy his new looks for a moment before resuming his anger. And to top it all off, his hair had finally gotten long enough to put in a decent ponytail. Despite his hair having really nothing to do with his other changes, he decided to just lump it in with the rest of his body related complaints as that made him feel better.

He put the hoodie back on and nabbed a nearby hair tie off his sink. After putting his hair in a ponytail and giving his reflection one more disgusted glance, he cut off his light and walked towards the front of his room. He caught sight of a person and with a yelp of surprise, leapt back and summoned two fireballs to his hand. The figure held up its hands in surrender and it was then that his brain finally kicked in and he recognized the figure as being Miguel.

"Dammit Miguel! What do you want?! And don't you knock?"

Miguel gave a small smile of apology which only caused Xavier to increase the size of the fireballs to that of two small boulders.

"Whoa, whoa, whoa! I'm sorry broski. I just wanted to check up on you. When I got here, you were busy giving yourself the stank eye, so I didn't want to interrupt."

Xavier slowly extinguished the flames though his scowl stayed right where it was. "What. Do. You. Want?"

"Yo, what gives with that though? You're pretty good looking. The fellas out there ain't gonna know what hit them man."

"Out where? Oh, you mean my prison. I'm sure we'll have plenty of dates at the mess hall. I can see if Nate will pirate whatever new movie is out. Ooh, maybe we can have a picnic in the gym!"

Miguel face softened into such an expression of sadness that Xavier almost forgot how angry he is. Almost.

"I know dude. But you have to understand, Serea really is trying to look out for you guys. There's so much ugly out there, man."

"Let me guess, we're just not ready for it."

"Hey that's a good thing. It shows that you're still human. Everyone here's forgotten what that's like."

"You included?"

"Nah, I've never known what that's like. But I saw it in others. It was beautiful. Humans are such amazing creatures. I just wish more of you would realize it. Enjoy your heart while you have it. In this place, that's always the first to go."

"I can't imagine why."

"Hey don't knock it. A heart is the most powerful thing that human beings have. The capacity of love is a gift only you have. Don't let it go bro."

Something about Miguel's words were both comforting and infuriating. Xavier couldn't quite put his finger on it and he was eager to see the conversation end.

"I'm gonna go out on a limb here and say that you actually had a reason for being here."

Miguel chuckled and nodded. "Dude, I have a reason for everything I do. You guys just never bother to ask."

"I'll bite, why are you here?"

"To wish you good luck on your first solo mission!"

Xavier felt that if he had rolled his eyes any harder that they would have stayed in that position. Before he could retort, Miguel pulled him into a sudden embrace. It felt warm and kind, but Xavier could see that Miguel was tense. It seemed as if Miguel was genuinely concerned. Xavier wondered if this is what it felt like to be held by a worried parent.

Miguel broke the embrace and stared directly into Xavier's eyes. His eyes looked almost golden though the sheer amount of fear they displayed caused a twinge of alarm.

"You're about to walk head first into an ugly and terrifying world." Xavier had never heard Miguel sound so serious. "The moment you walk out those doors, there's no going back."

"Miguel, I've known the world was a terrible place for a while now."

"You've only seen a taste of it. And the moment you realize that, you'll realize that there aren't any re-do's. There isn't any turning your back. I promise you that."

"What do you know?"

Miguel walked a few steps back and then disappeared. A few seconds his voice filled the room. "After this mission, you guys won't be able to bring yourselves to run. Brace yourself Xavier."

The words hit Xavier like bricks. He wasn't sure what disturbed him more. The fact that Miguel knew they intended to escape or the fact that what awaited them was so terrible that they wouldn't want to. After taking a few moments to calm himself down, Xavier looked at his door and took a deep breath. He opened it and began to walk to his office, determined and terrified.

6:

"Hey! Xavier!" A voice called sternly.

Xavier shook himself out of his current mental space and looked to his left to see Cassie looking at him with a bit of concern.

"You ok?"

"Yeah. Sorry."

He really wasn't. Miguel's words echoed through his head every few seconds, shaking him to his core. After their conversation, Xavier had decided to not tell the rest of his team about the ominous warning he had received. He didn't want everyone else to be as distracted as he was. The subsequent plane and car rides had been uneventful though he had barely paid attention to either. Now as they were walking down a nearby street, he knew he needed to get his head in the game.

"I may not be able to read your emotions, but it doesn't take empathy to see that something's bothering you."

Xavier needed to come up with a decent lie. Unfortunately, the only thing he could produce was, "Just going over everything in my head. Trying to make sure I didn't miss anything."

"We'll be fine." Nate replied, clapping him on the shoulder.

Out of the corner of his eye, Xavier could see that Cassie didn't look completely convinced. A light brush against his hand caught his attention and he turned his head to see Adam had a similar expression on his face. Xavier gave a small smile and looked directly ahead, determined to not look at either of his accusers any longer. As they crossed the street, they caught sight of their other group coming from the opposite direction.

The other group arrived a little before they did and all of them produced cash to present to the bouncer. The man looked like any other stereotypical bouncer; buzz cut, large build, disinterested gaze. He took the money from everyone with a grunt and waved them inside. As Xavier's group walked in, they heard very audible gasps followed by a mix of vomiting and cursing. Without thinking, he rushed forward only to have his mind scream out one clear line. "It's a trap!"

Xavier watched as the bouncer kicked Nate further inside the building, which caused him to crash into everyone else. The bouncer let out a grumbling laugh and as he closed the door, Xavier could see his face distort into a horrid demonic copy of the original. Xavier mentally berated himself for not noticing it earlier but decided to get to the others to ensure their safety. After checking to see if Nate was alright, they pressed ahead into the main body of the club. They pushed aside a red curtain and Xavier felt his heart drop into his stomach. Behind him he heard Cassie gasp.

Everywhere he looked, there were dead bodies. Some were cut to ribbons while others had their necks snapped in horrendous ways. Xavier likened the scene to what a Tarantino film might look like if it were real. He snapped out of his shock and began to look frantically for his other teammates. He saw them in a corner, all huddled with a look of terror on their faces. Max had his face in his hands and was crying uncontrollably, Danny was wiping his mouth with a puddle of vomit not too far off from where he was, and Justin seemed to just stand there with his eyes wide. Ophelia was the only one who seemed to be only one not affected as she walked towards the rest of them.

"I'm sorry I didn't see this earlier. If I had been paying attention…"

Xavier shook his head. "We can't worry about that now. We need to get out of here. I doubt they locked us in here just to show us this."

"Got that right Witch." A voice growled.

Upon hearing the voice everyone seemed to snap out of their shock and revulsion. A figure stepped out from the back of club and smiled at them. He only had the general shape of a human, but that did nothing to assuage Xavier's concerns. The man's face looked distorted. His nose had elongated into something that looked like a snout, his mouth seemed wider than usual and was full of fangs. His hands were also bigger than usual and sporting long black claws. Xavier recognized this monster as a Possessor Demon. They killed humans and possessed their fresh corpses. While they lacked the human's mind and memories, they could still blend in well enough to escape detection.

Xavier saw additional movement and saw seven more Possessor Demons come into sight. Xavier felt a twinge of both dread and annoyance. He didn't know who was pulling the strings, but it was obvious that someone wanted a display. He chanced a small look at everyone else and saw that each of them was slowly spreading out. Glad that they had caught on to what was going on he was returned his full attention to the demons. Each of them had begun to mirror the moves of his team save the one who had originally spoken. He was staring right at him with a grotesque smile. A few moments of silence ensued; each side waiting for the other to move. Then one of the demons accidently knocked a chair over and that was all he needed.

He launched a basketball sized fireball at the demon's head, determined to end this as soon as possible. The demon dodged it and flung himself at him, claws outstretched. With one fluid motion, he drew his sword and bisected the demon. He was elated that Justin had managed to learn the spell embedding process, as it made it possible that all of them were well armed without notice. In a flair of annoyance, he set the corpse on fire with such an intense flame the it was reduced to ash within seconds. A blur of motion caught his attention and he looked up in enough time to see Adam behead his demonic opponent. Adam wielded a Chinese guandao that, while huge, was exceptionally deadly in his hands. Initially, Xavier used to make fun of him for choosing such a bulky weapon, but he soon changed his tune. Adam practically danced when he used it and would even tie a piece of blue cloth to it when he practiced.

As he looked around, he noticed that everyone else had finished up their opponents with similar ease. They all congregated and all of them wore the same worried expression. He really didn't want to say it, because saying it always guaranteed the opposite. But unfortunately, he wasn't the only one thinking it.

"I hate to be that guy," Max murmured, "but wasn't this way too easy?"

A collective groan rang through the club as everyone looked at Max with annoyed stares. A sudden chuckle over a P.A. system prevented anyone from saying anything. Xavier could feel his body tense as he strained his ears to see if he could hear where the voice originated. The club wasn't that big, so he knew the person couldn't be far. The P.A. system's volume rose and fell before the person spoke again.

"Didn't anyone ever tell you little Witch? You shouldn't ever be that guy." The voice was smooth, yet Xavier could swear he heard a level of malevolence. "But to answer your question, yes. I suppose that was a bit easy. I wanted to see what your merry band could do."

"Are you satisfied?" Adam growled.

"Hm. Not quite."

A shriek announced itself from the back of the club and something zipped through the air. Before Xavier could say anything, Cassie lifted her hand and stopped the projectiles midair. One look at them and Xavier felt his heart drop. They were light blue and green feathers. Two figures burst into the room and he swore under his breath.

"Harpies!" Nate screamed.

Xavier had always assumed harpies were beautiful half-woman half-bird creatures that just had a nasty violence streak. The truth was a little more gruesome. Harpies had a bird like head that sat atop what only vaguely appeared to be a female torso. Their arms were long as their whole body that ended with two sets of incredibly sharp looking talons. Their legs resembled the arms though shorter. What stood out visually was their wings that sprouted from their backs. Having four wings with brightly colored feathers that were easily larger than their bodies made them all that much more menacing.

Xavier racked his brain for the best way to kill them. Harpies were infamous high-level demons that required equal parts skill and luck to take out. If their enhanced strength and speed weren't enough to deal with, they had the ability to shoot their feathers as projectiles and had a scream that could induce dizziness and lethargy. Fortunately, there were only two of them present. Whoever was testing them, wasn't serious about killing them.

"Justin, you and Nate are our best spell-casters. Do you two think you'd be able to hit them with some sort of muting spell?"

"We can, but a spell like that requires that we stay focused on keeping their voice boxes from vibrating. We won't be able to fight." Justin whispered.

"Do it. Cassie, hang back and shield them."

The harpy with the light blue feathers surged forward, apparently tired of being ignored. Danny walked forward with a smirk. He dodged the harpy's talon and punched it in the gut. The moment his fist made contact a crackle of lightning flashed and the harpy was sent flying with a squeal. Danny's weapons were simple but still as deadly as any of theirs. He wore a pair of steel gauntlets and a pair of boots with a steel toe and heel. Using his powers, he would send volts of electricity to his hands and feet which caused him to strike with the speed and power of lightning bolt.

"Nice." Xavier said, keeping a close eye on the other harpy who had stopped short after seeing its companion get sent flying. "Cast the spells. Max and Danny, you take that one. Adam you're with me. Ophelia, you stay with Cassie."

Ophelia nodded while taking off her leather jacket. A row of throwing knives was strapped to her arm, though it looked like a few were already missing. She withdrew two and stood in front of Cassie.

Xavier gripped his sword and looked at Adam who nodded. After hearing Justin and Nate mutter "Silence" he watched his harpy reel back in confusion. It opened its back to shriek, but no sound came out. It began to thrash about, evidently dismayed at its sudden loss of making sound. Similar sounds of shuffling and tables being knocked over announced the other harpy's discovery of the same thing. Xavier couldn't help but smile. The harpy caught sight of it and stared Xavier square in the eye. Though its eyes were completely black, he could tell it was enraged.

"Stop making it mad and kill it!" Cassie hollered.

"Jeez. You even tick off demons." Adam chuckled before looking serious. "Careful! Feathers!"

Xavier had only mere seconds to move to his left to avoid the oncoming attack. The harpy's wings were fully extended, nearly hitting the ceiling and with a small flap, the next wave of feathers sped towards them. Ever since he realized he had the ability to generate waves of intense heat, he had worked for weeks to use the ability to generate what he called a 'Heat Shield'. Generating that level of heat was dangerous in close quarters to someone else, so he only summoned a short burst which disintegrated the feathers.

Adam jumped back with a yelp before instantly reaching for his eyebrows. He flashed a glare at Xavier which elicited an apologetic smile.

"Mind not burning my face off?"

Before Xavier could answer, a flash of movement out of the corner of his eye required the attention of a bit of fire. Almost moving on reflex, he lifted his hand shot a torrent of flame. The harpy tumbled backwards. If it could make sound, he was sure it would be screaming in agony. As it stood, it just thrashed and writhed in pain.

"Hot." Adam chuckled.

"Been waiting long to use that one?"

"More or less."

"Please focus more on killing the demon and less on killing me with bad puns."

"Well…finish up. It's nearly done."

Xavier looked at the harpy and he felt his heart twinge. He understood that they were demon slayers, but seeing the thing suffer made him feel monstrous.

"You know that's why they taught us to strike to kill. Our powers can inflict ridiculous amounts of suffering if we pull our punches." Adam looked at the demon and orb of water appeared around its head. Xavier flinched as he heard the tell-tale crunch of bones being crushed.

Adam elbowed Xavier lightly before turning to the other side of the club. Xavier turned as well to see how his teammates were doing. His eyes widened at the sight. Max had chosen a chain dart as his weapon. Despite becoming a very capable combatant, Max claimed that he hated the feeling of hitting someone. So, when choosing a weapon, he decided to use one of the most complicated weapons to keep his opponent at a distance. What caused Xavier to stare in wonder was the fact the Max had not only mastered the weapon but had used his powers to dramatically extend the length of the blade and as such, every single was a beautiful display of deadly ice and cold.

Xavier felt a swell of the pity for the other harpy. If it tried to get it close, Danny would electrocute the thing with his strikes. If it stayed at a distance, it would fall prey to the icy sting of Max's weapon. Someone heaving a sigh soon caught Xavier's attention.

"Danny. Can I please kill it? Now really isn't the time to try out new moves." Max huffed.

"Just keep pressuring it. I'm almost fully charged."

Max clicked his tongue in annoyance. With a small throw, he sent his dart flowing directly at the harpy. The harpy dashed to the left which was unfortunate. Danny had sped in that direction the moment Max threw his dart. He smiled and lifted his foot. The moment the harpy came within range, he started launching kicks. Despite his eyesight and his brain's ability to process information reaching nearly super human levels, Xavier still could not see how many times Danny kicked the harpy.

Ten seconds is all it took Danny to reduce the harpy to a hole ridden corpse. He let out a little laugh before beginning to struggle for balance. Max rolled his eyes before going over to help him. Danny murmured his thanks as he grabbed his leg, which spasmed randomly. Xavier cocked an eyebrow which earned him a triumphant grin.

"Chun-li who?" he asked.

"That was unnecessary." Xavier replied, annoyed at the risk. "You had no idea whether or not your leg would be able to discharge the ambient voltage. Just because you can channel electricity doesn't mean you should risk overloading a vital body part for some flashy moves."

"Oh, come now. You have to admit it was quite entertaining to watch." A voice replied

Xavier didn't wait. The moment the first word hit his ears, every fiber in his being told him that he was in danger. With only a glance out of the corner of his eye, he ignited a humungous blaze around the source of the voice. Everyone else let out exclamations of shock and confusion.

"Xavier! What the hell?!" Adam screamed. "He was human!"

"Then why isn't he screaming?"

"What?"

"I only ignited flames near him. If he was human, he should be burning."

His answer was laughter. The figure within the flames then clapped his hands together which created such a force that the flames were immediately extinguished. The figure was revealed to be a male in a three-piece suit. He looked to be in his thirties. His golden-blonde hair was swept back which revealed his unusual eyes. Almost all of his eyes were colored black except for his irises which were gold. He gave a hearty chuckle while adjusting his suit jacket.

"Don't be too angry with your friend here. He has the sharpest instincts out of the bunch of you, though it's a travesty that none of you saw me coming."

"I did." Ophelia replied from behind the figure.

With one swift motion, she sunk two of her throwing knives into his back. He stumbled forward a step and then looked back at her with a scowl. She instantly withdrew a knife and threw it up, causing the figure to dodge to his right. How he had gotten so close to her face without Xavier even seeing him move was a cause of significant concern. Cassie seemed to share this feeling as she quickly lifted her hand in Ophelia's direction. Ophelia went flying right into Cassie's arms. Xavier's heart dropped into his stomach when he saw Ophelia's scared face.

"My… Your psychics are awful protective of each other." The figure said, chuckling. "I must say, your seer is well trained. Alas, she put holes in my suit. It's very expensive, Versace. You understand."

Xavier blinked, and the figure was mere inches from Cassie, his fist directly next to her jaw. Cassie's face wore an incredibly strained look as she no doubt using a phenomenal amount of energy to keep the figure in place. Danny soon appeared from her left and placed both hands in the figure. Electricity then began to shoot from his hands directly into the figure, sending him flying into a nearby wall. After a few seconds, he stood back up. After giving his hair a few tentative touches, he clicked his tongue in annoyance before beginning to dust off his suit.

Xavier didn't bother to wait; he launched two fireballs before running forward. He knew they would be ineffective against whatever that thing was, so he wondered how blades would fair against it. As soon as the fireballs collided, he swung his katana towards the middle of the figure's head. A hand raised itself from crackling flames and caught the blade between its index and middle finger. Xavier's eyes widened as he felt a foot collide with his stomach. His back clenched in protest as he collided with a wall.

He groaned as he forced himself to get up. He felt a hand touch the small of his back before hearing a muttered, "Heal, restore." He looked at Adam and gave a small smile before turning his attention back to the figure. Nate had begun to engage him, using a mix of his tonfa and small seismic waves; he had managed to secure an opening. Before Xavier could shout that it was a trap, something whizzed through the air causing both Nate and the figure to take a step back.

The figure looked in the direction of the new assault and smiled at Justin.

"Well, well. Aren't we impressive? Shooting arrows made out of compressed air? And let me guess, the bow can split apart into two daggers in case someone gets in close?"

Justin's only response was to shoot two more air arrows at the figure's head. With a flick of his thoughts, Xavier ignited the arrows when they were a few inches away. He had noticed that their opponent liked to dodge at the last possible second, so Xavier decided to create an explosion big enough; he could at least catch this thing off guard.

"Excellent timing. Unfortunately, you haven't really grasped the true extent of my speed."

Xavier felt his blood chill. Another reason he set the arrows on fire was so he could at least catch a glimmer of movement. Xavier swung his katana in equal parts frustration and fear. He was determined to land a blow; he had to land at least one blow. The blade never found its target. Xavier felt all the air and all of the fight leave his body as a fist crashed into his stomach. His legs soon gave out and he fell forward, only to be caught by his assailant. Despite being in excruciating pain, he summoned up enough strength push the thing off him and threw a fireball. The fireball was knocked aside with such a casual flick that it completely infuriated him. He leapt forward with a roar, but a hand appeared on his face. The impact the back of his head withstood as it collided with a wall nearly knocked him out. His vision went white and his limbs all went slack.

"I've had quite enough of that thanks. Why don't you calm down like the rest of your friends?"

Xavier turned his head as far as he was allowed, and his heart nearly stopped. None of his team was on their feet. Some were bleeding slightly, but he didn't think they were dead.

"Wut arr hu?"

The figure chuckled, and it seemed as if his eyes were almost glowing. "Well that's rude. But I suppose you can't help it. What I am should be fairly obvious. After all, possessors and harpies don't obey just anyone. As to *who* I am, my name is Alexander Kiras. I am the scion of House Asmodai and as far you're concerned little witch, the enemy."

"Then why are you letting us live?" Xavier spat, his face having been released.

"Simple, I don't wish to kill you yet."

"Why?"

"You seem to be very curious as to my reasoning for letting you live. You know what they say about curiosity and the cat?"

"Missed that lesson."

"So, it would seem. Well if you must know, I'm equally curious. I want to know how a full coven was able to be formed under my nose. I had become quite adept at arranging the deaths of fledgling Witches you see, so to see all of you was quite the surprise for me. Unfortunately, you don't have those answers or else I'd be torturing you or that blonde you're so fond of."

Xavier's stomach twisted into the most uncomfortable knot. He felt like he was suddenly back in high school, dealing with the various idiots who always tried to convince him that he cared for someone. Usually the person was repulsive to think about in any romantic manner, and the trend had continued.

"Oh, grow up. You can kill demons, but the idea of liking another man is what gets your panties in a twist?"

"What now?" Xavier growled, determined to get off the subject.

"Kids today." Alexander sighed while getting up. "I've seen everything you can show, and I look forward to seeing your growth. No worries, I'll kill you before you become a proper annoyance, but it will be interesting to see how quickly that day approaches. I'm sure you'll try your best to thwart my numerous plans. Word of advice, we are literally everywhere. I'm not even bragging here. I have about three hundred nests across this country alone. That doesn't scratch the surface my friend."

"I'll look forward to burning them all to the ground."

This was the first time Xavier had seen him look agitated and it pleased him immensely.

"Is that so? Well it looks like I'm going to have some entertainment. Don't disappoint."

Alexander walked past Xavier and headed towards the hallway that led to the door. Before he rounded the corner, he stopped and looked back at Xavier. "Silly me. It seems that I've forgotten my manners. Your name is?"

Xavier managed to expel a mirthless bark of laughter before answering, "Mike."

"Short for Michael…" Alexander hissed.

"What's the matter? Don't like my name?"

"Not particularly. Well, see you around little Fire Witch."

With a final look, Alexander walked out of sight. Xavier waited nearly fifteen minutes after he heard the demon leave before struggling to get to his feet. He immediately pulled out his assigned field cell phone and dialed the only saved number in there. After calling in an extraction and giving a brief synopsis of what happened, he hung up and began to check on the others. None of them seemed to be horribly wounded. He got to Adam and touched his forehead.

"Restore." He chanted, hoping he had the energy to wake up his team medic. His magic circle appeared, and he let out a sigh of relief. That sigh however, took out the last of strength. He felt the world shift before everything faded to black.

When he woke up, he was back in the medical ward. The sound of slurping caused him to turn his head so fast that he felt a crick in his neck. A hand suddenly dropped down and smacked him on top of his head.

"Idiot! I just got done healing you and you create more for me to do?!" Serea snapped.

"Sorry! I just heard you drinking and I… Serea?"

"Hm?"

"What are you drinking?"

"Blood packet." She lifted it up to Xavier's face where he could see. He didn't know what was worse, the fact that she was drinking it, or that the packet had a straw in it.

"Oh."

"Using my powers and my magic to rapidly heal eight people left me famished."

"But the straw though?" Xavier replied, winching because he moved his neck the wrong way.

"Isn't if nifty?" Serea asked, grabbing Xavier's neck. "We first made these about forty years ago. Super convenient and makes clean up a breeze."

Xavier felt the pain in his neck fade away and he rolled his head from side to side, careful to do so slowly.

"Thanks, but was it necessary to drink it now?"

"The alternative would have been me draining you dry."

"Ah. Point taken."

"Almost literally if I hadn't found this." She snickered going back to her drink.

"Heh, that one was actually pretty good."

"Thank you. So…can I be your boss now?"

Xavier felt his chest tighten as he began to replay the night's events in his mind.

"The others didn't tell you?"

"The others aren't in charge. But yes, they told me all they knew. But you interacted the most with this demon."

Xavier grew silent. He realized that they had only been in the field for a short time, but he had allowed himself to feel powerful, truly powerful for the first time in his life. He hated feeling helpless and not in control. He knew it wasn't his fault, but he blamed himself completely for his weakness.

"Xavier." Serea said, touching his leg.

"Sorry. The demon's name is Alexander Kiras."

"I'm sorry? Did you say the demon had a name?"

"Yeah. He's the scion of House Asmodai evidently."

Serea's face paled and she sat back in her chair with a look of honest fear on her face.

"Is that bad…?"

Serea looked him and her face adopted a stoic expression.

"Miguel. I know you're listening. Come out here. You have about as much to throw in about them as I do."

Miguel appeared right next to her, a sad expression on his face.

"Hey big guy. How you feeling?"

"Like I just stumbled backwards into the apocalypse."

"Not quite that bad buddy." Miguel replied, sitting down on the edge of bed Xavier was in. "But it's not the best either."

"Understatement of the year." Serea scoffed.

Miguel's expression seemed to grow sadder which made Xavier extremely worried.

"Well, it's like this. Only the most powerful demons have enough sense of self to name themselves. Among them the elite are assembled in the six noble houses. This Alexander guy claimed he was a scion, right?"

"That's what he said. What is a scion?"

"A scion is kinda like an heir. Every house has a Harbinger which is essentially the leader. After a few centuries, they name a member of their house as their scion. The scion must do something to prove their worth which almost always involves slaughtering innocents. Asmodai is one of the worst. Though it's kinda strange that a new scion would pop up so quickly."

"When did the last one pop up?"

"1941.

"As in…"

"World War II. Yeah."

"Are you telling me, the last scion was a demonic Nazi?"

"No. The last scion's mission was to get America involved. So, it helped execute Pearl Harbor. Lost a lot of good folks that day…"

"Still wasn't anything compared to the carnage of the Civil War." Serea intoned, looking off in the distance.

"You fought in the Civil War?" Xavier asked, honestly surprised.

"I've fought in every war held on this continent since the English came. The Civil War was a crown jewel among their accomplishments. By the time that bastard was done, we were even fighting our own people. Needless to say, they aren't one of my favorites."

"Well, whatever Alexander is planning, it's big. Also, he's the reason why there weren't any Witches. According to him, he's been arranging deaths."

"Depending on how long he's been active that might explain the shortage here in the states though I wonder if he's been active globally…"

"Maybe. But I'm a little more worried about why he left Xavier and the rest alive." Miguel replied.

"I asked. He said he wants to know how a full coven appeared under his nose. Don't worry though," Xavier added bitterly, "he'll kill us before we can become a proper annoyance."

"Well, we'll just have to prove him wrong. We'll intensify your training." Serea intoned, giving Xavier a small smile.

"I feel like we need to be on your level to beat him."

"Oh. I'm not trying to sound narcissistic but…I'm over eight hundred years old. I've travelled the globe a few times over. I've learned styles and secrets alike that are more ancient than most countries. Witches may be long lived, but you'll be at the end of your lifespan before you can touch me."

"Really not helping."

"I know. Sorry. But I will say this. Alexander is right in thinking that there's more to you boys. You're here for a reason and I don't believe it's to die at that hands of what sounds like a very pompous demon. You're more powerful than you know."

"Yeah, but I would actually like to start knowing."

"Learn at your pace dude." Miguel cut across, ruffling Xavier's hair. "Take every step as you're meant to, and you'll be amazed at how easy you walk."

A sudden knock at the door caught everyone's attention. The door opened to reveal Xavier's teammates as well as Cassie and Ophelia. The room then filled with talk of if everyone was ok and how Serea was proud of everyone. She excused herself as she still had a lot of coordination with D.C. police to assist with. A club full of dead bodies raised a lot of questions that she needed to answer. Miguel also bade them farewell, stating he had "stuff to do".

After a little more conversing, Ophelia and Cassie decided to go back to head back to their room to rest. They thanked the coven and told them that they would submit a request to be assigned as the coven's permanent field psychics. After they left, silence slowly descended on the room.

"Well, I thought we had gotten a lot stronger." Max huffed.

"We have." Nate replied. "We just came across someone who outclassed us."

"Danny, once we get out of here, I'll write a full report. I want you to dig up everything you can on this Alexander douche and his 'noble house'." Xavier ordered, still feeling as weak as ever.

"Alexander?"

"The demon in the suit that kicked the crap out of us."

"You got it boss."

"Hold up." Justin barked. "Why is that important?"

Xavier looked at Justin and heaved a sigh. He knew what Justin was really asking. Why are they concerning themselves with this when the plan is to run?

"There's no running from this." He stated, echoing Miguel's words.

"Excuse you?"

“There were dead bodies Justin! Literal dozens of them!”

“Your point?”

“Can you honestly walk away from that and not want to do anything about it?”

Justin opened his mouth and quickly shut it. His face showing that he was searching for the right words. When he spoke again, his deeper tone of voice made an appearance. “Xavier, the world is an evil place. It’s terrible but stuff like that happens. Demons or no demons.”

“We need the protection that Zora can offer. Alexander isn’t the sort of demon that’s just gonna let us go. We’re weak Justin. He took us down in seconds.”

“I know! I know. It’s just…the longer we stay here, the harder it will be to leave. I don’t want to spend my life fighting a battle that will never be finished.”

“No one does.” Adam replied. “But we may have the ability to drastically reduce the demon fighting power and actually have lives. Tell ‘em Max.”

Max nodded. “He’s right. According to my research, when the Witches were active, they were able to lead normal and sometimes extraordinary lives. Writers, movie stars, astronauts.”

“Wait, wait, wait.” Danny chuckled. “We’ve had Witches in space?”

“Twice. One French and the other Russian. My point is that we might be able to have lives. Did you know that only thirty percent of members of Zora actually live in their Branches? Most of the time its new recruits or people who just don’t like living among humans. But even they get to go out and do things.”

“Most of them don’t have the violent starts we did.” Justin snapped.

“Not true.” Danny snapped back, visibly irritated at Justin. “Most shifters who don’t know they aren’t human or psychics who never got trained. Zora covers up a lot of things. And we have hefty connections.”

“How hefty?” Xavier asked, honestly curious. He had known an organization like Zora had to have friends in high places, but Serea had refused to share any particulars.

“Near Heads of State hefty. There isn’t a developed country out there that we don’t have our hands in. A few underdeveloped too. Kinda scary how quick we can fake someone’s identity…”

“Either way. There could be a life for us out there.” Max said, looking almost hopeful.

“There might be a life, but we’ll never be free from this world.” Nate replied.

“That was guaranteed the moment we found out we were Witches.”

"Alright guys." Xavier said, eager to get some sleep. "This is something we can talk about tomorrow after training. Go get some rest. We're gonna need it from the way Serea was talking."

Everyone groaned but started to file out of the room. As Xavier got out of the bed he was in, he noticed that Adam stayed behind.

"Something I can help you with?"

Adam fixed him a peculiar look before answering. "Why did you wake me up first?"

"Simple. You're the medic. You've studied medical magic a lot more than I have. If anyone was really hurt, you'd be the best person to help them."

"Hm. Maybe you aren't stupid."

"But you're still a jerk."

"How else am I gonna keep you on your toes?"

"Maybe by not being a jerk? The shock alone may kill me."

"Hmmm. Nah."

7:

Xavier had become accustomed to taking a punch to the face, but he still didn't like the feeling. He especially didn't like it when the fist belonged to a massive panther shifter. It felt less like a fist and more like a sledge hammer. His cheek flared in protest as he flexed the rest of his muscles to keep from being knocked unconscious.

"Come on Xavier!" Beatrice growled, "You've got to stop leaving these openings. It's like you're asking my fist to hit you."

Xavier bobbed out of the way of another punch took a few steps back. Since being beaten by Alexander, he had spent the following weeks redoubling his training. Even though his coven had managed to exterminate three demon nests, he still felt an overwhelming sense of weakness. He had gotten to the point of starting his day with sparring matches with one of his three trainers; martials arts with Beatrice, powers with Serea, or combat magic with Szakiya. When he wasn't sparring or working, he was training with his coven.

"Sorry Bea." He replied, tasting blood in his mouth.

"Sorry won't save your life kiddo. You need to focus. Alright let's mix it up."

Xavier nodded. As everyone had continued their training, Beatrice and Serea had introduced them to a method of physical sparring while wreathing one's arms and legs in their powers. Witches and certain Shifters had been sparring like that for centuries evidently. According to Serea, sparring like that helped the combatants exercise precise control of their powers while still in the heat of combat. Xavier took a deep breath and conjured flames that covered his arms from the elbow down. With another thought he covered his legs from the knee down. He squared his shoulders as Beatrice began to cover her arms and legs in shadow tendrils.

Beatrice rushed forward while swiping her clawed hand down. Xavier mentally scoffed while side stepping the attack. He was going to kick towards her head but found that his foot was stuck on something. He looked down to see shadows tendrils wrapping around his foot and leg. With a huff of annoyance, he throttled the flames on his leg to sever the shadows and sped forward. With a feral grin on both their faces, he and Beatrice began exchanging blows. Neither one could gain purchase with the other. Despite her being the better fighter, a Shifter's powers paled in comparison to the full might of a Witch. At his current level, he was glad he could hold Beatrice at bay. Neither could land more than a glancing blow on each other; which was beginning to irritate him. Evidently the irritation was affecting his fighting ability because soon Beatrice regained the upper hand. Even more irritated, Xavier did his best to turn the tides again, but it was too late. He left himself open for a grab soon found himself on his back with a pointed tendril pointed at as throat.

"You were doing pretty well there, kiddo. You've really got a knack for Karate, but you gotta stop getting mad. There are some fighters who become stronger when they're ticked, you ain't one of them. You get sloppy, real sloppy."

Xavier accepted her outstretched hand and she practically lifted him off the ground. He muttered "thanks" and told her he was headed to the showers. This had been a running theme with him. Every single time he would get angry or irritated, he would screw up whatever he was doing. He knew he didn't have the best disposition on life, but this had gotten ridiculous. As he rounded the corner someone stood in his way. It took him a full ten seconds to realize it was Justin.

"Oh. Sorry. What's going on?"

"Mmhmm. That's exactly what I want to know."

"I'm sorry?"

"What's wrong with you? And don't say nothing."

"But nothing is,"

"Boy bye. You been training like crazy, you been keeping to yourself, and you barely speak to any of us. What is wrong with you?"

Xavier heaved a sigh and leaned against a wall. He was terrible at the whole 'feelings' thing. He was even worse at talking about them. He steeled himself and looked at Justin. Out of everyone, Justin had been the only one who really went out of his way to interact with him on a personal level. He owed Justin some honesty for that alone.

"I feel weak."

"And?" Justin replied.

"And it ticks me off!"

"Xavier, we've been doing this Witch thing for like, five minutes. How powerful did you think we were gonna be?"

"More than this! Powerful enough to smack that grin off that demon's face."

Justin's face reflected an epiphany being achieved. "So, this is about Alexander."

"It's about all of them. What if we go up against something as powerful as him? You think a sick sense of humor is going to keep us alive then?"

"Xavier it's not,"

"Not what? That simple? Isn't it?"

"No, it isn't. Alexander was a rare case. Usually demons like him aren't in the field like that."

"No, their planning wars and who knows what else! How do we beat things that actually start wars?"

Justin looked caught off guard by his question. Xavier supposed that he hadn't really thought about it before. He heaved a sigh and shook his head.

"Look, I'm sorry that I've been out of it. I'm angry that I'm weak and I'm weak because I'm angry. So, huzzah for a whirlwind of idiotic feelings."

"I swear you're going to be the literal death of me. There is nothing wrong with you not being a super demon slayer. Honestly, if you were with your mindset, half the country would be in flames. Just…take your time. Also, Adam is looking for you."

Xavier felt his heart jump to his throat. Despite their grudging respect for one another, Xavier still didn't trust him enough to allow him to do any medical testing.

"I'm scared."

Justin burst into a laughing fit that Xavier couldn't help but join in.

"What are you scared of?"

"The robot with water powers having access to advanced medical equipment. That should scare the crap out of all of you."

"Oh my god! You're about as bad as a damn child! He's not a robot."

"I'm sorry, what else would you call an emotionless husk parading around like its human?"

"An android?"

"And this is better how?"

"They're designed to be more human like. Anyways, go see him. He needs a blood sample."

"Fine."

"Thank you."

Justin waved and sped off with a flourish of his lab coat which caused Xavier to roll his eyes. He had no idea when they became friends, but he was glad he had someone looking out for him. After showering and checking to see if he had any pressing emails, he made his unwilling journey to the medical ward. He walked down one of the main hallways he caught sight of Serea speaking to a woman. He waved, and she beckoned him over.

"Hello dear. Finally going to pay your medic a visit?"

"The Borg shall never assimilate me."

The woman next to her started chuckling but Serea did not share her humor.

"Honestly. I've met twelve-year old's with more maturity."

"Well I am only eighteen. Six years doesn't leave a whole lot of room for growth."

"Says the walking wildfire. Anyways, go see Adam, he's running an experiment and he needs a blood sample."

"When I go missing and come back as a hideous mutant, it's gonna be on your conscious."

It was now the woman's turn to scowl. "Hey now! You be nice! Adam has really done well in our department. He studies diligently and has a real talent for medical work. He's even got to sit in and view a surgery." She then turned to Serea. "Although I have to admit, he is a little…robotic"

Serea's scowl deepened. "Lucy!"

Xavier snorted and excused himself. After turning down the wrong hallway and doubling back to go down the right one; he found himself at the lab Adam worked at. Adam was looking into a microscope while simultaneously writing down what looked like notes on a notepad. Xavier knocked on the door frame which caused him to look up.

"About time you showed up. Come over here and sit."

Xavier grumbled under his breath as he did what he was told. Adam put on a pair of latex gloves, tied a piece of rubber around his bicep, and then proceeded to clean the inside of his elbow with an alcohol pad he grabbed from the table. After a thorough cleaning Adam grabbed a needle pack and attached one them to a syringe. With an additional look at the vein he was aiming for, Adam slowly inserted the needle into Xavier's arm. Xavier winced slightly at the pinch but made no other move. Adam looked at Xavier for a moment and smiled.

"Resistance is futile, human."

"Not funny. At all. Especially with a needle in my arm."

Adam snickered as he withdrew the needle. "Well, you're the one who compared me to a robot. Loudly I might add."

Xavier shook his head as put a finger on his needle wound. "Heal."

"Look at you, learning how to heal flesh wounds." Adam said, separating the blood sample into two test tubes.

"There's an insult in there somewhere."

"There is. It's called you suck at magic."

"Thanks. I hadn't kicked myself for that yet."

Adam gave him a snide grin before looking at his new sample under the microscope. After a few seconds of looking, he growled in frustration. Xavier knew he shouldn't pry as it was bound to lead to more insults, but he was curious none-the-less.

"Did the blood call you a bad name?"

"Thank God our illustrious leader is hilarious, we'll all feel better knowing he's defending the world with his razor-sharp wit."

"Wit beyond measure,"

"Not in your case. Anyways, no the blood didn't call me a name. Might as well have though."

"What are you looking for?"

"I've been talking to Max and Danny and the popular opinion is that our suddenly showing up all together is too crazy to be coincidence. Full covens don't just appear like that. In fact, the last time a full coven was formed like ours was,"

"1875, in Scotland. Queen Victoria demanded that they serve the crown. One of the few times Zora has ever butted heads with a head of state."

"Exactly and they were all related to each other."

"Cousins, right?"

"First cousins. So, it made sense for them. Their entire clan were all witches or psychics."

Xavier cracked a smile at the implication. "Justin better hope we aren't related. Don't think he'd be able to deal with the idea of never dating Nate."

Adam snorted. "Yeah, I'd hate to be there for that. But fortunately for him, there is zero chance for us to be related. Especially when all of us have different ethnic backgrounds. So, I had to think outside the box. Maybe it's more than just blood lines. Maybe it's a genetic marker. Or something else entirely. Either way, there's no way this just happened."

"Six people completely unrelated all within the Eastern USA branch's reach? That part should be obvious."

Adam nodded and then he looked at Xavier with a strange look on his face. Before he could ask what was wrong, he felt his body tense up. He tried to move but couldn't get his body to obey his commands. He heard Adam say "Sweet" before the feeling just suddenly stopped. Xavier took a few deep breaths before turning on Adam.

"The hell did you do to me?!"

"You know how Serea can control our bodies by manipulating the blood in our bodies? I got to thinking that I could do the same except by manipulating the water molecules in your body."

Xavier had to fight the urge to fill Adam's office with fireballs and settled for a stream of curses instead. By the time his tirade was done, he was slightly out of breath and entirely out of patience.

"That was…colorful." Adam replied, looking slightly worried. "I apologize for making you my guinea pig. But it was a quick test and it saved me the trouble of having to ask someone else to do it."

"And that was your alternative?! Because it's not like I have a say on what happens to my body, right?!"

"Admittedly, I could have done that a little differently."

"You think?! My body is mine! You have no right to play with it like a damn toy!"

Xavier didn't bother to wait for Adam's reply. He stormed out of the lab and without a backwards glance. As he approached a nearby elevator, his cell phone vibrated. He pulled it out as the elevator doors opened and saw a text from Max asking him to visit his office in the archives. This irritated him so much that when he huffed, literal flames shot from his mouth. Any other day this would have amused him, but his current mood refused to budge an inch. After going down to the appropriate level, Xavier trudged to his new destination.

As he passed by people through the various halls, he noticed that they kept shying away from him. All of them wore expression of concern and even fear. Now on top of being angry, Xavier felt self-conscious. He looked at a nearby window to see his if he could make anything out in his blurred reflection, but he saw nothing. He increased his stride in a bid to get to Max's office quicker; he really didn't want to be looked at like that anymore. He finally came across a familiar door and threw it open. He nearly fell forward as he had to suddenly stop short to avoid stepping on papers. Max's office looked like a library that had been hit by several hurricanes. Various books, bond documents, and random papers were strewn everywhere the eye could see. And in the middle was Max, typing furiously on a computer.

"Um Max?" Xavier asked, gesturing at the floor.

Max looked up with a start. "Oh! You got here faster than I thought. I'm sorry I – what's wrong with you?"

Xavier blood began to boil at this point. "Oh nothing. I love looking at your messy office."

"You need to chill before you walk in here. You're not setting anything on fire."

Xavier wanted to scream but resisted the urge. Unfortunately flames popped out from his mouth the moment he opened it. He closed his mouth with a snap out of fear of setting something on fire. At this point he began to shake, he couldn't even talk without fire happening. Seconds later, the temperature around him dropped so significantly that he gasped and dropped to his knees. The cold was nearly unbearable, but the moment he was about to give in, it stopped. He shivered as his body struggled to reacclimatize to the warmer temperature.

"Are you calm now?" Max demanded, now on his feet.

Xavier looked at his face and for the first time, Max actually looked intimidating. "What was that for?"

Max opened his mouth to retort before looking at Xavier with a confused look which caused Xavier to wonder what on earth happened.

"You didn't notice, did you?"

"Notice what?"

Max shook his head and heaved an exasperated sigh. "You were generating a ridiculous amount of heat. Any higher and you may have actually started a fire."

Xavier stood up and thought back to the people he passed by on his way there. "That would explain why people were keeping their distance while looking at me funny."

"Yeah. Because no one wants to go near a walking oven. Jeez. What crawled up your butt and died?"

"It's nothing. What did you need?"

Max shook his head and met Xavier's gaze. "No. You nearly set my books on fire and they demand an answer."

"Just Adam being Adam." Xavier mumbled, walking towards Max's desk.

"You've got to control your emotions better than that. We all have an off day, but most people can't set things on fire because someone got under their skin."

Xavier couldn't help but agree, despite Max's words annoying him. Max gave him one more critical glance before sifting through the multitude of papers on his desk.

"How do you find anything in all this?"

"I know what pile has what."

"Do you mind?"

Max pointed at the ground and barked, "Levitate. Sort. Order." Max's white magic circle appeared over his hand and the papers on the ground all rose into the air in a flurry. Moments later they arranged themselves in three neat piles near a bookshelf. Xavier entering the office chuckling as Max resumed his shuffling. He soon pulled out what looked to be an intelligence report. Xavier had been receiving a slew of them from Danny since their mission in the club, mostly containing information on House Asmodai. He had also asked Max to do research to back up any findings.

"I see we've kept Danny busy."

Max snickered. "Between hacking into government systems to working with overseas branches, he has been hating us."

"From what he sent me, Asmodai is only concerned with war, battles, and oppression."

"That's true. But their specialties are wars of attrition. Their best work was The Holy Crusades."

"Are you serious? They caused that? All nine? Seems counterintuitive considering they're demons."

"Some of the vilest demons in our world wear the guise of holy men."

The venom in Max's voice made Xavier slightly curious but he decided to leave that alone for the time being. He did nearly set the room on fire, after all.

"So why am I here? That's not really surprising info."

"You're here because I figured out their M.O."

"Outside of causing mayhem and death?"

"Besides that, yes. They're strictly reactionary. They only start up when another scion upstages them."

"So…you're telling me that they start wars because they're trying to one up another house?"

"Pretty much."

Xavier felt disgusted. He wasn't what he would call a humanitarian, in fact he hated most people, but he didn't think people they deserved to die in some horrid demonic contest.

"Wait, how does Zora not know this?"

"They do, they keep a lot of stuff from us. Half the time, Danny is hacking info out of our own systems."

"Viva la trust issues."

"We're still kids to them."

"So which house caused Asmodai to get Alexander started?"

"House Leviathan initially. They had their hands in the U.S.'s economic decline a little while back."

Xavier snickered. "And here I was, blaming Bush."

"He definitely facilitated the means. Evidently the initial plan between the houses was just cause a little stir. It's not unheard of for the houses to work together to assist with the ascension of a scion. But Leviathan got greedy and our country's debt grew, as did the people's resentment. Of course, Asmodai couldn't let that stand, but they already had a scion. I'm guessing it took them this long to have another one."

"Um Max."

Max looked up from the report he was reading over and gave a puzzled look.

"How do you know all of this?"

"Our Middle East branch caught one of Asmodai's highest ranked generals and…persuaded him to give up the information. Evidently Serea and Allister both were called in."

A chill crept down Xavier's spine. No one ever spoke about Allister in more than a few words. He was the chief of the West Coast Branch and Serea's counterpart, except he was the first sane Lycan. The only thing Serea would reveal is that they had history. He was widely known as cold, intimidating and absolutely ruthless when it came to hunting demons. He felt almost sorry for the mentioned demon. He was about to make a quip when something Max said caught his attention. His face must have given it away because Max nodded.

"You noticed that I said initially right?"

"Yeah… Almost wished I didn't. Let me guess since we showed up, Asmodai has been more active than usual since the club?"

"Oh yeah. Low to high level demons feed on humans by eating them, but they have no sense of self. Little more than slightly intelligent beasts. Demons like Alexander, ones who have a sense of self, they feed off human energy."

Xavier felt that if he rolled his eyes any harder they would have been snuck to the back of his head. "You can't be serious."

Max cocked an eyebrow. "You literally sneeze fire and yet this is what you have issues believing?"

"How does everyone know about that?!"

"Seriously? You sneezed fire. How can everyone not know?"

"What you all just secretly laugh about it?"

"Well, it really isn't secret, but yes. We all laugh about it."

"Back the energy sucking demons please."

Max chuckled which elicited a glare from Xavier.

"Demons like those feed on the energy of humans put in specific situations. For Asmodai, that's mostly war."

"That's a lot of negative vibes floating by."

"Yes. But our world is constantly evolving. Sometimes it's for the better. We haven't had any legitimate large-scale wars in a while. So, what do you do when you need the energy of violent conflicts?"

"You stir up trouble on a smaller scale."

Max nodded and logged in to his computer. A few mouse clicks later, he pointed at his screen. Xavier carefully stepped around his desk and looked at the screen. On the screen was a map of the United States that was dotted with red bullets. There were at least seven bullets per state though some had significantly more.

"What am I looking at?" he asked, slightly apprehensive of the answer.

“These are all reported cases of extremely violent crime. Killing sprees, torture, and bombings are only the tip of the iceberg.”

Xavier knew he didn’t want to know the answer. “How recent?”

“Yesterday.”

“I’m sorry, what?”

“Yesterday Xavier. I think the final count is somewhere in the mid-three hundreds. This is what meeting Alexander did.”

“And we’re sure these are demonically caused? I’m not trying to make light of this, but sometimes people are just bad.”

“Oh, trust me. I wish I could blame most of these on crappy people, but no. Intelligence has been working around the clock and they’re fairly certain. Danny probably just got done leaving their report on your desk since he forwarded this to me a little while ago.”

Almost on cue, Xavier’s phone vibrated. He unlocked the screen to see a text from Danny stating that he dropped off a report and had locked it in his desk. Xavier took a deep breath and began to mull over everything he had learned.

“So…what do we do now?” Max asked quietly.

Xavier was trying to answer that very question. His initial instinct was to have a team locate Alexander and have a small army waiting for him, but he waved it off as being foolish. He stood for what felt like hours, agonizing over every single detail he could think of. Finally, the pieces began to align themselves. After a few more moments of thinking his plan through, he became confident in his decisions.

“I want you and Danny to focus on these attacks when you aren’t training. Danny will be keeping track of current attacks while you research past ones. Everyone has a pattern. That includes demons. I want to find it and exploit it if we can. If we get a feel for how the attacks are ordered or when, then we can start taking small steps to strike back. I’ll assist when I can.”

“Understood. Should I include attacks coordinated with other houses?”

“Yes,” Xavier replied, walking out the office, “I want to know what the differences are.”

Max began to sift through reports as Xavier rounded the corner. He took out his phone and called Serea’s phone. After ensuring she would meet him in his office he got back on the elevator. After a few floors, the doors opened up to reveal a familiar figure.

“Hi Szakiya.” Xavier said, still half-way lost in his thoughts.

"What's up? You're just the Witch I wanted to see." She replied, braids bouncing as she strode in the elevator. She pressed her fob onto the sensor and then smiled in front of camera. She laughed as the elevator restarted its ascension.

"What did you need?" Xavier pondered, mentally trying to verify if he missed a meeting with her.

"It's more about what you need. Which is practice. You're still casting baby magic."

Xavier shrugged. "This is true. Not really sure what my issue is though."

"The issue might be the way you think. I got with Beatrice and she agreed to give you up all day tomorrow, so I can have you."

"Ok. That works because you're about to be busy soon."

Szakiya looked at him quizzically, which made him smile. Once they arrived at his desired floor, he bade her goodbye and zoomed to his office. He opened the door to find Serea sitting on his couch tapping on her tablet. She looked up and waved before resuming her tapping.

"Candy crush?"

"Bubble Witch."

Xavier snickered before closing the door. He nabbed one of the chairs in front of his desk sat down with a huff. Serea pressed the power button on her tablet before looking at Xavier expectantly.

"I need a favor."

"This should be good. Go on."

"I need the most powerful members of this and West Coast's branch to hit the field. Hard."

Serea cocked an eyebrow and crossed her arms. "Why?"

"Asmodai has been extremely busy since the club. Over three hundred reported cases of demonic inspired attacks. Media control alone has had to be torture."

"How do you know about that?" Serea replied, narrowing her eyes.

"I think the real question is why I don't know?"

"You aren't ready. You haven't even,"

"Serea." He cut across, starting to get annoyed again. "Ready or not, we need to be involved. You've been going on and on about how we need to be on the field. Well, here we are."

"It seems I'll have to have your spy watched more closely."

"He's used to being watched. Although why you think it's a good idea to have us fight both you and the demons is beyond me."

Serea paused a moment before replying. "Why do you want such strong fighters in the field? Keep in mind, your answer will affect how we move forward."

Xavier had to fight back the urge to retort with all his might. He took a deep breath and refocused his mind on his plan before he spoke.

"There are way too many attacks happening and they are only going to increase. Alexander is calling us out. Plain and simple. I want you guys to answer. By sending out our strongest to wipe out nests we,"

"Make it seem like we've lost faith in you."

"Exactly. Alexander will see that, and he'll start to get really bold or really safe."

"Which will make him sloppy. Sloppy enough to reveal a pattern anyways."

"Bingo. He's actually pretty miffed that the Coven exists."

"Of course, he is, he's a Witch Hunter. And a damn good one now that we know about his involvement. Alright. I'll talk to everyone here and get Allistar on the phone. Excuse me, his assistant. But you know what that means for you lot, yes?"

"Increased training to make up for you guys not being here at the same time?"

"Indubitably. And your magic is garbage, so I need you to really focus."

"Does everyone know I'm bad at magic?!"

"Yup. That and the fact that you sneeze fire."

8:

"Xavier come on." Justin said exasperatedly. "You've never hung out with everyone before. This would be a good chance for team building."

"I'm good. I don't like large groups." Xavier replied, equally exasperated.

Justin clicked his tongue in annoyance and leaned forward on both elbows on Xavier's desk.

"Xavier, what is this about?"

"Why do you always assume there's some hidden deeper meaning behind the things I do?!"

Justin's only answer was to cock an eyebrow and look at him expectantly. Xavier rolled his eyes and acquiesced.

"I've never been good at being in large social events."

"For real? Had no idea."

"You don't understand, I had one friend and the last time we spoke, I punched her in the face."

"So, don't you think this is a prime opportunity to be sociable? Especially when these are the people who're supposed to trust your leadership?"

"I don't know how. I always wind up getting into it with someone. In this instance, definitely Adam."

"Xavier…it's a pot luck. Seriously? You cook something you always had growing up and you try to have fun."

"No one cooked in my house. I served one function and cooking wasn't it. If it couldn't be made in the oven or microwave, I didn't eat."

Justin looked taken aback for a moment. "You don't know how to cook anything?"

"Ramen noodles?"

"Lord, gimme strength. Well, most of us are doing it as a bit of cultural thing."

"You're really not helping your case here."

"Are you serious? There's going to be so much food."

Xavier looked away from his computer at Justin before chuckling and shaking his head.

"You are such a fat kid."

"Gotta stay thick. How else is Nate supposed to notice me?"

"Your ridiculous intellect, your ability to build almost anything, or your capabilities as a Witch?"

"Aw. You so sweet."

"I aim to please."

"Then come to the pot luck!"

"Didn't you say it was gonna be a cultural thing?"

"Gurl yes! Nate's making pupusas, Danny is making…something with kimchi, Max is making shawarma and something called nihari, Adam is making a quiche and I'm making gumbo!"

"You're from New Orleans?" Xavier snickered, ignoring the growl of interest his stomach made.

"Born and raised suga." Justin replied, adopting a Cajun accent.

"Well yippie for you. I don't have a cultural dish to throw down."

Justin looked at Xavier with a tell-tale sign of concern. Xavier braced himself mentally. He hated having this conversation with people because they always threw pity at him or were always angry.

"Xavier…what do you mean?"

"Exactly what I said."

"You're Native American though."

"Navajo to be exact."

"And what? They don't have traditional dishes?"

"I imagine they do, but none were ever taught to me." Xavier knew it wasn't Justin's fault, but this subject was always a constant source of frustration. For as long as he could remember, his ethnicity has always been a source of conflict or annoyance. People either didn't believe him, treated him like some pitiful animal, or just plain blamed him for his significant lack of knowing anything about his people.

"Well suga, Google is your friend. I'm gonna look something up and you and I are going to make it."

The response wasn't what Xavier expected. There was no pity or anger in Justin's eyes, just a blatant determination to make sure Xavier was included. Even with his former friend, she had never gone out of her way to do that. There was just a silent assumption that Xavier didn't want to. The truth was that he didn't know how. The only answer he could muster was,

"Okay."

Justin smiled and stood up with an air of victory. He started typing his phone and within a few moments, nodded his head. He headed towards to the door and told Xavier meet him in kitchen two, as he didn't like kitchen one. As he turned to leave, Xavier felt his mouth open.

"Justin."

Justin looked back with a puzzled look.

"I just- Thanks."

Justin smiled. "We all have skeletons in our closet Xavier. I know it's new, but you don't have to face everything alone."

"Yeah…I appreciate it."

"I know you do. Punch me in face though, and I'll collapse your lungs."

Xavier laughed before going back to his tirade of emails. It took nearly twenty minutes to finish up and view the reports he was sent. After he finished, he shut down his computer and headed straight for the Justin assigned kitchen. The kitchens were massive and the filled with people. Due to the varied diets of the members of Zora, a lot of different food had to be prepared. Xavier had essentially survived off the cafeteria food offered. Some of it wasn't all that good, but he knew better than to complain to the Kitchens Section Head. The man was a behemoth Bear Shifter that stood at nearly seven feet tall in human form. Xavier had no intentions of finding out what his bear form looked like.

As he walked around looking for Justin while simultaneously trying not to crash into anyone he discovered a group people all snickering talking in whispered tones. Xavier was well acquainted with such groups as many of them had formed to tease him as a child. When he walked over to see what their target was, he felt his stomach drop to the floor. Justin was fussing over his phone and then looking at his assembled ingredients. Normally this wouldn't be cause for staring, but Justin was wearing a bright yellow apron complete with white ruffles. As he turned his head, Xavier noticed a yellow flower sitting on top of his right ear, snuggled neatly in his hair which had been pulled into a neat ponytail.

Xavier couldn't help himself and started roaring with laughter. His laughter had startled the small group of people who were whispering about Justin and they dispersed with smiles on their faces. Justin looked at him with a confused look and turned around. This caused Xavier to laugh even harder as the front of apron read "Gimme some sugar" and featured a big of sugar winking. After some extreme effort, Xavier managed to stop laughing and gave a meek apology to Justin who was visibly irritated.

"What's so funny?"

"Nothing. Absolutely nothing."

"Nah, you sittin there laughin your ass off. Somethin got to be funny."

Xavier fought the urge to chuckle as he gestured at Justin's apron. Justin looked at it and then glared Xavier which ignited a fresh wave of giggles.

"And what exactly is so funny about my apron?" Justin growled, his deep voice signaling that Xavier was in danger.

"It's just…really loud."

"And?"

"The flower doesn't help?"

"Nate grew this for me."

Xavier rolled his eyes before walking over and looking at the assembled ingredients. "So, what are we making?"

Justin said nothing and continued to glare at him.

"Oh, come on! You look a cartoon house wife!"

"And when I get my gorgeous Latino husband, I will make a wonderful house wife. Take it back."

"Take what back?"

"What you said about my apron."

Xavier bit back the urge to retort and bowed deeply. "I'm ever so sorry m'lord." He replied, adopting a cockney accent. "I don't know what came over me brain."

Justin's only response was to grab a handful of flour and throw it at Xavier. He let it land on his chest as he was sure that the only reason Justin wore the apron was because it matched the flower that Nate grew for him.

"So…when are you going to tell Nate that you're pretty much in love in him?" Xavier asked, dusting the flower off his shirt.

"We're making fry bread. I doubt this recipe is fully accurate, but a google search will only turn up but so much."

Xavier walked up to the counter smiling. "That's not what I asked."

"It's the answer you're going to get. Hand me that bowl."

Xavier grabbed it and hid it behind his back which caused Justin to glare yet again.

"Xavier…"

"When are you going to tell him?"

"Dammit Xavier! Never!"

Xavier was slightly taken aback but surrendered the bowl, which Justin snatched with snarl.

"Why not?"

"You get the gay vibe from him?"

"Dude, my gaydar is so broken. I have no idea."

"Well, mine isn't and I can't get a read on him."

Xavier clicked his tongue in annoyance. "So, ask him, idiot."

Justin poured the flour he had been measuring in the bowl and shook his head.

"Are you kidding me with this? You're like the most confident guy I know not to mention you flirt like every time you're near him."

Justin grabbed a liquid measuring cup and handed it to him. "Fill that up to one cup and then put it in the microwave for a minute."

Xavier took the cup but refused to move. Justin reached to his left, produced a knife and simply looked at Xavier. He knew it was an idle threat, but it still spurred him to do as he was asked. He filled the cup and slammed the microwave door after placing the cup in there. Justin narrowed his eyes before taking a deep breath and exhaling.

"Yes, I flirt. I damn near wear a sign that says, 'take me, I'm yours'. But he either isn't interested or doesn't see it. I'm not gonna risk the team by challenging that."

"Dude, it's a yes or no. You get your answer and you move on."

"Once again, I'm not sure I want that answer."

"So, you'd rather hang out in the 'I don't know' limbo? I've never had a boyfriend, but I've watched other couples before. That's a terrible place to be."

"I know, and if we were normal human beings, I'd ask. But we literally deal with life or death situations. I can't afford to cause to a rift now."

"I guess. I don't think it would be all that bad but…"

"Water please. I'd like to get this done within the next hour. And maybe you're right, but this how I'm handling it."

Xavier retrieved the measuring cup and gave it to Justin. For the next fifteen minutes, Justin taught Xavier how to mix ingredients and then how to knead dough. Despite being grateful for the lessons, Xavier couldn't help but be distracted. He hadn't really given much thought to the social connection that he and his team lacked. He barely interacted with people for fear of judgment or worse. He didn't remember when he started to hate people, but he was always comfortable with keeping everyone away. This was the first time in his life where he was put in a situation where he needed to be sociable.

As he continued to consider everything, he realized he barely spent any time with his teammates outside work related concerns. He didn't know anything about them. None of their birthdays, none of their backgrounds, he barely knew what they did when they weren't killing demons. He let out a mirthless chuckle as he started to really comprehend the depths of his failure as a leader.

Justin must have heard him laugh because he turned to Xavier with questioning look.

"Oh. Sorry. Not laughing at you, it's at me."

"What did you do this time?"

"It's more what I haven't been doing. Hey."

"Hmm?"

"When's your birthday?"

Justin stopping mid-knead on the bread and looked at him with a bewildered face.

"You honestly don't know? Serea knows."

"Zora in general knows who we are. It's customary to grab as much information about new recruits as possible. All six of us have huge files somewhere in her office."

"And you never read them?"

"Never saw any reason. Kinda felt like I would be spying or something. That's more Danny's thing."

"Wow. I'm not sure if I'm proud of you or disappointed."

Xavier shrugged. "Whichever it is I'll be bready."

Justin just stared which caused to Xavier to roar with laughter again.

"Oh, sweet baby Jesus that was terrible."

"I know." Xavier rasped, trying to catch his breath. "But it was so good."

After exchanging more terrible bread related puns, it was time to let the bread sit. Justin went to one of the large refrigerators and withdrew a large pot. He explained that he had made his gumbo the night previous and all he needed to do was heat it up. Xavier hopped on a nearby counter and started checking his emails on his phone.

"It's so sad that your Facebook is Microsoft Outlook. Although none of us are really allowed to have social media anymore. Aside from that wannabe Snap Chat they tried to make us use…" Justin chuckled

"Meh. There's always something Zora needs us to do. Besides, I'm not missing much. Never had any social media. Hell, I never had a cell phone before I got here."

"Quoi?"

"I'm gonna assume that was French. And yeah. My upbringing was…a bit dark. My uncle was…"

"No parents?"

"Died when I was seven. I can barely remember them. Any pictures or letters I had of them were destroyed."

"Um…I have no words. Words have completely failed me."

"Don't worry about it. The gumbo is starting to smell good."

Justin looked like he was about to object to the subject change, but a figure strode up which caught both of their attention. Adam waved at both nonchalantly before heading into the fridge. Xavier felt his chest tighten. He had avoided going anywhere near Adam since his last visit. Despite his internal protests, he swallowed his anger and was getting ready to greet Adam before he was cut off.

"Hey, Xavier?" Adam said, after putting his dish in the oven.

"Yeah?"

"About the other day…my bad." Even though Adam wasn't looking at him, Xavier could see that he was struggling to say that. It made Xavier curious as to why, but in an effort to squash any unnecessary drama, he decided to let it go.

"It's ok. I have a thing about people controlling me and I kinda freaked out."

Adam looked at him with a strange look before his face resumed its usual stoic state.

"I thought you weren't coming to the potluck?"

"Someone had other ideas."

Justin smiled smugly before giving a small curtsy.

"Heh. Yeah, he yelled at me too."

"That's because all you two do is work and work. At least Adam can cook."

"Yeah. It was one of the few past times I got pick for myself."

Xavier wanted to ask for more details, but his train of thought was interrupted by Justin telling them both to come over and taste the gumbo. Adam walked over after closing the oven and Xavier soon followed. Adam swallowed the contents of the spoon that was offered, and his eyes widened with shock. Outside of combat, this was the most expressive Xavier had seen Adam. He looked like a human being for once. Xavier was eager to have his taste and once he did, he understood Adam's surprise.

There was an explosion of multiple flavors that devastated his taste buds. Having spent his entire life eating low standard food, this was the most delicious thing he had ever tasted in his life. The bold flavor of the broth mixed with vegetables and shrimp to perform a symphony of ecstasy. And the grand finale was a pleasant spice that permeated everything. He had never had anything so decadent and eating it literally brought tears to his eyes.

"Um, Xavier? You ok?" Justin asked, looking extremely concerned.

"I've never had food this good before…"

Justin's only response was to stare with his mouth open in wonder. Adam grabbed a nearby paper towel and handed it to Xavier, looking just as concerned as Justin. Xavier let out a chuckle before wiping away the tears.

"I'm ok. It was really good. Can you teach me how to make that some time?"

"Any time you want Xavier. Just tell me when." Justin murmured.

"I'll help if you want," Adam offered with a small smile.

"If your food tastes as good as that, then yes please. That was life changing."

The sad part was that he wasn't exaggerating. Up until that point he didn't know that people could make food that good without being professionals. He mentally spat a curse at his uncle and gave thanks that a demon had eaten him. He looked up to see both Adam and Justin staring at him.

"Sorry. Crappy childhood and all that. I'm good. Honest."

Justin shook his head and went back to stir his gumbo. After a few more tentative stirs, he declared his dish was ready. He cut off the heat and then proceeded to hunt down a container to put the fry bread in. Adam checked on his dish which prompted Xavier to go over. After promising profusely that he wouldn't cry again, he was promised a taste of the Quiche. Xavier hopped on the counter and started swinging his feet, excited that he would get to try more good food. Adam started snickering which caused Xavier to cock an eyebrow in confusion.

"You like a little kid who's about to get a present." Adam wheezed, snickering turning into full laughter.

"That's not too far off honestly. You two don't understand. I thought food this good only came from those fancy restaurants. This is like food Christmas for me."

Justin snorted before cutting off a piece of fry bread and handing it to him. Xavier took and eagerly bit into it. It wasn't as flavorful as the gumbo, but it still tasted wonderful. It was light and fluffy while still feeling like it would fill him up if he ate enough. His stomach growled, demanding more and in bigger portions. Both Justin and Adam broke out with renewed laughter which caused Xavier's cheeks to burn, despite not being able to resist smiling as well.

After a few more playful jabs at Xavier's lack of food experience, Adam pulled his dish out of the oven. Xavier rushed to his side so quickly that he was sure that his feet barely hit the ground. Adam gave a small gasp of surprise before looking at Xavier with an exasperated smile. After fetching a fork, he offered some Xavier. After a few cooling blows, Xavier put his mouth around the fork's contents. The dish was divine. The vegetables and meat sung such a glorious harmony with the crust that Xavier was sure he was being blessed by a god.

"Oh, my god." He whispered after swallowing. "Freaking marry me dude."

Adam's roaring laugh rang through the kitchen. Xavier had never even known he could laugh that hard before that day, and now that he saw it, he wished Adam would do it more often.

Justin looked on, astounded by Xavier's reaction. "Damn Adam. What did you put into that? Cuz I need it."

"I know right?!" Adam replied, wiping a tear from his eye. "No first date or nothing. Just straight to the marriage proposal."

"I don't think you two understand how good this is." Xavier chuckled while trying to figure out a good angle to sneak another fork full. "I'm gonna have to lock this down so I have this level of cooking for the rest of my life."

Adam, spotting Xavier's looks, held up a nearby spoon threateningly while giving him a small smile. "First off, you wait till we're at the table and then you can have some more. Secondly, I will not be swooned that easily. So far as I can see, you're the only one who's benefitting from this arrangement. What's in it for me?"

"You get to marry your boss?"

Justin shook his head before handing Xavier the container with the fry bread in it. "That's a damn shame. Is that all you have to offer?"

"Well that's the only thing I've got going for me."

"I disagree." Adam said, placing his dish on top of a tray, "You're intelligent, handsome, and you throw fireballs. These are all very good qualities."

"You think I'm handsome…?" Xavier asked, causing Justin to smirk.

"Who wouldn't? Am I right Justin?"

"Absolutely. You couldn't be friends with me if you were ugly. I need to be surrounded by beauty at all times darling."

Xavier shook his head chuckled. "Both of you are high."

"Xavier… We really aren't joking." Adam said, his tone becoming more serious. "You're handsome, dude."

"Have you not seen yourself in a mirror hun?" Justin asked, also sounding a lot more serious.

"I look in a mirror every day. I think I'm average. I've never had a boyfriend or even kissed anyone, so I figured I was just too bland to be noticed."

Justin looked genuinely taken aback. "You ain't never kissed nobody? Lord have mercy. Hell, I think even Max has had his first kiss."

Xavier shrugged and grabbed his fry bread. "I don't see what the big deal is."

"Oh honey…"

"Yes, yes, yes. I'm so sad! Let's go! Food!"

Xavier couldn't help but smile in anticipation as he, Justin, and Adam all walked towards the meeting room Max had reserved for their potluck. This was the first time that he had been this excited for any social event. As they arrived, he could hear Nate's booming laughter from the other side of the door. Xavier sensed something akin to a disturbance in the force and instantly narrowed his eyes in suspicion.

"Justin…"

"Hmm?" Justin answered, attempting and failing to look innocent.

"What did you do?"

"I have no idea what you're,"

"What did you do?" Xavier repeated, with a vicious glare.

Justin's barely hidden smile did nothing but irritate Xavier more. "I may have told Nate you discovered your inner fat kid."

Though Xavier was no longer upset, he decided to milk it to teach Justin a lesson. He adopted the most malevolent glare he could muster and walked slowly towards Justin. Seeing his face, Justin began to look honestly worried, but defiantly stood his ground. Xavier got directly in his face, fighting the urge to laugh tooth and nail.

"How dare you?"

"Xavier, it's not that big of a deal. It was a joke."

"This is no joke. You said I was fat." Xavier dramatically lifted his shirt and gestured at his stomach. "Look at these abs! Look at them! These were gym made! You apologize to them right now!"

The silence that followed was profound. All three of them started laughing. Justin playfully swatted at Xavier.

"I can't stand you! I thought you was tryin to square up!"

"That's what you get! Serves you right for calling me fat. At best, I'm pleasantly plump."

"You're fine Xavier." Adam replied, still smiling. "Actually, you've toned up since we first got here. You were kinda scrawny back then."

Xavier shrugged. "I haven't really noticed outside of my abs. And I only noticed them because I can tank a punch from Beatrice now."

"Who is hungry so get your still scrawny butts in here!" hollered a familiar angry female voice.

"We better get in there before she eats everyone." Justin whispered.

"I heard that!"

Still snickering, Adam opened the door to reveal a large meeting room. Everyone gave a short greeting and Xavier noticed that everyone they interact with on a near daily basis was there. Serea sat at the head of the table, beaming at them. Szakiya sat her right and Eliade at her left. Beatrice sat next to Eliade, looking irritated which seemed to be scaring Max. Danny was glaring at Beatrice, presumably for scaring Max, but broke the glare to wave at them. Ophelia was inspecting Szakiya's hair closely, causing Xavier to wonder if she was asked to see how much the hair dye had faded. Cassie rolled her eyes before beaming. Nate was smiling broadly before he gestured.

"Finally. We're starving."

"Sorry. I'm cooking stupid." Xavier answered, before taking a seat at the other end of the table.

Adam sat at his right as Xavier was sure that Justin would kill him if he sat beside Nate. Xavier gave Adam a knowing glance before looking at the table's contents. His mouth instantly watered as several smells tantalized his nose the moment he looked. It was almost if the food was begging him to eat them and he was all too happy to oblige. A snicker broke his food motivated trance and caused him to look up.

"Good lord." Eliade said between snickers. "I've seen starving wolves look less hungry. Do you not eat?"

Xavier went to answer, but Justin cut across him first. "He's never had a good home-cooked meal before. His uncle wasn't that much of a cook and T.V. dinners take you only so far."

"Well he's had the opportunity to cook since then I'm sure."

"Don't know how." Xavier replied, giving a small smile though annoyed he had to explain this yet again. "When you don't know any better, cafeteria food seems like the normal."

For the first time in his memory, Eliade was speechless. The amount of sadness in her eyes was almost disturbing as all Xavier had ever seen her express was anger and condescension.

When she spoke again, her voice was so gentle and caring that even Beatrice seemed taken aback.

"Then I will teach you. I spent twelve years in Paris and I became a rather accomplished chef. You find the recipe; I will find the time. No one should be without basic cooking skills."

The only thing Xavier could summon to say was a small "thank you". He had never had anything better than a terse conversation with this woman, so he was ill-equipped to deal with her being so kind.

"Well, now that we've established that, can we eat?" Beatrice asked before placing a small kiss on Eliade's cheek.

Everyone murmured a form of agreement before they began uncovering containers and passing around plates. Xavier was certain that if he had a tail, it would be wagging madly. The food was so delectable. Even the salad that Eliade had made was bursting with so many new flavors that Xavier hadn't even imagined. But something was gnawing at the back of his mind that caused a new emotion to rise.

The feeling began to persist to the point where it was interfering with his meal, so he swallowed the current piece of chicken he was chewing on and looked around. Everyone was eating and having a good time. There was laughter and stories and a general good mood flowing everywhere. Xavier couldn't figure out why he felt a growing tightness in his chest. As he looked from person to person, he realized it. Tears threatened to start again before he felt a hand touch his. He looked to his right to see Adam smiling at him.

"This is the first time you've had a meal with people who didn't completely hate you isn't it?" he whispered.

Xavier nodded. "Is it supposed to feel so warm and welcoming?"

"It is when it's with the right people." Serea called from across the table, a grin dancing across her face.

Xavier was grateful when she shrugged off Szakiya's probing questions. After a few tentative sniffs and after Xavier was sure that the tears had stopped trying to embarrass him, he resumed eating with gusto. As second helpings or in Max's and Beatrice's cases, thirds, were finished the table settled into general conversation. Beatrice was regaling everyone with a story about how she and Eliade killed demons at the opera.

"So, I had been saving for an Alexander McQueen gown for years." She said adamantly. "It was black with silver accents across the bodice. I had to pay almost a grand extra to get it in my size. Eliade even found a black and silver tux! I cannot tell you guys how angry I was when I noticed the little buggers. Because one of two things were going to happen; one, Eliade was going to get demon blood on her tux or two, I was going to get demon blood on my gown."

"So, who did the deed?" Danny asked.

"We both did." Beatrice replied, scowling. "At the top of the second act, we noticed like ten people instantly vanish throughout the audience. Let me just say, fighting demons in a pair of Jimmy Chu's is as terrible as it sounds."

"Did you almost break your ankle?" Xavier pondered.

"God no. I once ran ten miles straight in six-inch pumps. No, they were ruined with all the blood. As was my gown. Damn day off, my face was made up for the gods, and I had a dress that made all my curves pop out."

"God yes." Eliade murmured, looking exceptionally pleased.

"And what happens? Damn demons at the opera. I mean who eats people at the opera? It's already dramatic enough."

"Hey, hey, I made it better though. Didn't I?" Serea jabbed, folding a napkin into a series of shapes.

"That's true. After we contacted HQ for clean-up, Serea bought me two more gowns and matching shoes."

"Two? Whoa, moneybags." Nate joked.

"Do you not know?" Danny asked, looking shocked. "Serea's a freaking billionaire."

"I'm eight hundred years old! I better have something to show for it. I've had several life time's worth of experience, you bet your witchy arse I put it to financial use."

Everyone started laughing before one laugh caught everyone's attention. Everyone turned the left corner of the room where Miguel was sitting on top of a shelf while biting into a left-over chicken leg.

"Dammit Miguel!" Xavier growled. "Use a door! It won't kill you!"

Miguel looked at him and simply shrugged. There was none of his usual joy and happiness in his demeanor which told Xavier everything he needed to know.

"How many this time?"

"Enough that you guys need to get dressed. Now."

Xavier nodded, and everyone got up and began to leave out of the room in a hurry. Xavier looked back at the table and his stomach lurched in longing despite his being very full.

"I'll make you a plate! Go!" Miguel called, making a shoo-ing gesture.

9:

Xavier had become accustomed to Miguel's cryptic warnings, but he still hated receiving them. He was especially anxious about this one. There was something almost sad in the way he looked that made Xavier almost scared about what they would find. After reviewing Miguel's intel, Danny informed them of a slew of missing children's reports. They centered mostly on Vermont but stretched to areas of the surrounding states. There was a rumor floating around certain social media circles that there was a daycare center that people would abandon their children at so Xavier decided to start that there.

After a silent drive and a quick flight, they arrived at the center in question a few hours later. Despite only being a little past midnight, the surrounding area was oddly lifeless. The town wasn't very big, but Xavier had at least expected the occasional car to pass by. But after nearly forty-five minutes of observation, not a single person had driven by. It was at this point that he had decided to use magic.

"Map!" he barked, holding up his palm.

A small ball of fire appeared over his magic circle and began to grow and contort. Soon he had a flaming replica of the building he was observing. It was one level with almost twenty rooms, two offices, and five bathrooms. All and all, it seemed normal.

"Identify!"

A small wisp of flame appeared within his map and began to whisk in and out of the rooms. After a few seconds, the wisp disappeared. There weren't any secret passages that he could find.

"Identify!"

This time he would scan for any life signs in the building.

"You have to cast two 'Identify' spells to check for people and secret passages? You and your baby magic. Thought you were getting better." Justin snorted.

"I'm sorry, and your finely produced map is where? I at least can say I suck at magic. You're actually good at casting and yet you can't seem to wrap your mind around how buildings are built." Xavier retorted.

"Your point?"

"You're an engineer. Your whole thing is building stuff. You can make me a sword that can light on fire and turn invisible, but you can't deconstruct a building schematic."

"It's easier when you're starting from scratch. Because the vision of what's it's supposed to look like is always the end goal. Starting with an already finished product and disassembling it is just something my brain has trouble with."

"So, you can build everything under the sun, but taking it apart is your kryptonite?" Max asked, his face stuck in a report he had printed before they left.

"What's with the double team?" Justin whimpered, pouting.

"You started it." Max replied, cracking a smile.

"I know right?" Xavier added, also smiling. "What's that phrase you're always saying? 'Don't start none, won't be none'."

"…shut up."

A buzz in his ear caused Xavier to cut on his com while dismissing his map spell, slightly apprehensive he couldn't pick up any life signs.

"Go ahead."

"Well?" Adam's voice asked.

"It seems normal, but you know how that song and dance goes."

"Yep. Should we generate a fog cover?"

"Yeah. Go ahead and start, I'll tell the other two."

After pressing the button on his com, he nodded at Justin and Max. Learning how to generate fog was one of the first things they were taught by Serea. Max would generate a cold wave that Justin would push into the air. Once the dropping temperatures reach the ambient moisture that Adam gathers, the fog would slowly be generated. Justin would then focus the fog around a central point about a half mile in diameter.

After the fog set in, Xavier and the others exited the car. They crossed the street and met up with the other half of their group. They got to the door before Cassie held up a hand. Everyone took several steps back and looked at Cassie. Using sign language Cassie told them that she can sense emotions from inside. She then asked if Xavier scanned the building. Already feeling that this was going to be another disaster, Xavier responded in kind and told them that he had in fact scanned for life signs, but he didn't pick anything up.

After a few seconds of rapid suggestions, the doors flew open at them. Cassie and Danny both held up their hands. Xavier knew that Cassie was a powerful telekinetic and he once witnessed her simultaneously lift herself, Ophelia, and six cars, but Danny was the one who truly impressed him. Danny had only discovered a month ago that he could manipulate electromagnetic waves to move ferrous metals. At first it was a struggle for him to lift a can, and now he could stop heavy metal doors mid-air with no visible effort.

Xavier didn't have a chance to say anything as something came flying at a high velocity towards him. He generated an extreme heat wave seconds before it reached him. In the split second before it melted, Xavier could see that it was a Lego. He felt a wave of confusion but otherwise watched the door for anymore projectiles. Cassie and Danny both tossed the doors they were holding onto the street. The noise from the doors must have caught whatever was in there by surprise as a feral snarl rang out from the darkness inside the daycare. Ophelia threw two knives while Justin let an air arrow fly.

Xavier slowly drew his sword. He had heard their return fire hitting their marks, but there was nothing else. No snarls or cries of pain. No thud of a body hitting the floor. The moment his katana was free of its sheath, quiet shuffling noises emanated from inside the daycare. Everyone drew their weapons at that point, except for Cassie who simply assumed her combat stance. The shuffling grew closer and the closer it got, the faster Xavier's heart beat. He hated this part. Why demons got a kick out of dragging things out like that was beyond him. He much preferred the ones who attacked immediately.

The shuffling was by near the door and he tightened his grip. The moment their assailant came into the light, Xavier felt all the fight leave him and he nearly dropped his katana. It was a child, a little girl. She looked like she was no more than maybe five years old. Her skin was grey and decayed and, in many places, just plain gone. Her tattered blue dress was covered in blood stains. Her expression was that of a wild animal. Xavier couldn't help but think that she looked like a zombie, but he knew the real explanation was far more sinister. Saddest of all, the girl was still griping her filthy and torn teddy bear. As if death couldn't make her let go of her favorite toy.

"Max…what the hell is this?" Xavier asked, praying to any god that would listen that the answer wasn't as bad he was imagining.

"Wraiths. Incorporeal demons who enter the brain at the moment of death and control the body. They then use the body to kill others. They're related to the Possessor Demon but whereas the Possessors take over the body, Wraiths take over the brain. The only issue is, the more developed the brain, the harder it is to enter. So they…oh God…they usually target children. It's been almost a hundred years since anyone has seen them."

"How do we kill them?"

Max's only answer was to start crying and hug himself.

"Max! Pull it together!" Xavier snapped, sympathizing with him.

"We can't Xavier. We can't! They're children."

"And they want to be let go." Cassie whispered, looking to be on the verge of tears herself.

"What?"

"The demons take possession in the moment before death. The children are at least somewhat aware of what these monsters do with their bodies. Fear, revulsion, sadness, and an overwhelming desire to escape. Max, we have to."

Max wiped his face and heaved a very heavy and shaky sigh. "God forgive us. We have to destroy the head. Completely. There can be no part of the brain left over, because the control will still be there. If one us goes down, same thing. It's the only way to prevent them from jumping into another brain."

"Smash the head and don't die. Got it." Danny replied, adjusting his gauntlet.

"Careful, there's more coming." Ophelia murmured drawing additional knives in her hand.

True to her word, a group of decaying children filed out of the building. The ages seemed to range from 2 years old to nearly ten. Xavier sheathed his sword and summoned fireballs to his hands. He would make this quick, for both his sake and the sake of the trapped children. It seems that everyone had the same idea and everyone except Ophelia followed suit. With a few short words she told them that she would provide back up and watch the fight closely.

There were no other words. Just the sounds of horrid work that had to be done. Xavier doubted there would ever be a time where they finished a mission that quickly or efficiently. He was incredibly grateful to Justin, Danny, and Cassie as their powers afforded them more speed than the rest of them. Though only a few short minutes had passed, Xavier felt like years had passed by. Once the last of the wraiths had been dispatched, Xavier used his flames to burn off any filth on his hands. He felt so unclean, but he was glad that the children had been freed.

He turned to say something to the team but the sound of snarling and things being smashed rang from the building. Adam and Nate only had a few seconds to get out of the way of the two enormous creatures the tore their ways out of the building's opening, sending bricks and rubble everywhere.

Justin and Xavier both launched a torrent of their powers at the beasts. Both dodged but created openings for Nate and Adam to fall back. Upon further inspection, Xavier identified them.

"Gargoyles." He hissed.

Gargoyles were a powerful breed of demon. They possessed monstrous strength as evidenced by their rippling muscles. They could walk on either all six legs and or rear back two and use the other four offensively. Their black and grey skin helped with their camouflage, which allowed them to hide from prey. Their large maws were lined with pointed teeth except for dagger sized top canines. Most impressive about them were their large wings. Gargoyles were roughly the size of extra-large bears, but their wings were easily triple that size. They had the ability to fold their wings over and over until they sat on their backs, but the moment they fully unfurled, any prey would be terrified.

“We need to kill them before they start flying!” Xavier cried, drawing his katana. He had started the night hoping that he wouldn’t need it. Now, he couldn’t wait to drive his blade into the monstrosities before him.

Everyone else must have had the same opinion as he heard everyone arming themselves. Max surged forward, all traces of his previous mood vanished and, in its place, a cold fury that Xavier had never seen. He jumped in the air and spun. His chain knife sprang to life. Using his powers, he added two longer blades of ice to the ends of the knife. The result was a flurry of chain and ice. The grey skinned gargoyle let out a howl of pain as the snake-like blade tore into its skin, slashing it repeatedly.

The black skinned gargoyle roared and turned in Max’s direction. Before it could even move, Nate surged forward and bashed his ton-fa into the demon’s head. Xavier knew that everyone had become stronger. His maximum bench press had grown from a hundred and eighty to nearly five hundred in the span of a month but, the strength that Nate displayed was on a completely different level.

Seeing Nate handle the black one, Max threw his knife at the head of his opponent. The gargoyle dodged but a smile from Max revealed that his plans were going accordingly. Xavier didn’t know what spell Max used, but the knife began to circle around the gargoyle’s throat before wedging itself in its shoulder. With a throaty yell, Max yanked on the chain. The grey gargoyle let out a gurgled chocking noise before lifting off its feet. With a mighty swing, Max sent his quarry into its comrade. Xavier’s jaw hit the floor. He expected that type of feat from Nate do to his massive size, but Max hadn’t really gained any muscle aside from being generally toned.

Adam must have seen a chance because in a flash of blonde hair, he leaped on top of the grey gargoyle and with two elegant swings of his guan-dao, removed the creature’s wings. If it wasn’t still being chocked by Max’s chain, Xavier was sure that it would have squealed in pain. Instead it just began to thrash and bleed, its purple blood spraying all over its back. The black gargoyle, seeing its partner being brutalized dislodged itself from underneath and swung at Nate. The blow never reached its target as a gust of wind surged forth. Its arm fell to the ground as if cut off by a blade. The resulting howl brought a savage smile to Justin’s face as he knocked an air arrow. He freed it and with a flick of Xavier’s thoughts, it became a fire arrow. The arrow lodged itself in the creature’s shoulder and burst, roasting the side of its face.

The grey gargoyle renewed its efforts and began to pull at the chain with all four of its upper arms. Max pulled at the chain which robbed the creature of all its fight. Max's face wore an expression of sheer contempt.

"You know, I'm usually more of a pacifist." Max spat, walking towards the weak gargoyle. "And if you had resigned yourself to your fate, I would've given you a quick death." Xavier felt a small shiver creep up his spine as he felt the temperature drop suddenly. "But now that I think about it, a quick death is too good for you. I had to kill children tonight. Children."

With every word Max spoke, a little bit of ice began to creep its way up the gargoyle's body. Xavier, who had been looking at the black gargoyle out of the corner of his eye, turned to look at the grey one. His eyes met with its and the terror contained struck something in him. He knew that given the chance, they would have killed him without a thought. He knew that they probably killed their fair share of the children inside the daycare. He knew all of that and hated them for it. But in that moment, he felt a small swell of pity for the beast. The beast understood that it had to die. It understood that its crimes were unforgivable in their eyes. But still its eyes seem to beg for one thing, to be killed quickly. For a moment, Xavier considered granting that request, but one look to the ground where the corpses were changed his mind instantly. He looked directly at the gargoyle and shook his head.

"I hate the idea of hurting anyone." Max continued venomously. "But as I encase your monstrous body in layer after layer of ice…I'm almost satisfied. I'm going to drag this out. I'm going to make you suffer like those kids suffered. I would say more, but you probably can't hear me at this point."

True to his word, the ice had worked its way over the entire gargoyle's body. Its face stuck in a permanent visage of terror. Max gripped his chain and looked as if he were going to pull it and tear the demon's head off, but he hesitated. Xavier figured that this was probably the most sadistic that Max had been in his life, and if he was being honest, he didn't want to see Max do anything else. He looked at Danny and nodded. Danny vanished in a blink of an eye and the sound of ice cracking filled the air. Deep cracks radiated from where Danny's fist had collided with the demon and a few seconds later the demon had been reduced an icy pile of rubble.

"Xavier, right!" Adam's voice hollered.

Never had he been glad for his improved reflexes. As Xavier dodged, a black blur raced past him. The black gargoyle's face was nearly unrecognizable due to Nate's ministrations and it looked like Justin had taken another arm. It leapt forward and swiped at Xavier with a growl. Xavier angled his katana and with one downward swing, cut its claws off. The demon let out a cry that sounded equal parts pained and frustrated. It reared forward and slammed its remaining front claw in the ground. With a gust of wind that nearly knocked Xavier off balance, its enormous wings unfurled. It leapt in the air and with one swing of its wings soared in the air.

"I got it!" Justin called, crouching.

"No!" Xavier screamed. "You have to keep the fog going and call for cleanup and control. I'll go."

"You can't fly Xavier!"

"Don't need to! Nate!"

Nate nodded and extended his right arm. Xavier sprinted and jumped in the air. Nate positioned his arm right underneath Xavier's feet just as he crouched. With one swing, Nate launched him in the air. The Gargoyle had been dodging projectile attacks from the other members of the team and had only noticed Xavier after he was already several feet in the air. The gargoyle had attempted to flap his wings but seemed to struggle. Xavier assumed that Cassie was preventing him from doing so. Xavier resolved to buy her a cake as he landed on the demon's back. He pointed the blade of his katana down and sunk it into the demon. Unfortunately, the gargoyle had managed shake some of Cassie's control and jerked to the left.

Xavier's sword still sunk down into demonic flesh, but it landed in its shoulder instead of the back of its neck. With another jerk it tossed Xavier off its back. As he fell, Cassie must have let go in preparation to catch him because the demon began to flap in earnest and unhindered. As he heard every flap, Xavier felt a single thought echo in his mind. "That bastard has my sword." He was unsure if he willed his powers to activate or if they acted in accordance to his feelings, but he felt flames start to shoot from the bottom of his boots. Instead of questioning it, Xavier increased the ferocity of his flames and in a short few seconds, he was right next to the demon. With a small laugh at the demon's astonished look, Xavier landed again on the demon's back.

Xavier yanked his sword free and with one swing, took the head off the demon. For about two point five seconds, Xavier had forgotten that he was several stories in the air. He let a yelp of terror before remembering that he could at least slow his decent. Doing his best to keep himself upright, he blasted his flames under his feet. He let out a sigh of relief when he felt himself slowing down. After a few tense moments, he gently landed on the ground. Before he could say anything else he felt something hard collide with the back of his head. After blinking away the stars, he turned around to see Justin glaring at him, having already hit Nate judging from the way he was rubbing the back of his head. Xavier gave a small smile which only made Justin's scowl deepen.

"What the hell were you thinking?!"

"Justin…"

"No! Hell no! Don't you 'Justin' me! You had two flight certified members on this team, but your dumb ass want to act like you're a damn superhero and,"

"But we kinda are." Xavier mumbled.

"No dummy! We're Witches. And more specifically you are the leader of us Witches. You have an integral part to play on this team! There was no reason, none, for you to risk your life like that."

"Cassie would have caught me if I fell!" Xavier protested.

"And the gargoyle would have gotten away. How are you so damn smart and stupid at the same time? And then this idiot over here," Justin shot a quick glare at Nate, "damn helping you."

"It seemed like a good idea at the time." Nate offered with a half shrug.

"Xavier, you are responsible for leading this team which means you can't make unmitigated risks with your life!"

"You act like I'm this amazing leader, but I'm really nothing special. One of you would've easily replaced,"

Xavier's sentence was caught off by the impact of foot colliding with side of his face. Ignoring the throbbing in his cheek, he quickly hopped on his feet and took his stance. He was surprised to see that Adam was standing there, red with fury. Before Xavier could ask what the hell was Adam's problem was, a blur in the corner of his eye caught his attention. He managed to block in the nick of time, but the force of Danny's punch still hurt his arm.

"Why are all of you hitting me?!" he screamed, dodging another punch from Danny.

"Do you know what we hate about you Xavier?" Adam asked, waving Danny off.

"What?"

"You have no sense of self-value. You've worked as hard as any of us. And you're talented as hell."

"I throw fireballs and swing a sword." Xavier said skeptically.

“You beat me in chess and beat Serea to a standstill dude.” Nate said, looking flabbergasted.

“And?”

“Oh my God. I was nationally ranked and Serea is eight hundred years old! She was probably around when the game was invented. And you tied with her.”

“So, I’m good at a game. So what?”

“For cripes sake Xavier! You’re a brilliant strategist! Are you honestly this stupid?! Justin I am so sorry. I only agreed to throw him at the gargoyle because I honestly thought he had something planned.”

“I did. I just didn’t expect it to shake Cassie so quickly.”

“It was still a terrible risk.” Cassie replied bitterly, clearly offended at what Xavier said.

“Can we please talk about this later?!” Max screamed.

Everyone turned to look at him and the mood instantly changed. Max looked pale and gaunt, if he hadn’t vomited, he would soon. Danny rushed over and Max dove into his arms. Max’s sobs reminded everyone of what occurred before the gargoyles had attacked. Xavier didn’t know how he should feel. He hated the fact the fact that he had to do it, but he hated that he wasn’t as affected Max was. He went over to Justin and asked how long before the cleanup crews arrived. To answer his question, a series of black vans with the FBI insignia drover through the mist.

Xavier was always astonished at what the Psychic’s and Shifter’s did to clean up a scene. Everyone was in flurry, some literally, to dress the scene up like the scene of a tragic crime. Cheetah and rabbit shifters would use their speed to disseminate the corpses into trash bags while psychics would begin to move rubble and cast a telepathic net which deterred all but local law enforcement. A field medic walked up to him and asked if they needed medical attention. He looked back at Danny, who was still holding an upset Max, and shook his head. He thanked the medic and went looking for the field commander of the crew.

The field commander was a lion shifter that Xavier had worked with prior named Xorn. He was a grizzled middle-aged man that exuded a commanding aura that Xavier had come to expect of men that looked like him. He was talking to a group and looked to be giving directions. By the time he got within listening distance that group had already dispersed. He turned around revealing a half-scarred face and salt and pepper beard. He waved before taking out his flask and offering it. Xavier thanked him and took a swig of the contents. The drink burned his throat, but he didn't care.

"Thanks." He mumbled, handing the flask back.

"Looked like you needed it." Xorn replied, putting the flask back in his jacket pocket and taking out a cigarette. He lit it and took a long drag. "Wraiths huh? Christ. I remember my dad scaring the crap out of me with horror stories about them."

Xavier looked at him puzzled which prompted a throaty chuckle.

"Lion shifters live to about one-seventy. I'm a hundred and ten."

"You gonna be retiring soon?"

"Hell, with what you just dealt with, I should be asking you that. You picked a terrible occupation kid."

"It kinda picked me."

"Yeah, I guess it kinda did. You alright?"

"Would you be?"

"I see sick crap like this every day. You ain't been here a good year yet."

Xavier took a deep breath and he felt a wave of sadness wash over him. "You know what's sad?"

Xorn exhaled another puff of his cigarette smoke before answering. "The fact that people abandoned their kids here to die? I can't tell you why people do that kid. Sometimes humans are just as terrible as the demons."

"Then why do we risk everything to protect them?"

"Because there are only some humans who are like that. Demons it's always guaranteed."

Xavier nodded and gave a few more details about what happened. After promising to have an official report written up after he had gotten a chance to sleep, he bid Xorn farewell and went over to his team. Now that things had calmed down, everyone looked exhausted. Max had finally stopped crying, but he still looked horrible. Xavier told everyone to get in the cars and head on back. The drive back was quiet and almost everyone took the opportunity to nap on the plane. Xavier decided to use the time to get a head start on his report as the idea of sleeping wasn't something his brain agreed with. He looked up from his tablet when Max walked over to him.

"I'm sorry I cried in a combat zone…again." He whispered.

Xavier shook his head and smiled. "Are you kidding? I'm still kicking myself for not crying. Miguel was right."

"About what?"

"He said the heart is always the first to die in this job. After tonight, I can see why."

Max sat on the chair opposite him and pulled his knees up to his chest before wrapping his arms around them. "I wish I was as strong as you."

"No, you don't." Xavier replied, a little more sharply than he meant. He softened his tone before adding, "Because what I have isn't strength. Just because I'm used to horrible things, that doesn't make me strong. In fact, it's the opposite."

"What do you mean?"

"It's easy to shut your heart off to the world around you after you've been hurt a few times. But that's just fear. You shut everything out because you don't want to hurt anymore."

"Kinda where I'm at now. I never want to go through this again. This pain."

"But your ability to empathize with those kids is what makes you so human. You're so free with your affections that I actually get jealous. I wish I could care the way you do. It takes a courageous and an incredibly strong heart to see the things we see and still care about people."

"But I lost it today Xavier… I'm not a violent person. But I train anyway. And every time I throw the knife, I tell myself that it's to protect the ones that can't protect themselves. But tonight? I was a monster. You saw."

"I did. You got justice for those kids."

"No Xavier. Simply killing those demons would have been justice because they wouldn't be able to kill anyone else. What I did was vengeance. And the terrible part is that I didn't feel bad for making that thing suffer. I still don't."

Xavier shifted in his seat uncomfortably. He knew that Max was right, but in the depth of his heart he knew that were he in Max's shoes, he would have done the same thing; if not worse. But he knew that wasn't Max's way and he didn't want Max to lose that.

"We all get vengeful. That urge to punch someone in the face because they ruined your day. Wanting to make something suffer for inflicting suffering, it's part of our nature. But what makes you so amazing is that you have the back bone to admit that isn't how we should be. Just remember this night and learn from it."

Max nodded and they both sat in silence for a few minutes. Max looked up from his knees and asked, "You honestly don't think I'm weak?"

"A bit sensitive and definitely a head case, but never weak."

"Thank you." Max unfurled his legs and got up. He was halfway to his seat to when Xavier heard him say, "Hey Xavier?"

Xavier looked up from his tablet.

"Hm?"

"You're more important than you think. You're turning out to be a pretty decent leader."

10:

"So, the melatonin surges through the brain and then sleep happens?" Xavier asked.

"Melatonin doesn't surge." Adam admonished, head still in his microscope. "Do you not do research or…?"

Xavier scowled. "Try finding time for research when you're neck deep in command meetings, powers training, fight training, magic training, writing reports for freaking everyone, reading reports from you guys and everyone else, tactics training, and to top it all off…cooking lessons with Eliade."

Adam looked up and gave Xavier a dramatic sad face, complete with pouting. "Aww poor baby. Does da widdle baby need saving fwom da bad deer wady?"

"First off, shut up. Second, it's actually not that terrible. I'm learning about a crap ton of dishes and techniques. She's just a perfectionist cooking Nazi."

"Das not guht." Adam replied, adopting an atrocious German accent.

Xavier narrowed his eyes in annoyance which caused Adam to snort in laughter when he looked up. Xavier stretched and hopped off the desk he was sitting on. Adam had called him in the office to take a skin sample. As Xavier was getting his butt handed to him in powers sparring match he was having with Serea, he was all too glad to oblige. Adam made a small gasp of surprise which caused him to look over.

"I knew it!" Adam exclaimed, looking excited.

"What is it doc?"

Adam's face contorted into a look of disgust. "Don't call me that, it makes me sound old. Anyways I've been investigating our rate of cellular regeneration and it's vastly improved since the last time I looked."

"I would have thought that this wouldn't be news."

"Are you serious? There's barely any medical records on Witches."

Xavier furrowed his brow. "How is that possible? Witches have been around for ages and Zora is at least five-hundred years old. There were plenty of Witches back then."

"Yeah, but the advances of medical technology and examination were negligible at best. We really didn't start seeing the kind of advancement we needed until well after the Industrial Revolution. By then, Witches were a rarity."

"Heretic Witches weren't. No one examined them?"

Adam's expression hardened so much that Xavier almost felt in danger.

"Oh, we did. We tortured and dissected them. Evidently, Heretic Witches are integrally different from us natural Witches."

"We tortured them…?" Xavier knew that in the early days of Zora, torture wasn't as frowned upon, but he would have liked to have thought that they would have stopped those practices.

"Not this branch, but yes. Despite Serea and the other branch leaders personally stopping it, they chose to keep the data. Reading through all the reports was…disturbing. But ultimately, Heretic Witches have either none or reduced amounts of our natural gifts."

"How do you mean?"

"Witches are roughly about five times stronger than the strongest human, give or take, with the strongest Witch record being one Elza Friedmarch. According to Max's research, she was strong enough to hit people with train cars."

"Whoa." Xavier murmured, wondering if Max could possibly match her. "What about Heretics?"

"They get about two to three times stronger. It's the same with their speed. They have almost none of our regenerating abilities, their strength with spells is…uncertain. Much like natural Witches, magic truly depends on the person casting it. The only place they have an edge in is their force."

"Really? I thought that's where they would be weakest."

"It depends. If a Metal Heretic tried to fight you, you'd beat them easily. Most of us would. But then you have Heretics like Szakiya. Her force is time. Time is such a primal force of nature that she is almost guaranteed to win every time if she truly decided to go all out."

"Which is why Serea has her here. To keep an eye on her just in case things go south. Serea is really the one I can think of that could take her."

"And she's a monster too. So that tells you something. But even Szakiya would have to use her powers to heal or improve her odds in a hand to hand confrontation with a fully developed Witch."

Xavier let out a mirthless chuckle. "We're surrounded by monsters."

Adam nodded and gave a small smile. "Depending on who you ask, we're monsters too."

"Yeah. So, how fast do we heal?"

"I'm going to have to do some more tests with Nate, but if I had to guess, I'd say maybe about eight times that of normal humans? Maybe?"

"Good. He might need that." Called a familiar voice.

They both turned to see Cassie in the door way. Xavier felt a knot form in his stomach. Cassie usually dressed in cute skirts and bright t-shirts, even when she worked out. Now she was dressed in a pair of form fitting pants and a sports bra, complete with fingerless gloves and boots.

"You and I have a date toots." Cassie's voice had none of her usual pep and energy and the intensity of her gaze told Xavier that she wasn't taking no for an answer.

"What the hell did you do?" Adam whispered out of the corner of his mouth, looking extremely concerned.

Xavier shrugged before walking carefully towards Cassie. "I don't remember us setting up a sparring match. Am I in trouble?"

Cassie's only answer was to turn and walk down the hallway. Xavier's sore muscles ached with protest as they came under quite a bit of abuse from Serea earlier that day. The walk and subsequent elevator ride was uncomfortably quiet. When they arrived at the gym, it was completely empty. Xavier's hair on the back of his head stood up. Ever since he and the others had achieved a basic level of control over their powers, other members of Zora had resumed their usual work out routines. The gym was seldom empty unless the gym had been declared off limits. When they walked to the middle of the middle of the gym Xavier decided that he had enough.

"Cassie what is this about? And don't even think of keeping up that silence bit because I'll walk out of here."

Cassie turned to look at him and held her gaze before answering. "Do you know what one of the main benefits of being an empath is?"

"No. But I suppose this is the part where you tell me."

Cassie's eyes narrowed but she continued. "I learned how to read people on an almost intimate level. The slightest glance, the way they hold up their hand, all of it becomes clear. I've gotten so good that I don't even need my powers in most cases."

"Ok?"

"That ability allows me to do a few cool things."

"Like?"

Cassie turned around and flexed her hand and a pink katana appeared in it. She made no move to strike which gave Xavier an extra moment to inspect her weapon. It was slightly translucent but seemed alive with power. As his eyes traced the full length of the weapon, they stopped at the tsuba. The shape looked so familiar that he couldn't look away.

"Is that…?"

"Your katana? Yes."

"How?"

"Telekinesis is by far one of the most powerful and versatile powers we Psychics have. What you see here is a weapon made of pure telekinetic energy. One day I was reading my favorite comic and I saw a character do this. I've using this technique ever since."

Xavier couldn't even begin to judge. He had also torn through several comic books when time allowed, desperately searching for more ways to use his powers. That still didn't answer his most pressing question.

"But why my sword?"

"Draw yours and I'll answer."

Xavier had begun to make a habit of always carrying his sword with him ever since Justin had embedded the invisibility spell on it. He was unsure of how Cassie knew that he had it, but he didn't question it. He wanted to get to the bottom of this as soon as possible. He reached and touched the tsuba with this right index finger, bringing his katana and the small harness holding it on his back into view. After some additional fidgeting and cursing at the harness for its impracticality for combat, he held his katana and prepared for anything.

The two of them stood like that for nearly thirty seconds before Cassie made the first move. She sped forward with a surprising amount of speed and brought the sword down in a graceful arc. With one fluid draw, he brought his sword up to meet hers. The instant the blades were inches apart Xavier realized his mistake. He quickly dodged the feint slashed upwards. The blades collided, and pink sparks danced across both blades. Cassie dislodged her blade and launched a quick roundhouse kick. Xavier used the bottom of his hilt to knock her foot down before slashing down. He had no idea why she would kick him when his guard wasn't down.

Cassie pivoted to recover her balance before charging Xavier again. Every blow they exchanged stoked the flames of a sense of familiarity. Everything from the way she swung her blade to the way she stood. Everything about how she fought him just screamed that he had seen this before. The locked blades again and Xavier looked her telekinetic copy of his sword and it all clicked. Cassie must have seen the truth dawn on his face because she cracked a small smile before dislodging her blade again. Spurred by the knowledge that he was essentially fighting himself, Xavier raced forward, letting out a feral yell.

He lost track of how long they fought, but his body was beginning to give out. Every cross of blades sent tremors of pain down his arms and his lungs burned with every breath he took. Cassie seemed no better as she was covered with sweat and looked like she was ready to keel over. Xavier readied his sword for another clash, but his right arm spasmed and he dropped it. He looked at Cassie and started to snicker. Soon the two of them started to laugh heartedly. They both collapsed, and Xavier rolled over unto his back.

“Satisfied. Yet?” Xavier heaved between breaths, fighting off more laughing as he was sure it was going to kill him.

“I should. Be asking you that.”

Xavier was. This was a unique opportunity for him. He got to see the flaws in his fighting style in active combat. But even as he enjoyed the training session, there was a still a pressing question.

“What brought this on?” he asked, reveling in how cold the floor was.

“Our last mission.” Cassie answered after a few deep breaths. “The fact that you didn’t even know what you excel at is a huge issue. Xavier you’re responsible for our plans and strategies when we go into combat. The fact that you’ve just been winging it ticked me off so bad. But instead of beating the snot out of you, I decided to turn it into something constructive.”

“You were that angry huh?”

“Our lives depend on you making the right call. How the hell can we trust you to do that when you refuse to see everything you’re capable of? I’m not trying to give you a big head or even boost your confidence. I’m trying to get you to think. We play a vicious game with death every day. And I’ll be honest, if one of your poor judgement calls kills one of you, or heaven forbid Ophelia? I’d kill you. Somehow, someway. I would kill you.”

Xavier didn’t blame her. Were he in her shoes, he’d probably say something to that effect.

“You know I’d rather die than let anything happen to the two of you. You’re the only Psychics that like us.”

“And you have Ophelia to thank for that. Usually she just has to pay attention to see, but on occasion she gets dreams of things. She saw you guys and was determined to align our paths with yours. I’m not too sure what she saw, but I didn’t argue.”

Xavier flipped over and rested on his elbows. “You trust her that much huh?”

“That woman was the only light in my life for a very long time. Nothing like being nowhere near ordinary and then being able to feel everyone’s discomfort, hate, and fear because of it. Even when I came to Zora, the home of the freaks, they still treated me like I was…well a freak. People here read minds, turn into animals, and suck blood but the girl who’s being honest to herself is the ‘strange one’.”

"Pfft, the only thing strange about you is your constant perky mood. Makes me wonder if you're not touched in the head."

"That can be said of anyone here."

"True."

The silence between the two of them almost became awkward before Cassie sat up.

"Xavier,"

"You don't have to say anything Cass. I know what we're risking. What I'm risking. You guys are the only friends I've got. I just have a hard time viewing myself as anything more than this…screw-up."

The sound of running feet snapped Xavier out of his current train of thought and before he could turn around to see who it was, he felt an elbow drive itself into the small of his back. The pain was so extraordinary that Xavier's vision blurred. Before he could recover his wits, the figure grabbed both of his feet and began to bend his legs backwards, causing another tidal wave of pain.

"Ophelia!" Cassie screamed. "What are you doing?"

Xavier didn't know why Ophelia was attacking him, but the pain his back prevented any higher brain function other than to scream.

"Say 'I'm not a screw-up'! Say it!" Ophelia hollered over her shoulder.

"What?! Why would I-aaaaaaaaaahhhhhhhhhh! Alright! Alright! I'm not a screw-up!" Xavier was sure she was going to break him in two.

"Say 'I'm the Coven Leader and I was given that position because Serea saw something in me'!"

"Ophelia, he isn't going to be able to say all of that if you snap his spine! Let him go!"

Xavier let out a yelp of jubilation when Ophelia released his legs. He curled into a ball and lay on the ground, contemplating why his life had lost so much control in such a short span of time. He heard Cassie shouting something at Ophelia, but he couldn't comprehend what was being said as the pain still blocked all higher brain function.

When his hearing finally returned to normal he heard Ophelia say, "Oh stop whining. It didn't hurt that much."

Xavier glared with all the venom he could muster. He was considerably pleased when Ophelia looked concerned for a moment. Cassie rushed over and helped him up, which was a painful endeavor. Xavier looked straight into Ophelia's eyes, determined to be as angry as he was hurt.

"Why the hell would you do that?" he spat.

"I was tired of hearing you dump on yourself." She replied nonchalantly.

"So, you try to break me?!"

"Pain is an effective motivator."

That was the final straw.

"So is fear." He growled.

With a surge of angry thoughts, he summoned flames to his left head which formed a blade. With the quickest slash he could manage, he cut the right side of Ophelia's hair. Ophelia jumped back with a small exclamation before noticing her hair on the ground.

"You go John Cena on me again and I'll make you bald next time." Xavier hissed, resisting the urge to join Cassie in her giggling.

"Really Cass? Really?" snapped Ophelia, looking none too pleased at the prospect of her new haircut.

"Aw babe, it's just…really funny. I'm sorry. I'll finish it up in our room and cut off the burned ends."

After several more assurances, threats, and a friendly shoulder to lean on, Xavier finally made it to his room. He contemplated taking a shower, but the sight of his bed proved too alluring to resist. He flopped on top of his blankets and savored the comfort they provided. He took a deep breath and then he heard a knock at his door. In some horrid form of rebellion, his entire body began to ache and throb, threatening cruel retribution should he rise from his throne of comfort. Gritting his teeth, he forced himself back on his feet and walked to door. He had hoped that whoever it was needed something really important, for their sakes. He looked at the screen that was connected to his door's front camera and saw Serea, looking impatient.

He opened the door, dreading whatever it is that prompted her to visit but determined to meet it with a smile and wave. Serea returned the smile before walking inside. She made a beeline for his comfy chair and threw herself in it with a groan of exhaustion. Xavier sat on his bed, much to the jubilation of his sore body. Upon closer inspection, Serea looked genuinely tired which caused him to ask her if she had a rough day.

"Something like that, yeah. In a bit of an awkward position these days. Usually the Chevaliers step in when things get too big or powerful for the Slayers."

"I'm gonna nod and pretend like I know what those titles mean." Xavier chuckled.

"Oh! Bullocks, sorry. Never bothered to teach you that because it doesn't involve you yet. The main difference between the two is how powerful they are. For shifters, it's the usually measured by their powers. Like Bea's ability to manipulate shadows or Eliade's ridiculous speed. We need more from them than just the improved strength and agility and shifting. Vampires are required to show that they can transform into mist, hypnotize a psychic, and go a full ninety-six hours without feeding. Psychics need to show absolute control of their powers as well as display a mastery of a martial art. Lycans must be able to tap into their immense strength in human form, have their hunting urges completely under control, and completed their grueling silver resistance training."

"How come I've never seen any Lycans in this branch?" Xavier asked, knowing full well what the answer was. He was just curious if Serea's tired state would yield more information than normal.

"The same reason you won't find any Vampires in the Western U.S. branch. There's bad blood. Score one for Hollywood actually getting something right. Though Kate Beckinsale's outfit is so impractical for combat. But surely you've heard the rumors by now?"

"Of course, but rumors can only be taken so seriously."

Serea scoffed. "Then why haven't you sent your little spy to find out the information?"

"I did." Xavier replied, shrugging. He figured being candid to a point would disarm her. "But some secrets guard themselves well. Figured I would just ask you instead of having Danny risk his neck with his trainer."

Serea let out a shudder before nodding her head in agreement. "I'm a Vampire and he still gives me the creeps. The old bat just has this gaze and since he's only got one eye you *have* to look at it. But to answer your question, Allistar and I have a past that spans literal centuries. Unfortunately, since he and I are the first of our kind to claim sanity, our blood lines have always had this…tension. We've never gone to war thank goodness, but it is sort of understood that a Vampire and a Lycan won't be anything more than co-workers so to speak."

Xavier wanted to press further but he thought better of it. "You said that Chevaliers are essentially the elite among the members of Zora."

"Ah yes. We step in when the demons involved are a bit too powerful or numerous. But since you lot arrived, you've been chiseling out this sort of middle tier."

"So, we're stronger than your average Slayer but not quite at a Chevalier's level? That's fair."

"Bingo, good sir. While it has been nice to go out on assignment nearly every day, the demon's we do fight are monstrous. Think of it like fighting a final boss of a video game over and over again."

"I've never played video games outside of the occasional app my school friend would let me play with on her phone."

Serea looked genuinely surprised which didn't shock Xavier in the slightest. "Truly? I've even had a go or two at them. Arcades were really popular in Japan. Wow. Anyway, the demons we face back to back are incredibly powerful. Szakiya and I took on three Ifrits yesterday. My bum's still singed."

"Ifrit as in the fire demon? I thought they supposed to be tiny."

"Traditionally they are." Serea groaned while stretching. "But once they consume a human's ashes, they grow. The one's we had to fight lit an entire apartment complex on fire and fed on over thirty humans each. By the time we got there, they were literally several stories high and nearly as broad. Your powers would have been greatly appreciated."

Xavier's brain flashed so many red flags in his mind's eye that he was sure his actual vision flashed red for a moment. "I truly don't like where this is going."

"Yeah… Sorry buddy."

"I thought you said that the ranks don't apply to us yet!" Xavier squeaked, almost panicked.

"And that's true. Witches have their own ranks. Apprentice, Master, and Paragon. The six of you have been learning at quite an astonishing rate. Despite certain short comings here and there, namely your baby magic, you all fight nearly at the level of Masters. The problem is that Cassie and Ophelia are Chevaliers. In order to really operate at their level, you need to be Paragons."

"That's another reason why Cassie sparred with me today." Xavier muttered, realization blossoming in his mind.

"She had her own personal reasons as well, but yes. Her ability to recreate the fighting styles of those she has observed for a time is extraordinary and extremely useful for training. But she will be spending this entire week fighting other members of your Coven to show them the same thing. She just wanted to nab you first because she was upset with you. A sentiment I somewhat share by the by."

Xavier let an exasperated sigh. "Let me guess, 'how can you not know you're a bloody tactical genius'?" He mocked, adopting his version of Serea's accent.

"Your accent is atrocious, and you are by no means a genius. You are gifted however."

"The difference being?"

"A genius is aware of their gift and knows how to use it. You lack those traits entirely. Which will be one of your many areas of focus. Strap in dearie. It only gets worse from here."

"Aren't we training enough as it is?!" Xavier cried, his muscles screaming in agony at the sudden introduction of tension.

"Yes, but we need you stronger. The demons are getting bolder and more brazen by the day and I assure you, that is never a good sign."

Xavier sunk further in his bed and groaned, which elicited a laugh from Serea.

"I felt the same way when I was selected to undergo my Paragon training."

"Hey, if you were a Paragon, why do you call yourself a Chevalier?"

"Because I am no longer a Witch."

"You're not really your typical Vampire either. They can't weaponize and manipulate blood or cast spells like you do."

"The same can be said of Allistar, though his powers are far more sinister than mine. And neither of us have the strength with magic that we once did. We're better than you to be sure, but not by much. So, it's easier to call myself a Vampire as I'm directly responsible for what they are now."

Xavier's brain saw another chance to procure information and his mouth moved before he could think better of it. "You're not really the 'Queen of the Vampires, are you?"

Serea cocked an eyebrow before answering. "Yes I am. I wasn't exaggerating when I said I was the first to regain my sanity. And anyone I turned after the fact retained their sanity as well. After a mere fifty years, I had a nation of followers. I even have a castle in Scotland. Though my second resides there now."

"Not England?"

"No. I love my homeland, but after the whole Dracula and Van Helsing thing, England became very…inhospitable. The Grand Coven Leader at the time had banished all Vampires from England's shores. Rather than go to war with him, I decided to just move next door."

"Wait? Dracula was real?"

"No one told you? Miguel still laughs at me about him. He was one of my worst ex-boyfriends ever.

"Hang on! Hold it!" Xavier had to fight the laughter down before continuing. "You dated Dracula?"

"Yes. Sweet merciful Mary, yes. The only reason he went after Mina was to make me jealous and after I didn't pay him any attention it turned into this awful thing and it was all over the papers. Then the book got written much to my abject horror. I hunted down that Irish cow too by the way. Miserable old coward. I made him tell people that Vlad the Impaler was his source of inspiration and threatened to eat him if he ever told the truth."

At that moment Xavier lost all semblance of control and began to roar with laughter. He laughed so hard that it started to hurt which turned his laughter into small giggles punctuated by groans. Serea flashed him a look of annoyance before getting up and heading to the door.

"Aw come on! You gotta admit it's funny!" Xavier wheezed.

"Indeed. Would you like to know what else is funny? The fact that you still have training with Bea tomorrow and you're as sore as you are. Even with your healing abilities, I doubt you'll be completely recovered. It's a shame you're horrid at healing spells and your powers have no medical uses. If only there was someone who wasn't irritated with you that could help. Oh well. Good night Xavier."

"That's cold Serea."

"Oh, bite me."

11:

"Why?! Why did you agree to this?!" Justin screamed, side stepping a tree as he ran.

"Like I had a choice!" Xavier screamed, looking back to see if their pursuer was still on their tail. "I wasn't asked so much as we were volun-told!"

Just as Serea had promised, their Paragon training had begun on the top of the following week. Their first exercise was to escape Beatrice in her panther form using nothing except their magic. It wasn't until Justin cast a sleep spell did they realize that Beatrice had Szakiya cast a spell that prevented direct magical attacks. One hungry sounding growl later, they were all running through a nearby forest. Xavier ordered everyone to pair off and split up. As such, Beatrice decided that chasing Justin and he was the best choice.

"You won't be beating me anytime soon if all you do is run!" Beatrice hollered, announcing she was only a short distance behind him.

Xavier turned around and looked at the leaves and pebbles on ground. "Levitate!" he barked, causing his targets to rise in a like a usual cloud. As Beatrice came into view he pointed at her. "Shoot!"

The rocks got to her first, colliding with enough force to be heard, next came the twigs and sticks which managed to trip their target. The leaves didn't do much, but Xavier really didn't care at that point.

Justin came up beside him and pointed. "Encase!" The leaves that Xavier thought were useless began to cover Beatrice's body, leaving only the bottom of her paws exposed. Xavier knew that wouldn't hold her long and began to run in the opposite direction, followed closely by Justin.

"Got any ideas?" he asked, sounding slightly worried.

"A couple. Isn't the river near here?"

"Encasing her in water won't work, she'll just use her shadows."

"She'll still be wet."

"What…oh! Got it."

They continued running until they reached the small river. As they ran towards the water, a shadow in the corner of his eye caused Xavier to move to his left, pushing Justin out of the way. Beatrice landed in the water and flicked her tail in annoyance.

"That was lined up perfectly too. Guess your reaction time has gotten a bit better. Alright let's get this over with. Unless you plan on using more twigs and leaves. Which, by the way, itches something awful."

"Justin." Xavier said coolly.

"Really? Encasing me in water will literally hold me all of two seconds."

"No need for that." Xavier smirked.

Justin had managed to get to the water without being harassed and placed a finger in the water. "Generate."

Beatrice's eyes grew wide as Justin's current of electricity hit Beatrice instantly. Unfortunately, a scream from behind them revealed that Max was also in the river nearby at that time. Justin quickly withdrew his finger and gave a Xavier an uneasy look. A second later a low growl reminded them that their task was not quite done.

"Gonna need more than a few volts to bring me down. Not for Max though. Poor guy. I don't like it when my fur is frizzed, so I'll be nice and give you a two-minute break while I fix it."

Xavier and Justin took off without a word and headed towards where they heard Max scream. A few moments later they found Nate carrying Max in his arms. Max looked at them with an incredulous expression.

"Really? You couldn't give any warning before you electrified the river?"

"In their defense Max, you were going to freeze it."

Max turned and glared at Nate before addressing Xavier again. "My lower body won't move, and we can't hang around here. I'd say we go invisible, but you can't cast that."

"It's still a good idea. Go invisible and find Adam. He can heal you. I'll be a distraction."

Justin shook his head. "That is the single dumbest idea I've heard today. But I can't think of anything else to do right now so come here."

Xavier walked over, and Justin placed a finger on his sternum. He muttered "improve" followed by "enhance". The sensation was extraordinary. Xavier felt his muscles harden while his lungs seemed to swell with the freshest air he had ever had.

"These spells don't last long, and they leave you twice as tired. Don't waste them. You got fifteen minutes."

Beatrice announced that she was done fixing her fur with a growl. Xavier didn't even wait and ran back towards her. He nearly ran into her a moment later as he hadn't adjusted for the additional boost in speed. He dodged to the right and let out a whoop of joy. Beatrice took off after him and if Xavier didn't know any better, she looked like she was happy, though her feline face made it impossible to truly tell. They ran through the forest, engaged in the strangest session of cat and mouse he had ever seen. He saw two particularly large trees pointed at each other.

"Break!" he shouted, hoping he was casting the spell right. Much to his relief two enormous cracks appeared in the trunks of the trees and they began to fall in his direction. He put more effort into his legs and managed to run past them just before they fell. Beatrice leaped out of the way of the large trees and let out a yelp of surprise. Xavier took the chance to jump up a nearby tree. Surprisingly, his first jump took him almost sixty feet in the air. He started to jump from tree to tree, feeling like one of the characters from the anime that Nate showed him one time. He looked down and saw that Beatrice was right on his tail. He knew she could easily climb the trees like him, but she probably refused to risk him breaking whatever branch she was on.

After a few moments of climbing the trees he found what he had actually been looking for. Before this training exercise he viewed a map of the forest and then cast a mapping spell himself. He had located a nearby cave and made a mental note of it. Now that he was being pursued, the cave gave a perfect opportunity. He looked down again and Beatrice was nowhere to be found. He smiled and continued his tree jumping until he arrived at the cave. It was on the side of a modest cliff and vines and moss lined the outside of it. Xavier guessed an Earth Witch had created it in the past. He carefully walked inside as the side effects from Justin's spells set in. It started to feel like he had run for nearly an entire day without stopping. His breathing became labored and his legs started to feel like lead.

He took a few more tentative steps and tried to quiet his breathing, so he could listen. Considering how tired he felt, he really couldn't afford to be wrong about his hunch. A low growl assuaged his fears and he stopped walking.

"Looks like you beat me here." He huffed, his lungs really starting to burn.

"I saw it a few yards off. Just didn't think you'd be dumb enough to go for it. I have night vision you know."

"I do actually." Xavier closed his eyes. "Illuminate!"

Despite his eyes being closed, it was like he could sense just how bright the ball of light was and felt a twinge of guilt when Beatrice let out a howl of agony. He cancelled the spell and ran as fast as he could towards the entrance. He got outside the entrance and turned to run down the nearby path. Unfortunately, his legs couldn't handle the sudden shift in direction and buckled. The cave didn't look that high off the ground when he was on the trees, but now the he was essentially falling down the cliff, he could see that it was a little higher than he expected. He tensed and braced himself for what he was sure would be a painful landing.

"Slow!" A familiar voice cried.

Xavier jerked and painfully turned to see Danny looking up worried. After a few moments, Xavier landed in Danny's arms. He was surprisingly solid and seemed to hold Xavier with ease. He thanked Danny for the save and got out of his arms as he felt a little awkward being held like that. He instantly regretted the decision as his legs gave out, causing Danny to grab his arm and put it around his shoulder.

"Where are the others?" He rasped, the exertions starting to really take their toll.

"Close. What hurts worse?" Danny whispered, leading Xavier away from the cave path.

"Legs. Save your strength. Just in case this doesn't work."

"What doesn't?"

A scream that sounded equal parts human and animal rang out. Beatrice shot out of cave and located them with a snarl. She leapt off the edge directly at them, rage dancing a morbid tango across her face. Xavier smiled, for the first time in a long time, he actually felt like he was good at more than one thing. This was the first time he had put thought into a plan and despite being the result of a questionable decision to play bait, Beatrice had played into his hands beautifully.

"Pin." He whispered.

Three basketball-sized rocks flew off the ground and slammed into Beatrice, pinning her to a nearby tree. Xavier knew the rocks would hurt, but they wouldn't break anything. The purpose of this exercise was to force them to think creatively in their use in their magic, so Beatrice didn't have the right to complain. Danny let out a small snort of laughter which was answered with an annoyed snarl. Rustling behind them announced the arrival of the others and Adam rushed over to Xavier. Justin and Nate both walked over towards Beatrice.

"I have to say Xavier," Justin said, looking at the placement of the rocks, "You're stupid lucky."

"Actually, from the moment I played bait, this was planned. Although Danny catching me because I fell off a cliff was super lucky." Xavier replied, relief spreading through his body thanks to Adam's ministrations.

"Not bad bro." Nate walked up next to Justin. "Ms. Beatrice. I don't want to sound cocky, but I think we have this one."

Beatrice, who had been struggling against the rocks stopped what she was doing and looked at Nate. "How do you figure? The idea was to contain me. Even if one of you picks up the spell, you guys can't keep this up forever."

"Oh, that's totally true." Justin replied, a triumphant smile gracing his face. "But what happens when Nate and I gather dirt particles and expose them to the appropriate amounts of pressure, to manipulate and increase the size and shape of those rocks into something a little more confining?"

Beatrice let out a bark of laughter. "Xavier isn't strong enough to hold the spell that long. Now run along and get. I was having fun chasing you."

Everyone else looked at Xavier who's only response to look Beatrice in the eye and smile. Beatrice met his gaze and started laughing again.

"Well I'll be damned. Guess you figured that if you can't cast complicated spells, you'll make the simple ones stronger. Alright you brats, you win. But don't get too proud of yourselves because…"

A gust of wind buffeted everyone and Eliade stood next to the tree that Beatrice was pinned to.

"You're not done with today's training." She finished, a smug smile adorning her face. Everyone let out a groan which caused her smile to deepen. She looked up at Beatrice and let out a short laugh. "Hello my love. I have to say, I don't like this look too much."

"You're hilarious. Now explain the next part so they can put me down." Growled Beatrice.

Xavier released the spell and as she fell to the ground, she resumed human form. Xavier was surprised at how many visible bruises she had. The sentiment was evidently shared as Eliade looked genuinely surprised.

"You let them bang you up this much?"

"They hit me with rocks like four times! And this one decided to blind me in a cave. And they encased me in leaves! Crafty little…"

"I see. Well then gentlemen, the next part of your training is to catch me. You may not use magic or your weapons. You must use your powers." As soon as the last word left her lips she vanished and reappeared on the other side of Beatrice. Xavier looked at the ground where she was and noticed an abundance of vines and frost.

"Well done you two." Eliade replied. "But it's a little rude to cut someone off when they're explaining things to you. Anyways, since you finished things up with Bea a lot sooner than expected, I want to see if you can do it again. For every fifteen minutes that you haven't captured me, I will start to counter attack. I'll start with a push and progress from there. I'd say you have an hour before I start dropping you like flies. Good luck!" And with a small nod, she disappeared again.

Beatrice stretched and chuckled. "You guys better get moving. Elly's blows feel like a truck."

"Got any advice?" Nate asked hopefully.

"Wait fifteen minutes so you can see how she attacks. It'll hurt, but it won't put you on your butts." And with that a circle of shadows appeared under her. She sunk down in them with a smile and wave and then she was gone.

"What do you think Xavier?" Max asked.

"I'm inclined to agree with her. But that doesn't mean we do it blindly. I know Justin and I are flight certified, but what about the rest of you?"

"I hate heights." Nate grumbled.

"I'm afraid of heights." Max squeaked.

"I go in for mine next week, but I pretty much have the hang of it." Adam said.

"I just finished a few days ago." Danny offered. "Our flight instructor is jerk."

Xavier snickered, although he agreed. The flight instructor was an ornery eagle shifter that accepted nothing less than absolute obedience. Any deviation from his instructions resulted in a swift a smack in the back of the head with a stick he named Mr. Obey.

"Alright Danny, when it gets closer to fifteen minutes, get in the air and watch. You process information a lot faster than the rest of us do. Nate, can you create small bumps in the ground? Like not big enough to be generally seen, but enough to feel?"

Max looked at Xavier with a puzzled expression. "She's going to be moving too fast for that to work."

"Not necessarily." Justin called, inspecting the area near the tree Beatrice was pinned to. "With her hitting us, she has to slow down to prevent herself from killing us. The problem is we don't know how fast she can actually move. Judging from the way the ground looks over here, it's ridiculously fast."

"Serea said something like that." Xavier replied, which earned an approving nod from Danny.

"Her top speed is closely guarded, but I stumbled across a video of her breaking the sound barrier like it was nothing."

Nate let out a low whistle. "For a shifter to be able to withstand speeds like that is amazing. The air friction alone would set most people on fire."

"Surprisingly, her speed isn't that uncommon in Zora's history." Max replied. "Most of your 'prey' type shifters develop higher speed improvements. Rabbits, deer, horses to name a few."

They discussed other options before Danny looked at his watch and shot in the air to a nearby tree. They all gathered in a small circle with their backs to each other. Justin soon told them that he heard the sound barrier break in the distance. Xavier tensed and readied two fireballs in his hands. The first one to be struck was Nate who she sent flying into Justin. Eliade had slowed herself down to be seen which Adam had decided to capitalize on. He pointed a clawed hand in Eliade's direction.

Eliade let out a gasp and stopped moving, her face bearing a pained expression. Xavier felt his skin crawl. Adam had developed his ability to manipulate the water molecules in a person's body to such a degree that he could stop someone like Eliade and Xavier hated every second of it. He knew that Adam would never use this technique on him again, but seeing it still made his stomach turn.

"Justin! Trap her! She's vibrating and it's getting hard to maintain a lock on her!" Adam hissed through clenched teeth.

"Serea does something similar and I can shake her off. You'll be no different." Eliade growled.

Justin lifted his hands and a bubble of wind formed around Eliade. Xavier blinked, and she had disappeared. Something in him told him to produce his heat shield and the moment he did, he felt a hand collide with his shoulder. The impact wasn't as bad as he thought it would be, but it still sent him barreling a few feet. He rolled back on his feet and shot a fireball in the direction she thought she was headed, which was towards Max as he was the easiest to move. She deviated course which caused the fireball to hit a nearby tree. Max used the distraction to surround himself in a cocoon of ice. Eliade's face contorted in annoyance, but she adjusted course and sped off back into the forest.

Danny landed next to Max's ice cocoon, let out a snicker, and knocked on it to alert Max that she had gone. Xavier shook his head and rolled his eyes.

"So…you guys want my honest opinion or one of those white lies that makes you feel better?" Danny asked.

"We're not gonna catch her?" Adam asked, putting out the fire the Xavier caused.

"Not with the frozen scaredy-cat over there." Nate joked.

"I panicked ok?!" Max squealed, crossing his arms.

"You can face down a gargoyle no issue, but the deer lady terrifies you?" Justin asked.

"In his defense, she is kinda scary." Xavier instinctively rubbed his knuckles. "Whenever I mess up a recipe or technique, she hits my hand with a wooden spoon. Pretty vicious."

"Our real issue," Nate cut across, giving Xavier a smirk, "Is that if we use the type of power we need, we'll destroy this forest. And as your duly appointed tree hugger, I can't let that happen. Especially Ser Firestarter over there. Smoky the Bear is gonna snipe you if you're not careful."

"Point taken. There's an empty plain about a klick south of here. The ground would be pretty messed up, but overall damage would be minimal."

"Ok, that's a little over a half mile. How do we get there without being attacked by Eliade?"

Xavier pointed towards the sky which caused Nate to frown and began to vigorously shake his head.

"Dude no. Such a bad idea."

"We kinda don't have a choice. And I figured you could create a rock big enough to hold you and Max. It's easy."

"And it looks stupid…"

"Wait…are you honestly throwing a fit because you have stand on something to fly?"

Nate looked in the other direction before mumbling, "Everybody else can just fly through the air…"

Xavier rolled his eyes so hard that he was sure everyone could hear it. “Get over it. Max needs a ride although,” he turned to Max, “you need to learn how to fly properly too. But for now, let’s get in the air.”

Nate mumbled something in Spanish that Xavier was sure was an insult before walking over to Max and leading him a few feet away from the others. He lifted his hand the ground shook temporarily. With a large crack, the ground began lift and the two of them rose in the air on what looked like a large boulder. The moment they began to rise Max ran into Nate and buried his head in his chest while holding tightly. Both Danny and Justin glared at Xavier before they lifted off the ground to follow. Xavier huffed an exasperated sigh that caused Adam to laugh at him. They both rose into the air as well.

It had taken Xavier two full weeks to master flying, but the moment he did he was elated. He loved the way the air felt on his skin. Maybe it was how free he felt when he was in the air, but something about flying always made smile in delight. After they got a few hundred feet in the air, the empty plain he talked about came into view. Still acutely aware of the glares he was receiving from Danny and Justin, he sped off hoping to get everyone on the ground and out each other’s arms as soon as possible.

As they traveled Xavier saw something move below him, seconds later something collided with his shoulder. Justin flew in front of him and generated a huge sphere of air that engulfed everyone which several rocks collided with.

“You let that one hit me on purpose.” Xavier growled, clutching his now stinging shoulder.

“You deserved it.” Justin whispered, before grunting. “How can she throw things at such a high velocity from the all the way down there?!”

Adam lifted his hand and an orb of water started to form around Justin’s wind shield. After the orb finished forming Max looked up from Nate’s chest long enough to freeze the orb except for a small spot that Xavier could see out of. Despite being defended by two levels of protection, small rocks still pierced through.

“We’re almost there! Danny, grab Max! Nate, the moment we land; we need a rock wall!” Xavier ordered.

Danny flew over to Max and practically leaped into his arms. Max wrapped his arms and legs around Danny, which caused him to get very red. Nate started to snicker uncontrollably, which Adam joined in on. A collision of several rocks on the shield saved Xavier the trouble of having to scream at them to focus. The moment they arrived, Justin and Max opened a hole on the bottom of their sphere. Nate sped out and landed on the ground with so much force that a small crater was formed. He lifted his hands and a large circle of rocks nearly thirty feet high and around erupted from the ground. Once they were safely on the ground, Justin dropped his shield. After convincing Max to finally let go of Danny, he followed suit. Xavier looked at Nate to congratulate him on how quick he erected the wall, but when he noticed how intense his face looked, he faltered.

"Nate?" he asked, a little concerned.

Nate shook his head to shush him. "Growing a crap ton of weeds around the wall. Hopefully they'll trip her up."

"Don't push it."

"I'm fine bro-bro."

Nate's face finally relaxed after a few more minutes and everyone spread out, ensuring that they had enough room to fully utilize their powers. The silence that followed was almost unbearably tense. Xavier knew that they would at least hear her coming, but that didn't mean they would have enough time to react. After a few more moment of silence Xavier heard a faint noise coming from his left. He ducked as Eliade's fist swung through the air that his face had occupied a moment ago. Xavier leapt back and launched a tirade of fireballs in her direction. She dodged all of them and sped towards Justin.

Justin waited until the last second before managing to duck while simultaneously twisting and kicking her in the stomach. While the kick didn't look like it struck that hard, a gust of wind signaled that Justin coupled his powers with his strike. Eliade let out a small wheeze and flew backwards. Nate walked into her flight path, seeds in his hand. Xavier saw a glint in Eliade's eye which stoked a mighty panic in him.

"Move! It's a trap!" Xavier screamed.

Eliade's face switched from confident to annoyed as Nate had managed to raise a smaller rock wall immediately. She back flipped and landed on ground just short of the wall before speeding off. Xavier's mind raced as he desperately tried to figure what Eliade's attack pattern was. After realizing that she was trying to cripple the team instead of defeating them outright, he turned and hollered for Adam to be careful. The moment the words had left his mouth he saw

Eliade run past him with a small smile on her face. He cursed as he realized it was a feint. She appeared in front Max and launched a blow. With a crack of lightning, Danny appeared in front of Max and blocked her attack.

"You really think you can keep up with my speed?" She laughed, taking a stance.

"Not for long, but long enough for them to bring you down." Danny growled.

"If you don't electrocute them first."

Xavier blinked and both disappeared. Several cracks of lightning were the only way he could keep track of where they were as they moved far faster than he could see. He was impressed that Danny could move his body that fast for so long, but as a lightning bolt landed a few feet from him, he knew that this fight couldn't continue for much longer.

"Max!" he called.

Max, who had been trying desperately to watch the fight, looked and ran over, side stepping a stray lightning bolt. "What?"

"How quickly can you throw down a flash freeze?"

"I can't Xavier! You all will be,"

"I didn't ask you that!" Xavier snapped, causing Max to jump. He took a breath and reigned his tone in. "How fast can you throw it down?"

"If I concentrate and don't hold back? Milliseconds."

"Guys!"

Everyone looked at Xavier as he began signing directions for everyone to levitate a few inches off the ground. Everyone nodded and soon were floating. Xavier looked at Max and he nodded, kneeling to the ground.

"Danny!" Xavier screamed.

Danny and Eliade suddenly appeared in front of them. Danny looked worse for wear, bleeding from his nose and head and breathing hard while Eliade looked simply winded. Max slammed his hands to the ground and a torrent of cold air shot forth, freezing everywhere it went. Both Eliade and Danny jumped in the air. Eliade turned in enough time to see Xavier kick her in the stomach. The moment his foot made contact he ignited a small explosion. She would have shot backwards, but Danny moved and caught her. A flash of lightning and a brutal scream later, Eliade laid on the ground twitching. Nate landed on the gradually thawing ground and locked Eliade in a rock cocoon.

"Do we win?" Xavier asked, knowing that she wasn't nearly as hurt as she alluded to.

Eliade looked up and smiled. She suddenly appeared next to him before giving her hair a few tentative touches. "I suppose I'll let you guys have this one. You certainly did more than I thought you would. Danny should have shocked me harder if you really wanted to put me out of commission."

"I didn't know how quickly you healed and didn't want to risk actually killing you." He huffed, holding to Adam for support while Adam healed him.

"That's fair. Well boys the first day of your initial training is over. There is a cabin east of here. Xavier knows where it is."

"I do."

"You will sleep there for the night. I would suggest you spend the remainder of today discussing a battle strategy."

"Let me guess. We'll have to fight Szakiya using nothing but hand-to-hand and then we fight Serea after that?" Xavier asked, hoping only one of his guesses was true.

"You are correct and if I may be frank, you had better bring your best. We have all trained under Serea, but none quite so closely as Szakiya. She's going to hold back, but not by much. Good luck gentlemen." With another gust of wind, she disappeared. Everyone let out a groan of exasperation and began to head towards the cabin.

12:

"You're in luck Xavier!" Justin called from within the kitchen. "There's enough pork chops for everyone except Max and Danny. There's some Portobello in here. Y'all want that?"

"I want some!" Danny answered before giving a questioning look to Max who nodded. "So does Max!"

"Mmkay."

Xavier stretched and sunk lower into his spot on the couch. While the cabin looked rustic and worn on the outside, the inside was a completely different matter. It was chic and modern in design and had an enormous living and dining room with a matching couch and table. Xavier felt his stomach rumble impatiently and yelled,

"How long is it going to take? I be hungry!"

"Boy, you will not rush me! Now sit there and be quiet before I decide to not make you anything!" Justin snapped, causing everyone else in the living room to chuckle.

"I apologize!" Xavier chirped, honestly penitent, "You are a wise and gracious lord and I throw myself at your mercy!"

"You are doing the most…"

Xavier chuckled and turned before dodging a speeding pillow. He turned to see Max looking at him angrily.

"If I don't get my fancy southern fried Portobello, I will drop the temperature in your underwear to sub-arctic levels!" he hissed.

"No worries, I love Justin's cooking as much as everybody else does." Xavier replied, eyeing the area for any nearby pillows.

"It's been a little bit since our potluck." Nate mused. "It kinda reminds me of my family dinners."

"I know what you mean." Max replied, dodging the pillow that Xavier managed to find. "We used to have them every Friday night."

"My mom used to buy all these different cook books from different places and we would all pick out a recipe for her to cook."

"That sounds amazing! Did your mom travel a lot?"

Nate's face saddened a bit.

"Nah. She had a crippling fear of flying. After she was kicked off her fiftieth plane, she kinda gave up. So once her parents had died and left her a huge brownstone in New York, mom decided to become a foster parent. She learned over twelve languages and got a degree in anthropology. So, every time that she got a kid who's 'origins lie elsewhere' she'd do her best to help them speak English while learning about the culture they came from. In my case, she taught me how to speak Spanish. I didn't know anything about my culture, but she definitely hit me upside the head with it. Almost literally."

"What about…" Danny trailed off, looking uncertain.

"My actual parents? Birth mom was a junkie and literally tried to throw me in a trash truck as a baby. My dad did alright by me, but some evil ass old lady who lived next door to us hated having us there. She kept calling the cops on him and eventually he snapped and punched her. Last time I saw him was when they were cuffing him. Evidently, he was illegal and punching old ladies is a one-way trip back across the border. My mom tried to find him for years, but never could. Honestly I think she was more hurt by it than I was."

"She sounds amazing." Xavier replied, wistful.

"Sounds better than my folks anyways." Danny chided.

"Oh, don't tell me they were the stereotypical Asian parents?" Nate joked.

"Nah. But both of my parents married each other because it was the stable thing to do. There was no happiness in our home. So, I said forget that. I started partying, dying my hair. I got this sweet ass gig at a club where I was a DJ."

"What was your stage name?" Max asked.

"I went by DJ Mystic Surge for a while. But after Prince died, I died my hair purple and started going by Purple Skye."

"Oh my god!" Nate exclaimed. "I knew I had seen you before! I was at your show in New York! Your music was so good."

Danny's eyes lit up as a proud smile worked its way across his face. "For real? Thanks man. It's crazy. I go from being a DJ to a Witch to a spy Witch."

"Your instructor is creepy as hell dude." Xavier said, echoing Serea's words.

"Who? Barty? He's just lived the life too long. When you know the things he knows, it messes with you a little."

"Didn't he come this branch during the fifties?" Adam asked.

"Yeah. Zora may not get involved in world politics too much, but it doesn't mean we aren't affected by them. Some Russian Shifter from the Intelligence Unit named Bartok Ivanov knocks on our door during the peak of the Cold War? Caused one hell of a splash. But his lessons have gotten me out of a few jams."

Xavier felt a twinge of guilt. He was always asking Danny to gather Intel on things Zora preferred they didn't know. Everything from suppliers to work schedules, Xavier had initially wanted all of it. Danny never let him down. He always smiled and took it as a challenge.

"Danny, I'm" whatever Xavier was going to say was cut off by Danny shaking his head.

"You ever get that feeling that someone is always listening to your conversations no matter how low you whisper? That's what it's like working in the Intelligence Unit. You learn to just roll with it." He winked at Xavier who nodded in affirmation. "But on the plus side, it gives me a chance to find new ways to use my powers."

"Yeah!" Justin called from the kitchen. "Like you being able to keep up with Eliade."

"Keep up?" Danny chuckled mirthlessly, "You're too funny dude. She's so much faster than me, it's stupid. And her techniques? I thought I was a damn good fighter. My weapons are literally my hands and feet. I couldn't touch her."

"Imagine what Szakiya and Serea are going to be like." Max sighed. "Beatrice and Eliade are actually scared of those two. Hell, everyone is."

"Jesus if that ain't the truth." Nate stretched before continuing. "I work with a bunch of scientists. Men and women who literally study how our world works and all it takes is a surprise visit from Szakiya to make everyone lose their crap. Not only do they get deathly quiet, but they start getting flustered and what not after she leaves. They're that terrified of her."

"Can you blame them?" Xavier asked, sad that he came to his current thought pattern. "Most of them have been taught from birth to fear Heretic Witches. Despite being legit friends with the woman, Serea only has her here so she can be watched. Can you imagine what someone who has lost their minds could do with her kind of power?"

"They have a failsafe for that." Piqued Danny.

"I know. They have a failsafe for all of us. At least the ones that can cause the most damage. Anyone who hits Chevalier or Paragon rank."

Xavier's face was once again the target for an oncoming pillow projectile. This time it was from Adam.

"Stop with the doom and gloom. And I thought I was moody. Jeez."

"Do you even have any emotions outside of sarcastic and nonchalant?" Max asked.

Adam feigned a look of outrage. "Hey! I can feel a wide range of emotion good sir!"

"And all of them are negative." Quipped Xavier.

Adam lifted his hand and formed a gun shape that pointed at Xavier. Soon a small ball of water appeared in front of his finger. Xavier mimicked the action and smiled as a small ball of fire hovered near his finger.

"You really want to start this?"

"What's the matter? Scared?" Adam growled with a smile matching Xavier's.

"You should be, you're outnumbered." Danny said, having gotten up without notice and had a small ball of lightning pointed at Adam.

"I think not good sir." Nate mocked, standing up and pointing a ball of dirt at Danny.

Max heaved a sigh before lifting both of his hands. "I'm Switzerland."

The four of them looked at each other, all poised and ready. Nate shifted slightly and that was all the warning they needed. Each of them set off multiple shots while trying to find a more defensible location. Xavier let out a small grunt as a water bullet collided with the back of shoulder, leaving a wet spot. Xavier leapt behind the dining room table before returning fire. He laughed as he saw his shots land on both Nate and Adam. Danny suddenly appeared beside him and they took turns exchanging fire.

The living room began to show signs of damage as missed shots collided with pillows, the couch and nearby shelves. One particular shot knocked a picture off the wall. The subsequent crash and silence was enough to get Justin to holler,

"What was that?"

"Nothing!" The rest of them said in unison.

Justin swung around the corner and a look of bewilderment came over his face.

"The hell happened in here?"

"Nothing." Xavier repeated, smiling wide.

"You realize you're gonna have to explain this to Serea."

Xavier shrugged. "If she doesn't already know she will soon. Probably just take it out of my stipend."

"Your money." As Justin turned around to go back in the kitchen, Adam fired a water bullet at Justin's butt. Justin let out a yelp of surprise before turning around with a glare on his face. In unison, everyone pointed at Xavier.

"Nice try," Justin snapped. "But if he did it, then why is my butt wet?"

"Yeah Adam." Xavier added, taking the opportunity to absolve himself. "Why is Justin's butt wet?"

"I plead the fifth." Adam replied, barely containing his smile.

Justin lifted his hand and a gust of wind launched Adam a few feet into the air. Though Adam landed on the couch, Justin's threat was apparent. He stormed back in the kitchen. Everyone giggled and declared a temporary ceasefire. As they cleaned up some of the mess they made, Justin told everyone that dinner was ready. Everyone quickly help set the table and soon the room was filled with the delicious aroma of Justin's cooking.

Xavier tore into his food with gusto as everyone thanked Justin for the food. After first helpings were securely finished, conversation continued between them. Justin was telling them about possible upgrades he wanted to make to their uniforms.

"Did you build a bunch of stuff in school?" Nate asked, tearing a piece off the croissant he had in his hand. "You seem like a natural."

Justin nodded. "I was always tinkering when I was younger. I actually made a robot one time. But I kinda gave all that up."

"Why? I can see you winning competitions easy." Max asked.

"There's not a whole lot of room for a nerd on the streets. Been fighting almost every day of my life. I just got tired of it. Then I came out and that was a whole new reason to keep fighting. It's easier to hide being smart than it is being gay, you know?"

"How do you hide something like that?" Adam asked. "I mean, I'm not trying to be insulting or anything. I just don't get how you can pretend to be stupid. Especially when you're probably the smartest person at the table. No offense Nate."

"None taken." Nate replied, smiling. "You're right."

Justin took a deep breath before sinking into his seat. "When you live in the inner city and you're a person of color, there's this expectation that gets put on you from birth. And it encompasses everything. The way you talk, the way you live, the music you listen to. Everything. This is especially true about your intelligence. Being smart was a 'white' thing to do. And they make you feel like you're not supposed to be intelligent. Like you stole it from somewhere."

"Trust me, there are dumb white people too. Intelligence isn't something we invented, I promise." Adam chuckled.

"I know. But there are some folks in the community who don't see it that way. Do you know how depressing and discouraging it was to have to bring my internet browsing history to school to prove that I didn't plagiarize my research paper, despite citing my sources? Who wants to go through that year after year?"

"Was it really that bad?" Max asked, aghast.

"For me it was."

"Wow..."

"It's like that all over." Adam replied. "You've never been asked if you're going to be a doctor or own a 7-eleven?"

"I have, but it was usually from the people who went to that racist church up the street from us. I never really got that from my family or community. Our only stipulation was that whatever you decided to do with your life, you committed to it fully."

"Oh goodie, racist Christians."

"No." Max said firmly, catching Xavier by surprise. "Those pigs were not Christians. It may not be my faith, but I have studied it closely. What those people do and believe in was not the teachings of Jesus Christ. Much like Islam, Christianity is a religion of peace and understanding. Anyone who doesn't want to do that, doesn't want to be Christian or Muslim. Period."

A few moments of silence set on them which caused Max to get very red before muttering a small apology.

"Don't apologize man!" Nate said, clapping him on the shoulder. "I think we're all shocked because that's the first time we've seen you get up in arms about something not Zora related."

"Yeah. And it's a surprisingly mature stance to take." Adam replied. "Wish my family had gotten that message a long time ago…"

Xavier wiped his mouth with his napkin, his second helping polished off. "Story time?"

Nate's eyes got wide and he shook his head slightly. Adam looked up and laughed.

"It's ok Nate. Um, where to start. My family is the epitome of high class white America. I never had much say in what I could do, but I never really had wonder what it was like to have the latest and greatest of everything. At the time, they were grooming me to be a pianist. It was the first time we ever agreed on anything. But…"

"My sister happened." Nate mumbled, much to Adam's shock.

"She was your sister?!"

Nate nodded, looking at the table. "Yeah."

"Um…more details?" Justin demanded, looking both concerned and interested.

"It was the New York state competition. It came down to me and his sister. I had never heard her play before. I just knew that she was good. But the moment her fingers hit the keys, there was no question who was better. I still remember that performance. It brought tears to my eyes."

"Let me guess." Danny cut, "She was just some nobody from the wrong end of the state and they very well couldn't have her outshining the son of some prominent New York family."

Adam gripped his napkin so tightly his knuckles looked sheet white.

"They called my name and for the first time, I felt like my world had been turned upside down. I argued with the judges before my dad got me. He told me that she should be glad that she got to compete on the same stage I did."

"Heh. He told us the same thing when he offered his hush money." Nate retorted with a snort.

"I had never really experienced racism before that. It never dawned on me why the staff was always Hispanic, or why I hardly saw people of color at our parties. You could say my little perfect world got shattered that day. I started looking around and the more I looked, the more disgusted I became with my family. I started rebelling. Got into trouble a lot, stopped playing piano, and started bringing people home, got arrested a few times. But it still didn't do anything. I didn't know what else to do."

"Things like that are never easy to do something about." Nate replied, finally looking up. "After what happened, my mom and I started petitioning to have the competition looked at. Her performance was all over YouTube, so it wasn't like we didn't have evidence. Your family threatened us several times. To the point where they sent some guys after me."

"Wait what?!"

"Yeah. It was this red-head dude and his cronies. Didn't want to break his arm, but he kept trying to find things to hit me with."

Adam started laugh heartily, much to everyone's surprise. After nearly doubling over, he managed to regain some composure.

"So that's how my brother's arm got broken. He told us he broke it in a riding accident. I mean I knew he was lying, but this is so much better! I don't know what he was even thinking! No one in their right mind would try to jump you!"

"I'm not that big…" Nate muttered, shifting uncomfortably in his seat.

The entire table broke out in laughter. Danny was the first to speak.

"Are you serious? The only person bigger than you in Zora is Beatrice! I was surprised you could even fit through the door."

"Alright, alright. I get it. I've always liked the gym. It feels great to work out. And when I realized my size gave me an edge in wrestling, I just kept at it."

"I seriously think you're the only one out of us whose body didn't change after training."

"Actually, that's not true. I've gotten more definition surprisingly."

Xavier snorted.

"Like you need it."

Nate smiled and winked. The conversation continued for another hour before Xavier suggested they all get ready for tomorrow. As they each filed upstairs, it was revealed that the cabin had enough rooms for each of them. Further inspection showed that there were extras of their uniforms provided on their beds. After a particularly vicious bout of rock, paper, scissors to determine the order in which they used the bathrooms, everyone began to unwind. Having successfully won the first bout, Xavier showered and brushed his teeth with one of extra toothbrushes stored in the bathroom. He got to his room and was surprised to see Adam waiting on his bed, shirtless.

Xavier's face instantly grew warm as he cleared his throat to announce his presence. He had no idea why seeing Adam with his shirt off was affecting him so strongly, but he didn't appreciate it, at all. He had seen plenty of shirtless men in his life and none of them did anything, other than catch his mild interest. Adam stood up, revealing a rather well fitted pair of pajama pants, which caused Xavier's face to practically burn as he couldn't keep himself from looking.

"Oh hey," Adam replied, "Sorry for intruding, but I wanted to ask if you had any plans for dealing with Szakiya."

Xavier was determined to not meet Adam's eyes and started to stretch. "Not yet. I've been running some scenarios, but nothing's really stuck out as a winner."

"Xavier, is everything ok?" Adam asked, increasing the burning in his cheeks.

"Yeah, just a little light headed. But to answer your earlier question. Nothing I think of, short of attacking her together is going to get us through this exercise. Truthfully, I'm tempted to have us give up against Szakiya, so we don't waste energy when fighting…Adam?"

"Hmm?"

"Why are you so close?"

"Checking to see if you have a fever. You're red as hell."

Xavier's heart felt like it was going to burst as Adam reached up to touch his forehead. On pure instinct, Xavier grabbed his hand. He answered Adam's inquisitive stare with a slight shake of his head.

"Xavier, we need you in peak condition. If you're sick, then you need to tell me, so I can see what I can do to heal you."

"I'm fine. Stop worrying!"

Adam wrenched his arm free and gave Xavier a stern look. "Let me look."

"I'm good."

"Dammit Xavier!"

Adam went to grab him, but Xavier saw it coming and dashed past him. Unfortunately, he dashed the wrong way and was now trapped with Adam barring the door.

"Tell me what's wrong."

"It's nothing. I promise."

"It's not nothing!"

"Yes, it is!"

"Oh my god! Will you two get a grip? He's not feverish, he's blushing." Screamed Justin from down the hall.

Xavier felt his stomach hit the floor. How did Justin even know? Why on earth would he reveal that? Xavier resolved to rethink his friendship with Justin as soon he managed to get Adam out his room. He finally looked Adam in the eye and everything seemed to stop. He couldn't place the look Adam was giving him, but for some reason that didn't seem to bother him. That was until Adam opened his mouth again.

"What are you blushing for?"

There was a massive groan of exasperation as everyone in the cabin seemed to be listening in on their conversation. Adam's face contorted with agitation and he pointed to the door and barked "Silence". Once he seemed content with the room's soundproofing, he looked expectantly at Xavier. After a few moments of internal deliberation, Xavier answered.

"You have your shirt off ok? Don't know why I'm blushing like some little girl with a crush but I am! You're beautiful and you're nice to look at! Happy?!"

Adam's eyes widened and soon his face began to grow red. For some reason Xavier took a vast amount of pleasure watching Adam blush. Adam mumbled something that Xavier couldn't hear. After an awkward moment of confused staring, Adam repeated himself.

"I think you're beautiful too…"

"Oh god, why? You've got to have," whatever else Xavier was going to say was cut off by a water bullet smacking him in the face.

"Shut the hell up! I am sick of your self-deprecating crap!"

"Well, excuse the hell out of me! But I don't think I'm all that attractive!"

"That's what's the most irritating! You're so damn gorgeous it's stupid. Who lied to you? You told you that you were ugly?"

Unbidden memories flooded into Xavier's mind. Without meaning to, he reached up and began hugging himself tightly. A light touch on his arm made him look up to see Adam giving him a concerned look.

"Xavier, what happened?"

"I'm not…I'm not ready to talk about it."

Adam looked a little disappointed, but still gave him a smile. He cupped Xavier's face with his hand and before Xavier knew it, he was kissing him. Just as suddenly as it began, it ended.

"When you're ready to talk about it, I'll be here ok?"

Xavier let out a small laugh.

"You take my first kiss and that's all you've got to say?"

"I have more I want to say. But this is serious issue. I don't want to even consider moving forward until this can at least be talked about."

"It's not that simple."

"It never is with us. But I've waited this long, little longer won't hurt."

Xavier looked him in the eyes again. Why were his eyes so blue?

"And what if I decide that this is a bad idea?"

"Then I expect you to be big enough to tell me."

Adam went to leave the room, but Xavier's hand reached out and grabbed. Without thinking and without caring, Xavier kissed Adam back.

"I'll try. It's the only thing I can promise right now."

Adam flashed a grin.

"I can live with that." As he undid the spell on the door he looked back with a mischievous glint in his eye. "Can I ask one thing?"

"Sure?"

"Next time, can you take your shirt off?"

Xavier snorted before firing a fire bullet at Adam, who quickly ran out of the door with a giggle. He sat down on the bed and deeply sighed. As he tried to relax and unwind from all the earlier tension, he caught a flicker of movement out of the corner of his eye. He didn't need to identify who it was.

"I am so ticked off at you right now. Enter at your own risk."

Justin started chuckling. "We can spill the tea with me being right here. Now come on, I need to get my life before I go to sleep."

"That's a shame. Because I don't feel like telling you anything."

"Gurl, if I didn't say anything y'all would've still been fighting about you having a fever. I did you a solid."

The truth of his words irritated Xavier into silence.

"Let me guess, y'all not even gonna talk about it until you get your emotional baggage under control? Which makes sense."

"Well good for you, you know everything that happened."

Justin's only answer was to cock an eyebrow.

"We kissed." Xavier mumbled, finally giving in. "Twice."

Justin let out a joyous shriek before racing into the room and hugging Xavier. "I knew it! Gurl yas! Praise the baby Jesus you finally kissed somebody. And it was somebody fine too! Won't God do it?"

"Ugh. Shut up. …Justin?"

"Hmm?"

"Thanks."

"Anytime."

13:

The next morning came far quicker than Xavier would have liked, but he grudgingly got out of bed when his phone's alarm rang. After coordinating bathroom usage and securing a decent breakfast, he began going over the ideas he had for fighting Szakiya. Every plan had one glaring problem, Szakiya was just too strong. After establishing who their best hand-to-hand combatants were, they decided to assign a back up to each of them and together they would try to pressure Szakiya into a corner.

As if waiting for them to finish, Eliade appeared inside in the cabin to issue instructions to where they would be finishing their training exercise. With a warm wish of good luck, Eliade vanished. Solemn, but determined, they filed out of the cabin and walked towards the clearing in the forest that was indicated. Very few words were spoken as most of them were stretching their arms and shoulders or mentally preparing themselves. After thirty minutes of walking, they arrived at the clearing where Szakiya was sitting in what seemed mediation. Her eyes flicked open upon their arrival and she smiled.

"Good morning boys. How'd you sleep?"

After a couple minutes of general greetings, she stood up and dusted off her pants.

"Well I'm glad to hear that. Well I'm going to be nice. Since you guys did such a good job yesterday, I'm going to give you the same objective I did the first time we fought. Land a hit.

No powers. No magic. If you guys break those rules, I'll do the same at my discretion. Word to the wise, don't. Well if y'all are ready."

She assumed her combat stance and waited.

Everyone looked at Xavier and with a nod, he set their plans in motion. Adam, Max, and Danny all raced ahead with Xavier, Nate, and Justin following close behind. Danny reached striking distance first and launched a flurry of punches. Even without his powers, his natural speed had evolved to impressive point. Szakiya displayed an even greater speed by bobbing and weaving from every single punch. Max surged forward in what they all assumed was her blind spot, but Szakiya's foot to his chest dispelled that assumption.

She twisted to her left to dodge Adam's kick and ducked under Danny's roundhouse. She turned and slugged Danny in the gut which caused him to double over. Seeing the opportunity, she used him as a small springboard and kicked Adam in the face. In less than a minute, she had dropped their best fighters. Shrugging off his feelings of inadequacy, Xavier sped towards her before crouching for a quick leg sweep. Szakiya simply blocked the kick with one of her own and their shins collided painfully. Justin leapt in the air and with an impressive show of gymnastic ability flipped forward while bringing his foot down for a crushing axe kick. Szakiya blocked it, but it didn't prevent her from feeling the force of the kick. Justin's leg strength was nothing to sneeze at as Xavier had seen him leg press a car, just to prove he could.

For the first time since they started training with her, they saw Szakiya actually straining. That was all Nate needed as he sped forward. He stopped short and launched a brutal hook right to Szakiya's side. His first collided with her open palm. Fortunately for them, she wasn't ready for the sheer amount of force Nate possessed and she actually lost her footing. Xavier didn't wait and ran past Justin to kick her right in the chest. Instead of catching her balance, she simply fell backwards and caught herself. As soon as Xavier was clear, she hopped back up.

Danny was waiting for her, and seconds later she was blocking another kick. Max used the opportunity to get close and with a simple open palm thrust, he sent her flying through a nearby tree. Everyone looked at Max incredulously to which he meekly shrugged. Szakiya let out a groan as she got up.

"I didn't expect you guys to get this strong physically for a few more weeks. And here I was going easy on you. Well I'm afraid I'm going to have to change things up fellas. Your objective will be to last a whole minute. Starting now."

All Xavier heard was something colliding and a gasp, he turned to see Szakiya with her fist in Max's stomach. Max had an extremely pained look on his face but held on to her hand with all his might, preventing Szakiya from moving. With a smile she cocked back her left hand and backhanded Max away. Danny let out a snarl of rage and unleashed a barrage of vicious blows. At first it seemed that the two of them were evenly matched, but as the exchange continued Szakiya began to gain more and more ground and with a well-placed hook to the jaw, she dropped him.

Justin and Nate both attacked in tandem. Justin began to pressure Szakiya with a blur of kicks which allowed Nate to grapple her. As he threw her over his shoulder she landed on her feet and used the momentum to throw him. Justin appeared and swept her feet from under her, but she simply back flipped before launching her own kick. Justin dodged to the left and assumed a handstand. Xavier had always found Capoeira to be beautiful but extremely difficult to master. This was obviously not the case for Justin as he began to vault through to air while delivering blows that would have killed a normal human.

Adam caught Xavier's attention and they both joined in the fray. Szakiya eyes seemed to light up as she fought off all four them. While they tried valiantly, they all ultimately fell. Xavier, who had been hit with a particularly hard kick to the face, groaned as he forced himself up. Szakiya was beaming as she looked at her handiwork.

"Oh my god, you guys did so well. Five minutes! Five! I'm so proud of you! I think you guys are actually gonna make Serea sweat!"

"Forgive us if the pain in our bodies prevent us from expressing our excitement." Max mumbled, still holding his ribs.

Szakiya's smile deepened as she snapped her fingers. In an instant, all the pain disappeared from Xavier's body. He sat up, bewildered at how she had done this.

"How?" Justin asked.

"I sped up time on your bodies." Szakiya replied with a wink.

Max did not share her excitement as his face paled.

"You what?! Do you realize how dangerous that is? What if you had aged us? What if you had regressed us?!"

“Chill.” Szakiya snapped. “I’ve been doing this for sixty years now. I knew how much I hurt you and how much time you needed to heal from those injuries. I’ve pretty much gotten this down to an art form.”

“I’m sorry, you’ve been doing this for sixty years? How old are you?” Adam asked.

“I celebrate my eightieth birthday in December.”

“How are you that old?”

“I’m like this because of my powers. I may be a Heretic Witch, but I successfully tapped into one of the most primal forces of our universe. It came with certain drawbacks…”

“Immortality…”

“Close. The best I can figure it out is that my own personal time has stopped. Or it’s stuck on the moment I received my powers. Any wound I receive gets rejected and I can’t mature past this point. On the one hand, I was extremely powerful when I received my ‘gifts’. On the other, I won’t ever be able to exceed my limits. All these years, all I’ve ever learned is control over my abilities and traits. The only thing I could ever improve in was magic as its knowledge based.”

“Wait, are you telling me that you’re this strong and you’re still technically a fledgling Witch?” Justin asked, as surprised as everyone else is.

“For sake of argument, yes. Scary isn’t it? Serea said that if I had been able to increase my power, I could have surpassed her in fifty years. Oh well. I’m fine being right behind her. Anyways, you’re all healed up. If you head west, you’ll see a path. Take it and you’ll reach Serea. One more thing.”

A crunch of leaves from behind them caught their attention and Beatrice stood, leaning against a tree, their weapons in hand.

“Serea wants you to attack her with everything. Treat this as you would a real demon hunt.” Everyone walked over to Beatrice who looked none too pleased with them. “I’m gonna put you boys through hell in training. I know you guys were going against Szakiya but come on. I recorded the whole fight, so we’ll be able to point out everything you did wrong.”

“Thanks.” Xavier retorted sarcastically.

“Enough of that. You need to focus. Serea is going to give you maybe a few minutes to figure out how she fights before she starts coming at you seriously. Think quick Xavier. You’re gonna need it.”

He nodded as he strapped his katana to his hip. With a nod and another wish of good luck, Szakiya and Beatrice disappeared inside a shadow. While they walked down the path, Xavier started to bounce ideas off the team. After a few tries, they all seemed to agree on a plan and soon arrived at the end of the path. A large cave stood before them ominously. The air was quiet and there was no sign of life. It seemed that nature itself was warning them of the danger that lied within.

Xavier felt his stomach flip as he walked forward. They reached the middle of an extremely large cave where a solitary figure stood. Illuminated by a half dozen flood lights. Serea nodded at their arrival while she finished putting on her glove. There was an intricate spear laying on the ground next to her which caught Xavier's attention. After checking the feel of her gloves, she picked up the spear and faced them. No explanation was needed or any needless conversation. The only thing she said was "Begin ."

Justin let out a flurry of arrows which Serea dodged by rolling forward. With an elegant sweep, she forced Adam, Xavier, and Nate to step back. Nate threw several seeds at her, one of which landed on her arm. Seconds later she was tangled in what looked like a thorny vine. A flash of crimson cut the vines from her body a moment later, but Adam was already approaching. The two of them seemed to dance as they exchanged blows with their respective pole arms. Knowing Adam would get defeated in a few seconds, Xavier signaled Danny to begin.

Danny vanished, and after narrowly dodging thrust aimed at his leg Adam disengaged. With a crack of lightning Danny began landing blows on Serea. Serea's eyes began to glow and stuck out a clawed hand. Danny let out a strangled gasp as he was caught by the throat and thrown across the cave. Serea suddenly leapt in the air and back flipped as two hands made of stone attempted to grab her. Xavier was waiting on this he bathed the nearby area in the hottest flames he could produce. With a small yelp of exclamation, Serea stopped short of the ground and began to float into the air.

Justin flew into the air and blasted a torrent of air at her. She cut her hand on the edge of her spear and soon a large red rectangle appeared in front of her. The wind collided with the rectangle with monstrous force. Though the wind Justin produced was impressive, Serea seemed unfazed.

"Is this it?!" She screamed.

Justin responded by slinging his bow over his shoulder into his quiver. With a snarl on his face he renewed his attack, this time blasting Serea's shield with nearly four times the force. Serea was clearly taken aback as she first showed surprise and followed with an intense look of focus. Xavier nodded at Adam who slowly rose into the air right behind Serea. He shot what looked to be a high-pressure jet stream of water. It crashed against another red rectangle, and Serea looked over her shoulder with a sneer.

A familiar crack rang through the air and Danny's lighting collided with yet another red rectangle. Serea looked above her at where Danny was flying and rolled her eyes. Xavier couldn't help but smile as he blasted at Serea from directly below. The rectangles elongated and contorted until Serea was surrounded by a red sphere. Upon seeing this, all four of them doubled their efforts and in a display that impressed Xavier, began to batter Serea's defenses. Serea's eyes were now fully glowing and with a roar, she increased the size of the sphere until it pushed all of them back.

Xavier felt the air leave him as Serea's hand appeared around his throat.

"You know, you really shouldn't be so obvious when issuing instructions." She growled, kicking Adam in the chest.

"Point taken." Xavier smiled and thrust his hand forward. While he was used to stabbing demons, it felt almost profane to stab someone so human looking. Though her glowing purple eyes certainly helped. Serea hissed and pushed Xavier back, clutching her leg where a steam of blood was pouring out. Xavier couldn't help but giggle a little.

"Get it? Point taken?" he murmured, still trying to recover lost oxygen.

"You really think you've the time for puns?" Serea replied, clearly healing her leg.

"Yup."

The sound of something racing through the air rang through and suddenly Serea's arms were constrained against her side and a new cut would appeared in her shoulder. Max gripped his invisible chain and with a turn began to swing Serea around like a toy on a string. After a few seconds he let out a growl and slammed her into the ground. Despite creating a large impact crater, she was still conscious and clearly annoyed. A gust of cold air announced Max's powers and the ice soon revealed the chains wrapped around Serea's body. She began to struggle in earnest which earned a giggle from Justin.

"Those links are tungsten. You're strong, but you aren't going to break them. And before you mention the cold from Max's powers, I treated them with magic."

"I know." Serea replied. "Which is why I just undid the spells." With a final heave she snapped the chains and pulled the knife out of her shoulder.

Before she could say anything else the ground opened right beneath her. She fell some distance but managed to catch herself before landing in the hole entirely. Unfortunately for her, Nate had a giant boulder poised and ready and promptly closed her within the hole.

"What now?" Adam asked Xavier, looking unsure.

"Now, she wins. Brace yourselves."

No sooner than the words left his mouth, Xavier felt as if someone had set his blood on fire. Every single inch of him cried out in agony. He dropped to ground with a scream and was soon joined by the rest of his team. The boulder suddenly crumbled and Serea burst through the rocks before slowly descending to the ground. She caught sight of something and cocked and turned. Xavier forced himself to turn and look and he was surprised to see Adam slowly getting to his feet.

"You're trying to counter my control of your blood by controlling the moisture in your body? Clever if you actually had the will to resist me. You don't." And with the final word, Adam let out a howl of renewed pain and dropped to a knee.

"I won't give in." Adam replied threw gritted teeth.

"Yes, you will. All living creatures bow before me. Even Witches." She placed a finger in the middle of his forehead and all the light left his eyes. Adam fell to the ground without a word, his limp body signaling the end of their battle.

The pain in Xavier's body began to subside as Serea walked over to a nearby light. After a few moments of rummaging, she was drinking one of her infamous blood packs. She strolled over next to Max and relief washed over his face. After walking by everyone, she sat on the ground and finished her pack.

"All things considered, that was actually pretty good." She replied, looking slightly pleased. "I heard what you said earlier Xavier. How'd you know I'd finish the fight that way?"

"I do my homework." He replied, determined not to reveal anything more than that.

"Indeed. While there's certainly room for improvement, ending this battle on your terms speaks well of your progress. I'm not sure if I'm proud or angry that I was stabbed twice though."

"You said treat this like a real demon hunt." Max offered.

"That's the one thing you didn't do unfortunately."

"What do you mean?"

"Let me rephrase." She nodded at Xavier. "*He* didn't treat this like a demon hunt. Why didn't you stab me somewhere vital? I had no idea about your blade and you had the perfect opportunity."

Xavier shifted uncomfortably. "If I had moved my hand back any further, it would have telegraphed."

"And your reason for not stabbing one of the arteries in my leg?"

"You held off attacks from us using a small cut on your hand. Didn't want to give you more ammo."

Serea narrowed her eyes which caused Xavier to huff and relent.

"Fine! I didn't want to hurt you. You're still human. Ish. It felt wrong to stab you. It would have felt worse to stab you somewhere- AH! What the hell is wrong with you?!"

Serea's fingers wedged themselves deeper into his shoulder as a response. He unleashed a pillar of flame that washed over her body. Xavier extinguished the flames mentally and went to help her before feeling a hand on the back of his head. He didn't think his nose was broken, but it still throbbed painfully, and he struggled to breathe in the dirt.

"Just when I think you've moved forward, you take ten steps back!" Serea hissed. "I'm still human?! That's your reason?"

Xavier could only grunt defiantly.

"I look human. But I'm a damned monster. There are more out there just like me. I know because I made them. I can tell you right now, you show mercy and you're going to die. There will come a time when your enemy will look just like you. You get hung up on some idiotic shite like looks and it'll be a bloodbath. Now get back to base and get to work."

The pressure on the back of his was gone but he just laid there, face in the dirt. A few minutes later he felt a hand gently touch his shoulder. He sat up to see Adam looking worried.

"You ok?" he asked, healing Xavier's shoulder.

“I’ll live.”

“She didn’t have to do that. She,”

“She’s right Adam. I shouldn’t have held back.”

Adam fell silent and looked down. “I know. But she didn’t have hurt you.”

“She was trying to make a point.” Xavier replied with a smirk.

“Did you just…?” Justin narrowed his eyes and shook his head.

“What is with you and puns today?” Max asked.

“I don’t know. I just had a punny feeling.”

Xavier let out a laugh as everyone just groaned.

14:

“I knew we would run into something like this sooner or later, but really? An actual cult?” Xavier asked, hoping what he heard was incorrect.

“That’s what Miguel said.” Danny replied, looking equally apprehensive. “And his Intel has never been incorrect. I’m just wondering why he would give this to us and not Serea.”

“Probably because he knows something that would cause Serea to ignore this.”

Danny shrugged. “Either way, we’re headed to Missouri. Their next gathering is in two days.”

“I’ll make the arrangements and brief the rest of the team. Thanks Danny.”

Danny nodded and turned to leave out of the office before stopping and giving Xavier a curious glance.

"What?"

"Well, worst case scenario we might have to…"

"Kill them?"

"Look, I know that you don't like hurting humans, but if they really are helping demons,"

"I'll be fine." Xavier barked, "I value the lives of my team a little more than some demon worshipping hicks."

Danny still looked unconvinced, but he nodded and left. Xavier took a deep breath and sunk back into his chair. Ever since their last training exercise with Serea, he had gotten a mixed batch of reactions from his team. Max and Adam agreed that hurting humans wasn't a great prospect, while Danny and Nate agreed with Serea. Justin was unusually ambivalent towards the subject and simply told Xavier to do what was best for the safety of their team. He knew that if it came down to it, he would do what needed to be done and he hated it. Deep down, he valued human life and the whole reason he had resigned himself to be a Witch was because he wanted to save innocent lives.

He sat up and did his best to shake off the heaviness in his heart. With a practiced speed, he began to fill out the numerous requisition forms for their mission. After receiving a response from the appropriate departments, he got up and headed to each of his other teammates. While it certainly would have been easier to have them all meet in a conference room or have Danny brief them, he really didn't want to be at his desk. He enjoyed visiting the different units and it gave him an excuse to walk around.

He stopped by Justin's lab first and was able to sit in on Justin running a durability test on his protection spells. The uniform being tested only began to show signs of tear after nearly five tons of force had been applied. Xavier hated to ruin the accomplishment with a mission brief, but Justin seemed excited at the prospect of trying out their new uniforms. When he arrived at Nate's lab, he was pleasantly surprised to see Max there. Evidently the two of them had been tracking Max's strength and comparing it to known records. Though they weren't thrilled to get a mission briefing, they were still happy to see Xavier outside of training.

That left Adam, he stood outside of Adam's office for what seemed like an eternity. They hadn't spoken of what happened in the cabin, but every time they would be in a room together, he swore he saw Adam stealing glances at him. Despite Justin's insistence, he just couldn't bring himself to unload all his emotional baggage on Adam. No matter how much he wanted to.

"Are you walking in or not?" Adam asked, snapping Xavier back to reality.

With a last-minute steeling breath, Xavier walked in. Adam looked up from the notes he was writing and smiled. Xavier smiled back and sat down on a nearby chair.

"How did you know I was there?" he asked, praying that his cheeks weren't as red as they felt.

"You know how you can sense and see nearby sources of heat? I wondered if I could do the same with moisture. I can sense a source, but if it's smaller than a human, I have a hard time pinning it down. But if someone decides to stand awkwardly outside my office, that's a whole other matter."

Xavier snorted. "Well, aren't you cool?"

"Not really." Adam shrugged. "You can actually shift your eyesight to see thermal readings. I can point and say, 'there's water over there'."

They both laughed, and Adam's hand brushed against Xavier's. They both sat in a pleasant silence before Adam looked at Xavier expectantly.

"Oh! I guess I should tell you the actual reason I came here. Other than to see your gorgeous face."

Adam cocked an eyebrow. "Are you…flirting with me?"

"And I'm probably being hella awkward about it so please save all judgements until after I leave."

"…Proceed."

Xavier launched into the mission briefing before he let himself say anything else that was stupid. After a few minutes of talking he finished and decided to leave quickly to spare himself from further embarrassment. As soon as he reached the door he heard Adam say:

"You know, your face is pretty gorgeous too. I'd like to see more of it."

Xavier stopped and nodded before nearly sprinting away. He had no idea why he was so bad at this. He had spent an entire lifetime watching other couples and had been confident that when his time came, he would be able to do better than they ever did. Now that he stood at the precipice of a relationship, he was as clumsy and foolish as the very people he ridiculed. He made a beeline for the nearest elevator and headed for the Psychic's floor. Fortunately, Cassie and Ophelia managed to get an office right next to the elevator, so Xavier never had to go down their hall.

Though having two psychics assigned to their coven by request went a long way to improve relations, there was still an underlying level of hatred that Xavier simply didn't know how to address yet. He got to their office and Ophelia greeted him at the door with her usual nonchalant wave After briefing both of them, he spied a plate of cookies on Ophelia's desk. Even though he was several times faster than her, Ophelia still managed to knock his hand away in the nick of time.

"No! My cookies!" she hissed, standing in front of the plate. "My baby made these for me!"

Cassie shook her head exasperatedly lifted a finger. A cookie whizzed from behind Ophelia and Xavier snatched it and immediately shoved it in his mouth. While it wasn't as good as Justin's cooking, he still felt satisfied getting to eat it. Ophelia glared at Cassie who looked her up and down defiantly.

"I made them, I get to decide who eats them."

Xavier decided to interject before a full argument started, "Would it be ok, if I made you cookies to make up for second one I'm about to eat?"

Ophelia seemed to fight the urge to smile but eventually gave in, "I want chocolate chip."

"Will do."

After securing a second cookie and a look of appreciation from Cassie, he headed back to his office. Serea was waiting for him, furiously typing on her tablet.

"What can I help you with?" he asked, already knowing the answer.

"Who cleared you for this mission? I can't find any record of this."

"No one. Miguel brought this directly to us."

Serea stopped her typing and looked at him with a strange look. It was soon replaced by anger. "And you just thought you would go gallivanting off and not say anything to me about it?"

Xavier felt a familiar wave of irritation but forced it aside. A shouting match was the last thing he needed right now.

"I'm a Section Head. I was presented with a mission from one of our chief intelligence agents and I responded accordingly. I didn't see any reason to go running to you for permission to do my job. It's not like you weren't going to find out, as all mission requisitions have to be sent to you. I fail to see the issue here."

"Don't get smug. I'm still very upset that Miguel went behind my back..." Serea responded, her eyes narrowing.

"Miguel didn't go behind your back. This mission would have been something you would have assigned to us anyways. So, he cut out the middle man and oh look, we're going to go do the mission. Believe it or not, we don't need you micro-managing us."

Serea stared directly into his eyes and met her gaze unblinking. She finally relented began to scroll on her tablet. "Has Justin finished those durability tests?"

"Yes."

"Good. I expect all eight of you to be outfitted. Be careful and report in when you get to the safe house."

Xavier grunted in affirmation before walking back into his office. Every time he would think he had Serea figured out, she would do something to that would throw him off. He supposed it was appropriate that their frustration with each other was so similar. After sending a mission notification to the appropriate parties, he headed to his room. As soon as he got there, he sensed the heat of a live body inside. With an eye roll he unlocked his door to see Miguel, sitting crossed legged on his bed, eating a sandwich.

"If you get dirt or crumbs on my bed, I'm burning your hair off." Xavier snapped, noticing the bottom of Miguel's sneakers.

Miguel finished chewing before answering. "That's what they invented washing machines for bro. Besides, we still haven't dished about you and a certain blonde hottie."

Xavier shook his head. "Why am I not surprised that you know about that?"

"Because it's kinda my job to know everything?"

"And your purpose for being here?"

Miguel smiled wryly. "To make sure you were in one piece after dealing with Ms. Grouchy Fangs."

"I wouldn't have had to deal with her if you hadn't gone behind her back."

"Yeah, but this isn't something she needs to be directly involved with."

"Because?"

“Allistar will be there. Missouri is one of the border states between the East and West Branches. When those two get around each other, well let’s just say it’s better if that doesn’t happen.”

Xavier’s ears perked up. Despite going so far as to send Danny to the West Branch, they were never able to find out more than the absolute basics about the branch’s leader and his relation to Serea.

“Anything I should know about dealing with him?” he asked, hoping Miguel might slip up.

“The dude’s kind of a monster. He’s taken out a small army’s worth of demons by himself with nothing more than a smile. Just play nice and don’t screw up. He might actually like you. He was a Fire Witch and leader of his coven too.”

“Oh?”

“Yeah. Although anyone who isn’t a Lycan hates working under him.”

Xavier tried pressing Miguel for details but gave up after being deflected several times. After exchanging a few more pleasantries and occasional threats due the amount of dirt on Xavier’s blanket, Miguel disappeared. Xavier grabbed his bag, packed some clothes, grabbed a travel pack with toiletries, cleaned off his blanket and left without a backwards glance. Only when he was on the elevator, headed to one of the Zora transport vans, that he realized how strange it was that he was able to get ready so quickly. His room was always bare, and his clothes were plain. Originally, he had done this to prevent himself from feeling at home at Zora; now it was just simple habit. This had become his life and he hadn’t really noticed until then.

As everyone met at the van and piled in, everyone seemed to be calm. He wondered if this had become just as much of a habit to them. Every time they got in one of these vans, there was always the understanding that they could possibly never return. Yet as the van left, no one seemed to have the fear or tension they used to have. He watched them during their flight and wondered at whether or not he should be glad. As they landed, he turned his attention to the town at hand.

The town wasn’t very large but being directly off the interstate made it so strangers went unnoticed. Justin and Xavier flew high above the town to properly map it, while the others went through the town, collecting what information they could. After a few hours of work, they met up and exchanged notes.

“It seems like your run-of-the-mill town. Which pretty much tells us that the cult is here.” Nate said.

“There’s no question. It’s here.” Danny replied, pulling out his phone and putting it in the middle of the table. “Cassie and I came across this weird sun symbol in town. When we asked some of the locals about it, they got really stand-offish and afraid. After some invisible spying on some old ladies, we figured out that the cult meets out in the corn fields.”

“The ladies seem to think that cult is just a bunch of ‘goths’ and ‘hipsters’ being weird, but the police think otherwise.” Ophelia snorted in disgust which earned a small smile from Cassie. “To be so insular of a town, the police and mayor’s office have done a great job in covering up the fact that there have been nearly two dozen disappearances in the past two months. My bet is that someone in one or both factions is in on it.”

“You would be correct.” Max replied, pulling out several pieces of paper. “We were fortunate that the mayor spends most of his time among his constituents. Probably out picking who goes next, the bastard. After a few sleep spells and Adam picking the lock with water, we found multiple instances of the mayor claiming the property of the missing people for the city and selling it off. My theory is that the mayor doesn’t know exactly what this cult is doing, only that they’re making people he wants gone disappear.”

Xavier felt a wave of anger but chose to focus. “I know the cornfields they’re talking about.” He held out his hand and detailed map made of fire of the surrounding areas appeared over his magic circle. “If we look over here, these are the fields. Off the northeast, we have a pretty big clearing and what appears to be a large farm house. I’d hate to think that they would meet somewhere so obvious but considering there are only two ways in by driving, I suppose they could actually guard the place.”

“Does anyone else get the feeling that we’re about to walk into a scary movie?” Ophelia asked.

“We fight demons. Our lives are an ongoing scary movie.” Adam replied.

“Sad, but true.”

After discussing a breaching strategy and the possible demons that they may face, Xavier suggested that they all go out that night and investigate before the meeting was to take place. As they had a handful of hours to kill, they all decided to pass the time by doing different things. Nate, Max, and Ophelia went off to go get them food, Justin was double checking the spells he put on their uniforms, Danny was doing what he could to remote access the city's servers, meanwhile Adam, Xavier, and Cassie were checking on everyone's weapons.

"Why don't you use a weapon?" Xavier asked after confirming with himself that he had never seen Cassie bring one into combat.

"Oh, I have one. I just don't like bringing it out for routine missions. I can't turn my weapon invisible like you can."

"Yes, you could." Justin called, closely inspecting Nate's uniform. "All you would have to do is telekinetically warp the light around your weapon."

"Do you realize how much focus and effort it takes to do that for extended period of time?! No thank you. I'll just get you to cast a spell."

Justin grunted in response, brow furrowed. Xavier let out a snort of laughter before he went back to inspecting his katana.

"What about you?" Cassie asked. "Why do you use a Japanese weapon when you could have learned a style from your people?"

"Says the pot to the kettle."

"Hey! I'm half Chinese so I had every justification to learn Kung-Fu."

"Well, you identify with your culture. I don't have much to go on. I was taught a few things when I was a kid, but after my parents died that stopped. Everything I learned beyond that point was through internet research. But I always felt like an outsider looking in. Besides, I'm good with my sword and it suits me."

"It's the same with me." Adam replied, looking a little sad. "My family is proud to be descendant of French nobility, but I don't know anything about France or its culture. And I thought about learning Savate and using a rapier, but it just didn't feel right. So, I decided to learn Wushu as I've always thought the art was beautiful."

"It suits you." Xavier found himself saying. Seconds later, he realized how that came across and started to inspect Nate's ton-fa very closely. Out of the corner of his eye he could have sworn he saw Adam smiling at him.

As the hours pressed by, they all got dressed in their uniforms and armed themselves. Xavier was inspecting how his new boots felt when he felt a surge of body heat near him. He looked and surprised to see that it was Adam, blushing furiously. Once he caught sight of Xavier's stare, he immediately turned to the opposite direction. Before Xavier could thoroughly enjoy his new-found confidence in his looks, he felt a gloved hand smacking him upside the head.

"Focus." Ophelia chanted, walking by.

Though annoyed, he knew she was right.

"Alright. If memory serves, only ones not flight certified are Ophelia and Max, right?"

"I've got Ophelia." Cassie called.

"And I'm flight certified!" Max squeaked. "I got it a few days ago!"

"So why do you still look pale as a sheet?"

"Because it's still scary!"

"This coming from the guy who threw a gargoyle…"

"Why are you always bringing that up?! I don't like heights…" Max mumbled. "Besides, all I had to do was generate a disk of ice and levitate it."

"You know you can just ride with me, right?" Nate offered.

"I'm fine! Can we go?"

Xavier lifted his hands in defeat before smiling, which only earned a glare from Max. They filed out of the safe house and after a quick scan from Xavier, all rose high into the air. A cloud cover soon enveloped them, and they sped towards the farm. Xavier felt every inch of him tingle with glee as he felt the air around him. While he did occasionally fly around Zora, it still wasn't the same as when he was in the open air. His excitement was short lived as he caught sight of bright lights.

The farm in question was lit up like a Christmas tree with a surprising amount of people walking in. And true to Xavier's prediction, two cop cars were stationed at either road entrance.

"I thought Miguel said they were meeting tomorrow." Nate whispered.

"Something may have changed. Let's land a few yards off. Justin, Nate, and Max cast invisibility spells on us."

After everyone was properly invisible, they all landed. As quietly as they could, they all came up to the barn. Xavier quickly cast a mapping spell, and in conjunction with his powers, identified that there were nearly sixty people nearby, but no signs of any living demons. Seeing two possible breach points on the upper floors of the barn, he instructed half the group to use one while he and another used the other. After seeing the small indents in the dirt walk away, he flew into the air. Being invisible was great for infiltration, but it made tasks like opening a window slightly difficult.

Once they were comfortably inside, Xavier began to observe the people down below. Upon entering, the people were handed white robes to wear over their clothes. Once the robes were put them on, they found a seat and would begin conversing with those near them. The first thing that Xavier noticed was a lack of children, though he tempered his hope with a memory from his recent past. As more people piled in, two tall figures walked from a back room and stood on their make shift stage. They wore white robes similar to everyone else's except that theirs possessed the same sun symbol that Danny had shown them. The figures' faces were completely hidden by hoods. A profound quiet fell over the congregation immediately.

No sooner than the quiet fell, another set of footsteps echoed. A man walked in and stood in the middle of the two figures. There was no doubt that this man was the leader. His robes had gold trimming and a matching long scarf that went to his feet. His hands were adorned in fine golden rings that gleamed, even in the bland lighting of the farm. He wore golden spectacles upon the bridge of his long nose and even his thin lips were painted gold. Dazzling still, was hair that seemed to be made of the metal that he clearly had a love for. And in the middle of his robes, there was a dazzling rendition of the sun symbol. With a flourish of his arms, a large banner unfurled behind him with the same symbol.

"Welcome to all. My dear Children of Light."

15:

The congregation erupted in applause and began whooping and stamping their feet. The man lifted his hand and the noise stopped almost instantly. The man smiled before continuing.

"You do this humble Arch Bishop a great honor. But this great praise is not mine to bear, for it is The Light that deserves your worship. Its gentle rays shall bless each of you. No more shall you have to throw your prayers to a silent god. No more shall you have to engage in mindless hatred and prejudice. For all shall bathe in the joyous rays of The Light!"

The congregation once again erupted in cheering. Xavier could see why something like this would be appealing. It took all positive parts of most religions and did away with their negative aspects. But something still didn't seem right, and he watched on.

"Tonight, my fellow children, we usher another sacrifice into the embrace of the light."

Xavier felt his stomach clench as his suspicions were confirmed. A door opened, and an elderly woman was dragged out by two robed figures.

"You damned cultist bastards! How dare you take my son! George! George honey please! Don't let them do this!"

A man near the front row bowed his head but made no move to assist the woman. One of the figures holding her withdrew a needle and sunk it in the woman's neck. The expression the woman had almost moved Xavier to tears. As loathsome as he was to allow this to continue, nothing demonic had occurred yet. No matter what they may believe, they weren't permitted to interfere in human crime. Unfortunately, not everyone on his team held to that. A burst of cold shot through the entire barn and Max landed on top of one of the figures holding the older woman. The other figure went to draw a weapon, but Max grabbed the figures wrist and broke it with a simple squeeze.

Other members of the cult raced towards Max and he brought down every single one. He broke bones and sent people flying, but fortunately none of his strikes seemed fatal. After fifteen people had been dealt with, the Arch Bishop lifted his hand and eerie quiet fell over the barn again.

"I see we have a young man with something on his mind. Young one, what angers you so?"

Max's only answer was to swing his chain knife at him. Though the blade did not cut the man, Max did send his spectacles flying across the room. Xavier's hair stood up as the man made no attempt to move, in fact, he didn't even blink.

"Your aim is marvelous. Such talent for one so young."

"The next one is going to take an eye." Max growled. "I'm taking this woman. If any of you try to stop me, I'll start slicing off body parts."

The Arch Bishop merely smiled. "Hmm, I see. Well that does pose a bit of a problem. I can't have you injuring anymore of the faithful. We worked tirelessly to break ground here you see? Dear Children, please depart. When time and circumstance allow, I shall call upon you again."

Xavier pulled out his field phone and used the camera to record to as many faces as he could. He knew that Zora would have to find these people and erase their memories as soon as possible. The congregation all walked out obediently with the exception of those who retrieved their members that were unconscious before leaving. The two police officers closed the doors to the barn and silence again. This silence was different, full of apprehension and anger.

"You really know how to spoil a night; you know that?" The Arch Bishop said, his voice changing dramatically. "Do you have any idea how hard is put on this whole bit for these idiots? And here you come waltzing in, beating the tar out of my disciples and ruining my favorite pair of spectacles? You know what?" He turned to the two figures behind him. "Kill him and bring me that fancy weapon of his. It'll make a nice trophy."

The figures nodded and drew a pair of ornate gold-plated daggers and advanced menacingly. Four knives came from the upper level, announcing Ophelia's involvement and stopped the figures dead in their tracks. Xavier whispered to have his invisibility dropped and leapt from his perch to the ground. The Arch Bishop scowled at his approach.

"Just how many of you, oh wait. I had heard whispers of a new coven. You two must be members of it. Well, since you enjoy playing with demons…"

A growl tore its way through the barn, causing Xavier's heart to miss a beat. With his focus having been entirely on Max, he had forgotten to continue to scan the premises. He looked at Max, but he couldn't catch his attention. Max was fixated on the Arch Bishop and didn't even looked fazed by the demonic growling. The wall behind the Arch Bishop exploded inwards, spilling debris and pieces of wood everywhere. The Arch Bishop smiled as a white beast let out a roar. Its entire body seemed to be rippling with powerful muscles. Claws the size of swords on each of his four paws clacked on the wood as it walked. It had a wide maw with two huge fangs jutting upwards out of its mouth. All around its neck and head was a mane that shone like gold. Xavier was getting real sick of that color.

“Am I supposed to be intimidated?” Max spat. “You bring a simple Field Demon whose skin has been dyed and all of a sudden you think you’re at an advantage? Just when you couldn’t get more pathetic.”

The Arch Bishop’s face turned an impressive shade of scarlet. “Kill them!”

“Take care of the demon!” Max shouted, dodging to the left of its outstretched claws.

One of the figures ran at him, thrusting one his daggers at Max’s head. Max blocked the blow with his chain before quickly running behind the figure putting them in a choke hold. A moment later, the figure slumped to the ground. Xavier tried to yell for Max to stop, that those people could be drugged humans acting against their will, but the Field Demon’s claw presented an issue. The demon took another swipe at him; to which Xavier responded by slicing its arm. This demon’s blood was an unusual brown, but its wound quickly healed.

Xavier let out a frustrated growl as he bathed the creature in flames. While it was writhing in pain, Xavier used his speed to get close to the creature. In the moment before his sword reached it, their eyes met. Though a demon and a beast, Xavier could swear that he saw a look of relief on the demon’s face. Even as its heart was pierced, its face was calm and contented.

“To your left!” Adam screamed.

Xavier didn’t even bother looking, he just brought his sword down, causing his assailant to dodge to their right. The Arch Bishop snarled before getting off the ground, saber in hand.

“How dare you force me to touch the dirt in this outfit! Do you know how much the dry cleaning for this is going to be?!”

“Send me the bill.” Xavier replied, looking for Max. The other figure proved to be formidable and was mildly successful at dodging Max’s attacks.

The Arch Bishop’s blade proved far quicker than Xavier expected and nearly took his eye. He dodged and threw a fireball which was blocked by what appeared to be a shield made of golden light. Horrid realization fell over Xavier as the Arch Bishop smiled.

“We’re not so different, you and I.” he cooed.

A knee collided with his face and sent him flying to the opposite side of the barn and through its wall. Max landed, and Xavier caught sight of blood dripping off his knife. He looked back and saw the other figure on the ground, still.

Max went to the hole in the wall and let out a stream of curses. Xavier walked over and saw that the Arch Bishop was no longer there.

"He's a Light Heretic Witch. That could have easily been a hard-light construct."

"You would be correct." called an unfamiliar voice from inside the barn.

The first thing Xavier noticed was the man's mane of snow white hair. It was shaggy and wild, held back by a simple hair tie. The man was no larger than Xavier, but something about him seemed almost bestial. His ice-blue eyes possessed a hunger that made Xavier feel that he would eat anything. Even his walk was different. Less a human, and more a predator approaching prey.

"Allistar." Xavier replied, with a courteous head nod.

Allistar flashed a toothy grin and nodded back. "Figured out who I was just by looking at me. Impressive. If I knew you were going to figure it out that fast, I wouldn't have given your spy such a hard time. Speaking of which," he pointed towards the roof, "are they coming down or…?"

"The humans who congregated here may still be about. It's bad enough they've seen Max's face. Don't need them seeing anybody else. The less our psychics have to erase the better."

Allistar clicked his tongue in annoyance. "You lot are Serea's ilk alright. Always with the cloak and dagger bit. But no need to worry about the humans who got away. Me and the boys took care of them."

Xavier's heart sank into his stomach. He scanned the area but couldn't find any other Lycans. What he did see were the fading thermal signatures of dozens of bodies. His eyes widened, and he looked back at Allistar who was still smiling.

"How? Why?" Was all Xavier could bring himself to say.

"Easy questions." Allistar hopped a small distance back and snapped.

Seven balls of light appeared, each a different color of the rainbow. The balls begin to twist and shape and soon seven hulking, translucent Lycans stood before them. Xavier had seen photos and videos of Lycans in the past and he realized they didn't them justice. He was just grateful that these ones weren't real.

"So, this is what your magic turned into after you were bit?"

"Yup. I call it Spirit Magic. Not only can these babies inflict actual harm on people, but their bites also do different things. And they're rainbow! You should see how popular these guys get during Pride Month. It's awesome! But you know what's not awesome? Not introducing yourselves! Seriously, I will send them up there to eat you lot!"

The rest of the team all leapt down from the upper level and none looked pleased.

"My you're dour bunch, aren't you?" Allistar scoffed.

"We watched you kill all those people." Cassie hissed.

"Of course I killed them. There were no children and all of them had seen Max's face. If you want to blame anybody, blame him for breaking protocol for an old woman. Bad ass entrance though, I'll give you that."

"I know what he did." Xavier retorted, "But,"

"Actually, you're the Cover Leader so technically it's your fault that those people had to die. It's plain to see that you're nowhere near strict enough. If one of my pack decided to pull what Max did, again very nice entrance, I would have beaten him to the River Styx and back."

Xavier's rage had reached its point. "I'll admit that he screwed up. But that does not excuse mass murder! Our Psychics could have erased their memories, our Shifters could have covered up evidence! We have people in place for exactly these types of events!"

Allistar's face wore an expression of disinterest, but his voice held a quiet anger.

"And that's some pitiful human thinking. Do you realize that by the time they got to their cars, they were already texting and tweeting? This would have gotten well out of your control if I hadn't stepped in."

"You don't know that! All Max did was beat up some people. At worst they would have just thought he was crazy!"

"You're delusional."

"And you're paranoid. And a damn murderer."

Allistar's Lycans began to growl in unison which caused everyone else to draw their weapons.

"Be careful of who you name call, little Witch. The boys are still hungry."

"Be careful of who you threaten. You're kidding yourself if you don't think Miguel isn't watching. Whatever your history is, you're not gonna risk directly attacking someone so close Serea."

Allistar's scowl turned into a wolf-like snarl which only caused Xavier to smile. Without a single word, Allistar turned and left out of the barn.

"What's our clean-up team's E.T.A.?" Xavier asked, after convincing himself to breath.

"Fifteen minutes tops." Adam replied. "I've already informed HQ of what happened."

"Great. More than likely they're sending Xorn's team out here. When they get here, assist them however you can. Adam please see to the woman. She's drugged, but alive. We need a moment."

"Xavier." Danny mumbled, "Take it easy,"

"Don't," Xavier warned. "As much as I hate to agree with that murdering ass, Allistar had a point and I have a job to do."

Danny looked crestfallen but nodded in agreement. Xavier walked up to Max who hadn't moved from the hole in the wall. As he approached, the air grew colder. Xavier quickly blasted his heat shield before continuing his approach.

"I know what you're going to say Xavier." He croaked.

Xavier walked around saw that Max's eyes had grown red and puffy.

"I'm sure you do. Max, you're a pacifist at heart. What the hell happened that made you snap like that?"

Max sniffled before answering. "When my family moved our new neighborhood, everything was supposed to be better. Better house, better jobs for my mom and dad, better schools. But it wasn't all better. There were these people. I won't call them Christians because they weren't, despite pretending to be. They were terrible. They would harass my mother and sisters. They would vandalize our house. When the police finally arrested one of them, they sent their children after us. My big brother was always the strong one. They…hurt him. They hurt him so bad that he can't walk. They took a sledge hammer to his legs!"

"So, it wasn't the cult you were seeing."

Max shook his head.

"No. When they brought that poor old woman out against her will. I lost it Xavier. I couldn't stand by and watch people like them hurt someone else. I couldn't. Nothing else mattered. All I wanted to do was turn that stupid Arch Bishop into an ice cube."

"Hurting someone who hurt you is a natural reaction. But those cultists weren't the people who hurt your brother. As much as it would have sucked, that Arch Bishop probably would have called the demon in the back of the barn and we would have killed it then. No one else needed to die tonight."

"Allistar,"

"I'm not talking about that! I'm talking about the two that you killed! In cold blood! More than likely they were human Max!"

"I know!" Max screamed, assaulting the area with a fresh wave of cold air. "I know, I swear I do. I don't know what came over me Xavier. I just knew that I had to kill that Arch Bishop. I kept thinking, if that if I took him out all of that would end. That no more people would have to die."

"The problem is that you don't see what flawed logic that is."

"What do you mean?"

"Let's start with the Arch Bishop. Until I had told you, you didn't know that he was a Heretic Witch. Which means, you fully intended to kill a normal human, again in cold blood."

"Our job is to protect people!

"From demons! And everything else that goes bump in the night, which doesn't include crappy humans! If that man had not revealed his underworld connections, then we would have nothing to do with this!"

Max stared at Xavier with disgust.

"You can't possibly believe that."

"Whether or not I believe in it is not the point. If we cross that line, if we start making those decisions than we are no better than the monsters we kill. There has to be a line and you nearly crossed it!"

"And if I had, this cult would have been stopped!"

"That is not how humans work and you know that! They would have used his death as lightning rod to bring more people to their cause. And let me ask you something, who's to say that this is only chapter of that cult?! Weren't you listening? They 'worked hard to break ground here'. That isn't something someone would say about their only location. You would have committed murder, again, and it would have done nothing."

Max's eyes widened and immediately began to leak tears.

"Xavier, what have I done?"

Xavier went and gave Max a tight hug.

"I'll help figure this out. But you need to get counseling."

Max nodded before breaking the embrace.

"I think I need to be alone for a while."

With a pat on the shoulder, Xavier headed back and saw the gnarled face of Xorn looking at him. He waved away the smoke from Xorn's cigarette and greeted him.

"Allistar huh?" he rumbled in his low voice.

"They told you?"

"Didn't need to. I know that whack job's handiwork anywhere. But those two," He nodded near the remains of the stage. "weren't. I'm guessing that's why he's all messed up."

Xavier nodded, trying his best not breathe in the cancerous fumes.

"Boys like him weren't meant to kill. Make sure you take care of him. I'm gonna write in my report that those two died because of the demon. If that damned idiot Miguel keeps his mouth shut, Serea won't know anything."

"Thanks, Xorn."

The grizzly Lion Shifter nodded before walking towards one of the members of his crew. After spending nearly an hour assisting the cleanup crew they all flew back to the safe house. They all elected to leave that night as staying near the town seemed distasteful. Once they were safely on the plane headed back Xavier chanced the question that he been wanting to ask.

"I know tonight was kinda rough, but you guys ok?"

Ophelia looked up from the book she was reading. "We just watched sixty people get slaughtered by the head of the West U.S. Branch. 'Kinda rough' really doesn't cover it."

Xavier didn't say anything else for the rest of the trip. Despite being exhausted, his mind refused to let him sleep when they returned. Instead, he retrieved his laptop and began work on his report to Serea until exhaustion finally took him. He awoke an hour later, finished the report, and submitted it. When they got back, and he was comfortably in his room, Serea soon called him and told him that she was giving him and the other's the day off. He attempted to sleep for a couple hours but continued to wake up intermittently. After locating comfortable pants, he went to a nearby mess hall in search of coffee.

When he arrived, he was surprised to see Szakiya sitting at a table with her own mug of coffee, reading something on her tablet. It was unusual to see her in anything that wasn't a Zora issued uniform, but she looked very comfortable in her pajamas, complete with purple robe. She looked up and greeted him.

"Hey hon. Welcome back."

"Thanks." Xavier replied, filling a cup with the delicious nectar that was vanilla flavored coffee.

"Heard that last night was rough."

Xavier sat down at her table and nodded.

"Rough really doesn't cover it." He said, echoing Ophelia.

"Well, we're not gonna talk about it. What do you plan on doing with your day off?"

Xavier shrugged.

"Same thing with all my other days off I guess. I want to go see Max, but I don't know how to cheer him up."

Szakiya looked in thought for a moment before her eyes lit up. "I remember him mentioning a book series he wanted to get."

"That's great and all, but Amazon doesn't do same day delivery out here."

"That's why you can come along with me to go shopping and get it."

Xavier stopped mid-sip and narrowed his eyes.

"You just need a pack mule, don't you?"

"Sure do. And I've been meaning to take you shopping. Your wardrobe is depressing at best."

"Your kindness knows no bounds." Xavier sarcastically replied. "Though this will be the first time I've left the compound for something not mission related."

"I know. Well I'm going to get dressed. Meet you in the garage in forty minutes."

Szakiya got up with her mug and tablet and took a step before looking at Xavier.

"Hon, we may not be technically human anymore, but that doesn't mean we have to be Witches all the time. It's ok to take a day and pretend to be a normal human being. It's the same for your team."

As she left, Xavier pulled out his phone and called Justin.

"This had better be good." Justin's voice was deeper than anything Xavier had heard in the past and he nearly dropped the phone.

Very quickly, Xavier explained that he wanted to have another team dinner and asked that Justin send him a list of groceries that he would need. Justin sat in silence before saying that he would send it once he slept a little more.

"Xavier?"

"Yeah?"

"This is actually a good idea. And I'm proud of you for thinking of it. But if you wake me up out of good sleep again, it better be important. Because if it isn't life threatening, it soon will be."

"Yes sir."

16:

The sound of weapons clanging filled Xavier's ears as he exchanged blows with Nate. Xavier blocked a blow with the bottom of the hilt before swinging his blade down in an arc. Nate used both ton-fa to block and they locked weapons, both refusing to budge.

"Both of you need to watch your footing!" Beatrice called, holding Max in a headlock. "I know you're tired but that doesn't excuse poor foot- ow! Did you just bite me?!"

Xavier and Nate still stood firm. Xavier tried to force Nate back, but he refused to budge. The two then disengaged with a flurry. Ducking under Nate's left ton-fa, Xavier jammed the bottom of the hilt directly into Nate's abdomen. Nate doubled over, but soon followed it with another strike towards Xavier's head. Xavier moved to the right and launched a kick at Nate's side. His foot throbbed painfully as it collided with Nate's weapon.

"And time!" Beatrice called, holding Max in a Full Nelson. "Match goes to Nate. You were sloppy Xavier."

"Yeah, yeah." Xavier replied, shaking Nate's hand.

"Good match. The stomach shot was brutal though." Nate said, wheezing slightly.

"My bad. Got a bit carried away."

They walked out of the ring and nabbed water bottles while watching Max get what looked like a very painful lesson in grappling. Nate decided to be helpful and tap in which yielded disastrous results. Xavier could barely keep himself from laughing as Nate was being manhandled and folded in many painful ways. After fending off a particularly persistent fit of giggles, a pair of hands grabbed him from behind. On instinct, Xavier leaned forward and threw his would-be attacker on the floor in front of him. He was unsurprised to see that his attacker was Miguel, who was groaning rubbing the back of his head.

"Dude! What gives? I was giving a buddy some love."

Xavier shrugged. "You scared me and grabbed from behind. In the middle of training. What'd you expect?"

"True. I should count myself lucky. Beatrice used to pile drive me into a wall." Miguel replied, hopping to his feet.

"And you survived? I'm impressed."

"Aw thank you bro. When you get cleaned up, can we talk in your room?"

"I'm sorry what?" Adam said, surprising both of them.

One look showed that Adam wasn't too happy to hear about Miguel visiting Xavier's room. Even though it was born from a misunderstanding, Xavier was still really happy to see Adam get jealous over him.

"Whoa no!" Miguel said, holding up his hands. "Nothing like that! Xavier's my bro and we chill out. No worries, he's totally got his eyes on you. And may I say, he's got great taste."

The amount of snickering that followed made Xavier wish he could turn invisible right that second and considered casting the spell despite not quite mastering it.

"Miguel…" he growled, opting instead to stick with threats or maiming and/or burning, "Find somewhere else to be that isn't here."

"Gotcha. We still cool to have that discussion?"

"If I don't blow up this entire floor first, sure. Please go."

Miguel gave Xavier a wink before disappearing. Xavier refused to meet Adam's gaze as the snickering continued. With a few hasty words, he excused himself and practically sprinted for the elevators. When the doors were securely closed he turned around and began knocking his head against the wall.

"That wasn't the smoothest bro. Just saying."

"Miguel, I will literally blow the elevator up just kill you."

"Sorry, sorry. So, I found something kinda funky."

Xavier stopped hitting his head against the wall and looked at Miguel.

"The last mission you brought us didn't end too well."

"I know… But you guys are stronger because of it. And this one may not have demons involved at all. It's just really strange."

"Alright, what is it?"

"A mental institute out in Georgia has had a rise of violent behavior from its tenants. While not inherently strange for a place like that, the violence is erratic and often from patients who have no history of violent behavior. Also, the attackers are almost…rabid when they do it.

Now it could just be another case sucky humans, but I would feel better if you guys check it out."

"Alright." Xavier replied, leaning against the wall he was banging his head on. "Simple Intel gathering. The girls are on another assignment, so I'll have no Psychic help. That gonna pose a problem?"

"I can't say for certain bro. Go in prepared anything. Good luck."

Miguel disappeared as soon as the elevator opened. Xavier walked towards his room and went straight to his laptop. Whenever Miguel collected data for a mission, he always managed to upload everything he found. True to form, there was a dossier's worth of information on the hospital already, including a video of a patient being attacked. Rabid was certainly the word Xavier used to describe the attack. The woman's eyes were wide and wild, and she attacked with her hands and teeth like a wild animal.

He picked up his phone and called Danny, who he had look over all of the data.

"There is definitely something odd going on." He said after viewing the video. "But I really don't like this Xavier. You know how our last mission from Miguel went."

"I know. Which is why this going to be an Intel gather mission."

"Then let me go in myself."

"No. If someone is directly responsible for these attacks, you could be outnumbered or cause a security breach."

"I've snuck into harder places than this Xavier."

"I know. But trust me on this one ok?"

Danny remained quiet for a few seconds before acquiescing and hanging up. A few more minutes and a half-dozen forms filled out, Xavier went to clean himself up and get ready for their next mission. Admittedly, he was just as worried as Danny. Max had barely gotten back to his old self after their last mission, and if anything happened on this one, he wasn't sure if a set of books would help.

When he met up with everyone, his fears seemed to abate as Max was fussing at Nate for poking fun at their training session earlier.

"At least I didn't run out the gym, my face redder than a hot dog because the boy I like happened to be nearby!" Max snapped, unaware that Xavier was directly behind him.

Xavier blasted a burst of hot air forward and Max went ridged.

"I didn't quite catch all of that Maximillian. Mind repeating yourself?"

"Ooh gurl," Justin said, "He called you by your government name. You in danger gurl."

"Don't be silly Justin." Xavier replied, lowering his voice to little more than a whisper, "After all, I know where he sleeps. And since I'm a Section Head, I can override door locks."

Justin started snickering. "He gon come for you in the dead of night. Dressed in black on black on black. You gon *die*."

Max turned around and Xavier had to bite his tongue to keep himself from laughing at how pale he turned.

"In my defense," Max squeaked, "You were really red."

Xavier bent forward so that his mouth was right next to Max's ear.

"And your face would be too if the guys found out that you play with your Disney Barbie collection when no one's looking."

"I do not!" Max yelled, his face beet red. "Those are totally unfounded accusations!"

Max stomped off and got into the van, still very red. Justin gave Xavier his signature "we're gonna talk about this later look" and followed. Xavier had to bite his tongue to keep from laughing as he felt Max and Danny both glaring at him.

When they arrived at the mental institute, nothing seemed out of the ordinary. In fact, the place seemed still and serene. They snuck to the back entrance and Xavier mapped the building. His stomach tightened as he immediately noticed something wrong.

"Why are there so many large-scale heat signatures?"

"Water heaters?" Adam whispered.

"Even with a building this size, the max you need is like three. Not twelve."

"Twelve? Dammit."

"Take a picture of the map and go in pairs. Identify it if you can. Keep coms open but be quiet. Fully staffed night shift in there."

Learning from their last mission that invisibility spells should only be used sparingly, Justin had enchanted their gear with several spells to aid in stealth. Everyone left, and Xavier saw that Adam was his partner. His heart skipped a beat, but he overrode his immature joy in lieu of the mission. Xavier pointed to a heat source near them on an upper floor and they headed inside. Floating a few feet in the air, they flew down the hall until they reached the stairs. A guard was standing nearby. When it became obvious that he was content to stand and play on his phone all night, Adam caused the nearby water fountain to explode.

Once the guard was distracted, they flew past. The heat source was inside an empty room and was positioned on the wall. Further inspection showed that it was some sort of tank with pipes leading to the air vent on the wall. Adam placed his hand on the tank and cast a quick identification spell.

"Well?" Xavier whispered

"It's some sort of chemical compound. I don't recognize most of it except for the Epinephrine."

"What's that?"

"One of the major chemicals released by the brain when we're angry."

"So, this stuff is anger mist?"

Adam nodded. "That's my guess. And they're pumping it through hospital."

"That explains- hold up." Xavier tapped his buzzing ear com. "Go ahead."

"Xavier." Justin said. "Those signatures are,"

"I know. We found one too."

"What do we do?"

"As messed up as this is, there isn't anything demonic about it. We need to pull out."

"Understood."

Xavier beckoned at Adam and they went to leave the room. As they looked out the hallway, they noticed the security guard was on the ground, motionless. A thermal scan showed that the guard had been killed recently. A feral growl echoed down the hall and Xavier spotted three patients. Much like the woman in the video Miguel took, they looked rabid. One particularly large man suddenly stopped and began sniffing the air. He turned around and their eyes met. To be so large, he moved with a surprising amount of speed. Realizing that there would be no time to cast an invisibility spell, Xavier dodged the strike and kicked the man in the temple. As the man dropped, he took a small sigh of relief that he had held back enough to ensure he didn't kill the man.

Adam's fist whizzed by his face and collided with jaw of another patient. As the man fell to the ground, Xavier's heart finally resumed a normal rhythm.

"I didn't hear him coming."

“Neither did I.” Adam said, watching the last patient as she approached. “You sure there isn’t anything demonic going on here? Humans can’t move that fast without making noise usually.”

“Not sure.” Xavier replied, wincing at the elbow strike Adam hit the woman with. “But I don’t like this. We need to destroy these pumps.”

Xavier tapped the bottom button of his com and once he heard everyone check in he issued orders to for them to destroy the vats and to be careful of the patients. He turned back into the empty room and began to melt the vat with an exorbitant amount of heat. Unfortunately, he did it too quickly and burned a hole in the wall. With quick curse he stopped the heat. The chemical however, began to flood the room. Adam pushed him aside and formed a large water bubble that captured the ambient mist. With a flick of his wrist he funneled the water out of the nearby window.

“Really?! Why is your answer for everything to burn or melt it?” he hissed at Xavier

“Cuz fire?”

Adam rolled his eyes and they headed to the next nearby chemical tank. After a clearing out all the tanks, the team began their exit. As Adam and Xavier went down a hall, his thermal sense reared in alarm. There were nearly twenty people around the nearby corner. Despite checking for and disabling the cameras, Xavier couldn’t shake the suspicion that they were being watched. His com buzzed, and he answered, after ducking into a nearby utility closet.

“Let me guess, a small army is blocking your way too?”

“Yup.” Danny replied. “Can you do another full scan?”

Xavier summoned his map and his heart sank. All of them were surrounded.

“Get to a nearby window. We’ll just fly out.” Xavier said, annoyance pushing aside anger.”

In response, alarms began to blare throughout the entirety of the building, nearly deafening him.

“Danny! I thought you said you took down the security systems!”

“I did! Someone must have remote restarted them!”

“Then generate an EMP. Wipe everything out. Our coms should still,”

“Ah-ah-ah, little Witch.” A familiar voice crooned. “No tinkering with my toys.”

Xavier felt his blood go cold.

"Alexander."

"Indeed. I must say you've quite the penchant for ruining things. Especially my expensive ones. Well, *Xavier*, I've a bit of a proposition for you. If you and your cohorts manage to fight your way out of there, I won't send the pack of angry Howler Demons I've got nearby to eat everyone. Refuse, and well, you know how that song and dance goes. Bye. Don't forget to put on a good show for me."

"Alexander, you sick, twisted,"

The com line cut out before cutting back on.

"Xavier?" Max asked, voice shaking.

"Do as he says. They've been made rabid, but they're still human. Just pull your punches. Meet where we came in. Destroy your coms."

When everyone issued their affirmative, Xavier snatched the com out of his ear and crushed it in his palm.

"We'll figure this out." Adam said, touching his hand.

Xavier nodded and they both exited the closet. Moving as quietly as they could, they raced around the corner. They each managed to drop four people before the rest of the horde noticed them. Xavier grudgingly admitted to himself that he enjoyed how easy it was to bring down his opponents. Between the training and the natural enhancements to his body, the practically floated from opponent to opponent. One strike was all it took. In a few minutes they were racing down the stairs.

After taking out two security guards, they ran into Justin and Nate who left a trail of unconscious bodies behind them. With small nods they resumed their hasty exit. When they finally got to the bottom floor, they noticed Danny and Max engaged with a group of nearly fifty patients and guards. With a leap, all of them began to fight off the feral army.

Xavier's heart leapt with a savage type of joy to see his fellow Witches fighting by his side. A little more than six months ago, they were just these kids who could barely hold their own in a single combat and now they were fighting off a huge group of people without so much as breaking a sweat. He remembered some of the older members of Zora referring to the thrill of battle alongside their comrades-in-arms and wondering if he was feeling the same thing.

As the final attacker fell to the ground, Xavier's exhilaration fell straight through the floor.

"This the police, we know you're in there. You're more than welcome to come quietly, but I really enjoy shooting idiot kids making trouble. Choice is yours."

"Of course, the cops show up as soon as we win." Justin sighed, "Why wouldn't they?"

"We need to hide our weapons. No way can we explain these off." Danny replied, taking off his gauntlets.

Nate used his powers to lift and small section of the floor up and they all threw their weapons inside. They also threw all their cell phones and any other Zora specific equipment in the hole. After replacing the floor, Xavier melted the concrete back into place as gently as he could. When they opened the doors, they were met by nearly a dozen officers with their guns trained on them.

"Aw, y'all took the easy way." One officer strode forward, putting down his megaphone. "Well no matter. One of y'all want to tell me what the hell y'all were doing in there."

"We were looking for a cool place to shoot our music video." Xavier replied immediately.

The officer gave him an honest puzzled look. "Now I can buy the fact that y'all are a band. Ya even got matching outfits. Let me guess, death metal?"

"Thrash." Danny snapped.

"And y'all convinced a black man to join?"

"I'm the lead guitarist." Justin growled, his deeper voice announcing his irritation.

The officer chuckled. "Is that right? Well, strange as that might be, I can believe that. So how did y'all go from checking place out, breaking and entering I might add, to beating the snot out of innocent security guards?"

"The people in there attacked us!" Max yelled, "They're crazy!"

"You don't say? Well maybe that's why they're here. In a crazy house."

"Yeah but, all them attacking us? That isn't strange?"

"Oh, it is. One of the guards said that everybody in there done lost their minds. But I want to know how you bunch made it out without a scratch? The guard said that the patients had killed a few people."

"We all studied martial arts together," Xavier called, "it's how we met."

The officer clicked his tongue before beckoning some officers to them.

"I have to take y'all in for the breaking and entering, but we'll investigate the rest of this. Y'all high school kids are going to have to learn that your actions have real consequences."

17:

The handcuffs were so incredibly uncomfortable that it took all of Xavier's self-control not to break them. Once they arrived at the station to be processed, their lack of any identification caused a bit of a stir. Finally, the officer in charge decided to register them all as John Does until a parent came for them. When Xavier was given his one phone call, he called the Zora hotline. As arrests were an occasional occurrence, Zora set up a hotline that allowed field agents to call for help. Unfortunately, due to their being Witches, his call went straight to Serea.

"Jason?" Serea answered, sounding honestly concerned.

"Hi mom."

"Sweetie, where are you?"

"In the Brook River County jail…"

"And just what are you doing there, young man?!"

Xavier put an ashamed expression on his face, which caused the nearby officer to nod approvingly.

"We were looking for a cool place to shoot our next music video, so we broke into the nearby crazy house."

"Jason! The proper name to use is Mental Institute and you and that damned band of yours are in so much trouble. When I get there, you and I are going to have a long and possibly painful discussion of your life choices!"

"I know mom. I'm sorry."

Serea hung up the phone and the officer escorted Xavier back to their cell. When the officer offered to let others make a call, Xavier informed him that his mother was on first name basis with all their parents. They'll know by now. The officer laughed as he shut the door.

"Was your mom angry?" asked Justin.

"Positively livid." Xavier replied, mimicking Serea's accent.

"Yay. I can't wait until she tells my dad."

"Your father is actually in your life?" the officer asked.

Justin's scowl was so intense that Xavier was sure he was going collapse the man's lungs.

"Yes." Justin replied through gritted teeth. "I have a father."

"And he ain't ashamed of you?"

The mood inside the cell instantly worsened. Even Xavier found himself glaring at the ignorant officer.

"What does he have to be ashamed of?"

The officer gestured at Justin. "Well at ya. If I had a son who was such a sissy, I'd shoot him myself."

"Well thank God you haven't procreated. I doubt humanity could afford having a little version of you walking around."

One of the other officers nearby started roaring with laughter but was soon quieted by the look he received. The insulted officer stomped up to the cell and Justin stood up defiantly.

"Since you dress like a lady, maybe you ought to act like one and keep your pretty much shut."

"You know I would actually be insulted by that if it wasn't obvious you've never had a lady."

The officer tore open the cell's door. "You know what? I think this one has something to tell us in the interrogation room!"

Danny and Adam both stood up, but Justin stopped them with a look. As they turned around the corner Justin mouthed the words "I'll be ok."

"Xavier we can't let them take him, they'll beat him." Max cried, grabbing his arm.

"Beatrice can dish out more punishment when she's sick, than those clowns can on their best day. He'll be fine."

“See?” Max said, pointing to his face. “You don’t even believe that!”

“What do you want me to do?!” Xavier hissed. “Knock down the door with my super strength and set this place of fire? Tell me, how do think Zora is going to cover that up?”

“They’ve done it in the past!”

“Yeah but think how far back that was.” Danny intoned. “Things are different now. Technology is different now. In order to cover something like that up, people would probably have to disappear. It’d be Missouri, all over again.”

At the mention of their last disastrous mission, all the fight left Max and he sat down on the bench quietly. An uneasy quiet fell over them as no one dared say how worried they were. The tension only increased as the minutes continued to pass by. Nearly twenty minutes had passed when they saw officers sprinting towards the entrance of the station. Soon a low rumbling started to vibrate through the whole building.

“Nate! Rock Cover! Now!” Xavier screamed.

In the seconds before two hollow boulders encased them, Xavier could see the form of a giant tornado through the window. Nate’s Rock Cover was shown to be able to withstand ballistic fire, yet he was struggling to hold firm against the gale force winds outside. After seeing a particularly large crack, Xavier nodded at Max. Max went to the crack and filled it with ice as the winds continued to batter their shield. When the winds finally abated, Nate chanced a small hole and reported that the tornado was headed away.

Nate then used his powers to bring everyone underground. Using Xavier’s flame as a light source, Nate tunneled under the ruins of the police department until they reached where Justin was. Nate opened the ground right beneath him and Justin landed without a word. The moment their eyes met, Xavier knew. He quieted everyone as they barraged Justin with questions and told them to focus on getting out of there.

With a few short orders, he had Nate and Danny go back to the mental institute and retrieve their gear from underground. Adam was to go to a nearby building up the street and pose as a tornado victim to give Serea an update. The rest of them would wait nearby under an invisibility spell. After nearly an hour they all regrouped and headed towards the nearby airport. Serea had just arrived and looked none too pleased to see them. Once safely in the air Serea grabbed Justin the scruff of his vest.

“You better start talking. A tornado? What were you thinking?!”

Xavier's speed impressed even him as shoved Serea to other side of the plane. Serea looked at Xavier with glowing eyes, but they soon went back to normal the moment she looked at his face. With a curt gesture, Xavier took Serea to the back of the plane.

"Xavier what the in nine hells happened?!" Serea whispered. "A little mishap with your powers is one thing. But a large scale natural disaster is quite another. I suppose I should be grateful that he managed to destroy the police station, but what on earth would make him do such a thing? In Georgia! Georgia doesn't even get tornadoes!"

In a low monotone Xavier explained what he believed happened. Serea placed her hand over her mouth in horror.

"Oh my god. In all my years no one was ever brave enough to… And I was so cruel just now… I've got to,"

"No." Xavier barked, grabbing her arm,

"Well someone needs to make sure he's ok!"

"I can tell you with certainty that he isn't."

Serea looked at Xavier with a puzzled look before the realization dawn on her.

"You too?" she gasped.

"Not tonight. But yeah. So, trust me to handle this. I don't care what paperwork I have to fill out, or who I have to talk to. But please, let me handle this."

"Of course. I'm here if you need me."

Xavier took the opportunity to inform her of Alexander hacking their coms, news that she didn't take well at all. After telling him that she would handle it, Xavier went back to his seat. The rest of the plane ride went in complete silence. Once they landed, Xavier told everyone to get some rest as the sun had already started to rise. After being told that Serea wanted to talk afterwards, he made a beeline for Justin's room.

He knocked a few times and overrode the door lock when he received no answer. Justin had certainly made a home out of his room as the walls were covered in various posters. Some Xavier recognized, and some he didn't. He walked towards the bathroom where he could feel the heat emanating from the door. Past the sounds of the falling water, he could hear Justin crying.

"Justin, cut the water down." Xavier called, feeling a pang of worry of how hot the water was.

"Xavier go away!" Justin yelled after sniffing. "I don't want to talk!"

"Then listen. The water will never be hot enough. There's no point in giving yourself burns."

The water shut off and all Xavier could hear was Justin's small sobs.

"You?"

Xavier leaned against the bathroom door and sunk to the ground.

"Yeah. I told you that my parents died. Once my uncle got ahold of me, that was it. Almost every day."

"So, when you said that you served one function…"

"Yeah. You can imagine how happy I was to see a demon eat him."

A small silence broke between them.

"Xavier?"

"Hm?"

"Do you ever stop feeling the hands?"

"Eventually. Every person is different. That was my life before all of this so I'm still struggling. It might take you a little shorter."

"I'm sorry about the tornado… I didn't know what else to do!"

"You felt weak, like you couldn't defend yourself. Which hurt worse because you're this powerful, kick-ass Witch."

"All I wanted was for them to stop."

"I don't blame you in the slightest. Knowing me, I would have wound up killing them."

Justin took a deep breath before releasing it.

"I wanted to. Jesus be my shield, I wanted to. I wanted to break their little scrawny necks. But if I did that… If I went there, into that place. I know I wouldn't come back. So, I just sat there…"

"I get it. I really do. Which is why I'm here. Because you need two things right now. Things I wished someone had given me."

"What's that?"

A shuffling to his right caused Xavier to look over where he saw Nate, holding a bouquet of assorted yellow flowers. He smiled which Xavier returned before answering.

"A hug, and someone to tell you that this isn't your fault. It was never your fault. I would give you a hug, but there's a chiseled Latino god with flowers here that I think you'd want to hug more."

Justin let out a small gasp and Xavier saw his shadow get closer to the door.

"Are the flowers yellow?" Justin whispered.

"Uh-huh."

"Dammit. Now I have to come out."

"Yeah. They look like he grew them too."

Justin let out a small laugh.

"Thank you, Xavier."

"It won't be easy, but it will get better with time and support. You know where to find me if you need me."

Xavier stood up, dusted off his pants and walked up to Nate clasped him on the shoulder.

"I feel like I need to offer one of these to you." He said jokingly.

"Nah. I don't like yellow or flowers." He lowered his voice to a small whisper. "Look, don't ask him if he's ok and don't press him for details. Just be here and make him feel safe."

Nate nodded, and Xavier walked out of the room. When he closed the door, a body collided with his and held him close. After his brain recovered from the initial shock, he saw that it was Adam. As he hugged Adam back, he felt something wet hit his neck. A few seconds later Adam was crying on his shoulder.

"Um, Adam? What's wrong?"

"I'm so sorry!" Adam hiccupped. "I didn't know. I acted so damn high and mighty and you were dealing with something awful."

"It's ok. Really. You didn't know. You were right to say that we should talk. I just didn't know how until just now."

"It's not your fault." Adam whispered.

"What?"

"It's not your fault! It was never your fault!"

The words hit Xavier right to his soul. He knew that it wasn't his fault but hearing it from someone who genuinely cared for him stirred something within him that he hadn't felt in a very long time. And as Adam continued to sob apologies into his shoulder, Xavier felt his own tears well up. He had once told himself that crying would solve nothing. He had vowed to be strong, so that he could help other people who went through the same thing. He never considered how doing that would affect him. He held on to Adam tightly and they both stood there crying into each other's arms.

After what felt like hours, Xavier finally calmed down enough to break the hug and look at Adam. Even when he was crying, Xavier thought he was beautiful. After wiping the tears from his eyes, Xavier placed a soft kiss on his Adam's lips.

"We take it one step at a time?" Xavier offered.

Adam laughed. "Yeah."

There was a small giggle from behind them and Xavier turned to see a bright brown eye peering through Justin's open door. Xavier kicked the door lightly, which elicited another giggle from Justin before the door closed. Xavier looked at his phone and noticed that Serea had asked when he was coming to see her. He gave Adam another kiss and told him to get some sleep. After a few minutes, he arrived at Serea's office.

Her office was always an experience to visit. Usually there a half dozen people flying in and out of the door, sometimes literally. But it was quiet, still even. Xavier wasn't sure if he liked that but knocked anyways.

"Come in Xavier."

Xavier walked in and found a collection of four people around her office; Beatrice, Eliade, Bartok, and much to his consternation, Sumna. As the Section Head of all the Psychics in the branch he had found it the height of irresponsible that she did nothing to improve relations between Psychics and Witches. Any effort he made to sit down and discuss things were instantly rebuffed. Though he'd be lying to himself if he didn't appreciate her fashion sense. Despite being clad in an emerald green bathrobe and pajamas, her hijab and make up matched perfectly. She greeted him with a curt nod which he returned, attempting to keep himself from scowling.

"Thank you for coming. We've something of grave importance to discuss."

Xavier closed the door and perched on top of the arm of her couch.

"We potentially have a spy." Xavier responded indifferently.

Bartok began to chuckle. "I like this one. Right to the point."

"Well it's the one of the maybe three conclusions that makes sense. Our com links are engineered to prevent an outsider from hacking our communications. It's possible that Alexander just got lucky, but unlikely."

"And what do you think happened?" Sumna replied with an eye roll.

"Someone who really doesn't like my Coven sold us out. Rather, someone who doesn't like the idea of Witches. We already know that Alexander has a history of killing new Witches. And he was so good that the idea of a whole Coven forming without his knowledge surprised him." Xavier looked at Bartok and Serea. "Why are we having this conversation? Between the two of you, this should have occurred to you."

Serea nodded her head. "Yes. The Psychics and the Intelligence Unit have been working very hard on this since you told us."

"Which means the traitor is among those two factions."

"Don't you think we investigated our own first?" Sumna asked in biting tones.

Xavier looked at her impassively. "No. Not really. From what I'm told, your telepathy is so strong that you can read the minds of nearly every person in this country. How have you not torn through the minds of everyone here?"

Serea cut across before Sumna, who was visibly enraged, could answer.

"Some Psychics, Vampires, and particular Shifters are harder to read than others. Even for someone like Sumna."

Xavier turned to Bartok, "And your investigations?"

"Intelligence work takes time, little morsel. Besides, we're hitting a bit of a blind spot."

Xavier heaved a sigh as he realized the real reason he was called.

"Us. You think one of us sold his soul to the Devil. Well, demon."

"It's possible."

"Start your investigation with Max and Justin."

The entire room seemed to be stunned into silence which Xavier laughed at.

"Don't get it twisted. I know none of us did it. But since you're going to investigate us anyways, I may as well help you. Faster we get cleared, the faster we can catch the real traitor."

Bartok started cackling madly. "Oh, following you will be a treat!"

Xavier felt a chill go down his spine.

"You're really creepy, you know that?"

"Sure do."

18:

"And thus, it is my finding that the Coven is completely innocent. The only thing suspect about them is Nate's internet history. Guy's into some weird stuff." Bartok answered, tossing his files on Serea's desk.

Xavier shifted uncomfortably in his chair. He knew that Bartok was the Head of Intelligence for a reason, but it was still extremely uncomfortable to have someone know every tiny detail of your day-to-day life. Bartok was almost obsessively meticulous in his profiling. He was even able to make dietary suggestions to Xavier based off his bathroom usage.

"Spasibo, Bartok." Serea replied.

Bartok nodded and turned into bat before flying out of the office. Serea shuddered soon after.

"I am *so* sorry I had to subject you to that. But we did need to be sure."

"It's ok. He's just very…thorough."

Serea nodded.

"I once had him profile me, when I suspected that I might have fallen under some type of control. It was not pleasant."

"At least he's on our side?"

"It took nearly a year of international investigations to confirm that, but yes."

"Does this mean you're lifting our mission embargo?"

Serea smiled.

"It does, and just in time too. Miguel brought something to me that I want a few of you to back me up on."

Though relieved that they were no longer under suspicion, Xavier was shocked to hear that Serea wanted them to accompany her on a mission.

"I thought Szakiya was usually your partner on missions?"

"And she still is. But I haven't gone on a mission with you lot in ages… and she's currently doing a favor for me in Switzerland."

Xavier rolled his eyes which earned a sheepish grin from Serea. She beckoned him to come around her desk and pulled up a video once he did. The video was of two men in a ring and after exchanging a few blows, the men started attacking each other like wild animals. Xavier felt his stomach flip as he recognized the look on their faces.

"It would appear that our friend Alexander as resumed testing of his rage inducing gas. So far only a handful of people have died. I suppose they finally figured out that a gratuitous amount of dead bodies is akin to a giant neon sign that says, 'demons are here'. But not even culling the number of dead could really keep them from Miguel for too long."

"Really?"

Serea's face suddenly grew hard.

"I've known that man for centuries and I've never seen him that angry. When he learned what happened, he was furious. Now mind you, Miguel may be lazy and a hippie, but he is infallible as a spy. He's the only one that can actually surprise Bartok. So, if he truly wants to find someone. Anyone. It's not really a matter of if, as it is when. He found this place about a week ago and has been running recon on it since. He's quite fond of you lot."

"We noticed. He's like the annoying big brother we never asked for."

"Indeed. But back to matter at hand."

Serea laid out a plan that Xavier and two others would infiltrate the arena the fights were being kept at while she went in as a contender. Their job would be to find the source of gas quietly and grab a sample. When asked if she would succumb to the effects, she informed him that she was be taking a low dose mood stabilizer. With it she was confident that she could stave off its effects.

Xavier stopped by Danny's office and was temporarily mesmerized at how quickly he had gotten access to Congress' network. After complaining about how they still refused to do anything useful, Xavier asked him to come along on the mission. Though surprised that Serea wanted them to help her, he agreed.

Xavier then went to Adam's office. Before walking in, he checked his face in a nearby window's reflection to ensure he looked presentable. And he walked in, he saw Adam looking through a book, his brow furrowed deep. After knocking and clearing his throat, Xavier finally had to tap him to break him from his concentration.

"Xavier! Jeez. Scared me half to death."

"Didn't mean to," Xavier replied sheepishly before sitting on a nearby stool, "but you were really into that book. What is it?"

"Anatomy. I was assisting with a surgery and nearly screwed up. Can't have that happen again."

Xavier felt disappointment wash over him.

"Oh well then I guess you won't want to go on a mission with Me, Danny, and Serea?"

"Did I say I didn't want to?"

Xavier instantly felt better.

"Really?!"

"Oh god, you looked like I just told you Christmas was coming early."

"Well…I really wanted you to go."

"Are you sure that our relationship is the basis that you want to make that decision?"

"Hey! Your medical skills might be needed on this one! I'm not completely hopeless."

After explaining the details of the mission, Xavier noticed a gleam that crept into Adam's eyes.

"So, we get to dish some payback to that jerk? I'm definitely in now."

"Never mind that your boyfriend asked you to…"

Adam gave Xavier a stern look which stopped any other comment short.

"When we're on a mission, I'm not your boyfriend, I'm your teammate. You cannot lead us in a life or death situation while trying to be my boyfriend. Love and affection are ultimately selfish. You can't afford to be weak in choosing between me and the mission."

"I know." Xavier mumbled, acquiescing to Adam's logic. "I was just being funny."

Adam's face softened as he leaned forward as placed a kiss on Xavier's cheek.

"I'm just making sure babe."

After establishing more specifics about the mission and when they were due to leave, Xavier kissed Adam to leave him back to his studies. It was still unusual that he was dating anyone. Almost all his life he told himself that no one would find him good enough to date, not with his emotional baggage. Now that everything was out in the open, he felt lighter and surer of himself. Since then he finally indulged himself and started to buy things for his room. He was shocked to see several tens of thousands of dollars in his account when he finally decided to check. Once he had gotten over the minor heart attack of joy, he went on something of a shopping spree.

He decided to stop by his room to pick up one of the sodas he had bought from himself when he sensed that Miguel was waiting for him. He expected Miguel to be eating something messy with a huge grin on his face, so he was ill-prepared to see Miguel in a Zora uniform with his hair pulled into a ponytail. Though he appeared to be quite skinny in his normal clothes, the form fitting Zora uniform revealed a surprising amount of muscle. The more Xavier looked at Miguel, the more he disliked what he saw.

"Hey bro." Miguel greeted solemnly.

"No."

Miguel blinked a few times, his face looking quite confused.

"What?"

"No." Xavier repeated firmly. "I don't like this."

Realization dawned on Miguel's face.

"Well even I have to get serious sometimes. So, about this mission,"

Xavier wasn't having it. He bolted forward and gave Miguel a big hug. Miguel let out a small laugh and returned the hug. When Xavier stepped back, Miguel's face seemed to go back to its usual self.

"That's better."

Miguel nodded. "Yeah. I don't get mad often bro, but when I do its kinda intense. Thanks for that."

A bright light shone around Miguel and his regular clothes soon reappeared.

"I didn't know you were even capable of getting angry." Xavier replied, sitting on his bed to prevent Miguel from sitting on his blanket.

"Oh yeah dude. When my kind get angry, like really angry, the earth trembles."

“And what exactly is your kind?”

“Nothing you need to worry about now bro. Anyways, you guys need to be careful with this mission. This Alexander is a piece of work. He’s worse now than ever. I’m like eighty-five percent sure that he’s expecting you. If things get hairy call me, and I’ll pop in.”

“Do you and this demon have history?”

Miguel grew very quiet and slowly nodded.

“When I first faced him, he was just another demon general. It seems the years have been good to him.

“Why didn’t you kill him?” Xavier asked, honestly curious.

“Not that simple buddy. Either way, you guys need to go in expecting a trap. If you can see the trap before it happens, you can turn it to your advantage. Everything about this screams that something isn’t right.”

Xavier agreed, though he was loath to admit it. Alexander’s machinations had put him on edge. What was troubling still was that neither Max or Danny could pin down his activities. The mental institute was the first real lead they had in months. His plan to lure Alexander into revealing his hand had all but failed. Despite walking into Alexander’s hands, he was determined to strike a blow to that egotistical demon’s plans. Miguel soon left, citing having to go talk to Serea. Despite looking to be in a better mood, Miguel still looked worried. Xavier shook it off and went to Justin’s office to check on him. Despite claiming to be fine, Xavier still insisted on checking on him every day. After being satisfactorily threatened for disturbing his latest project, Xavier went to prepare for their mission.

The arena was inside a huge casino right outside of Baton Rouge. When Serea successfully registered for the fights, thanks in part to her slightly revealing outfit, they each snuck into the casino. When Xavier had mapped the building, he found five large heat sources in the general shape of what appeared to be a large tank. When Serea assigned one to each of them, Xavier felt his pride bristle. He had become accustomed to issuing the plans and was unused to following orders in the field.

Though invisible, all three of them waited until the fights started to begin. Not surprising, Serea was first. The roar of nearly every man cheering as she walked to the ring was deafening. Xavier rolled his eyes as he flew to his target. He was grateful the building was so large, trying to weave through the ocean of people below wasn’t an intriguing prospect and it gave him an opportunity to refine flying using condensed heat waves. It achieved the same effect, but with none of the flash.

A surge of the cheering caused Xavier to look to the ring to see Serea standing on top of an unconscious man, her hands raised in victory. Even though he knew it was for show, he couldn't help but laugh she bounced around, the blonde curls of the wig following suit. He landed by an employee entrance and noticed that the door was locked. After verifying that no one was around, he rammed his shoulder into the door. What he didn't count on was the door being in poor repair and was dismayed to see it fall completely to the ground. The people nearby all came to investigate and Xavier felt his heart leap into his throat. It was only after he watched several people pass by him that he realized he was still invisible. He sped past the assembled people and once he was safely in the back halls, he let out his extremely pent up breath.

"Please tell me that wasn't you." Danny's voice queried through their new coms.

"Alright, I won't tell you." Xavier whispered.

"Evidently you forgot the definition of covert." Serea hissed under her breath.

"It was an accident. Didn't think the door would…whoa."

When Xavier had come around the bend of the hallway, a blast of heat battered his newfound sense. Now that he was closer he could properly see the shape and the source was nearly the size of a room. It was hidden behind a fake wall that, upon inspection and a burning a hole through a bookshelf required a palm scan to open.

"Guys, converge on my location. I found it, but I can't get this open without tripping every alarm."

"You boys be careful." Serea whispered, "All of a sudden they kicked out all the other fighters."

Before Xavier could ask why, the feedback of a P.A. system rang through the building.

"Ladies and gentlemen." A male voice pompously called.

"Isn't that…?" Danny asked.

"Yup."

"What was Miguel saying about this being a trap?"

Xavier felt his rage swell as Alexander continued to address the casino.

"We want to thank you so much for your patronage. Unfortunately, we've come to the part of tonight's event that is V.I.P. exclusive. Those of you who are not, please exit the arena to enjoy the many other splendors of the casino. Thank you again. Oh, and if a certain firebrand would visit my office, it would be most appreciated."

The P.A. cut off and Xavier spat a stream of colorful and well thought out curses.

"How the hell did he know you're here?" Danny asked frantically.

"It doesn't matter. Get what we came here to get. Serea? You ok?"

"Yes. Evidently, I'm a part of the V.I. P. event. Lucky me."

"I'm gonna uncloak myself out there and let his goons come to me."

Xavier raced out of the door and felt something zip by his face. Even though he was invisible, he was sure it was Adam. Once he got back out to the arena, he dropped his invisibility spell. As predicted, two large men in black suits came for him.

"Don't make any sudden moves Witch or you're lunch." One of the guards said motioning for him to follow.

Xavier scoffed and summoned a small fireball to his hand. "You'd burn before your teeth ever reached me. Now shut up and take me to your jerk boss."

The guard's face distorted slightly at Xavier's fireball, but it soon recovered and scowled. They led Xavier to a service elevator and moments later it opened to a luxurious office which had a clear view of the entire arena floor. Alexander was sitting in the middle of office with his back to them, sipping on a glass of wine.

"Leave us." Alexander commanded without looking backwards.

The guards left without a word, though the one Xavier threatened flashed its distorted jaw before leaving. Once the elevator closed again, Alexander beckoned Xavier closer with a finger. Fighting the urge to set the entire office on fire, Xavier grudgingly walked forward until he was beside the demon. Alexander was wearing a deep cut V-neck that was accented by a collection of silver necklaces and bracelets.

"My, how you've grown." Alexander purred, his golden eyes alight.

Xavier beat back the desire to gag.

"Yeah well, daily training does wonders I guess."

"Especially in your case."

"Enough." Xavier snapped, eager to steer the conversation into more comfortable waters. "I doubt you brought me up here to flirt. How the hell did you know I was here?"

Alexander smiled before taking a sip out of his cup.

"Every night that we've been here, I've had my security team monitor for any unusual spikes in thermal activity. You flying about my casino definitely qualified as strange."

"Well aren't you so smart?" Xavier retorted bitterly.

"I certainly think I am. Now considering she registered the same night you arrived and has handedly defeated every person she's faced, I assume the blonde is one of yours?"

Xavier simply looked at out at the arena.

"I thought so. I've paired her up against a fellow who I believe isn't inherently human either. There are even some whispers that he's the legendary White Wolf of the West."

Xavier's eyes nearly popped out his head when he saw familiar nest of white hair walk out onto the arena. Every fiber in his being wanted to scream. To tell Serea not to go out there. It was too late. From his vantage point he could see the shock on both of their faces followed by an unmistakable rage.

"I wonder how long your friend will last? Especially when I dose them both with my improved formula?"

Xavier grabbed Alexander by the shirt and threw him into a nearby bookshelf. Alexander only laughed as he got up.

"Stop the damn gas!" Xavier screamed summoning two huge fireballs to his hands.

"Be mine."

"What?"

Alexander suddenly appeared in front of him and his lips came close to Xavier's. Unbidden, and quite by accident, Xavier shot a torrent of flames out of his mouth. Instead of questioning where this power had been hiding since his early days of being a Witch, Xavier opened his mouth wider and increased the strength of the flame until he ran out of breath. He was dismayed to see that Alexander remained unharmed, despite his shirt being completely burned off and his necklaces glowing red.

"Ha! Yes! There it is! That spirit that makes me feel more alive than I have in centuries!" Alexander's eyes were wide which gave his face a crazed look. "Think of what we could do together! Think of everything I could teach you! Why bother living your life in service to humans who would never accept you when you can be by my side! I will make you a king and give you the greatest Empire you ever,"

"SHUT UP!" Xavier screamed, launching another torrent of flames. "I will never join you. Your hands are so bloody I'm surprised you can even see them!"

A hand gripped Xavier by the throat and he found himself pinned to desk with Alexander over him.

"I could just take what I want, you know. It'd be so easy."

Xavier let out a strained bark of laughter.

"You can, but you won't. Because what you want isn't this. You want me to want to join you. You want it to be my choice. And I can promise you right now, I'll never make that choice. Ever."

Before Alexander could answer, a powerful stream of water blasted open the elevator doors and forced Alexander to dodge with a yelp. Adam walked out of the elevator looking absolutely enraged.

"Jealous boyfriend to the rescue? I'm definitely the better-looking blonde." Alexander sneered.

Adam said nothing, and a second later Alexander was dodging another stream of water. The stream cut threw everything in its path, carving a small wound into the office.

"I'll thank you not to do that. This office wasn't cheap."

Adam smiled savagely and whipped a jet stream in a large V-shape, following Alexander. With a groan of metal, the entire section within the V slid back and fell to the ground to abject horror of the people below.

"I suppose you should count yourself lucky that everyone down below is a demon. Thank you for providing my exit. Xavier, think about it."

"Not a chance in hell!" Xavier screamed hoarsely, as Alexander suddenly disappeared.

Adam walked over, placed a hand on Xavier's throat and healed it.

"Thanks."

"No time for that. We need to,"

"Guys!" Danny yelled via their coms. "I need you!"

Xavier looked down at the ring and he saw Danny holding Allistar and Serea at bay with two metal plates. Even from there, he could tell Danny was struggling.

"We're on our way!"

"Hurry! These two are legit trying to kill each other and I don't know how long these demons are just gonna sit and watch!"

Xavier leapt out of the hole and flew down to the ring with Adam right on his heels. A few of the braver demons that remained began to throw various objects at them. Once a chair had been thrown, Adam shot another jet stream, making them scurry away. Xavier flew over to Serea, whose eyes were already glowing purple.

"Serea, you've got to calm down!"

"No…" she replied huskily, while still struggling against her restraint. "It's his fault. He left me. He deserted me! I needed him! I'll kill him!"

Danny, having reached his limit, flinched as both Serea and Allistar knocked away their impediments. No one moved as the two titans stood before each other, glowing purple eyes staring into glowing white ones.

"Boys..." Serea huffed slowly. "I'm going to tell you this once and only once. You get in my way and I'll drain every drop of blood from your veins. Now move."

19:

Allistar's red Lycan smashed into Serea's blood shield with monstrous force. Serea's face wore a grimace as she struggled to remain standing. She tapped the shield and long spikes shot forward and impaled the Lycan. Allistar let out a howl as the Lycan disappeared. Blood began to pour from numerous cuts that suddenly appeared along his body.

"How fitting." Serea taunted. "Both of our magic demands a sacrifice of blood."

"Sounds like grand fun for you, eh?"

"No but spilling more of yours does!"

Serea's shield dispersed into small red diamonds and with a wave of her arm sped towards Allistar. His yellow Lycan appeared and in second before the pointed diamonds found their mark, whisked Allistar away. Serea let out a snarl and leapt after him. Xavier had never felt so puny in his life. Looking at those two fight was like watching the mountain battle the sea. But even as he watched, he knew he had to try and stop them.

"Dammit!" Danny yelled, hanging up his phone. "Even with her magic, Szakiya won't be able to get to us for another four hours."

"Then it's up to us." Xavier replied, his sense of self-preservation protesting every word.

"It's up to who?! Uh-uh. The only thing waiting for us in there is death."

"But if we don't do anything, they'll kill each other. Zora loses two of its most powerful members and potentially the Vampire and Lycan support. We have to do something."

"Dude, have you seen the way she snatches blood out of people?!"

"I can stop her from doing that." Adam said quietly.

"Last time you did that, she crushed you."

"She won't be able to fight you two and Allistar and maintain the concentration needed to fight me too. Especially with that gas making her crazy like this. It'll take me out of the fight, but I can keep your blood in your bodies."

Despite Adam casting protection spells on them to prevent the gas from affecting them, Xavier still had a hard time believing he was strong enough to combat a monster like Serea. He swallowed his doubts and turned towards the two warring beasts.

"Good. Danny you take Allistar, I'll take Serea. Maybe they'll leave themselves open enough that we can actually do some damage."

Xavier drew his katana and took a few deep breaths to steady himself. He nodded at Danny and they both raced off towards their opponents. With every step he took, he kept telling himself that he was crazy, that he was running to his death. But when he considered the enormity of what was at stake, he quelled those fears and moved forward. Serea and Allistar were caught in another gridlock. This time Allistar's blue Lycan was protecting him by projecting a force field out of its mouth and Serea was smashing into it with two giant, red, spiked hammers.

Xavier, mustering all the strength he could, shot Serea with his strongest fire blast which forced her to shield herself. As Allistar dropped his guard to go in for an attack, Danny suddenly appeared and pumped him full of lighting. Despite all the flames, Xavier could still see Serea's glowing eyes fixated on him. There was no doubt that she was going to try and kill him. Maintaining the flames, Xavier began to raise the heat in the area near where she was shielding herself. If he could only knock her unconscious, then they would only have to deal with Allistar.

"Xavier behind you!" Adam screamed.

A metallic ringing filled the air as Xavier barely held the green Lycan's claws at bay. A flash of red told Xavier to dash to his left as a red javelin skewered the ground. Serea rose in the air and Xavier could see her burns slowly healing.

"Serea think about what you're doing! What this could do to Zora! To the Vampire Nation!"

Serea narrowed her eyes and lifted her hand producing at least twenty more javelins.

"You were warned…"

Danny appeared right in front of Xavier and the suddenly the world was a blur of lights and sounds. The moment everything stopped, he felt a wave nausea wash over him.

"Sorry about that. Keep forgetting that other people can't handle that type of speed."

"I would throw up, but I think you left my stomach over there."

Allistar screamed again and Xavier saw the green Lycan slowly disappear as the javelins meant for him had instead impaled it. New wounds appeared on Allistar's body which caused Serea to smile.

"Two down, five to go."

"You blood sucking cow!" Allistar laughed. "You really think it'll be that easy?"

The yellow Lycan appeared right behind her and unleashed a barrage of lightning fast strikes, landing with brutal intensity.

"For every one of them you take out, the rest get stronger!"

Allistar then looked at Xavier and Danny and his smile widened. Xavier didn't wait and shot into the air with Danny in his arms. The fangs of the purple Lycan just barely grazed his leg but it was enough. Unimaginable pain coursed its way through Xavier's body and he felt himself scream so loud that his voice gave out. Fortunately, Danny had begun to fly on his own and he held on to his teammate. The pain soon subsided, and Xavier took a few calming breaths.

"And that was just a graze!" Allistar laughed. "Imagine what'll happen when he bites you for real!"

"Oh my god do not let that thing bite you." Xavier rasped, finally trusting his body to fly on his own.

"Yeah I noticed. I, holy crap…"

Xavier turned around to see the yellow Lycan being held by its throat by a now very muscular Serea. Though covered in an assortment of small wounds, she now looked more dangerous now than ever. With a snarl, she broke the neck of yellow Lycan, causing Allistar to double over in a coughing fit.

"You're being optimistic if you think I've reached the peak of my powers." Serea growled, rising slowly in the air. The blood from her wounds rose into the air and Xavier felt his jaw drop. Serea had formed an entire armory of several hundred different weapons. Even Allistar looked taken aback as his remaining Lycans all went to his side.

“I’ll give you one chance to surrender so that you may die painlessly.” Serea called, as every weapon pointed directly at Allistar.

His only response was to lift his hands. The purple Lycan turned into mist and soon formed translucent gauntlets, with its fangs forming spikes along his knuckles. The blue Lycan wrapped around his waist and became a belt. The orange Lycan became a pair of boots while the indigo one wrapped around his head, forming a wolf-head helmet. Serea laughed and the weapons bolted forward. His belt began to shine and wrapped his entire body a blue force field.

Xavier was in awe of the sheer determination Allistar showed. Despite Serea’s weapons flying at ridiculously high speeds, He had managed to stand his ground and fend off most of the onslaught. Even with the few weapons that managed to sneak past his defenses, Allistar’s force field held strong.

“Xavier, while she’s distracted.” Danny whispered.

“I’m not. I just had to locate what was interfering with me.” She called and pointed to where Adam had been hiding.

Adam had already been moving and Danny managed to shield off any additional weapons by shooting random bits of scrap metal at them. Xavier had never felt such rage in his life as he did that moment. Danny let out a yelp and vanished with a crack of lightning before reappearing next to Adam. Xavier barely noticed that chairs and nearby tables were either melting or catching fire. Even Serea and Allistar noticed as both ceased their fighting. Xavier let out a roar and shot his flames. The blast was gargantuan, bigger than anything that Xavier had ever summoned before.

As the flames soared across the arena, they burned everything they met to a crisp. Both Serea and Allistar let out exclamations of shock before shielding themselves. For some reason, this angered Xavier further and the flames grew more intense. He began to drift near them as he wanted to see their faces as they burned, Especially Serea. She was the one who tried to kill one of the few sources of happiness in his life and she needed to burn for it. He smiled when he saw small cracks in both of their shields. He would soon burn them to a crisp. He heard someone calling his name, but he didn’t care. It wasn’t until he felt familiar arms wrap around him from behind that he diverted his attention.

“Babe please! You have to stop!” Adam cried, his eyes watering as small burns appeared on his face. “You’ll kill them!”

Seeing the burns on Adam's face stopped all the rage and replaced it with an even greater sense of regret and worry. He extinguished the flames immediately and pulled Adam into a close hug.

"I'm so sorry! I didn't mean to hurt you!"

"I'm fine, we need to worry about…them…"

Xavier turned around and let out a gasp. Both Serea and Allistar were covered in burns and barely moving. The ground around them was scorched and glowing red. Xavier tried to scan them, but to no avail. He had almost believed he had killed them when Serea's body jerked suddenly. The jerking continued until Serea had turned over on her stomach.

"You damned Witch!" she gasped. "I'll kill you. I'll kill you. I'LL KILL YOU!"

A pair of giant leathery wings burst out of her back and began flapping. With each flap of her wings her body began to change. Her muscles began grew even larger and her mass started to increase. Her hands began to grow bigger with matching claws. Her skin slowly began to shift to all black and her mouth began to grow wider showing the armory of fangs she now had. As the sounds of her bones snapping and getting larger permeated the air, Xavier felt himself drifting backwards. When Serea finally finished changing she had grown to be nearly the size of the arena. She spread her wings and let out a vicious roar. Her now enormous purple eyes fell on him and Adam and she smiled.

He didn't know what she hit him with, but the impact sent him barreling into a wall. Every inch of his body cried out in pain and all he could manage to do was look up.

"Now stay put." Serea said, her voice now a garbled abomination of what it once was. "I'll kill you after I kill,"

Her words were drowned out by a giant furred, clawed hand wrapping around her throat. Allistar had become a giant Lycan with fur as white as snow. Serea slashed downwards causing Allistar to move out of the way with a surprising amount of speed. As they began to exchange blows, Xavier struggled to get up. His body refused to move more than a few centimeters before the pain threatened to knock him unconscious. He looked around to find Danny or Adam but saw that Serea had dealt with them in much the same manner. He had almost given up hope when Miguel's face suddenly popped into his mind. In all the fighting, he had forgotten that Miguel was nearby. Even though he knew it was a long shot, he gathered what little energy he had and weakly called,

"Miguel. We need you."

A bright white light flashed, and Miguel appeared right between Serea's and Allistar's hands; his foot blocking Allistar's and a gold and silver broad sword blocking Serea's.

"Finally!" he called, "I thought I was gonna have to watch from the sidelines forever! As for you two, why don't we all calm down?"

The same bright light started to emanate from Miguel's back until it filled the whole arena. The light felt warm and welcoming, like being hugged by an old friend. All the pain in Xavier's body started to melt away and for the first time in his life, he felt truly at peace. Unable to resist its pull, Xavier closed his eyes allowed himself to head further into the light's embrace.

When he finally awoke, he found himself in the medical ward. He looked around and saw Serea sitting directly next to him, with tears in her eyes. She rushed forward and pulled in a tight hug which caused his body to protest slightly by aching everywhere. Upon hearing his groan of pain, she immediately let go with a gasp.

"I'm so, so sorry Xavier. Dear god, I don't even know what to say. There's no excuse."

"Well in your defense, you were gassed with that angry mist."

"That's no defense. It wouldn't have affected me so much if I was facing anyone else."

"So…considering I almost died behind that, mind telling me what your beef with each other is?"

Serea grew quiet before taking a deep breath.

"Before Zora, before I was turned, before everything, I was a young woman freshly married. Allistar was my husband. We were married young to cement an alliance with our families, but it didn't matter. I had loved him since we were children."

She sat back in her chair and crossed her arms.

"Then my sixteenth birthday came, and I discovered that I was a Witch. I thought he would hate and scorn me. But it was the opposite. He was a Witch too. I couldn't believe my luck. Back then, Witches trained their fledglings in schools called Arcadieums. When we arrived, they allowed us to stay in the same room because we were wed. For some reason, that made it better. We studied together, trained together, and fought together. Eventually we finished our training and we formed a Coven with friends we had made."

Xavier sat up as Serea drifted into a silence, her face extremely pensive.

“That was the beginning of the end. Every Coven was assigned an area to protect and ours happened to be where The Twins decided to nest. The twins were these brother demons; one bat and one wolf. Their demonic bites could turn a human into a horrid copy of themselves, completely under their control. At first it was the occasional skirmish here and there, but it got worse. Then we lost Paul. Allistar blamed himself for Paul’s death and he became obsessed with killing The Twins. So much so that he didn’t notice I was pregnant.”

“Did you tell him?” Xavier asked incredulously.

“Of course I did! Twice! But he was always looking over a map or a report. Then he found their nest. I prepared with the rest of them to fight. To finally end this so that I could get my husband back, but I was starting to show.”

Serea let out a small chuckle.

“Leave it to him to notice my baby bump when I’m putting on armor. We fought for nearly two hours. Now he wanted to be my husband, now our child mattered. He ordered me to stay behind. But I couldn’t. They were fighting in a forest, a place where my powers were strongest. I followed. We should have known it was trap. I remember that battle like it was yesterday. Our friends fell beneath their numbers one by one. I had gotten desperate and opened a giant hole within the earth, some terrible last-ditch effort to kill them all. It almost worked.”

She reached up and touched the side of her neck gingerly.

“I had killed all but two. The bat had sunk its fangs into me, while the wolf took Allistar. They separated us, to feed on two powerful Witches. I’ve never fought so hard in my life. All I knew is that I had to kill that thing to save my husband. To save my baby…In end I failed them both. There is no cure for vampirism, even with the advances of modern medicine and science. It’s same with lycanthropy. The moment the virus enters your body it begins rewriting you on the molecular level. Unfortunately, it’s not process an unborn child can survive. It was such a horrid thing. To feel your body changing and just knowing you’ve lost your child.”

“Oh god, Serea I’m,”

She shook her head with a sad smile.

“Your ancestors weren’t even born yet love. No need to apologize. The days to follow were some of my darkest. I’m not sure if it was because I was fighting it, or because I was a Witch, but I was aware of everything my body was doing. Because I had slew my sire and fed on him, I had no orders to follow. No one to control me. I attacked and turned people indiscriminately. I nearly took over all of Wales according to some old reports."

"And then Miguel showed up."

Serea nodded.

"At that time, he was called Mihai. Despite my best efforts to kill him, including growing to the size of a castle, I couldn't so much as scratch him."

"Yeah about that, since when could you do that?"

"Since this new thing called always? Has no ever told you that I can do that in demon form? From what I understand it's something of a joke nowadays. Oh lord when Godzilla came out? People were literally betting on whether I could beat him!"

"Not gonna lie, I would've done it too."

"At least you're honest about it."

"So, happened after?"

Serea took another breath before leaning forward to rest her arms on her legs.

"Miguel used his powers to bring me back to sanity. Once I reestablished my control over my own body I resumed human form. I wanted to leave to rescue my husband immediately, but Miguel refused to help me until I had learned to master my powers, all of them."

"He wanted you to stop all the other vampires you had created."

"And there was were quite a lot. But one power I had stolen from my sire was the ability to exert my control over those who share my bloodline."

"Wait…"

"Yes. Which means whether they like me or not, every vampire in the world has to bow before my whims."

"Every vampire?"

"Every vampire. And don't think there aren't factions who despise me for that. Were I to fall in battle, I daresay the Vampire Nation would become the biggest threat the world has seen since the demons."

"Called it. So wait, does that mean Allistar can do the same with the Lycans?"

"Yes. But he seldom uses that power. He's always been a charismatic leader. Which is why I suppose, Miguel stopped me from killing him when we found him terrorizing Ireland. When I saw him as the beast he was, I thought it better to put him out of his misery. I know now, that was simply my cowardice. In truth, I was overjoyed in getting my husband back. Once he got back to human form, I dashed over to hug him. The first thing he did was punch me into a tree. He kept asking where our baby was. He knew the answer, but he still asked me anyways."

Fresh tears started to fall from her face.

"I told him that our baby was gone. And he tried to kill me. He said it was my fault. That I had killed our child because I couldn't be bothered to listen to anyone but myself. My selfishness killed our baby. I argued back. I told him that if he hadn't been so obsessed with those damned demons that we wouldn't have been turned. If he was just humble enough to ask for help after Paul died. That I couldn't stay because I knew they were going to their deaths… With Miguel's intervention and training, we managed to regain much our lost skills and master our new ones. Allistar left and told me to only speak with him when humanity needed him."

Serea took a moment to wipe her eyes and steady herself before continuing. Xavier managed to lean over enough to grab her hand, which she squeezed affectionately.

"I travelled the world after that. Turning key people that I knew would be able to help start my empire. I would turn the Vampires into a force of good. Who better to protect humanity from the dark then those immersed in it, I thought. Allistar evidently had the same idea. Then along came Africa. It was there that I had learned that those I had sired had inherited my dislike for Lycans. There was a powerful Spider Demon in Kenya that needed killing. Our forces practically tripped over each other. If the Spider Demon hadn't attacked at that moment, we would have torn each other apart. That was the first time we had spoken in nearly eighty years. We entered an extremely uneasy alliance and defeated the Spider."

"Did you think of Zora after that?"

"I did indeed. I also saw this as an opportunity to unite the world's Witches on a global front while combining our forces. The Witches, Vampires, and Lycans working together. Demons wouldn't stand a chance. Of course, ideas are often easier said than done. My people refused to work with his people and the Witches didn't trust either of us. It was, how does Szakiya put it? Ah yes. A 'hot buttered mess'. Miguel had been instrumental in cementing alliances, through agitation alone in some cases. And then it came time to sign The Concordant. The night previous, Allistar came to my chambers. He offered to get re-married and to have another child. He or she would be the great beacon between our people. I slapped him. I couldn't believe that he wanted to get married for such a reason and not because he still loved me. He told me that I owed him a child and left. Since then, we've only worked together a handful of times. The last time we spoke was a few centuries ago when he asked if I would mind his being in the same country as me."

"Whoa. That's…a lot of baggage."

"Yeah, no kidding. Thanks to Alexander's little chemical shower, all the rage and aggression I had towards him, just came out. I doubt he knew about our history, but the timing was still uncanny."

"What was Allistar even doing there? This is the second time he's been in a state in our territory."

"Well, Missouri was just a coincidence, but evidently Alexander has been causing issues on the West Coast too. So Allistar was trying to ferret out information while enjoying beating up clueless humans."

Xavier nodded, but then noticed that the light shone slightly different on Serea's arm. When he pointed it out, Serea laughed and lifted her forearm up to his face. There he saw a shiny patch of skin, which he realized was a burn scar.

"How?"

"Well…you evidently don't like it when people try to kill your beloved. This arm was the closest to my shield when you were throwing hell fire at us. It's the first wound that I've gotten in nearly a hundred years that required me to heal myself with magic. I wanted to savor it a little."

"Yeah sorry." Xavier replied, feeling a little guilty for nearly killing her and Allistar. "I don't know what happened. I just got mad. Like angrier than I've ever been. I have no idea how I managed to do that."

"I do. But it's one of those annoying 'you have to find the answer from within yourself' type things. Well, I've stolen enough of your time. Oh, and before I forget. To make up for nearly killing you boys I transferred some additional funds to your accounts."

"Oh Serea, no! You don't have to do that."

"Oh hush, it's only a few million. You can start house hunting for a vacation home. I am sorry to say that it will still have to be on the East coast. But at least there's Florida. So long as you don't mind all the racist old people… Well anyways, I'll speak you later. There's a blonde outside tapping his foot so impatiently."

Serea stood up and opened the door. After exchanging a few words with Adam, left with a wave. Even though he knew Serea was exceptionally wealthy, Xavier was still in shock that she would just give him that type of money.

"Babe?" Adam asked, placing a hand on his.

"Sorry! Sorry. I was still processing that Serea just made us millionaires."

"I know! Ten million. Each. She even gave it to Cassie and Ophelia. I'm a former rich kid and I still don't know what to do with that kind of money! But more importantly, are you ok? Last night you were…scary."

Xavier felt a swell of sadness. He could still see the burns on Adam's face clear as day in his mind.

"Yeah. It's just when Serea tried to kill you, I don't know. I lost it. I couldn't focus on anything else but trying to hurt them for trying to hurt you. I know I shouldn't have let feelings get in the way during a mission."

Adam shook his head.

"You shouldn't, but I can't yell at you about it without being a hypocrite. When Alexander had you against the desk… I just kept thinking 'not again, I'm not gonna let it happen again, not while I'm still breathing.' I didn't even care about the fact that there could be humans nearby. All I wanted to do was kill that slimy demon for touching you."

"That's sweet babe, but I'm a big boy Witch. I can take care of myself. I don't need you protecting me."

Adam's face contorted in annoyance.

"Just like I don't need you protecting me. But you did it anyways. That's what couples do Xavier. They protect one another, they have each other's backs no matter what. I want you to feel as safe with me as I do with you."

Xavier wanted to argue, but Serea's history with Allistar still stood vividly in his mind. So instead he leaned forward and kissed Adam.

"I do feel safe with you. And I will always have your back. I…care about you."

"Thank you for catching yourself. Still a little too early to use the l-word right now. But I care about you too."

Adam then motioned for Xavier to move before getting in the bed and snuggling into his arms. Xavier kissed his forehead before reveling in how amazing it felt to be held by someone who cared about him.

"Hey Xavier?"

"Hmm?"

"Why are you always the last one to wake up? Like literally every time we get hurt, you're the last one. "

"Am I really?"

"Yes." Adam laughed.

"Huh. No clue. But it's convenient."

"How?"

"Everyone else has to come to me and tell me what happened."

"Wow, that is so lazy."

"It's a gift."

20:

"Focus Xavier!" Szakiya barked.

"I am." Xavier snapped through gritted teeth.

A bead of sweat formed as he struggled to complete his assignment; namely, compressing a rock. He combed over all the information he remembered about the pressure generated in the earth but couldn't quite recall how the minerals set when they're compressed. This lapse caused the spell to backfire which exploded the rock. Szakiya used her powers to restore the rock to original form before clicking her tongue in impatience.

"Really? Really? This is the seventh time! You have got to do better."

Xavier huffed out of frustration. After the disaster at the casino, all his trainers had stepped up their training regimens, but none quite like Szakiya. According to her, magic could have prevented things from getting as bad and his "baby magic" was unacceptable. Xavier gave in, though he believed that his magic was at a higher level than she made it sound. He had mastered basic healing, identification, and sleeping spells. And he was unmatched when it came to mapping spells, yet this wasn't enough for Szakiya.

"I'm not a scientist like you. You do remember that right?"

"Oh, trust me honey, no one is going to confuse you for a scientist. But this is high school level stuff. Stuff you should have learned already!"

"Geology is boring!"

"No, its not!"

"It's literally a science studying rocks!"

"Rocks are cool!"

Xavier groaned and rolled his eyes which caused Szakiya to swat at him.

"I'm serious Xavier, you need to get better."

"I'm trying, it's just that I'm not good at stuff like this."

Szakiya pursed her lips before retrieving her phone. After sending a quick text message, Serea showed up a moment later.

"Absolutely not!"

Szakiya rolled her eyes.

"He needs more specialized help Serea."

"But it doesn't have to come from him. He'll say I owe him a favor. I don't like owing him favors!"

"Who? Allistar?" Xavier asked, thoroughly confused.

"No!" They both replied before rounding on each other.

"Serea, he needs to be able to do more with magic than map things."

"But he's really good at it. Why stare a gift horse in the mouth?"

"Serea…"

The women stared at each other for a few moments before Serea finally broke,

"Ugh! Fine! But you're doing the favor. Whatever it is. Xavier!"

Xavier straightened up.

"You need to pack some clothes and choose a member of your team to be your second-in-command. You're going off to get tutored for a while."

"Do I have to?"

Serea pointed at Szakiya who whose scowl was so fierce that Xavier felt like he was a small child getting scolded. He nodded and once excused, bolted out of the office and headed to his room.

"Are you really that bad at magic?" Adam asked, arriving after Xavier's text message.

"According to Szakiya I am. I don't who this Asreaon guy is, but he's supposed to be some type of miracle worker. Assuming of course you can stand the training."

"Lovely. And why do you want me to be your second-in-command? You know, aside from the fact that we're together."

Xavier looked at him, puzzled that Adam thought their relationship was the reason he made his choice.

"Us being together had nothing to do with it. You're level-headed, pragmatic, and you put the mission first. You've actually come a long way from the uncaring jerk you used to be, and it shows. The team respects your input because you take the time to think about what you say."

Adam's face turned extremely red.

"Oh. Well, thank you."

Xavier chuckled and planted a small kiss on Adam's cheek, which only made him blush more.

"Stop being cute!" Adam yelled, hiding his face behind a nearby pillow.

"Not when it makes you blush like that." Xavier called, retrieving his bathroom amenities.

"Bleh. Remind me why I fell for you again."

Xavier walked forward and kissed Adam passionately before resuming his packing.

"You can't kiss me like that and then leave for an undisclosed amount of time!" Adam yelled, throwing the pillow he was holding.

"Well you asked me to remind you! What else was I supposed to do?"

"It was rhetorical you butt-head!"

Adam threw himself on the bed with a huff. After gathering a few more things and placing them in his duffle bag, Xavier sat down next to Adam and ruffled his hair.

"I'm gonna miss you." Adam muttered.

"And I'm gonna miss you. But Szakiya does have a point. What if I'm on a solo mission somewhere? Fire isn't always handy in some situations."

"Aren't you the one who whines while I'm the logical one?"

Xavier chuckled again.

"Not today evidently."

Adam sat up and kissed Xavier on the cheek.

"Just hurry back ok?"

Xavier packed the rest of his stuff before he and Adam walked down to the garage. After receiving his travel itinerary and giving Adam a final kiss goodbye, he headed out. He wasn't happy to be heading back to Louisiana so soon after the casino. Despite Zora using their connections to quiet the media and keeping the police away, Xavier still felt that he shouldn't be anywhere near the state for another month at least. As his plane landed in New Orleans, he caught a taxi to the given address.

The house was a large Victorian style abode which possessed a very odd paint scheme. The borders of the house were painted red, while the majority was painted sky blue. And the window shutters ranged from hunter green to black. Xavier walked up the steps of the porch and quietly tried to map the house. The spell backfired immediately. Xavier looked around to ensure no one was looking before he tried again. When the spell backfired a second time he attempted to scan house for thermal signatures. He caught sight of a few people before a massive heat source nearly overloaded his eyes.

Fed up and slightly apprehensive, he attempted to expel the ambient heat only for it to be increased. As if someone was doing it simply to throw him off. Focusing his now growing agitation and sharpening his will, Xavier completely suppressed the additional heat. A moment later someone threw open the door.

"Dammit kid! Take a hint! We don't like people prying! If you wanna know what the house looks like, knock on the door!"

The man had crimson hair and matching eyes. His face looked like it came right out of a fashion magazine with how symmetrical and chiseled it was. As the man's shirt was off, Xavier could see that nearly his entire upper body was covered intricate and tribal looking tattoos. What was most impressive was the two glittering and translucent wings coming out of his back.

"S'matter?" he asked. "Never seen a Fae before? Name's Asreaon. Guessing you're the newbie Witch."

Xavier nodded, still in shock that the man would so casually walk to the door in broad daylight.

"What? Now you can't speak?"

"Sorry." Xavier replied hastily. "I'm Xavier."

Asreaon looked him up and down and shook his head.

"Yeah, you're not gonna last long under me. Let's get this over with."

Though annoyed at the fairy's snap judgement, his curiosity still pressed him to ask certain questions.

"I thought Fairies were smaller?"

"You're thinking Pixies. They're the spirits of Fae with exceptional magic. Their spirits get preserved in a tiny body made entirely of their magic and they continue their work. You'll see a crap ton of them coming to see me."

"What about other Fairies?"

Asreaon stopped and turned to give Xavier a puzzled look.

"Didn't those Zora chumps tell you what this place is?"

Xavier shook his head, as hulking shadow down the hall caught his eye.

"This is The Final Chapter."

"That's not ominous at all."

"Heh, I thought it sounded cool a few centuries back. This is the place where you go when you don't fit in with the 'underworld'."

"Why is it called The Final Chapter then?"

"Because it was first founded by those who were the last of their species."

Realization now dawning on Xavier, he bowed his head and mumbled his apologies.

"You didn't kill us. We did. Nothing for you to be sorry for. Except for how weak Witches are. Without us to teach you, you're a joke."

"Kinda big coming from someone who doesn't fight."

"We actually do. Just not for Zora."

Asreaon led Xavier up a flight of stairs and into a simple room. All it had was a bed, night stand, dresser, and mirror.

"It ain't the Marriot but you're getting my services for free so no complaining. Since you're an active member of Zora, you get paid. Food is on you. In fact…"

Asreaon waved his hand at the back wall and it began to move backwards extending the room considerably. With a snap, a complete kitchen set up appeared with brand new appliances.

"There. You've got a pretty decent kitchen. I suggest you grocery and make the best of leftovers."

Xavier turned and looked at Asreaon shocked and unable to speak.

"People always do that when they see true magic."

"How did you?"

"Believe it or not, it's not that different from the magic Witches use today. I just have to think less and move more. But we'll explain that in training squirt. Drop your stuff and let's figure out what you can do."

Xavier tossed his bag and jacket on the bed and looked at Asreaon expectantly. With a laugh and a snap, Xavier found himself in a huge room. The walls were lined with shelf after shelf filled with books and in the far-right corner, a desk covered in papers. Asreaon tapped his foot and the rugs underneath their feet vanished without a trace.

"Alright kid, define magic for me."

"Just how old are you?" Xavier asked, his pride raging at being called "kid" that often.

"Old enough to call Serea 'kid'. So, you're definitely dealing with it. Now answer my question."

"Magic is the ability to change the world around you while still being bound by its laws."

"A bit text book, but essentially correct. Magic isn't just changing the world, its change personified. It's understanding the ebb and flow of all things and knowing the exact way to make a ripple."

"Then how did you create a kitchen? That would be impossible for even Szakiya to do."

Asreaon laughed before a cigarette appeared in his mouth and lit itself.

"Simple. I asked. That's actually the key difference between our magics. Take turning a rock into a diamond. In order for a Witch to do it, he or she would need to have extremely in-depth knowledge of how they're formed naturally and then force the rock to compress and minerals to gather to make it happen. Me? I just ask the rock to do it and offer a little of my energy to make it happen."

"It can't possibly be that simple?"

"What the magic? Yeah it is. It's the asking part that's hard. Humans often lack the humility and the patience to fully connect with the world enough to wield true magic. Their magic is proof of that actually."

"How do you figure?"

“Human magic is based on verbal commands. Instead of asking for the change with your soul, you demand it. You bark orders at whatever it is you’re changing and give it ridged instructions on that change. I suppose that’s good for people who have minds of science. Science is after all, your method of understanding the world around you. But for those rare few with a mind of magic, this is the better path.”

“And I have a mind of magic? Cuz I definitely don’t have it for science.”

“That’s what you’re here to find out. You could be neither.”

“That’s a thing?!”

“Yep. They’re called Mundane Witches. I think you can tell from the title that they don’t have the best rep.”

Xavier felt his chest tighten. He never considered that he could simply be an inept Witch. The thought scared him more than a little.

“Stop.” Asreaon called.

“Stop what?”

“That train of thought. Stop it. It’ll cause you to make mistakes you wouldn’t normally do.”

Xavier narrowed his eyes in suspicion.

“As the oldest living flame user on this planet, I have a unity with any who share my force of nature. And thus, I can feel your thoughts as my own. And if you call me that again, I’m kicking your ass.”

Xavier did his best to shield his mind. Though he couldn’t be affected by telepaths, Ophelia still insisted that they learn the basics of shielding their thoughts from prying eyes.

“That won’t work kid. I’m not reading your thoughts. I’m feeling them. Neither of us can control it so just make peace with it and let’s move on.”

“Fine.” Xavier growled through gritted teeth.

“Now as I was saying, human magic uses verbal commands because they order things around. But there’s a collection of true magic spells that use a verbal cue as well. Only difference is that it’s a genuine call for help. These are called Peerless Spells. And they’re the epitome of magic. Because a person has to be truly humble and truly need help to cast them.”

“Can you cast a Peerless Spell?”

"Don't ever ask that to anybody else here who can cast. Barely anyone knows about these spells and those who do, sure as hell do not want to share that information. But yes. So far I can cast sixteen of them."

"How many are there?!"

"I honestly have no clue. Once you get past your first two, the rest kinda just flow to you? I got my most recent one last year. So yeah. Learn something new every day. Alright. I'm gonna put you through a series of exercises. The point is not to accomplish them all, but to simply see how you work magic."

The exercises started off with simple tasks; moving things from one point to another and identifying simple substances. Xavier was especially proud of how impressed Asreaon was at his ability to map the entirety of the city. But once things got more difficult, he couldn't help but become frustrated at his lack of progress. Some things he couldn't do simply because he lacked the knowledge and others because the knowledge didn't stay in his mind. After four hours of tests Asreaon brought them back to his room.

"It's still too early to tell, but I can tell you this, you're getting in your own way. A lot. Grocery store is a few blocks that way. You may want to get out there before dark. Beating the crap out muggers is fun, but it attracts police attention."

Asreaon disappeared without a sound which only served to irritate Xavier more. He flung himself onto the bed with a huff and grabbed his phone. After texting most of his team that he was fine, he called Adam.

"Hi babe." Adam answered, sounding distracted.

"I catch you at a bad time?"

"A bit. I'm helping the team that's investigating the chemicals that Alexander has been using. If we can identify all the components, we might be able to use them to track where he's making the stuff. But I have a few minutes. You ok?"

Xavier replayed Asreaon's words in his mind.

"Do you think I get in my own way?"

"Absolutely."

The speed of Adam's answer did more harm than good to Xavier's current mood, but he chose to press for answers.

"How?"

"Well it kinda goes back to that whole self-deprecating thing you do. I know why you do it, but I wish you wouldn't. But it's like clockwork with you. You make a mistake or forget something, and you just tear yourself a new one."

"Wow…been thinking about this a lot huh?"

"It's kinda hard to miss babe."

The sun hit his shudders just right that lines of amber filled his room. His stomach informed him that skipping dinner was not an option.

"I'll try to work on it. Well I gotta go babe. Need to get food."

"Just order pizza."

"Are you kidding?! After all those hellish cooking lessons with Eliade? Nah. I'm gonna cook."

"Ok babe." Adam laughed. "Well, be careful and have a good dinner. I'll text you before I go to bed."

"Alright babe, miss you."

"Miss you too."

Xavier fetched his wallet which held his fake I.D. and debit card and then nabbed the copy of the house key hanging on the wall before leaving the house. True to Asreaon's directions, the grocery store came into view after walking a few blocks. Grabbing a basket, he began to mull over what Adam has said to him. While he had always known he was hard on himself, he didn't think he had gotten to the point where it was interfering with his abilities. And even as he inspected two bundles of bananas to see which is riper, he couldn't really figure out why.

The rest of his shopping was spent in fruitless introspection much to his chagrin. As he rounded a corner he heard the sounds of a struggle. Despite knowing that he had no place in human affairs, the prospect of knocking some sense into muggers seemed too good to pass up. He found two red-headed men attempting to shake down a middle-aged gentleman. To the man's credit, he had already bloodied one their noses.

"I like this one. Feisty." One of the men snarled, holding the man by his throat.

"Well if you're looking for feisty, then boy are you guys gonna love me."

Both men looked startled for a moment and in that moment, Xavier saw one of their faces distort. A smile slowly crept across his face as two demons backed away slowly.

"I got it from here sir. You may want to beat it before this gets ugly."

The man nodded, gathered his belongings and ran as quickly as his portly size would allow. As he passed by Xavier he whispered,

"Give 'em hell kid."

Xavier snorted at the man's unintentional pun and began to slowly advance on the two demons.

"Sorry fellas, but I'm gonna have to end this quickly. Can't have any witnesses."

He sped forward and with a single punch caved in the chest of the demon that spoke. His partner opened his maw to tear out Xavier's neck, but his fangs never met their mark. With a sweeping kick to the demon's jaw, Xavier broke its neck. He placed one on top of the other and quickly reduced them both to ash. As he turned to quickly retrieve his groceries he saw Asreaon waiting for him, his groceries in hand.

"Hi."

"Um, hi?"

"Problem with me helping you with your groceries?"

"Um, you could have put on a shirt. And shoes…"

Xavier was grateful that Asreaon had enough sense to at least cloak his wings.

"Most people would leap at the chance to be escorted home by someone as gorgeous as me."

Xavier scoffed.

"I've seen better."

"You take that back or the milk gets it."

"You spill my milk, you're buying me a new one. I didn't spend my hard, demon-slaying earned money for nothing."

Asreaon laughed and nodded towards the street. After Xavier secured his milk and eggs they headed back to the house. The walk was pleasant even though neither of them said anything. The fireflies buzzed around them and scent of magnolia and juniper was heavy in the air. As they continued to walk a gentle breeze blew through and Xavier could almost feel himself gliding with it.

"Hey! Come back to earth!" Asreaon yelled, yanking on his shirt.

Xavier finally snapped to and realized that he had in fact begun to fly in the air.

"Sorry. Don't know what came over me…"

"You had a hippie moment." Asreaon replied matter-of-factly.

"Wuzzat?"

"It's when you have a moment of genuine connection to nature. You didn't really think you'd go through this whole Witch thing and not have a moment like that?"

"I guess it's kinda hard when you're either in an office or in the field."

"What's your role?"

"Coven Leader."

"Bleh. Paperwork, paperwork, and more paperwork. Usually Coven Leaders are stuffy and the hardest to train. But you…there's something in you. And I think I know how I'm gonna bring it out."

Something about the gleam in Asreaon's eyes made Xavier uneasy.

"Am I gonna die?"

"…maybe?"

21:

"How was this a good idea in your mind?!" Xavier screamed, dodging a fireball.

"I told you that it might kill you! Now focus!" Asreaon hollered back, throwing another fireball.

When Asreaon first brought up the idea of Xavier having to dodge his fireballs, he was perfectly fine with it. He was confident that he wouldn't even have to dodge. Then he found out that Fae Fire could actually harm him, and his perspective shifted. Now he was scrambling and jumping out of the way of Asreaon's attacks. He was surprised at himself. He had already forgotten what the fear of being burned felt like. Even when he was cooking he never really worried about it and even went so far as to pull things out of the oven without a mitt. Now that he faced something that could burn him, he felt humbled and slightly weak.

"There it is!" Asreaon beamed, flying down to the ground.

"There what is?" Xavier panted, his arm still stinging from the fireball.

"Your humility. When we wield a force of nature we kinda forget to respect it. I wasn't sure if my flames would burn you, but I'm glad they did."

"Lucky me." Xavier retorted, wincing at his arm's throbbing. "Why does your flame burn me?"

"No clue." Asreaon waved his hand at Xavier's arm causing relief to surge through it. "My guess is my age. Something as ancient as I am, might have some hidden perks to my powers."

"How do you not know?"

"Because I'm literally thousands of years old. Do you realize how boring self-discovery and introspection get? At this point, if I learn anything new about myself I take it as a pleasant surprise."

"Haven't you trained other Fire Witches before?"

"Yup. But I usually use grenades. You get bounced around enough and the humility usually just flows. But I ran out, so you got off lucky."

Xavier rolled his eyes. Though he admittedly had a newfound appreciation for his powers. He summoned a small fireball was shocked to see that the color had shifted to a deep red.

"Whoa. Haven't seen flames like that in a long awhile." Asreaon said, shocking Xavier with how close he had gotten.

"Why did it change colors?"

"Our powers reflect our journey. As we evolve and change, so do our powers. Something in you must have changed so now you got red flames."

"What does red fire mean?"

"That the flames you currently wield are red in color."

"Seriously?"

"Yup! Now then."

Asreaon held out his hand and a piece of paper appeared.

"Ask the paper to become an origami swan."

"Hey paper, mind folding yourself into a swan?"

Asreaon snorted and let out a small laugh.

"I asked for that one. But seriously. Remember last night. Remember how you were swept away. That's it. Now hold the feeling in heart. Let it combine with the power inside you.

Good, good. Now remember the humility you felt earlier. Remember that you're asking, not telling… Now open your eyes."

Xavier chanced one eye and saw a neatly folded swan sitting in Asreaon's hands. Xavier couldn't believe how it easy that came for him and instantly asked for additional tasks. Asreaon obliged and after an hour of working on small tasks, Xavier felt accomplished, but completely exhausted.

"So small fact about true magic, it definitely takes a lot out of you. So, head up to your room and catch a nap. Once you wake up, we'll work on more stuff."

Xavier nodded and slowly walked to his room. As he walked down the hall he saw someone standing by his door. The person's light blue skin shone in the sunlight which only served to highlight their pitch-black eyes. Their hair was an interesting teal color that occasionally looked transparent. The person caught sight of Xavier and nodded their head slightly.

"Hello Xavier." The person said. Though their voice sounded unmistakably masculine, their lithe build and feminine features caused Xavier to make no assumptions.

"Hi. I don't think we've met." He replied, extending his hand.

The person let out a small laugh which Xavier swore sounded like ocean waves before taking his hand and shaking it. Their hand felt slightly damp and yet the moment they let go, Xavier's hand was dry.

"I and some of the others in the house have been watching you closely. It is rare that Asreaon takes an interest in his students"

"Has Zora sent a lot of people to him?"

"More often than he would like, but the favors they owe us keep things civilized. Many of the inhabitants here bear a great deal of ill-will towards one or more of the factions housed there."

"That explains why I haven't seen anyone."

"Yes. They are observing. To see if you are different."

"And you?"

The person smiled.

"I already know the answers to the questions I sought. But I did not come here to simply exchange pleasantries. I have two pieces of advice. Would you care to hear them?"

"Yes." Xavier replied.

"Answered so quickly? You've no idea what or who I am."

"I can tell you're an Ancient. And that you wouldn't be speaking to me unless you truly felt that I needed to hear what you had to say."

The person smiled warmly.

"You show a wisdom that few your age ever see. Very well. My first piece of advice is that you love hard and love free. Love is one of the greatest bonds in the world. It mocks time and spits in the face of death. My second is that when you face Alexander, remember that he is only a demon."

"How did you,"

"Farewell Xavier."

The person vanished, and Xavier let out a groan of exasperation. He hated the "mysterious" types as they left him with more questions than if they had simply left him alone. As he plopped on the bed, he chose to take the advice in the spirit that he thought it was given and promptly went to sleep. He awoke to the feeling of something tugging on his nose. When he opened his eyes, he let out a yelp when he came face to face with an inches tall person floating in front of his face.

"Rude." The pixie said with a huff and extremely deep voice. "Asreaon says wake up."

Xavier had to rub his eyes to make sure he wasn't dreaming and when he identified that he wasn't, he nodded. The pixie flew off with without a backwards glance. Xavier stretched and headed for the door. As soon as he crossed the threshold, the hallway turned into a forest path. After looking around frantically for any sign as to what transported him he wondered if Asreaon was to blame and called for him.

"I'm in the clearing." Asreaon's voice called back.

Xavier ran down the path, equal parts irritated and astonished. When he finally reached the clearing, he found his tutor sitting in front a massive fire pit. In it the flames danced to and fro, forming fantastic shapes that he never thought possible. As he continued to stare into the flames he felt something stir from within him. A soft and warm song that resonated with his very being. He felt himself walk forward as if bid to do so. As he approached the edge of the flames, he reached his hand towards the flames. A tendril of fire slowly crept out and wound itself around his hand.

The flames suddenly roared with new intensity and began to shift in color. Seeing the parade of lights, he decided to offer his new flames, so that he might add to the beauty before him. The flames seemed overjoyed and snapped and crackled jubilantly before assuming the same red color of his flames. They began to change and contort until they assumed the form of a large bird. The bird's head leaned forward until it was level with his. Any other day, Xavier would have been wary of all of this, but the only thing he could bring himself to do was to touch his forehead to the creature. An overwhelming sense of calm and reassurance fell over him, and he closed his eyes.

When he opened them again, he was back in Asreaon's study, and the Fae was sitting on his desk smoking. Tears welled up in his eyes as he genuinely missed the comfort and peace he felt when embraced by the flames. Asreaon handed him a tissue with a small smile.

"What was that?" Xavier croaked.

"Would you be mad if I told you I truly didn't know? The legend states that those are the first flames of this world. Whether it was Prometheus' or a drop of pure sunlight, who knows? But it has always been tradition that the most powerful Fire Fae protect it. As I'm the last one, it fell to me. Whatever it is, it seems to resonate with fire users that are sensitive enough."

"Is it alive?"

Asreaon chuckled, "What do you think?"

"I think that was the first time I ever felt at peace. Evidently, I did something right, because it felt like it liked me."

"I don't bring many of my students out there. And even when I do there isn't a guarantee that things go smoothly. Some run away. Some simply stand and stare. One guy tried to make it less intense. But only a few have ever had the courage to physically interact with it. And out of those few only five others offered their flames as you did."

"Does that mean I'm special?"

"Not particularly. Just means you aren't a punk and have a great connection with your force of nature. If anything, you did what you're supposed to do."

"Oh…" While Xavier was glad for the experience, he was still a little crestfallen that it didn't really mean anything.

"Trust me when I say that being the 'chosen one' sucks. A lot." Asreaon replied. "You don't want it. Because it never ends well."

"Ok, then why did you take me out there after only two days of training?"

"Because you have a crap ton of potential and I've noticed it's easier for my students to tap into that potential after visiting the First Flame. Jeez, stare a gift horse in the mouth why don't you?"

Xavier mumbled a humble apology which was waved off. Asreaon set Xavier to the task of more training exercises before dismissing him for the night. When he awoke the next morning, he found that the previous days tasks came much easier. As the days progressed, Xavier found that he could do far more than he envisioned. After successfully materializing a soda, Asreaon declared that he was starting to make real progress. Though he wouldn't be able to do any mass materializing any time soon, the fact that he had come that far was impressive.

Just as Xavier was starting to feel good about this training, a blue pixie woman flew in with Xavier's phone and informed him that Zora had been trying to contact him. He thanked the Pixie and saw that Adam had called several times.

"Finally!" Adam barked, once Xavier called back. "Been trying to reach you all day. We found a lead. The gas is being held in a warehouse in Maryland. We need you back."

Xavier was loathe to leave but he knew they couldn't let a lead like this go by and he knew he needed to be there.

"Understood. I have my uniform with me, I'll meet you all there."

Xavier hung up the phone and smile apologetically at Asreaon who smiled back.

"It's all good kiddo. Just promise me two things."

"Shoot."

"That you won't overdo it in the field and that you'll come back to finish your training."

Xavier nodded his head in the affirmative and promised. Asreaon waved a hand and Xavier was by the front door with all his belongings. With some small muttered thanks, Xavier walked out of the door.

22:

As their team approached the warehouse, Xavier couldn't help but feel uneasy. The company that owned the building was directly linked to the Kiras family, so there were likely demons posing as workers. When he scanned the building, there were a handful of people loading crates into trucks. What stuck out was seven individuals scattered throughout the building. While their thermal readings were human shaped, Xavier sensed something completely different about those seven. When asked, Cassie said their emotions were very much skewed but still human.

"We might be dealing with Heretic Witches, though it's always hard to tell."

"We are." Ophelia whispered. "And you shouldn't do that Xavier. The one near this wall will sense it. Somehow. Better to sneak in."

Xavier nodded and hit his com.

"We're dealing with Heretic Witches. Stealth for now."

"Copy that." Adam replied.

After Danny opened the door they all proceeded with their investigation. Fortunately, their door was blocked by a number of crates. Cassie slowly brought one of the crates towards them and opened it. After a quick identification spell, they determined that the cannisters inside the crates held Alexander's gas.

"Can you use your magic to empty these crates?" Danny asked Xavier

"Maybe. But not the whole warehouse. Still in training."

"We might be better off taking everyone out and then just destroying everything after."

"Crap!" Ophelia hissed.

The hairs on the back of Xavier's neck stood up as the whole warehouse was filled with the sounds of a man's scream.

"What happened?"

"One of the Heretic Witches got bored…"

Xavier's com buzzed on and Justin's bass rang through.

"Xavier, the workers are under some kind of trance, but they look human. If these Heretics are just gonna start killing willy-nilly…"

Xavier understood what Justin was actually telling him and hated how true his words felt.

"Cassie, with my direction, can you pinpoint an individual's emotions?"

"I'm already putting the workers to sleep. However…"

"However?"

"The three of us here have killed humans in the past. I know you and Max have an issue with it, but now isn't the time. These people…their emotions. They'll kill if you don't kill them Xavier."

"I'll do what I have to."

Cassie nodded, and a row of crates moved forward, allowing them further access to the rest of the warehouse. After seeing the workers all slump and fall to the ground, someone began to scream.

"What the hell are they doing? Why are they all sleeping?! Get up!"

"It's them…" replied a low husky voice. "They've come…"

"Come out! You sneaky pieces of,"

"Hush…"

Cassie growled. "Oh, I do not like him."

"Left!" Ophelia screamed, pushing Cassie and Danny aside.

Xavier's senses flared, and an explosion set off right where they standing. Someone cackled and jumped to the ground in front of them. The man wore skin tight red leather pants and matching boots with no shirt. His hair was a dirty blonde and greasy mess matched only by the dirt on his face. And stretched across his chest was a wide scar. His eyes met with Xavier's and he smiled. Xavier's senses flared again, only this time Xavier stopped the explosion cold. Cassie took the opportunity to blast the man across the room. Before he hit the wall, the man stopped suddenly in the air. A figure in blue cloak floated down, their face completely hidden.

"Are you ok…?"

"Dammit Richie! I told you not to interfere with my fights!"

"It's Richard, Fred…"

A large tornado tore through the room and tossed them aside. A tremor began to shake the room as another person landed on the ground. Nate tapped his foot on the ground and the shaking stopped. As Xavier looked around he noticed that they outnumbered the Heretic Witches by one. He nodded at Ophelia who slowly backed away and disappeared into the shadows.

Fred let out a vicious howl and sped towards Xavier. Xavier side stepped his strike and slugged him in the gut. Fred growled and directed a clawed hand at Xavier. Already foreseeing what would happen, Xavier had already begun to prevent the explosion. A crack of lightning caught his attention for a second, which Fred used to slam into him. While this person was certainly strong, he had nothing on Beatrice. Xavier kneed him in the face before following it up with series of blows to the face.

Fred fell to the ground and started to laugh.

"He said you were strong." Fred wheezed after spitting the blood from his mouth.

"Whatever Alexander promised you, it won't be worth what you will have to pay."

"Yeah it will. You don't kill,"

Xavier swung his sword so fast that it impressed him. Unfortunately, the sword never reached Fred's neck as the blade was stopped mere inches away. Xavier turned with a snarl to see Richard looking in their direction. Cassie then appeared behind him and kicked him with such force that he crashed through a nearby wall. A glint of silver caused Xavier to block with his blade. He had to give Fred points for trying to take him on with a butterfly knife.

"This is awesome!" Fred panted, looking crazed. "And here I thought you were gonna be boring!"

"Why are you doing this? Alexander can't be paying you enough to die."

"I wanted to fight someone strong. And since Alexander only wants me as a guard dog, he gave me you."

Xavier felt his face contort in disgust and pushed Fred back. They began to exchange blows, with Fred showing an impressive amount of skill using his butterfly knife. Despite having a strength and speed advantage, Fred's raw skill with his weapon made him an even match. Frustrated, Xavier used his powers to coat his blade in flames. Fred's eyes grew wide and he renewed his attacks with a savage joy. Xavier blocked everything else in the background out and focused solely on taking this man's head.

When they clashed again, it was a flurry of steel and flame. Remembering his duel with Cassie, he began to watch Fred closely, to see if he could pick up on any patterns. Sure enough, he noticed a certain flourish Fred did after blocking a strike. When Xavier saw it again, he went for a thrust. Fred locked eyes with him and smiled. Xavier's heart skipped a beat as Fred produced another knife from him pocket. At worst Xavier was going to lose the use of left arm for the remainder of the fight, but that was still enough to turn the tide unfavorably. The knife never made it further than being taken out Fred's pocket. One of Ophelia's throwing knives embedded itself in Fred's left hand.

Taking advantage of Ophelia's expert sniping, Xavier pivoted and swung his blade up. Fred's scream seemed to drown out everything else and everyone stopped fighting to look. Xavier cursed his merciful nature as he looked at Fred. He could have easily have let Fred bleed out, but at the last second, he cauterized the wound. Fred gripped his left stump and snarled at Xavier. Xavier replied by bringing the tip of his blade to his throat.

"Tell me what I want to know, or I'm taking a leg next."

Fred spat on the ground.

“I knew you were weak! You could have killed me just then! You could have,”

Xavier gripped him by the face and slammed him so hard into the ground that it cratered around Fred’s now bleeding head.

“You have something I want. Which means you’re more useful to me alive. And if you happen to be a quadriplegic, all the better. Your call.”

Fred’s face went from shock to sheer elation. The look he gave Xavier was so euphoric that Xavier couldn’t help but recoil.

“I take it back. You’re perfect.”

Something whizzed near Xavier’s head which caused him to leap back. A person in a rainbow shirt with matching short shorts and hair landed in between them and glared at Xavier.

“Leon! What are you doing?!” Fred snarled, sitting up.

“Look what he did to you darlin’! I’m not letting him touch you again! Archie! We’re getting out of here!”

Fred let out a roar of frustration and tried to run towards Xavier, but Leon stopped him and held him down. Soon a pink portal appeared underneath them and they began to slowly descend. Fred managed bite Leon on the leg and punched him away.

“Xavier!” he screamed. “We’ll finish this! And next time, there won’t be anything or anyone in the way! Next time, you’ll have to kill me! Alexander is shipping the gas to D.C.! Tell him we quit!”

“Fred!” Leon whined.

Fred smiled and flashed a rude gesture at Xavier with his remaining hand before they disappeared completely. Adam flew over and let out a small snort of laughter.

“What’s so funny?”

“You attract the weirdest guys!”

“It’s true he does!” Justin yelled, checking on a sleeping worker.

“Focus!” Xavier hollered, extremely uncomfortable at this newest revelation. “Ophelia, you got a read?”

Ophelia put down the canister she was holding and nodded.

“That Fred guy was right. The general energy surrounding these is that they’re headed to D.C. Not sure for what though. No one who handled these knew anything. I’ll head up to the ops center and see what else I can learn.”

Xavier nodded.

"Danny go up with her and see what you can pull from their systems."

Once they left, Xavier called Xorn and signaled him to move in with his team. Despite this not being the caliber of scene Xorn's team would handle, Xavier had grown to like the old Lion Shifter and appreciated the way his team handled things. Xorn eventually walked up to him and pointed to the ground.

"Who'd you maim?"

"Some Heretic named Fred. Likes blowing up things. Definitely nuts"

"Oh, well that explains the blast residue we found. Still should have killed him though. Might come back to bite you on the ass."

"He had information I needed."

Xorn turned and smacked Xavier upside the head.

"What was that for?!"

"Xavier, I know good and damn well you know better than to feed that crap to me!" he growled, taking out a cigarette. "If torture was really what you were after then why did you cauterize the wound? And don't tell me it was an accident! You still can't bring yourself to kill a human."

Xavier shushed Xorn before looking to see if anyone was paying enough attention to hear them.

"Look, killing demons is easy. They're monsters."

"So are we." Xorn looked him square in the eye and put a clawed finger in his chest. "You better stop with this 'they look like me' bull. You hear me? Drop it right now. Because what you've done is create a problem that's just gonna get worse later. You said he was nuts right? Then it's almost guaranteed that you're gonna see him again. Because now you've given him a goal to work towards. Next time you see him, you take his head off. You hear me?"

Xavier nodded and rubbed his chest. He knew Xorn was right and he had every intention of ending that fight, but when it came time to swing his sword, he just couldn't help it. After the first time that he failed, he knew he wouldn't have it in him to make the killing blow again. He pushed the thoughts out of his mind and attempted to refocus himself. Fred and his friends would stay under the radar to lick their wounds, but Alexander was still on the move.

Ophelia and Danny weren't able to recover much else aside from the drop point which was right outside Arlington. When they investigated the area, it was completely scrubbed. They sent Miguel out in search of where they moved that much product but informed them that it may take time. Xavier poured over every report they had since they encountered Alexander, but nothing came to mind which frustrated him greatly. Forming strategies was useless if he didn't know what he was planning for. Now questioning his strategic abilities, he slumped down into his chair and contemplated taking a nap when he heard a soft knock at his door.

"Come in."

The door opened revealing Eliade. Something about the way she walked in seemed off and caused Xavier to sit up. She said nothing but beckoned swiftly. With a nod they both walked to the nearest elevator. Eliade touched her fob to the panel inside the elevator and pressed the talk button.

"Eliade. Identification: zero, zero, six."

She nodded, and Xavier walked over and mirrored her.

"Xavier. Identification: zero, one, two."

A speaker on top of the elevator buzzed on.

"Acknowledged."

Xavier leaned against the wall as heart nearly beat out of his chest. Their destination was one Xavier had hoped he would never have to return to. As a Section Head, he had access to some of the most secret places in their branch, provided Serea actually allowed him to go. One such place was called The White Room. An interrogation chamber that had so many spells weaved in it that it practically hummed with magic. They reserved this room strictly when all other interrogation methods failed them. The room strips away everything but the truth from a person. In order to assume his position as a Section Head, he had to be subjected to questioning inside the room. It left him emotionally devastated for a week. Now that they were returning to it, he felt sick to his stomach. He felt Eliade wrap her arm around his shoulder and looked up to see her smiling gently.

When the elevator finally opened, Beatrice and Sumna were waiting on them. Sumna's version of the Zora uniform possessed a skin tight, black, long-sleeved undershirt which looked very hot and uncomfortable to him. When they arrived, she nodded and looked directly into Xavier's eyes.

"I owe you an apology Xavier." She said quietly. "You were right about my not trying hard enough."

Realization struck Xavier hard.

"The traitor was close to you?"

"My second."

Xavier clapped her lightly on the shoulder and she nodded sadly. Quiet as a tomb, they all walked down the hall until they came to two twin doors. They stood in front of the door and a loud buzzer announced that the doors had been unlocked. Szakiya turned to greet them, though none of her usual cheer was present. They faced a large two-sided window were a man sat inside The White Room, sobbing. Serea was standing in front of a microphone, with a stern look on her face.

"Identify yourself."

The man flinched before answering.

"I-I-I don't know anymore…"

"Then state the name you were born with."

"Corbin Kiras."

Xavier felt his stomach plummet at the mention of the man's last name. Beatrice grabbed his arm to keep him from saying anything.

"And how did you manage to sneak your way into our organization?" Serea growled.

The man's sobs over took him for a minute before he could answer.

"My family held the lover of the Psychic Section Head at the German Branch hostage. They forced him to plant false memories in my mind, so I would actually believe that I was Corbin Hertz. So, when I came to this branch and had my memories examined, no one would be any wiser."

"Implanted memories would not fool our top telepaths."

"They would when they replace everything else in my mind."

"What were your orders?"

"They changed as time went by. First, I was to get close to Sumna. If I couldn't seduce her romantically, then get close professionally. If someone got too close to the truth…oh god…I had to deal with them. I was responsible for the attack on Apollo Hernandez. I forced those Tiger Shifters to…to…"

Corbin started coughing as he had chocked on a sob. When he finally stopped, he started rocking back and forth.

"What else were you told to do?"

"I'm responsible for the death of over seventeen new Witches. Every twenty or so years, the Kiras family would place a plant in a Branch. Whenever we got word of a fledgling, the agent would report it."

"Then why did you not report the whereabouts of our current coven?"

"I've been trying to fight the conditioning. I became aware of it one day when I discovered that I knew Muy Thai. I never studied it. I didn't want to be Corbin Kiras. I didn't want to go back. I liked helping people! Everything seemed like a giant nightmare. So, I managed to delay my reports in a way that you all arrived just in time to save them. I'm so sorry!"

"Enough!" Serea barked, before taking a breath to regain her composure. "What does Alexander plan to do in Washington D.C.?"

The man grew deathly still.

"He means to expose every member of Congress to his compound."

"What will that gain him outside of a room full of angry men and women?"

"I don't know."

Xavier pulled out his phone and quickly searched for any news on anything happening with Congress. When he found what he was looking for, he felt a mixture of relief and anger. He motioned at Serea and she nodded.

"I will return shortly, in the meantime write down every name of every plant that you are aware of."

Serea strode over and everyone turned to listen.

"Congress is voting whether we'll have an armed response to that recent attack one of America's army bases."

"And?" Beatrice asked, looking confused. "They'll be too busy beating each other up to vote."

"Will they?" Sumna asked. "What if Alexander improved the formula? Instead of full blown rage, its agitation and annoyance? You couple that with the fragile egos of most politicians…"

"And they give that orange idiot permission to launch another war." Szakiya hissed. "Because clearly that worked out so well last time."

"Do we have the kind of pull to stop a congressional hearing?" Xavier asked, grasping for hope from anywhere he could find.

Serea shook her head. "No. We have few friends in this administration. The most I can guarantee is access. Get your teams ready. I'll finish here shortly. We end this tonight."

Everyone left in a flurry and Xavier's mind kept racing. House Asmodai was infamous for causing costly wars which resulted in terrible causalities. The more he thought about how many would die if another war were started, the more his resolve hardened. Despite Alexander being so much more powerful than he is, he knew he had to kill him or the entire country would pay the price.

He called everyone on their phones and informed them of what he found out. Though shocked and enraged, each of them went to go get prepared for their fight. Xavier went started to head to his room when the words filled his mind. The words of the one with blue skin rang as clear as a bell in a quiet sky. He turned and headed to where he knew he needed to go.

"Xavier? Why are you out of breath?" Adam asked, after opening the door.

Xavier's only answer was to grab him and kiss him passionately. Adam gripped him tightly and returned the kiss just as passionately. When they finally broke apart, Xavier placed his forehead gently against Adam's.

"I'm not telling you this because we might die or out some stupid sense of romantic timing. I'm saying this because it's what I feel and I'm not gonna hold it back. I love you Adam."

"Xavier…"

"It's ok if you can't say it back. I don't want you to say it unless you mean it anyways. But I mean it."

"I really don't know what to say but…thank you. And I do care. But…"

"Hey! What did I just say?" Xavier chuckled.

"Ugh! You're horrible and I hate you. And you're stupid amounts of cliché."

Xavier pulled Adam into a tight embrace.

"Adam?"

"Hm?"

“We have to win. No matter the cost.”

Adam squeezed him tightly and nodded.

23:

“Are we really, really sure that we need three assault teams for an attack on a Congressman’s home? Because we’re talking almost thirty people and that many people can’t be trusted to be stealthy.”

Serea looked at Xavier sternly.

"Miguel reports that the entire mansion is filled with demons. So yes, we're sure."

"Ok, but how? The house belongs to someone married to a member of the Kiras family. There's no way that Alexander hasn't prepared for a Zora raid.

"Xavier has a point Serea." Eliade replied. "We haven't heard from our advance agents. We have no information coming out of this except from Miguel. This feels like the quiet right before a predator pounces on its prey."

"Alexander won't have anything that can keep occupied me for long.

"You say that, but he's been one step ahead of us this entire time. It just seems unlikely that his base of operations for all this wouldn't be well defended."

Beatrice grunted. "Going in head first seems a bit reckless. I'd bet that weasel has been expecting this."

"Considering the spy he sent in didn't see fit to uncover any real secrets about us, our true abilities should still be something of a shock."

"And how much of your fight with Allistar do you think he saw?" Xavier quipped.

Serea paused and pursed her lips.

"Almost forgot about that."

"This just doesn't feel right. If his goal is to agitate the House and Senate into war, then why not be at the Congressional Building. Why be holed up in some mansion?"

"A question you'll have to ask him." Adam mumbled bitterly.

"Hey! It's not like I want him to like me!"

"But we might be able to use that to our advantage…" Serea mused. "Send you in to distract him while Szakiya or Eliade finish the job."

"No. He'll see that coming. I can almost bet money that he has high tier demons waiting on you. He's gonna make it so it's just us."

"Not a chance in hell!" Adam snapped. "You know you're gonna need help!"

"I wasn't saying we give him what he wants. But he's gonna make sure that all of our big guns are busy. Remember, he was a Witch Hunter for years. And that egomaniac will want to finish what he started."

The room grew quiet as everyone seemed to be caught in introspection.

"Boys…" Serea started but stopped when Xavier shook his head.

“Don’t. We’re surviving this and we’re going to have another potluck.”

“You’re such a fatty.” Justin snickered.

Once the tension was broken, everyone filed out. Xavier was retying his boots when he felt a familiar presence nearby.

“Here to wish us good luck?”

“Something like that bro.”

Xavier turned around and saw that Miguel was back in his Zora uniform.

“You gonna be fighting with us?”

“Yeah. But I won’t be able to come with you.”

“I figured, or else you wouldn’t have that look on your face.”

Miguel nodded and smiled sadly.

“I wish I could. I hate that I’m sending you in to fight that thing by yourselves. But I can make sure you know what you’re in for. Alexander’s speed is ridiculous, but it’s inherently different from Eliade’s. Once he’s committed to killing you, he’ll transform into his demon form. That’s when you can kill him.”

“Anything else?”

“Sadly, I can’t tell you anything more. Just trust in yourself and those that care about you.”

Miguel’s words stayed with Xavier the entire time they drove. Since they had so many, each team would use a different means of transport. The van his team was assigned to was uncomfortable, but he was glad that they all were together. After an hour of silence, Cassie decided to start singing. It was a simple song, one that Xavier had heard on the radio a long time ago, but the way she sang it made the inside of the van come alive. Max and Adam soon joined her and the harmonies they made Xavier’s soul leap.

After the song ended, they began to laugh and talk as they always did. Max began to regale them with a story of a misadventure involving falling books and a very concerned mouse shifter. For the next few hours they continued to share stories and memories and even convinced their driver to join in with a story of her own. When they crossed into the city lines, all laughter was replaced by a quiet determination. Everyone readied their weapons. Cassie retying a strap caused Xavier to look over and see the hilt of a sword sticking over her left shoulder.

“Is that?”

"A Jian? Yeah. Told you I have a weapon."

"It's awesome!" Ophelia cooed, showing an uncharacteristic amount of excitement. "She got Szakiya to enchant it, so it enhances her telekinesis. Last time she used it, she disintegrated fourteen demons at once. Fourteen. She's so beautiful when she slaughters our enemies."

Cassie giggled and kissed Ophelia on the cheek.

"You dork."

"Mmhm. But I'm your dork."

"You're my dork who can snipe a demon through a wall, from a window, in the dark, while it's raining outside. But I'm the impressive one, right?"

"Actually." Xavier said, remembering their last battle. "I forgot to thank you for your help against that guy Fred."

"The Heretic? No problem. It was actually fun to snipe so many targets."

"Next time, try to avoid my hair." Justin added, suddenly scowling.

"Your hair or your head. I had to choose. Kinda wishing I had chosen the latter."

"Ha. Ha. Ha."

"It could have been worse. Could have gotten it wet."

Everyone snickered, while Justin seemed to be doing his best to keep a smile off his face. When the driver let them know that they were fifteen minutes to their destination, Xavier activated his com. Serea's voice came booming through, frustration dying her words.

"You better take that pompous demon's head off Xavier."

He heaved a sigh.

"What are we dealing with?"

"Damn near every sort of demon seen on this continent. Including Ifrits! They're not even burning anything, he just put them there to taunt us!"

"I don't think he cared that much Serea…" Szakiya's voice came.

"Oh yes he did! Either way Xavier, the moment we go in, we're fighting hard. I still don't know how anyone hasn't noticed this racket."

"Let's count our blessings and be grateful."

"The voice of pragmatism!" Szakiya called.

"Oh, shut up. When you arrive, signal us. With any luck we'll draw the bulk of the horde and go from there."

As their van turned coasted down the nearby driveway, a massive force collided with the van. Xavier's head throbbed in utter protest as he forced himself to get up. His thermal readings showed the shape of a gargoyle. As it reared up on its hind legs, Xavier enveloped it in fire. As the gargoyle lay dying, he looked around to check on everyone else. Though sore and caught off guard, everyone seemed ok. Their driver instructed them, to proceed on foot and that she would see to any other demons in the area. Against his better judgement, Xavier agreed. Max kicked open the indented door and they all hopped out.

Two more gargoyles bounded towards them with vicious roars. Justin flicked his hand and a burst of wind surged forward and beheaded them. Xavier cocked an eyebrow which elicited a shrug from Justin.

"They aren't my favorite type of demon. Brings back bad memories."

Everyone nodded and mumbled their affirmations while Xavier mapped the building. The amount of demons that he could sense was alarming. Instead of trying to distinguish the difference between the demons, he frantically searched for any signs of individuals. He finally located one in a random office to the west.

"Alexander has a trap waiting for us. Be ready." He tapped his com. "Serea? We're going in."

"Affirmative. Good luck."

Xavier could see the thermal signatures of the two other teams begin to engage the demons. With a small prayer for their safety, Xavier dissolved the map and began to head inside with the rest of them. The moment they entered the door, a gaggle of small imps screamed the alarm. A second later they were completely cloaked in ice. Nate tapped his foot and with a seismic wave, shattered them. They ran down the hallway and four harpies dropped from the ceiling.

"Ooh! Dibs!" Cassie chirped.

All four harpies went slack and fell the ground slain. With a triumphant smile, Cassie skipped before resuming her trek down the hall. Almost every corner and door they passed held a demonic surprise but none of them could stand up to their might. Xavier had almost allowed himself to feel confident until he heard a bestial snort. The wall exploded outward and revealed the hulking mass; a giant Minotaur.

"These are a thing?!" Xavier asked incredulously as he dodged a piece of rubble.

"Cassie, Ophelia, and Nate! This one is ours!" Justin yelled, blasting the demon with a tornado.

"Wait! This is what Alexander wants!"

"Exactly!" Nate replied, launching seeds after seeing the Minotaur shrug off Justin's attack.

"What?!"

Max grabbed Xavier's arm with bruising strength and proceeded to drag him away. Xavier tried to pull his arm away, but Max tightened his grip to a near unbearable degree.

"Easy!" he hissed, feeling his fingers spasm.

"Sorry…" Max whispered.

As they rounded the nearby corner, Max finally slacked his grip enough to allow Xavier to break free.

"What hell are you guys doing?! This wasn't part of the plan! Did you see that thing? They can't handle it by themselves!"

"Then I'll go and back them up." Adam replied.

Xavier stared into Adam's eyes before nodding.

"Be careful."

Adam kissed him on the cheek before dashing off back to their comrades. The rest of them took off and dispatched more demons as they went. They finally arrived at the hall where Alexander was waiting, they were greeted by a solitary demon. Cold dread crept up Xavier's spine as he recognized what it was. Shades were notorious Witch killers in the past as they could absorb most of the powers used against them. This particular shade was human in shape and lacked any defining traits. From head to toe it was just a black blur. It bowed its head slightly before pointing at Xavier and then pointing at the office.

"Go ahead." Max murmured. "Me and Danny can handle this."

"Are you sure?"

"I know everything about these demons. We got this."

Danny winked at Xavier before stepping forward. The air began to crackle and pop and Xavier's arm hairs began to stand up. The shade still pointed at the office though it appeared its attention was centered at Danny. Xavier walked past and closed the door as he heard a bolt of lightning crash. The office was larger than his flame-based projection had let on, which Xavier was grateful for. Alexander sat on top of the desk holding a glass of champagne.

"Xavier!" he said with a bright smile. "Welcome!"

"Not that warm of a welcome outside." Xavier replied, shying away from a blast of cold air.

"What? Them? They're no match for someone I have declared mine."

"Again with that, still don't really remember agreeing to that."

A glow of anger crept into Alexander's eyes, but his smile persisted.

"The only way your friends make it out of this alive is if you join me Xavier. They're outnumbered and outmatched. If you listen closely, you can hear the Minotaur sweeping the floor with them. And I'd like to finish this up before the vote tomorrow. The clean-up alone is going to cost a fortune."

"Yeah I was kinda surprised that those actually existed. Did you import him from Greece or…?"

"Did you not hear what I just said?"

"I did. I totally did. And you know how I hate to upset you, but they're gonna win."

Alexander's glare was so deep, that it completely revealed Alexander's demonic heritage.

"Why? Why?!" he roared.

"Gonna have to be a bit more specific."

"Do you realize how many in the demon and human world wish for my attention?! Do you know the things they've done to earn my favor?!"

"Hmm, nope."

"And you stand there, smug with no reason when you should be thanking me!"

"I thought it was my spirit that attracted you to me in the first place? Remember? You tried to kiss me, I said 'ew', and then I breathed fire in your face. Still haven't figured out how to do it again…"

Alexander placed the glass on the desk and started to laugh. The laugh was hearty, but it dripped with evil. When he finally stopped laughing, his eyes were glowing gold.

"You're right Xavier. That spirit is what caught my eye. But you misunderstand. I don't want that spirit, I want to break it."

"I'll die first."

"We shall see…"

Xavier erected his most powerful heat shield directly in front of him and Alexander snarled and leapt away. Xavier started to unleash a barrage of fireballs which Alexander dodged. One fireball nearly stuck him in the face, but he managed to avoid it at the last possible second. Xavier smiled as he been watching closely and understood with Miguel spoke about. To test his theory he rushed forward, launching more fireballs. Alexander once again dodged them but this time, he ran directly into Xavier's blade.

"How?" Alexander groaned, gripping his new gut wound.

"You don't actually have super speed. You project a path of energy and then move your body along it. The problem is that you can't deviate from the path."

Xavier held his sword chest level and smiled.

"I see you."

The air was violated by Alexander's horrific laughter.

"You think you've won?! This is when the fight gets interesting!"

A circle of golden energy appeared around Alexander and his body began to morph and change. The energy began to glow brighter until Xavier was completely blinded. When the light finally subsided, Xavier felt his mouth drop open. Alexander's demon form was that of a huge anthropomorphic lion with a black mane.

"How?" Xavier found himself saying.

"My mother was a lion shifter. All demons in line to become possible scions are half demons. Makes our abilities stronger. For instance," Xavier felt the back of a fist collide with his face and blast him into the nearby book shelf. "Did you see *that*?"

Xavier coughed and spit the blood from his mouth. He did actually see it, but the speed in which Alexander was traveling had increased beyond his reaction time. He shot in the air and summoned his full heat shield. He had to be careful to keep the shield as near to his body as possible or he'd set off the sprinklers. Something collided with his shield that brought his full attention back to Alexander. The hairs at the end of his mane with sticking up and hardened and which a cruel smile, Alexander shot them all. Xavier tried to dodge, but the needle hairs were too quick and numerous. Eventually they overwhelmed his shield and struck him in the leg.

He dropped to the ground as his body was racked with unimaginable pain. Alexander walked over and picked him up by the front of his vest.

“All you have to do, is give in to me and the pain stops.” He purred.

Xavier’s reply was to shoot his flames in Alexander’s face. When he was released, he kicked the demon away with his uninjured leg before sending another torrent of flame crashing into Alexander’s body. A feral roar blasted the flames away and all Xavier saw was a blur. He blinked, and a clawed hand was aimed straight for his chest.

Xavier smiled and rolled away as Alexander’s shriek pierced the air. A pile of dust landed on the ground as Alexander gripped his shoulder. Electric blue blood began to leak profusely causing Alexanders’ breath to become haggard. Adam uncloaked himself with a wry smile and pointed the blade of his weapon at Alexander.

“I saw you go back to the Minotaur!” Alex screamed.

“You sure did. Should have worked on seeing if I cloaked myself directly after.”

Alexander turned to Xavier and narrowed his eyes.

“Yeah, he’s been here the entire time. And let me tell you that it’s kind of awkward to have a demon throw himself at you while your boyfriend watches.”

“He won’t be for too much longer…”

The world slowed to a standstill. Alexander had managed to project an energy trail directly behind Adam and was already half way there. Xavier’s legs refused to move faster than snail’s pace and he became enraged. Didn’t they know Adam was in danger? Didn’t they want to save him? Alexander had nearly finished his trek and Adam began to turn around with his eyes open wide as he saw Alexander’s clawed hand. The rage gave way to fear. He couldn’t lose Adam like this, not after everything they had endured.

As the claws grew closer and closer to Adam’s body, tears began to stream down Xavier’s face. He opened his mouth, but no sound would come out. He reached for his magic and begged and pleaded that it would save Adam. He was willing to die himself if he had to, but he just wanted to get to Adam. No one deserved to die like that. Something in his mind bloomed and one word came to his mouth.

“Transmission.”

The white-hot sensation of his flesh being rent hit Xavier’s hip as he held Adam tightly in his arms. Adam looked around frantically before giving Xavier a puzzled look.

“You won’t get lucky a second time.” Alexander snarled.

“Won’t need to.”

Alexander projected another path right in the middle of them. Xavier uttered the word again and brought them back two feet. As Alexander came into view, Xavier slashed him across the chest with his katana. The hairs in his mane prevented a strike from being lethal, but he still staggered back. The two looked at each for almost a minute before Alexander began to chuckle.

"In all my life, I have only met one other person who could stand before me as you do now. What's funny is that he told me that a Witch would finish what he started."

"Any last words?"

"I really wish you had joined me. I could have saved you from what's coming next. Ah well…"

Alexander projected his path directly forward and as Xavier moved into position, a wide smile graced the demon's face and in the instant before his head flew off he winked at Xavier. Alexander's body fell to the ground and Xavier released his pent-up breath. Adam walked over and placed a hand on his shoulder looking concerned.

"What was that?"

"I'll explain it when we're done. Mind getting these things out of my leg?"

Adam covered the wound in an orb of water and with a small pull, removed every needle from his leg. Xavier let out a sigh of relief. As he was about to ask how the others were doing, a small bit of movement caught the attention of his periphery. As he turned, the entire world went black with Adam's muffled cries being the last thing he heard.

24:

Xavier woke up and let out a disgusted groan with was met by a familiar chuckle. Serea was smiling and struggled to stifle a new set of giggles as she caught sight of his exasperated face.

"How come this only happens to me?!" Xavier cried.

"I have no clue love."

"What happened to me this time?"

"Um...how to put this mildly... Nate sent a rock flying through the Minotaur; which killed it, but also went through several walls until it reached your head."

"I kill the Scion of House Asmodai, and then get taken out by a rock. Yeah sure, why not?"

"Oh sweetie, I'm so sorry. But I am so proud of you! Do you have any idea of what you accomplished in that fight?"

"Yeah. And please don't tell anyone. I'll tell the team when I'm ready, but right now I kind of want to finish up my training first."

"Oh, thank god!" Serea, releasing a large breath of relief. "Saves me the trouble of explaining it you. Asreaon did something right for once. I truly hate to turn back to work so soon, but we need to speak about what Alexander told you right before you beheaded him."

"My guess? The other Houses are moving."

"Yeah... Remember when I told you to find a vacation home? You might want to do that sooner, rather than later. It appears you're going to be very busy and your training still isn't even remotely close to being done."

Xavier let out another groan which Serea responded to with a small kiss on his forehead. Once he was up and dressed, he went to find his team. He was more than pleased to find them all in one of the kitchens, cooking for their potluck. Nate sheepishly apologized and which Xavier graciously accepted. When Nate wasn't looking however, Xavier lit a small flame which consumed the back side of Nate's pants and boxers. Justin beamed at him before offering his apron, so Nate could go back to his room with some modicum of dignity.

Once clothes were procured and food was made, everyone got together and enjoyed another meal. Eliade even went so far as to congratulate Xavier on his homemade garlic bread. Xavier accepted the praise and chose to ignore the fact that it was store bought and he had simply added a few ingredients to it. Once everyone had eaten and Miguel was given an appropriate amount in a doggy bag, people excused themselves for various reasons. Adam had remained, though his face was no longer smiling.

"You still mad at me?" Xavier asked sheepishly.

"A bit. That plan was so risky."

"But we won in the end."

"Only because of some power of love bull. We can't rely on that to win every battle."

Xavier rolled his eyes.

"Well, excuse me for caring about your wellbeing."

Adam's eyes widened before he hugged Xavier.

"Oh babe, no! I'm still really grateful that you saved my life! I'm sorry."

"Uh-huh…"

"Look, we both heard what Alexander said. We can't afford to expect tiny miracles every time we face down a powerful demon."

"You just can't take a victory and run with it, can you?"

Adam laughed before leaning forward to kiss him.

"You wanna go to the beach?"

"Now?"

"Soon?"

"Yeah sure. Gotta look at houses evidently."

Adam snorted with laughter. After talking a little while longer, Xavier excused himself and headed to his office. A red origami flower was sitting on his desk. After spending few frustrating minutes to open it, it contained only one sentence: "Good job." Xavier smiled before throwing the paper away.

"Miguel." Xavier called, sitting down behind his desk.

The sound of loud chewing filled the air, as Miguel appeared on couch sitting crossed legged. He grunted a greeting as he tore into a piece of pork chop.

"And they call me a fatty…"

Miguel's face announced his offense and he began to rapidly chew his food while tearing off his shirt.

"Excuse you?!" he barked, finally swallowing. "I am the pinnacle of in shape. Look at these abs. Look at them!"

Xavier fought the urge to laugh as he shook his head. Of course, he would remember when Xavier did that.

"I'm good. Please put your shirt back... You take off your pants and I'll burn your leftovers to ash. I don't need to see the whole package."

Miguel looked positively aghast and quickly put his shirt back on before racing to his container of food.

"Miguel, I think you know why I called you here."

"Duh. Cuz we're bros and you kicked serious demon butt."

"Miguel..."

Miguel's face suddenly grew serious and he shook his head.

"I can't promise you answers Xavier."

"Can you at least tell me what we're in for?"

"What makes you think I know?"

Xavier's look made Miguel chuckle.

"Ok fine, what makes you think I can tell you?"

"Because I'm telling you I need you to."

"Doesn't work like that. Because you don't need to know."

"Dammit Miguel! Come on!"

Miguel shrugged with only exacerbated Xavier's irritation.

"What do you want me to do dude? I got rules and junk..."

"Which we still don't know about."

"Part of the rules."

"Is there anything useful you can tell me?"

"You're my favorite?"

A small silence crept between them.

"Really?"

"For now. If you get grumpy a few decades from now, then I might kick you to the curb."

Xavier couldn't resist the urge to laugh despite knowing that Miguel was deflecting. After he finished laughing one question burned at the front of his mind.

"Are you really on our side Miguel?"

Miguel wore an amused expression. "For now."